JENNIE MOENCH

NEAR FUTURE E3

The Third Episodes of the Science Fiction Short
Stories of Near Future by Jennie Moench

Warrior Publications, Inc.

Warrior Publications, Inc.
P.O. Box 127
Grand Blanc, Michigan 48480

ISBN 978-0-9854905-7-7

Dedicated to my son, Ivan.

Preface

In this third book in the Near Future series, a storm is brewing. Mother Earth is trying to shake off her parasites. The first story starts with the funeral for our heroine, Janet, but you soon get to know her cousin, Aarar, as he looks for her killer. In the second story, Millie establishes her band of helpful, Watchers, who use Remote Viewing to locate and offer aid to endangered travelers. Jay travels to Australia when the Unique Idendifier is identified in a group of Aboriginals. Dave's new client is a Transmorphic, as he identifies as a female robot. Finally, in the last story, Liam and Arthur meet Jak for the first time.

I hope I didn't spoil the stories for you. I hope these stories inspire you to consider the future and what you want it to look like. These things need careful consideration and planning. All of us need to work together to create that wonderful planet that our children deserve!

Table of Contents

Transporter

Aarar was distraught, as was everyone around him, at his cousin's funeral. She was so young, only 3 years older than he was. The two were close online, even though they hadn't seen one another in person, recently. It was Janet's father, who pushed the button that ignited the fire on the cremation chamber. Janet's mother, grandmother, and aunt all let out wails as the fire instantly ignited. Tears streamed down everyone's faces. It was a very sad occasion.

Afterward, the small crowd of mourners gathered at Pia and John's home. Aarar felt sad for the older couple when he realized that they were now childless. They lived in a neat, one story house, that was now, much too spacious for the couple. There was a whole wing of the structure that was empty. He hated the sad look in his Aunt Pia's eyes whenever they met. She seemed to be especially kind to him, he wondered if it was because of her loss that she now looked a bit envious at him. Like she wanted to keep him, in place of her perished daughter. "You know, Aarar, Janet had the very latest technology and equipment. If you ever want to come by and use it, you are more than welcome!"

He nodded shyly at his aunt. But, he could tell that there was something else that she wanted to ask him, and it was later, as he was about to leave with his parents, that she was able to corner him alone. "I think she was murdered," Pia stated very bluntly. "And, I think, the details are recorded in her computer system. I think if someone, who was good with technology, were to sort through her equipment, they might be able to find out who it was!" She said this looking very earnestly at the, nearly graduated, computer science major. Aarar didn't know what to say. Pia drew nearer the young man, "You could stay here for your last year, you could have Janet's room," the desperate mother implored. "You could use her transporter! It's all new, and now, it's paid for!" she wailed, then began sobbing anew. Aarar felt very awkward, he didn't know how to 'comfort' someone, but he tried. Hugging his aunt, and then patting her back as he began to cry himself. He promised to consider his Aunt Pia's proposition, but at that time, he just wanted to get out of that house. Away from the death, away from the reality that he would never see his cousin again, and away from his realization that death was real, even for someone as young as himself.

The ride home was quiet. Aarar didn't mention his Aunt's proposal, but after he helped Daadee into her favorite chair, it became the topic of conversation. His Aunt Pia had already discussed the possibility of him living with her for his last year of college.

"I think it would be good for my sister to have someone to care for," Alisha stated once everyone was seated in their living room. She was looking at her son with sad eyes. "I don't want to see you go, but, maybe it would be good for you. I know Pia would take good care of you." She looked away into a distant nothing as she continued, "I don't understand how Janet fell from a cliff, but, however it happened, maybe you could help," she finished quietly in the direction of her only child.

As soon as he was able to escape to his room, he noticed a tear run down his cheek. He turned his body as he sat on the edge of his bed, so that he could lay on his stomach and rub the tears off on to his pillow.

Aarar had always been a quiet boy, in person. He had inherited well balanced features from his Tamil mother and European father. His skin was a healthy tan color. His eyes were large and brown with a ring of gold in the centers, on bright days they shone like the sun. He was almost an inch over six feet tall, slim built with long legs. But, his shoulders were broad, and with a little bit of a regular work out, his chest and arm muscles became well developed. He was a handsome man, although, he, himself had no idea. He still only thought of himself as, 'that smart Indian kid,' from high school.

But...online, while his cousin's avatar had taken on the appearance of Kali the Hindu Goddess, he, was the Prince of Hind! The Prince was always dressed in royal colors with gold trim. He even had his own show where he interviewed people. His guests were fellow gamers, they would meet with him at his virtual set and the conversations would be about new and popular games. This was when his shyness disappeared. In fact, he had virtual girlfriends, many were fans. His dream was to have enough followers that he could attract more sponsors. But, as far as his family was concerned, this whole online thing was a distraction from his studies. And, to be fair, it was, Aarar admitted. Janet was the only one who understood what he was trying to do, and that there was a possible future in it, and now she was gone.

"NEXT LEVEL with the Prince of Hind is an alive interview with that asshole avatar that beats the shit out of you in your favorite game, every Thursday at six o'clock! This weeks interview will be with Sheba the Destroyer! Tune in if you want to discuss how she kicked your ass in Fairyland!" Boomed the voice of the Prince over a picture of an animated version of him giving his famous, twinkling eye wink into the camera.

The animation faded into a long view of him sitting on a gold and red velvet throne in his royal palace. It sat on an oriental carpet with a smaller, yet very ornate, guest throne beside his. They appeared in his courtyard of palm trees and colorful orchids. A light breeze kept the beautiful foliage astir. While behind and between the two thrones was a new addition to the set. It was a large statue of the multi-armed Goddess Kali, but wearing a red sari, black armor and the face of his cousin.

Sitting on the smaller throne was his guest, Sheba the Destroyer. She was dressed as a fairy with a green tunic, pointed ears and a set of transparent, but iridescent wings, that fluttered as she waited patiently for the Prince to begin his interview.

"Sheba! So nice to have the opportunity to talk with you! Thanks for being a guest!" the Prince leaned into her with a raised eyebrow and formed an enchanting smile with his thick, well shaped lips.

Sheba wondered if he looked anything at all like his avatar. "Thank you for asking me," she responded, "This is an amazing set!" She looked at the camera, "I don't know if the audience can see this, but there is a bluff in front of us that faces the west, and to what appears to be, the making of a beautiful sunset!"

"Every night! You should come here more often!" the Prince responded in a low voice. His avatar raised an eyebrow again and caused that eye to twinkle.

Sheba smiled and the Prince heard a faint giggle. There was a small hesitation before she spoke, "I also love the new statue! Is that a Hindu goddess?"

The Prince was glad that she noticed it, but didn't want to get emotional over the details, so he nodded, "Thank you for noticing! Yes, it is a new addition! But, let's talk about you! You have the high score in Fairyland right now! Isn't that right?" He bent his elbow on the arm of his throne and curled a finger under his chin, gazing at Sheba intently.

The real live Sheba was contemplating the amorous avatar, she wondered if it was his husky whisper of a voice that made him so alluring. "Ah, yeah, I'm now 3200 points higher than my closest competitor," she explained.

The Prince could tell by her halting voice that he was having an effect on her. He raised his perfectly formed black eyebrows, then pursed his large sensual lips for a second before asking his next question, "I heard a roomer that part of your success has to do with an unconventional way you use bogo berries, is that true?" he asked.

"Um, well, yeah. I throw them with one hand while using a sharpened thorn in the other. I made the thorn spear myself! It's a great way to defend yourself if someone sneaks up close to you. But, if you smash someone in the face with a berry in close contact, it blinds them for a few seconds."

The Prince looked pensive, "is that something you discovered while playing? Or is it somewhere in the documentation?"

Sheba was beginning to feel more comfortable, "No, it's not documented and I probably shouldn't be giving out my secrets like this," her avatar was smiling broadly. "But, if you wait until the last minute, then smash the berry square in their face, it stuns them for a just enough time to run them through with a spear!"

The Prince sat up, "oh! So it takes some real expertise!" He nodded at her with adoring eyes.

This flustered her for a moment, "a...yeah. It's definitely something you need to practice."

"Well, then I challenge you," the Prince announced with a flourish. "Then, you can practice on me! I would give a life in Fairyland, just to experience one of your famous bogo berry executions!"

Sheba laughed, "okay, I'll make you a thorn spear."

The Prince moved to the edge of his seat, "Would you really?" He asked excitedly. "I'd let you take my life twice for it!" he offered, then looked at her expectantly for an answer.

"Sure!" she shrugged, then wondered if they had just made a date.

The Prince smiled then sat back in his throne, "So, how long have you been playing Fairyland?" He asked as Aarar was secretly sending her a message.

MEET ME AT THE CYBER CAFE AFTER THE SHOW

"A few years..." Sheba considered, "I got a subscription for my birthday...I guess it's been 3 years now!" Sheba could hear the faint alarm that someone had messaged her off camera.

The Prince could see her looking down at her left hand, making it obvious that she was reading his message. "How long before you were playing at an expert level?" He asked, re-directing her attention to the sparkle in his large dark eyes.

She was feeling butterflies in her stomach, "Well, at first I just hid from other players and explored the forest."

The prince nodded again and made an agreeable sound, "So, you are the curious kind."

"Yes." She admitted, then noticed another message on her communicator.

I KNOW THAT I AM CURIOUS ABOUT YOU!

Sheba made an involuntary giggle. She hoped that the Prince hadn't heard it, but when she looked back at his avatar, she could tell by his smile, that he had. They continued talking for nearly an hour before the Prince looked into the camera, raised his eyebrow, and made his eye twinkle for the last closeup shot that signaled the end of his show.

Once the livestream was ended, the Prince smiled at Sheba, "we had a lot of viewers for that show! You were a hit!" he smiled at her adoringly. "So, do you have any time for me?" he asked in his deep whisper of a voice.

"Sure."

"Well then," he began, "why don't you attach yourself to me, and I'll take you to this cyber bar that I like to go to."

Sheba fought her nervous habit of giggling when aroused, and complied. The next thing she knew, the two of them were in a large room with red walls and round black tables with chairs arranged around an empty stage. Avatars and bots of all types were speaking loudly to one another, walking all around them, and some were sitting at tables together. A bar at the back of the room had every stool filled with both cartoon and realistic looking avatars as well as a group of three beautiful and very vivacious blonds who noticed the Prince when he appeared. 'Ah, the Tanoshi girls,' he said to himself with a smile as he gave each of them a twinkle wink. He knew the girls well and couldn't help but be a bit flattered, when he noticed them frown as

Sheba stepped in behind him. He fired off a message to them that he was having a business meeting and hoped they'd be around later. Giggles. He really enjoyed the three and how they liked to do everything together.

Unfortunately, Sheba noticed the exchange, but didn't say anything. He motioned to an empty table for them to sit, then took his golden seat as it was no longer a throne but had transformed into a common wooden chair. Aarar pulled the real live office chair on rollers up to the holographic table, close to Sheba. He pressed a button on his keyboard and the air was scented with sandalwood, so that he could imagine how her hair smelled, even though the scent was unknown to her. 'It was soooooo cool being the Prince,' he said in his head, as he inhaled deeply, 'I never want to be anyone else.' When he glanced back toward the bar, the girls were waving and throwing him kisses. He laughed and waved back. Sheba's avatar was without expression, sitting beside him and observing the action.

"Sorry," he apologized, "they are fans of the show," he explained.

It was obvious to Sheba that they were more than fans, but she tried to ignore them. "I'm sure you have many fans! Your show is becoming very popular. Is it a lot of work? Do you have help?"

The Prince sighed, "Yes, it is taking more and more time. I am a one man show," he admitted, "I do the editing too."

"Wow! Even the little animations?"

He nodded, "Yeah, but, once I have the programming down, I just use inserts." Then, he looked at Sheba, "So, what do you do when you aren't gaming?"

Sheba laughed, "that's what my parents keep asking me!"

"You too!" the Prince related.

"Yes! I keep taking classes, but I still don't have a major!"

"Well, it sounds to me as though you are being given a choice! My parents have decided for me!"

Sheba stopped laughing, "really?"

The Prince sighed again, "well, actually, I did choose, but it was so long ago! I am a different person now, but, my parents are old fashioned and think that I need to be in high tech, like my cousin was."

"What about the show? What do they think of it?"

"Not much. My cousin brought up an episode for them to watch and she tried to explain to them about my viewers and how I have sponsors, but they think it's just...well...nothing." The Prince said glumly, instantly regretting his mood killing honesty.

Sheba's avatar carefully placed her right hand over his and looked into his face, "What a shame! I think any other parents would be thrilled at your creativity and talent!" Aarar was touched. There was something about Sheba that made him want to kiss her.

It was at this time, as the avatars were close, that they heard the giggling of the Tanoshi girls. When they looked up, the three were standing near their table, but the one in the center was wearing a long coat, that she flung open to expose her curvy naked body, and as the couples eyes took in the spectacle and moved down to the area where her legs came together, they noticed that there existed a very engorged clitoris with a ring pierced through it, where there dangled a small Prince of Hind logo.

The Prince burst out laughing as the girls scurried away, glancing at him over their shoulders, and running out the exit. Aarar was quickly typing out an appreciative message to them, promising to be available soon. Sheba was silently smiling, but the spell was broken, and this was disappointing to him, as he had been enjoying her company.

"I'm so sorry!" he cooed. "Listen, lets go back to my palace and I can show you the beach. It's beautiful at night!"

Sheba agreed, and the two were instantly transported to a beautiful, wild beach where the sky was so full of bright stars that they lit up the night and shimmered on the breaking water. Each wave thundered as it hit the sandy beach. Boulders lined the shore and when she turned around, she could see that they were at the bottom of a tall cliff.

Aarar pressed a button that blew a gentle breeze on the avatars. 'How romantic,' she thought to herself, especially when she turned back around and noticed that the wind was buffeting his hair. A seagull cried. The Prince drew closer.

Sheba became a bit nervous, "are there ever any other avatars here?" she asked.

The Prince shook his head, "no, this is my kingdom, no one can come here without permission." For a sad moment he considered how this was now true, as his cousin had passed away. Then, he pushed the memory away and returned his gaze at Sheba, "You know Sheba, there was something that I wanted to do before we were distracted," he said in a whisper close to her avatar.

Sheba looked up at him as he grew closer still. Aarar moved his invisible right hand to his mouth and began to sensually suck and kiss the base of his thumb, pretending it to be her lips. After several seconds, the Prince pulled back while Sheba's lips were still pursed and her avatar eyes were close. He smiled and waited for her to open them. Then, bent closer to her face, "So tell me Sheba," he purred, "is your avatar complete?"

"Oh yeah," she answered softly. She allowed his avatar hands to gently guide her to the ground, and under him. With her delicate wings wrapped under her head like a pillow she writhed on her back, as the water lapped over her, and she allowed him to undress her. His gloved hand skillfully untied the front of her fairy tunic, and let loose the pink flesh of her bosom. Tiny sea foam bubbles lapped over them, the Prince made a humming sound, "Sheba!"

"No," she moaned, "call me by my real name! Cynthia!"

The Prince looked down on her, to study her breasts, "C-y-n-t-h-i-a," he sang out softly, then looked her avatar in the eyes, "You know, I think I like that even better than Sheba! It sounds soooo sexy!" he finished by bringing his face close to hers and kissing her. Then, he began kissing neck, and then chest, and then, he grabbed the front of her opened tunic and ripped it off. He laughed and threw it out of the way. And there she lay beneath him naked.

Aarar pushed a stack of books, that he had on the floor, with his feet, to get them out of the way, then continued to move down the body of the avatar under his left arm, careful not to crush her and the illusion. He held his right hand in his mouth, making a soft sucking sound that was barely audible to Sheba. She let out a little scream when he made it to her most private area. The Prince became excited as well, "Cynthia, Cynthia, Cynthia, ouch!" he hissed, then giggled as he had accidentally bit himself.

"What?" Sheba asked, puzzled.

"Nothing, my dear!" he laughed raising up so that he could see her face. "It's just that you are so beautiful that you made me hurt myself!" He started to return to his previous position, when Sheba stopped him.

"Wait, what is your real name?" she asked.

The Prince looked taken aback, "Why I am the Prince of Hind!" He made a sweeping motion with his arm, "and everything that you see around you is my Kingdom!"

Sheba laughed, "you know what I mean, your birth name! Who are you?"

He paused a moment, this was a question he usually refused to answer, but as he looked down on the beautiful fairy, he felt the need to comply, "Aarar." She repeated the name.

"Yes! But it's a secret! Don't tell anyone!"

"Is it Indian?"

"Yes."

"Do you really look like your avatar?"

The Prince sighed, he already wished that he hadn't told her his name, this conversation was a distraction. "Basically, you see, I'm an Indian guy! But, I have to admit, in real life my eyes don't really twinkle, I guess they are just the average amount of shiny. How about you?"

"Well, my skin is less green and I don't really have wings, but other than that," her voice trailed off as she unbuttoned the Prince's silk shirt. She opened the shirt and looked at his tight chest, "does your chest really look like this?"

The Prince laughed, "well, it did, I have to admit that I haven't been working out as often as I was when I photographed myself for this avatar."

"Are you fat?"

"No, if anything my problem is the reverse of that, I have a very active metabolism, so I stay pretty thin. How about you?"

Sheba was still examining the ripples of his taught torso. "I'm not fat, not thin, I look just about the way you see me."

The Prince nodded, but didn't know what he would do with this information. What difference did it make? Yet, for some reason, he didn't want to lie to her. So, she was drawing information from him that he normally didn't divulge. They continued with their love making. Pleasuring themselves while captivated by the other.

Aarar had given his show much thought before he created it. He felt that it was important for his avatar to show expressions that identified how he truly felt. Not just a delayed giggle or a surprised look, but keep it genuine and in real time! So, during the show, his avatar's head and limbs moved with his real body, except for his right hand, which was using a holographic keyboard of his own design that ran a program he wrote that caused his avatar to show a wild range of emotion on cue.

As far as the filming of the show, he programmed a system that filled the viewers screen with a closeup of whoever was speaking to, but with a second smaller screen in the bottom right hand corner that always showed a close-up of the Prince of Hind with his often comic expressions. He also enabled an app to run that gave every viewer the ability to add giggles, laughs, or boos to the audio of the live-stream. He felt that both of these practices were part of the reason for his growing viewership.

And... he loved it! He felt more alive as an avatar than he ever did in real life. More in control, and much better liked. Everyone who gamed had an opinion of the Prince, usually good, but there were some who thought Prince Hind was a bit of a smart ass, but that was okay too. It was all fun. As the Prince interviewed his guest, Aarar had his eyes on his monitor as the fingers of his, gloveless, right hand flew across the keyboard and made the audience roar!

In real life Aarar was very shy, crippling shy. From the time he was a small boy he had difficulty looking into someones face when they were talking to him. Especially girls. As he got older the problem became compounded as he noticed that he became aroused at even the sound of a female voice, so he made it a practice of not looking up at them, to avoid a bigger problem. Often the girl would mistake him as being from a religious belief that women should not be out in public, especially with his tan skin. But, that was far from the truth, the truth was that he loved women too much! So, he continued to spend most of his time alone and more often than not, online. Now that he was in college he could take all his classes that way. He rarely left the house and the only humans he interacted with were his parents and grandmother who lived with them.

His interesting life had become his online life, because, avatars can do anything! Be anyone! They were immortal! So, as an Avatar he could be fearless! And, despite Aarar's virginity, the Prince of Hind was a permissive, sexual beast! And all the ladies loved him for it!

After saying good bye to Sheba, he made good on his promise with the Tanoshi girls. They were always a good time, even the one with the suspiciously masculine voice. But, what difference did it make?

It was very late at night when he finally pulled off his goggles to attend to business. He had several messages, one was from a sponsor who wanted to renew their ad. This made him happy, he recorded the important information, then checked his bank balance. It was getting bigger as he only spent money that was related to the show. Not having a social life, in real life, was economical. His silver lining.

He returned to his messages. There was a new one from a fan who played Gladiator. This was his cousin's favorite game. The message was a request for a conversation. Aarar clicked on the tab that opened a window with a very excited fourteen year old, "I did it! I'm high score now!"

The Prince of Hind's face made an over the top excited look complete with steam coming out of his ears. "That's great!" then, "wait, you are top score on Gladiator?...Who did you beat?"

"Kali!"

Aarar was confused, "When?"

"Just a few minutes ago! So, can I be on your show now?"

Aarar didn't know what to think, how could this kid have beat his cousin, whose funeral he had just attended? "Um...sure! I'll get back with you!"

He then went to the Gladiator high score screen, and found that indeed, the highest score now belonged to 'Death Defier.' He checked the name on the message he had just received, 'Death Defier.' "huh?" he asked himself aloud, "how could that be?"

Aarar had worked even later on his school work, so it was the afternoon of the next day before he fell asleep. He woke up because of the pounding on his door. It was his mother telling him that dinner was done and he needed to come out of his room!

He got out of bed and then noticed all the books and things that were still sprawled across his floor. He arranged the books into a tower and dropped his dirty clothes into a hamper, then he threw a long, white, cotton shirt over his head. Once he opened his door, the smell of chicken and curry suddenly made him remember that he hadn't eaten. He walked through a small living room with a couch and blanket neatly tossed over it. Then an oval opening into the dinning room where his grandmother and father were already seated. His mother was dressed in a simple blue sari, and was walking around the table, placing a mound of white rice on each plate.

"So, he lives!" Aarar's mother, Alisha announced as he walked into the room.

"I stayed up all night finishing a project that was due," he explained as he found his chair near his grandmother. He automatically picked up a ladle and scooped up some of the curry and placed it on his grandmother's rice for her. Then did the same for himself. Alisha placed a lid on the pot of rice and then set it on a coaster on the table before sitting next to her husband, Tony.

"Homework?" Tony looked at his son, "that's not what it sounded like last night when I got up to use the toilet!"

Aarar sighed, he needed his own place. He had purchased and installed large sheets of sound proof material on the walls all around his room, but it was still a problem. Actually, it was this problem that was the reason behind the Prince of Hind's trademark, low whisper of a voice.

He partially removed a cloth that was covering a pile of flat bread, then he set a piece on his grandmother's plate. The old woman picked it up, tore it in half, then began scooping up the rice and curry, eating with gusto. After taking a bite, she noticed her grandson was watching her, so she made an ear to ear grin at him, that made him smile back. He loved Daadee, she was his favorite person now, even though she rarely spoke, but she loved him, he could tell. She was a small woman who liked wearing colorful cotton saris that she sewed herself. That seemed to be her only activity except watching shows from the couch in the front room.

"Well," Alisha started in Aarar's direction, "I sure hope you can behave yourself after you've moved in with your aunt and uncle!"

Aarar was embarrassed, his parents were always making him feel like a child.

"When am I supposed to make the move?" Aarar looked at one parent and then the other. He didn't like change, moving would be a big change, but with the way his parents were treating him, it made the whole idea more attractive. Maybe when he moved he could finally bring his voice above a whisper on his show.

His parents looked at one another, then Alisha explained, "your Aunt Pia wants to send Janet's transporter here to pick you and your things up. She will just have to transmit the emergency code to your communicator somehow. Could you help her with that?"

Aarar nodded. "So, they never did find Janet's communicator?"

Alisha shook her head. Aarar looked at his grandmother again, she was eating quietly. He scooped up a piece of boiled chicken and placed it on her plate. She looked up and grinned at him again, he smiled back. He was going to miss her, so he was happy that she had a good appetite. He wanted her to live forever, but, he was especially concerned now that he was going to be gone, and didn't know how long.

After dinner he went to his room and contacted his Aunt Pia. She had been anxiously waiting for his reply. He helped her with the transfer of the file on to his communicator. She told him that the transporter would be sent to him right away. His trepidation was gone, he had decided at dinner that he wanted to move. He needed to be away from his parents. His only concern was that he was afraid that his aunt was asking him to do the impossible, by hacking into his cousin's equipment. He consoled himself that if he gave it his best try and still was unable to find anything, maybe his aunt would except that the whole thing had been a tragic accident. But, he would deal with that then, right now, he just wanted to escape.

He started putting his clothes into bags and stacking his equipment into towers. Then, he carried his belongings to the front porch. His mother stopped him as he passed her to ask what he was doing. He explained that the transporter was on it's way there now. She looked up at him with concern, he wondered if maybe she would really miss him. They hadn't had a real conversation in years. They seemed to have nothing in common to speak about. She was his parent and told him what to do. He would answer her questions about school, but his heart wasn't in their only common subject.

She watched him with tears in her eyes. She was loosing him. Her only child. She was regretting the promise she had made to her sister, about him moving in with her. Pia had lost her child and now wanted Aarar, Alisha contemplated jealously. He had better not get behind in his studies, she ruminated while standing at the window, with crossed arms watching her son sitting on the steps of the porch.

When the transporter turned down the drive, Aarar smiled, it was beautiful. He watched the silver vehicle come to a stop near the house. He pulled his communicator out of his pocket and pressed the button that caused the door to slide open. Aarar sighed and then laughed as he joyfully stepped inside to look around. It was beautiful! Everything clean and shiny. He tried the couch, if felt wonderful. He turned and opened the shutters so that sunlight filled the little vehicle. This was exciting! He jumped up and began carrying his things inside. Then, his mother appeared in the drive, "weren't you going to say goodbye, even?"

"Yes," Aarar promised, losing the excited grin that he had been wearing.

She looked at him sternly and pointed toward the house, "don't forget about your father and Daadee!"

Aarar nodded and went back inside to locate his father's office. He knocked on the open door to get his father's attention, then reached out to give him a hug good bye and exchange a few words. Then, he found his grandmother on the couch with a blanket across her lap. He sat beside her and explained that he was going to stay with his Aunt Pia for awhile. "Pia," the old woman pronounced with a smile.

"Yes," Aarar nodded, glad to hear the old woman's voice, then he hugged the one who he would miss the most.

His mother was now inside, standing in front of the couch with her hands on her hips. Aarar stood up and hugged her, then walked out the front door, and for some reason, he knew that this was the end of his old life and the start of a new one. He shut the door without looking back.

He gleefully scooped up the rest of his belongings and stepped inside the open door of the vehicle, quickly shutting the door behind him. Then, he opened the console to type in his destination. He noted that the address was already listed as 'home.'

"Wonderful!" he said aloud, touching the option. He considered how it was probably Janet that had set it up and it was almost as if she were talking to him. This made him smile.

He started to look out the window, but stopped himself, for the fear that he might see his mother chasing him because she had changed her mind! He threw himself onto the sofa instead, and then just happily looked around himself. Even if it was only temporary, it was splendid!

He checked out the electronics, then flipped on a large monitor that covered the front of the transporter. A holographic keyboard appeared in front of him. Then, the default view popped on, it was an unimpeded view of the road in front of them, as the keyboard slowly disappeared. Aarar sighed.

But, the thing that Aarar found himself attracted to the most was the long side window. He sat sideways on the couch and watched life around him, knowing that those people couldn't see him through the metallic windows, or touch him through the metal skin of the transporter, it was a wonderful feeling of safety for him. People were such sharp, pointy things.

He enjoyed viewing the outside world, but he had no interest in interacting with it, he was becoming more reluctant every day. Since he finished grade school and became a full time, online, college student, he had no reason to touch anyone but himself. And, this behavior, and remaining a virgin, was now common place. Many people lived their lives in complete solitary, by their own choosing, especially as robots were becoming more and more affordable.

Aarar stretched, then decided to get up and explore the cabin some more. There was a small bathroom in the back! His families transporter didn't have that! Then, he noticed a set of shelves covered the back wall. He opened one cupboard and then another, finding a small refrigerated compartment. "Coooool," he shouted, and then pulled himself out a bottle of beer. He stopped before opening the bottle to consider if it would be appropriate, would his Aunt and Uncle approve? Then, he remembered that they had a different transporter and that this one would be used by him alone, so he opened the bottle, chuckling to himself. There was also an unopened bag of pretzels, so he took it, too, and made himself comfortable on the couch again. The window kept drawing him to it. It was so interesting when they were driving through an urban area, people would be walking on the sidewalks. Many of them had dogs. He always wanted a dog, his family had always had cats because that was his mother's preference.

But, he did notice, something strange ahead on the sidewalk, he strained his neck to keep his eyes on it as it passed. There was a beautiful woman with long, blond hair, wearing a short red dress, and carrying an older man in a suit. His body was limp, but the woman appeared to carry him without effort. Aarar marveled at the sight until it disappeared into the vegetation. He decided that she must have been a robot. He wondered where she was taking him, as he appeared to be unconscious. Life out of the window was quite interesting.

When he reached his destination, the vehicle opened a large door that allowed it to park on a charging pad inside the building. He opened the door to find his Aunt Pia standing near the transporter with her arm wide open for him. She hugged him warmly then asked if he was hungry. "Yes," he answered eagerly, not mentioning that he had already eaten one dinner that day.

He found his Uncle John sitting at the kitchen table with a half eaten plate of spaghetti. His uncle stood up and hugged him with a warm greeting. "Glad to have you!" he exclaimed before sitting back down. When he did, his Aunt set a plate of spaghetti in front of him, then she pointed out a platter of garlic bread in the center of the table. This was a treat for Aarar, and his Aunt Pia knew it, she had made the special dinner for him as she knew that it was something that her sister never prepared. Although, Janet always complained that her mother was old fashioned, Pia was much more 'Americanized' than Alisha, who always prepared traditional Indian food. Here, there was silverware even! Eating with utensils was a bit awkward for him, as he was out of practice. He watched his uncle spear the long noodles and then use a tablespoon to twirl it before putting it in his mouth. Aarar imitated him, happy to use his hands for the bread.

"So, how was the trip here?" Alisha asked as she sat down.

Aarar patted his chest as he swallowed a mouth full, "Wonderful! That transporter is the best!"

Alisha smiled, "I knew you would like it! Janet sure did!" Just mentioning her daughter's name made her eyes teared up, so she looked away for a moment.

Aarar turned his gaze down to his plate. It made him teared up to here her name. Pia noticed, so she reached for him, hugging his neck and breaking down into sobs. "I'm sorry Aarar, I just can't stop crying!"

He hugged her back and the two cried together for a few minutes. When Pia finally pulled away, they noticed that John had left the room. He came back a few minutes later with moist red eyes, he took his seat, and then reached across the table to pat his wife's hand without looking up at her. That first night was the most difficult, but it would soon get better for them, as they learned how to comfort each other.

It was as they were finishing dinner that Pia was able to compose herself enough to explain to Aarar that he should make himself at home for his first night, but that the next day, she wanted to have a talk with him about all the suspicious activity that preceded her daughters death. She knew that Aarar and Janet were close online and that he might have information that she didn't have, so that maybe they could put the pieces together and discover the true cause of Janet's death. Aarar nodded his agreement.

After his second dinner, Aarar unloaded his things from the transporter and began piling them onto Janet's bedroom floor. He looked around himself, she had a large room with the head of her bed pushed against the door-wall, and a desk pushed against the opposite wall with a large area in between that was surely used for VR. There were book selves lining another wall with two large windows on either side of her desk. Aarar stepped up to one of the large windows to appreciate the night time view of their wild back yard. He noted that the tall wooden fence that used to line the back edge of the property was gone so that he could see the neighboring yard and the tall trees of the nature park that were beyond that.

Then, he walked to her book shelf and was happily surprised to see a six inch replica of the Kali statue that he had designed for his show's set. He picked it up and marveled at the detail and color. One of the last interactions that he'd had with Janet, was when the two of them were at his palace and he was showing her his new design. She was delighted and asked for the file. He smiled at the thought, apparently she liked it so much that she converted it to a vector file and printed it. This made him really happy. After marveling over the statuette he carefully set it back on to the shelf.

It was then, that he looked down and notice pink chalk lines on the floor. Janet's floor was made of small pieces of wood that had been sanded and polished till the wooden seams were undetectable to the touch. He knew that the entire wing of the house was built by his Uncle John, who was well known for his craftsmanship with wood. Ironically, his daughter was also a carpenter, but online. Her job was to create interiors for rented homes in the Oogle History program. But, he knew that she also had a 'side hustle' that was transforming 2d video into Virtual reality. They often discussed some of her more interesting requests.

He walked to her desk, she had a large monitor hanging over it, with a stylus and thumb pad sitting neatly off to the side. He picked up the thumb pad, it was a new model that he didn't own but was familiar with. It was used with newer apps that no longer used thumb print images, but rather used a small program that the thumb pad created to measure pressure and other characteristics, adding extra security.

He picked up the device and turned it over in his hand, examining it before setting it back on to the desk. This told him that his first step into hacking his cousin's computer would be to get a copy of her DNA so that a 3d image of her thumb could be printed. He had read about the government program that would do this for the family of a deceased loved one, in an effort to combat the 'dark web' market that grieving survivors were having to resort to when trying to access their loved ones online information. He would have to discuss this with his aunt, who most likely possessed Janet's baby teeth.

He opened the top drawer of the desk, to find pencils, pens, etc all neatly arrange. In the back he noticed a journal. He reached for it, but then hesitated. Was this something he needed to give his Aunt, or would Kali want him to be the first to open it? He decided that it needed his inspection first, so he opened it. There on the first page, above a series of scrolling lines she wrote, 'Someday I will haunt you, and it will be electronically and through what I create.' This made him smile. It also made him realize that whatever else was written here, he needed to be the first to read it.

When he turned around, he noticed another pink chalk line, just under Janet's bed. He walked over and knelt down to examine the marks better. They were each, two lines that formed right angles. Together they would have made the bottom of a box. But, it was clear that they weren't made with a straight edge, but rather hand drawn...'to trace something?' Aarar contemplated. Then, he wondered why, his normally very neat cousin, would use chalk on the floor and then not wipe it clean when she was finished, with whatever it was, that she was working on. He looked around the rest of the room for more chalk marks, but didn't find any. He found this interesting.

He made his way back to the transporter room and started carrying more of his things to Janet's room. It was mostly clothing and tech equipment, but not too much of either. He had left his book collection and other sentimental things at his parents. Janet had a much larger book collection than he did, anyway, most of the books unopened, as reading was done electronically or through audio, but paper books were popular collectibles.

After a bit of organizing, he set his computer on the open area of Janet's desk and turned it on. There were always messages, but one from Cynthia got his attention first. He opened it up and read her thank you for the interview and the fun time afterward. She mentioned again how she would like to meet him in person. He smiled, 'so the Prince of Hind had made another conquest!' But, he had no intention of an 'in person' visit, although, he would continue to string her along since he enjoyed Sheba's company.

There was another message from the kid who had, somehow, beaten Kali for top score in Gladiator. He still didn't understand how this could have happened, but the kid was top score, so he responded with a message arranging for the interview. He sifted through the rest of the messages, there was also a message from the newest 4-star-general in the Army game. This guy was anxious for an interview, too, and Aarar did have a bit of an ulterior motive for this interview, as it was discovered that the guy was also related to a celebrity and Aarar had planned a few questions on that subject as well. He knew the interview would get lots of views. So, he quickly returned the message.

He worked late into the night again, finishing school work last. Sleeping in the new room was difficult, since he hadn't spent many nights away from his childhood home. All of the wonderful, new, changes were still unsettling.

He woke well into the next afternoon. He found his aunt anxiously waiting for him at the kitchen table. She had wanted to knock on his door, but was afraid to disturb him. He was her most worthy guest.

"Ah! Aarar!" his aunt chirped as he walked into the kitchen, "Alisha warned me that you were a late sleeper!"

"So sorry," he apologized, "I had a lot of work to finish last night, so I was up late." He stopped in front of her and nodded humbly. He was wearing his long white shirt again, it was his favorite garment.

"Don't worry, don't worry," his Aunt repeated. "You can make up your own schedule here!"

"Thank you!" Aarar smiled and took a chair at the kitchen table, looking at his aunt and not knowing what to do next.

"Would you like coffee?" she asked,

"Yes, that would be good."

Pia moved around the kitchen to get a coffee mug to pour him a cup, then she sat it in front of him. "How about something to eat?"

"Yes, I am starved," he admitted.

The two chatted about pleasant things as Pia made him an omelet with salsa poured over it and then sat across from him and watched him eat it. Aarar thought the salsa was a wonder curry, different. Finally, she took away his empty plate and poured more coffee for them both. Then, she sat down across from him again, and folded her hands in front of her.

Aarar felt uncomfortable, then remembered that he needed to tell her about the DNA. "Do you have any of Janet's baby teeth?"

"Yes, of course, I kept every one!"

"Great! We need them to collect DNA for a copy of her thumb," he explained. Pia nodded, not knowing how this would be accomplished, but trusting her nephew."

"So," Pia started, "First, I just want to thank you again for coming here. I'm really happy to have you!" she said quietly, in all sincerity. "Now, these problems all started with that terrible trip to Mammoth cave! Why she wanted to go there, I don't know! And why, alone? She told me that it was just something that she wanted to do, but then her transporter got stolen and she was kidnapped! That part of the country is no longer a safe place to go!" Pia shook her head and Aarar nodded in agreement. "She never identified the men. I don't know if she was scared or what, but she wouldn't even tell us!" Pia pointed at herself then made a hands up gesture. "There had to be some way for her to give the police more information than she did, I just couldn't understand it! No one has been arrested, the transporter was never found to this day! Then, as soon as she gets a replacement from the insurance company, she's off again, and this time for the last time! All alone, again! Why?" Pia tried to compose herself, she knew that tears were not helpful at that time. After a few moments, she wiped her eyes with her hand, and looked back at Aarar who was sitting quietly, listening. "I have a theory, I've read about something called the Stockholm syndrome, this is when a hostage falls in love with their capture," she looked up at Aarar, "do you think this could have happened?"

Aarar quietly considered this, "she never talked to me about what happened on that trip. When I asked her, she just said that she didn't want to discuss any of it."

"Did she talk about anyone new in her life?"

Aarar shook his head, then paused, "she did start taking an interest in Army." He explained slowly, as he was recalling the details, "there was someone else she played with that had built a tunneling system."

Pia looked confused, she didn't understand anything that he had just said, and didn't know how it was relevant. "Are you saying that she played a game with someone?"

Aarar hunched up his shoulders, "She believed it was a person." His Aunt looked even more confused, so he explained in more detail, "you know, whenever you are in virtual reality, you never know for sure if someone is an avatar of a person, or if it's a bot, but I think Janet knew this avatar was a person, someone who she might have even known in real life."

This made more sense to Pia. "Okay, what was their name?"

Aarar thought for a few moments, "I don't know. I don't think she ever told me."

"Are you sure?"

He thought about it some more, and shook his head, "No, I don't think she told me, because I remember asking her and she just ignored my question and kept talking about the game. I don't think she wanted me to know."

This only caused Pia to be more agitated and anxious, "did she tell you anything that could be a clue to his identity?"

Aarar could see the desperation in his aunt's face and he worried that he had caused it for no reason. "I don't know, I'm not sure that she even knew," he lied, trying to deescalate the situation.

"Do you know any of her friends? Were there some online that might know who the Army guy was?"

Aarar was very uncomfortable, his aunt was making him remember that last conversation that he had with Janet at his Palace, and it was suspicious, but he didn't want to cause his aunt more anxiety. "I can ask around," he promised.

Pia sat up in her chair, as she had been leaning closer to her nephew as they spoke. "There is another thing I wanted you to do for me, please attend some of her social groups. She had a few and I think that she must have confided to someone. Especially the travel group. I think if I went, they would be suspicious of me, but you could go and talk to them easier, as you are the right age."

"Do they meet online?" he asked hopefully.

But, Pia shook her head, "I don't know, but I want you to go in person, they may not even be aware that she...passed on."

Now Aarar became anxious, "I'll look online first —"

"No," Pia interrupted, "what if her killer is one of the members of that group? I want you to go in person and see what kind of reaction you get from them when you tell them about her death! You could just show up, and tell them as a group about why you are there in her place, then just watch the faces of everyone there. See if you can tell from their expressions if they know anything about it! I want you to attend every meeting this week. Go to all of them, her social group and any others, too!"

Aarar was now very uncomfortable, he couldn't do any of this in person, there had to be a way of attending the meetings online, he told himself, not wanting to disappoint his aunt by saying it out loud. But, she kept looking at him in the eyes, he knew he had to respond, so finally he nodded, "okay," he lied.

"Oh, and what do we need to do with her teeth?" she asked.

"There is a lab in the city, you could bring the teeth there and they will extract a bit from the inside of one of them with a tiny drill. You can wait while they do it, then take back the teeth. From that, they send you the file needed to print a copy of her thumb," he explained, but his aunt still looked puzzled. "To open her computer," he clarified.

"Ohhhh," Pia nodded, "you can go with me. Can you make the appointment for today?"

Aarar sighed, this was going to be tough, all of it, but how could he explain to his aunt that he feared being in public more than anything, so instead, he just nodded. He returned to his new room, then contacted the lab. He was told that he could bring the teeth by any time before 5pm, as the procedure didn't take very long, but Pia would definitely need to be there to verify her identity and that her daughter was indeed deceased. DNA had become a hot commodity for identity thieves, so strict laws to protect it had been instituted.

He stared at his computer screen for several moments, thinking about excuses; he was ill, he had schoolwork, he needed to take a nap...all of it was lame and he knew it. His aunt had been so kind to him, not just recently, but always, and now she needed him. It was his turn to help her. He needed to suck it up and go. There would be people, but he could just keep space between them and himself, he ruminated.

He got up and returned to the kitchen where he found his aunt with a collection of Janet's teeth, all in little, dated envelopes that were being stuffed into a larger one. She looked up at him and then mumbled something about hoping that they didn't get the teeth mixed up. He told her that they could leave any time for the lab.

"Great!" she said, stuffing the larger envelope into her purse. "We'll have to use Janet's transporter. John took the other one to his work site today." She looked up at Aarar with a smile, "it's like his little home away from home when he needs to be at a far away location." Aarar could tell that she was trying hard to be upbeat, but he could still hear little sniffles between words.

They met up in the transporter room. Pia looked around herself remembering when it used to be a garage. Time passed so quickly! Janet's set of rooms didn't even exist then! Aarar boarded the craft as, the door was already opened. He stood at the council and entered the address of their destination while Pia made herself comfortable in a padded, swivel chair opposite the couch. "This is nice! Isn't it?" she marveled, setting her purse on the table next to her, and then moving the chair to view her surroundings. Aarar made an agreeable sound, then took his seat across from her.

He was trying to stay calm and resign himself to the fact that he would have to leave the transporter and walk through another building that most likely will have other humans walking around that are not related to him. Strangers, scary, scary strangers. People were such sharp pointy things! Every real life encounter seemed to make him squirm, and get nervous. Especially women. He couldn't look a woman in the eyes and have a conversation, no, not in real life. It was always weird and embarrassing. They could 'see' him! There was no place to hide anything! No invisible right hand, controlling the show. Everything was exposed. He was starting to work himself up. He could feel his heart beating fast. He felt hot. He jumped up and walked to the back of the transporter, pulling a bottle of water out of the refrigerated compartment. He rubbed the cold glass bottle across his forehead before opening it.

When he returned to his seat, his aunt was looking at him with her head cocked to one side and a sympathetic look on her face. She reached over and patted his knee, then looked out her window. Aarar was a bit embarrassed, he could tell that she was thinking that his agitated state was over his cousin. He would be even more embarrassed if she knew the truth. He turned sideways and watched scenery pass by the window.

The lab had a transporter drive thru. The vehicle stopped mid way to let them out in a lobby before driving itself off to park on a charging pad. There was a set of elevators with a sign next to the doors that named each department and it's floor. Inside, Aarar pressed the button for floor two. The doors closed. He sighed, not one other person so far. Maybe this would be easier than he anticipated. The elevator let them out in an empty hallway, a sign with an arrow that pointed the way to the lab was in front of them. They turned to their left and a skinny man with a pink riding suit walked his bicycle down the hall passed them. This made Aarar smile. 'I can do this,' he told himself.

They followed the corridor, passed unmarked doors until they came to a larger entrance with a set of windows on one side and a sign on the other, indicating that it was indeed the lab. Aarar began to feel tremors, he backed away from the door, so that his Aunt could turn the knob and open it. Inside, on the right was a small lobby with two rows of chairs and a low table between them. A man was sitting with his back to the wall, peeking up at the couple as they walked in. On their left was a half wall of glass over a desk and at the desk, behind the glass was a woman sitting at a screen. Aarar immediately averted his gaze to the floor. He crossed his arms in a defensive pose with his back to the far wall. He looked up at his Aunt who looked back at him with a confused expression, as she was expecting him to take the lead and talk with the receptionist, but instead he just uncrossed his arms to point feebly at her purse. "You have the teeth," he mumbled in low voice.

As soon as she moved to the little window near the young woman behind the glass, he immediately returned his gaze to the floor, and recrossed his arms. Pia thought her nephew's behavior was strange, but addressed the lady behind the counter to explain their visit. She set her purse down and extracted the valuable envelope with teeth in it. Then, she was directed to have a seat in their lobby. Aarar followed his aunt and took the chair next to her. Then, the door to the room opened again, this time it was a middle aged woman with another, very pretty, younger woman.

Pia, took the opportunity to reach over and pat her nephew's knee. "Why are you so tense," she asked softly.

This kind of question always flustered him, as he didn't know how to respond. The two women left the counter and were moving toward the row of chairs. So, he just shrugged and smiled as though he didn't know what she was referring to. His arms still crossed tightly in front of him, and his legs restless, he fidgeted nervously, as he tried to look normal. The two women took seats at the end of his row. He felt hot and began noticing the feeling of nausea. Finally, afraid of being sick, he rocked himself to his feet and apologized to his aunt before bolting toward the door. "I'm sorry, I don't feel well," he explained, holding the door open, he turned again to his aunt, but with his eyes cast downward, "I'm going to sit in the transporter," he explained before rushing out.

She watched him with a confused, concerned expression. 'How odd,' she thought.

He summoned the transporter with his communicator from the elevator, and was so happy to see it turning into the circle drive of the drive thru, that he was able to ignore a small group of people who had just arrived. After climbing aboard, he slapped the door button at the top of the two stairs, then threw himself onto the couch. "Ah," he sighed, safety. His nausea disappeared with the hotness. The transporter remained still for a few minutes, then, for lack of direction, it lurched forward in search of a charging pad.

Aarar closed his eyes, he was in love with the vehicle, it had just become his sanctuary.

When they got back to the house, Pia promised to forward the email with instructions for printing out a copy of Janet's thumb, as soon as it arrived. Then, she speculated that, surely, as soon as he was able to open her computer then he would be able to find information on her social groups. "It will probably be good for you to socialize," she added. Aarar smiled and nodded, but he would be avoiding those 'in person' groups as much as possible. Maybe, he could attend online, he pondered.

When he got back to his room, he opened his computer to check his messages. After responding to a few he scrolled down to find the last one that Janet had sent him. It had an attachment, he knew what it was and had long ago responded back to his cousin. The attachment was her latest version of a villa that the two of them had been discussing. This would have been the last draft, but he hadn't taken the time to upload it to his Kingdom yet. He considered that he still didn't have the time, but the sudden urge to see it was too much to resist. After some technical issues were resolved, he put on Janet's goggles and gloves, as hers were the latest model.

The program first took him to his throne room. From there he moved forward, to the large vine covered balcony. It overlooked the sea and was especially beautiful as the sun was just beginning to set, making the sky a lovely pink color. He leaned over the railing to see farther down the coast, where there now stood an ancient looking, Italian, villa. He used his controller to hop onto the railing, then he spread his arms out and dropped off the edge, gliding to the sandy beach below, he loved the flying sensation. Then, he walked along the edge of the water, so that it would lap across his feet. It looked so real, he could kind of feel the water splashing against his ankles.

Soon he stood in front of the small but impressive dwelling. It had an enclosure of thick gray stone blocks. The entrance way featured a stone arbor that was covered in grape vine, with pink moon flowers, just beginning to open up amongst the purple bunches of grapes. He pushed open the rod iron gate to follow a terracotta path to the doorway. He stood and looked around himself to admire all the green foliage and the sound of birds, before opening the door.

Inside, were white plaster walls and several windows with wooden frames and shutters that were pushed open so that the room was bathed with the fading yellow light of the sun. The entrance way was a continuation of the red terracotta, with a set of stairs at the end and rooms branching off the main hall in both directions. He tried the room to his left first. It featured oriental carpet that depicted a snow covered mountain range in the center, with a lone horseman walking toward it. The edges were decorated with intricate designs that depicted wildlife and fauna. The only furniture was his golden chair, which had been converted to a shiny wooden one. The windows looked into the walled off garden.

He decided to go upstairs next. This area was all open on both sides of the staircase, with wooden floors that looked very much like the actual floors in Janet's room. There was an open air balcony at the top. He moved to the west side where the sun was now lower in the sky, as water lapped the sandy beach between great, black, boulders. 'So beautiful,' he thought, then he sent out his intentions to thank his cousin for the beautiful villa, hoping that they could somehow reach her. He wished that she could be there with him to see it installed.

It was as he was contemplating all of this that he noticed movement on the beach in front of his palace. Straining to see better, he slowly made out a red and black figure walking his way along the waters edge. His jaw dropped, it was Kali. He called out to her. She stopped and looked up at him. After they made eye contact, she suddenly turned and disappeared. Stunned, he flew down to the beach, but she was long gone. His mind raced as he tried to consider how her avatar could have been included in the program. But, no, it couldn't be. Maybe, she could have left her image there, but, not her avatar, that was walking and responding to his call by looking up. Aarar was confused, he searched the palace, then remembered to check his guest register. He pulled down a menu and chose it off the list. It appeared in front of him, he located his login, then there, under his handle was another, Kali.

Well after Aarar had taken off the goggles, he continued to ponder if his cousin could have somehow programmed her avatar into the villa code. She was good, she was creative, could she have done this thing that he thought was impossible? Was Kali, somehow, living on without Janet? It was only Janet and he that had access to his kingdom. The only way another avatar could visit was if it was attached to one of them or invited. The only thing new he had done recently was upload the villa program to his kingdom. Could there have been code hidden in that program that activated the avatar when it was loaded?

Then, he suddenly remembered how it was Kali that was defeated in the Gladiator game. Hidden codes were used to identify avatars by the games and site they visit, so, if the Gladiator game reported that it was Kali who was defeated, then it was Kali...or someone impersonating her.

Aarar slapped his forehead! That was it! The missing communicator! Someone had stolen her identity through her communicator! He remembered asking his Aunt Pia if she had contacted the bank when Janet's communicator hadn't been located and she had already done this, but, these actions would have nothing to do with Janet's avatar.

He jumped off his chair and put on his goggles again, he needed to take his cousin's rights to have full access to his kingdom! The Kingdom was in danger! He then, accessed his sites most sensitive information, he took away her right to access code or copy it. Then, he started to erase her avatar's ability to visit his kingdom altogether, but stopped short, maybe if he allowed Kali, and Kali only, to visit but not change or steal anything, then it could help him identify who this impostor was.

Meanwhile...on the outskirts of town in 1930 Oogle History, a beautiful, young Indian girl appeared, wearing a bright red sari under her black armor. She stood for a few moments, looking around herself. She appeared to be on a narrow dirt path, with trees and wild foliage all around her. She put a hand to her forehead to shield her eyes from the bright light of the electric sun. She could see the tops of buildings in the distance, so she followed the trail toward the buildings. Slowly a riverbank was revealed, where a row of small, tar paper shacks lined the shore. There appeared a large red #5 on one of the center houses. Kali considered this a moment, she was looking for suite #4, so, was it the one on the right or the left? She counted the houses, 1, 2, 3, 4, 5, 6, 7. "Ok! I got this mother fucker!" growled a deep masculine voice.

Kali walked to the door of the fourth shack and knocked. The door opened and a formally dressed butler in a tuxedo, bent his head under the low threshold of the door, and looked at Kali in an impatient way, "May I help you?" he inquired.

Kali hadn't thought about access with her new identity, "I'm on the list, I'm just using a different avatar, so, um...could you look me up under a different identity?"

"I'm sure, I don't know what you are talking about- excuse me!" The butler disappeared back into the doorway and shut the door.

Kali shook her head. She pulled a device out of the air and shouted, "Spore!" but the device displayed a, "?" to connote that it didn't understand. Kali became more aggravated, "Spore! At #4riverside, 1930 oogle history!" she shouted. Finally, the little screen showed the picture of an old, scruffy looking avatar, whose initial expression was one of surprise and interest, "Well, hello there!" he chirped.

Kali looked into the device, "Hey Spore, it's me!" the avatar hissed.

The little man on the device, made a face, "Kevin?"

"Yeah, Kevin! So, will you tell that damn butler to let me in?"

The scruffy man made a 'hump' sound then flipped off the video. The butler reappeared at the door and held it open for the Indian goddess. Inside, the empty building was an open elevator. Kali stepped inside and pressed the only button. The doors closed, and then, the bottom of the elevator seemed to fall out and Kali suddenly found herself standing outside again, but now there were other avatars all around her. The row of seven little tar paper houses still lined the shore, but there were people in little boats floating down the river, some avatars were rowing, some fishing. The doors of the little houses #1-3 were open and an older couple sat on the porch of #3 in rocking chairs. The occupants of houses #1 and #2 were sitting together in front of a large outdoor screen while a movie played. There was now a sign over the door of #4, "Spore's Emporium." Kali turned the knob and walked in.

Spore looked up from a counter that was inside. "So, what the hell's goin' on with you Kevin? Get a sex change?"

"Ha Ha!" boomed the gruff voice. "You can laugh all you want but, I'm tellin' ya', this chick has all kinds of access!"

Spore knew Kevin's game, it wasn't the first time his friend had visited him in disguise. Both men made their money on the dark web, and identity theft was big business for them. Stealing someone's online identity was like discovering a buried treasure chest, you never knew what you'd find inside.

Kevin continued excitedly, "You know who the Prince of Hind is, right?"

Spore just shrugged. Kali waved him off, "anyway," she continued impatiently, "this chick, has FULL access to the Prince's whole kingdom! Dude! It is soooo cool. I'm going back and looking to copy the programming. So, that's why I'm here, I need a little expertise and thought you might be able to help me out!"

Spore shrugged again, "I don't know, haven't seen the place."

Kali continued, enthusiastically, "Well, I've got full access. I'll just attach you to me."

"Sure, but, you gotta pay for my time! I don't just work for free!"

Kali moaned, "Listen, when you see what I have access to, you are going to shit! Then, I'll give you a copy of the code! We can both make a mint!"

Spore nodded, he had no reason not to believe Kevin. He consented to being attached to Kali's avatar before it disappeared. But when Kali reached the Prince's kingdom, she was alone. She started to message Spore, but before she could, she looked up to see the Prince of Hind standing in front of her. So, in a panic, she disappeared.

The Prince could not believe his eyes, but then, she was gone in a flash. Seeing her was unnerving for him, even though he had already figured out that she was an impostor. He considered his decision to allow her protected access, he hated the idea that someone else was using her avatar, but he also really wanted to discover who this person was and find out how they had acquired Kali's identity.

He pulled off his goggles and gloves, he really had a lot of business and school work to get to. Lately, there had been so many other things distracting him, that work was piling up. He sat down at the desk where his computer was already running. He saw a message from his aunt with an attached file that was Janet's thumb imprint. He got up and turned on the nearby 3D printer and made sure it was full of resin, then sent the file to print. He checked the rest of his messages while he waited for the printer to finish. There was a message from one of his sponsors. Part of his agreement with them included him appearing at their cyber cafe to host a variety show once a month. This was something that he always looked forward to. It was a way for him to advertise his show and fulfill the requirements of his cash sponsor, at the same time. Win/Win.

The printer made a beep sound as it was finished. Aarar retrieved the hardened piece of plastic and brought it to the desk. He pushed his computer aside and flipped on Janet's holographic one. The large monitor that was attached to the wall lit up. A prompt asked for a thumb scan. Aarar pulled the thumb pad near him and rolled the little plastic cast of Janet's thumb against it. It was accepted. A new screen appeared with several options. Aarar chose the Universal Communications Center, (UCC), it was a widely used app that pulled all communications onto one screen. Hopefully, this program would have a record of everyone she communicated with. But, to his disappointment, he quickly saw that the top most information was from two years ago!

He sat back in his chair and wondered if the Kali impostor was also responsible for cleaning her communication records. He sighed, then sat up and noticed, that there was something from that very day! He opened it up and learned that the impostor's name was Kevin.

In a small city in Kentucky, James Aldridge had noticed an advertisement announcing the newest four star general in Army was to be interviewed by the Prince of Hind. He didn't know who the Prince of Hind was, but he was interested in seeing what the guy had to say, sometimes they gave away secrets on these interview shows. He wondered what this guy, Voltar, might have to say about secret places in the game. He was always interested in stuff like that. He had planned to watch the interview live, as it would give him the opportunity to ask questions himself.

So, now, he was at the police station, where he worked, tuned into the site, that was a kind of network, of avatar based programs. He shook his head when a flashing image of the prince popped on, this was not his kind of show, he could already tell. Then, the Prince appeared on his throne, and that was when Jim realized that the theme of the set was Indian.

A twinge of guilt ran through his body, but he looked away momentarily and shook it off.

Slowly, the camera panned out to show Voltar's avatar sitting next to him in a slightly less ornate throne. After exchanging greetings the camera panned out a bit more, and that was when Jim noticed the beautiful Kali sculpture between the men.

His jaw dropped open, he froze the screen to examine the goddess more closely. 'Yes,' he concluded, it was her, it was her face, her body, except for the additional arms, it was Janet's avatar! And it did look like Janet!

"And for today's interview I have managed to book the newest four star general in Army, Voltar!" the Prince announced. The sound of several audience members pressing the applaud key ensued. "So, Voltar, how does it feel to be only the twenty-sixth four star in the history of the game?"

"Honored – well actually, there was a lot of work involved! I've clocked over 2000 hours! I'd say, it was about time!" More applause. The Prince's avatar blows smoke out of his ears.

"Now that you've made it through the ranks, are there any additional perks?"

"Now I can pick my battles, usually everyone wants me in their unit. And...I get paid for appearances and promotions! That's always a good thing! No more being told that I'm wasting time when I game!"

The Prince chuckled, he related more than he wanted to let on. "I hear that the girls really like a man with medals!" This time his avatar made the twinkle eye.

Voltar laughed, "I hope so! That's why I wear them everywhere!" He pointed at the metals on his chest. The Prince zoomed in on it and made a whistle. The audience laughed.

"You will have to go for drinks with me after the show, so we can try it out!" the Prince teased.

"Not that you need any help!" Voltar giggled, "those Tanoshi girls are wild!" Voltar wanted to elaborate, but decided that it might not be appropriate, as they were being taped.

"But, back to the subject in hand – I mean, at hand!" the audience laughed and applauded as the Prince's avatar made another twinkle eye.

"Could you tell us about that last victorious battle that scored you your last medal?" the Prince asked in a more sober tone.

Jim held his fingers over the keyboard, he had planned to ask about secret tunnels, but typed out a question about the Kali statue instead. 'Is your statue modeled after a real person,' he typed, then sent. The Prince was reading the questions to himself, as they appeared on a computer screen off camera, while Voltar discussed the game. He noticed the one about Kali, but chose to ignore it.

The conversation went over, as Voltar was very popular and received many technical questions about the game. When they had finally finished with the last of them, the Prince turned to his guest and asked the question that he had been most anxious to ask, "I hear you have a very famous older brother."

Voltar sighed, "Yes, but, don't ask me anything about him! I don't want to be a security breech!" he laughed, but no one seemed to get the joke. The Prince pressed the laugh button several times to make up the difference.

"Yeah, I hear that he is busy with those SAIN people! Don't suppose you could tell me about that either?" the Prince needled, as he knew that Liam Moore was a hot topic everywhere.

"No," Voltar stated, shaking his head vigorously.

The last thing that the Prince of Hind wanted, was to make this guest unhappy, so he let his final answer mark the end of the interview. Then, he looked into the camera again and added, "And now, I wanted to address all the questions that I've been getting about my new artwork," he panned the camera to the statue. Jim sat up in his seat. "This is Kali, she is the Hindu Goddess of death and time. People keep asking me if her image is based on a real person, and all I can say, is that if you think you may have met her, then you are indeed, a lucky person!" He brought the camera back to the Prince's face for one last twinkle wink to end the show on.

When Aarar finished with his interview, he walked out of his new room and headed toward the kitchen, where he knew his aunt was anxiously waiting for an update. He explained that he had an important conference call and couldn't be disturbed. So, now she and his Uncle John were sitting at the table with after dinner coffee. As soon as they noticed him Pia jumped up and made him a plate, then put it in the microwave to heat up. "Aarar, I made fried chicken with breading, the way you like it!" Pia announced with a smile. This was another dish that his mother didn't make. He was starting to wonder if his Aunt really was trying to 'steal' him, as his mother had complained before he left her home.

"Thank you! I am hungry! The call went over," Aarar explained, expanding on the fib he had told her earlier. He sat down at the table and between bites he told them that he had been able to create the thumb model and that it was successful at opening Janet's computer. But, then he had to tell them about how her communications had been erased for the last two years.

"What does that mean?" his Aunt asked in an alarmed way.

"It means that someone did take her communicator."

"Could there be another explanation? How do you know for sure?" his Uncle countered.

"No," Aarar shook his head, "the fact is, someone also stole her avatar. It's no kind of accident. Someone took her phone, cleaned the messages from the last two years, off of it, and began using her avatar."

Both parents looked at him in disbelief, their fears were confirmed. Pia began to cry.

"How do you know someone stole her avatar?" John asked, wanting to confirm the conclusion that both he and his wife were making.

"I saw her," he explained.

"Did she say anything?" Pia asked in a desperate voice.

It pained Aarar to see his Aunt and Uncle so distraught, all over again. "No. It's not Janet. It's someone else, a man, I found out that his name is Kevin, but that is all I've been able to figure out so far. Every time I see the avatar it disappears as soon as it sees me."

"Every time? How often have you seen...it?" his Uncle asked.

"Twice, just today. I think, most likely, they were exploring places that her avatar has access to, maybe looking for programming to steal," he shook his head, "but, I don't know yet."

Everyone was silent for several moments. Pia was holding a tissue to her nose, trying to keep from breaking down. John looked angrily into the distance. Aarar didn't know what to do. Finally, his Uncle reached across the table and took his nephews hand, "I can't believe how much you've found out after just one day! I was skeptical, but son, you have really come through for us! Thank you!" He looked deep into Aarar's eyes. It was all very emotional, but now it was clear. There was more to Janet's accident. In fact, it was looking to all three of them, like it wasn't an accident at all.

As soon as Aarar finished his dinner, he got up to go back to his room when his Aunt blurted out a reminder that Janet's travel club was meeting the next day, and he had promised to go. He started to mumble something about going online, but his Aunt quickly shot down his idea, as she felt that the visit needed to be in person. "They may not even know that she's passed," Pia reminded him.

So, reluctantly, he agreed.

When he got back to his room, he had work to do concerning another clue, that he had yet to mention, to his Aunt and Uncle. The message that was sent after the phone was cleaned. Kevin must have forgotten that he was using a stolen avatar, as he gave the name and address of his acquaintance within the message itself. Aarar had given the situation some thought and decided that the only way Spore would communicate with him is if he looked like the avatar Kevin had used. He was going to become Kali. So, now, he was retrieving the image of Kali that he had stored for the statue and was making a second version, but with only two arms. Then, he converted it to a file format that his operation system would accept as an avatar.

After donning his goggles and gloves, he entered the address of 1930s Ooogle History. It was an elaborate world in virtual reality that anyone could visit. It was a new adaptation of simply, Ooogle History, which used vintage satellite photographs to create an exact replica of anywhere in the US and some foreign counties. People often chose their favorite place and time period, rented their home and then, they often hired someone like Janet to customize the blank inside of this building that they then inhabited virtually. There were many places to visit, but most required you to pay membership fees to be admitted. Otherwise, you could only visit avatars that allowed you on their guest list. 1930 Ooogle History was a new version that allowed avatars to visit a stylized 1930 world. He was hoping that his appearance would give him a pass to enter Spore's suite.

When the program dropped him off in the middle of a field, he was a bit disoriented. He looked down at his feminine hands and noticed the shear, silk fabric of the red sari that he was wearing, gently followed his movements. It felt very strange to him. Then he noticed that he was actually standing on a narrow dirt trail that cut through a prairie of tall grass. He could see the roofs of buildings in the distance. He moved toward them, until the prairie opened up to a river with seven small, black shacks lining it's bank. He noticed how empty it was. No other avatars could be seen anywhere. But, there was a large number 5 written in red paint on one of them. So, he used that clue to lead him to the door of suite #4.

He knocked on the door. It was opened by the butler, who silently held the door open for him. Inside, there was only one place to go, an open elevator, so he entered. He pressed the one button to find himself suddenly transported to the outside of the building again. Perplexed, he looked around himself to find that the riverbank was now alive with activity. Avatars were everywhere, enjoying the dimming rays of an electric sun. He realized that he was most likely in a bootleg version of the program. The little shack must have been an illegal portal. This made him uneasy, as you could never tell if you were being secretly scanned in these types of places. But, he pressed on.

Now there was a sign, over the door of #4, that said, 'Spore's Emporium.' So, he knew he was in the right place. This time the door opened without the butler. The inside was nearly as shabby as the exterior. A rough looking, counter with a glass top occupied the wall to his left and behind the counter was a disheveled older man wearing a tattered, felt hat. He looked up from the counter as Kali walked over the threshold.

"So, did ya' figure out a way to get me access?" he asked expectantly.

This was the part of the plan that Aarar was most concerned about, his voice. So, he pantomimed talking without issuing any sound.

Spore wrinkled his brow, "say that again."

Kali repeated the performance until Spore stopped her, "your headset isn't working! I can't hear anything! Try turning it off and on," he grumbled, then paused, waiting impatiently.

Kali pretended to be doing something, then looked again at Spore and mouthed the words, 'how about now.' Spore shook his head and waved back at the avatar in a dismissive way.

"Just..tell me! Did you get shit figured out so that I can attach to you and go there? Did ya' do what I told ya'? Nod yes or no!" Spore stammered with an irritated voice. Kali nodded yes.

"Okay then, let's go! I got shit to do!" the annoyed avatar grumbled.

Kali quickly attached Spore's avatar to her own, then the two disappeared.

But, when they reappeared Spore was confused. He looked around himself in a panic, "What the hell?" he shouted before disappearing.

Kali transformed into the Prince of Hind. A VR police officer at a console looked up from a screen and reported, "we got it!" The other officer cheered. The Prince was especially happy. He had been in contact with the office right after he found the accidental message in Janet's UCC. He was advised to bring the avatar to the only place that could legally scan an avatar, a VR police station.

These virtual police stations were usually run from offices in brick and mortar precincts. They were a very necessary arm of the police force since most crime now occurred online. The FBI and CIA also had virtual offices. It wasn't enough to be at a computer keyboard, you needed to have agents at the scene, that meant using virtual officers as well.

The officer at the console now ran a check to see if the 'Spore' avatar was also stolen or if it could be connected to a flesh-and-blood person. At his earlier visit, it was an officer that pointed out to the Prince, that 'Kevin' sounded more like a real name than an avatar, so maybe the men knew one another in real life.

It only took a few minutes for the check to come back, "well, looks like it was not reported missing, and so a real police officer will now make a visit to find out, in...Kentucky," the officer at the console announced.

"Great!" the Prince sighed. He then went on to give them the address of the portal, it looked like Spore might also be on the hook for bootlegging copies of Oooogle History. One of the officers went into action to locate it before Spore could close it down.

Then, the officer gave him a bit of information that he was less enthusiastic to get, "If we confirm his online identity it will require an in-person deposition." The officer looked down at a device, "as soon as there is an arrest, you will need to report to the police department in Munfordville, Kentucky."

Aarar nodded his consent then pulled his goggles off and laid across the bed. This was all very exciting, but he wasn't sure if he really had anything to tell his Aunt and Uncle yet. And he was not happy about the deposition. But he wanted to tell someone! So, he called Cynthia, on a his communicator. They had been video chatting the night before. He had decided that he liked Cynthia better than Sheba. And he was becoming comfortable talking with her, even knowing that she could see him clearly on her communicator, him, not the Prince of Hind, and yet she acted like she still wanted him. Sometimes, as they spoke to one another, he even had the impulse to pull her through the device and sit next to him. Yet, later, when he considered being in the same room with her, it made his belly ache.

But, it was in the course of this conversation that Aarar recalled the officer saying that the avatar belonged to someone in Kentucky. This was the state that Janet had visited when her transporter was stolen.

And that, was how Cynthia ended up hearing the whole story about his cousin Janet and her suspicious death. Aarar didn't plan to tell her everything, but it was so nice to have someone to talk to. She wasn't Janet, but Cynthia had become a sympathetic ear for him.

They discussed what his strategy should be if he got another glimpse of the Kali impostor, or if the criminal would be frightened off by Spore being questioned by the police. Finally, it was decided that they should meet at the cyber cafe' just for little while. Both of the students had pressing assignments due, but they promised one another that they would only stay for a bit of entertainment, as it was open mic night at the cafe'.

Both donned their goggles and were transported to their favorite table. They sat in their golden chairs, enjoying the view of one another. Aarar really enjoyed that he had someone to confide in, so he came clean with his whole living situation to her.

She now knew about his small world, and was becoming suspicious of his anthropophobia, it was increasingly common among...well, everyone. Society was now structured in such a way that people could live their whole lives isolated from other people. Video, VR, RV, robots, electric transporters, communicators, and computers had caused human to human contact to be unnecessary. And no one knew how many 'shut ins' there really were.

What Aarar was finding out about Cynthia, is that she too felt that she was living in a very small world. But for her, the problem was that her parents had forced her to return home for online schooling as she was failing too many classes while living in a dormitory, and they felt that the problem was her social life. The truth about Cynthia was that she was the opposite of Aarar in this regard, it was lack of social contact that had led her to use virtual reality more often of late. And it was this hunger for contact in real life that started her to push for a real live meeting. The suggestion made Aarar uncomfortable, but he did enjoy her company and so he made her vague promises with no intention of following through. He would string her along like he had with all of the others, he told himself. While she was secretly formulating a plan to lure him into the real world.

In a police station in Kentucky, James Aldridge looks up from his desk when another officer tapped on the door frame to his office, as the door was already open. "Hey,

James," the man began, "we got a hot one! Ooooogle copyright infringement!"

Jim sighed, "yeah. Where?"

The man looked down to read off a small hand held device, "The VR police have sent a request for someone in our office to interview, Rupert Mosley at 444465 hwy 12." The officer looked up at James, "looks like it's about bootlegging software and the identity theft of Janet McDougal." Jim went cold. "Who do you want me to send?"

James tried his best not to change his expression, "I'll take care of it!

But the other officer continued, "I certainly wouldn't mind being your back up!" the man said then made the gesture of rubbing two fingers together, "Ooooogle Rewards! You know their's are up to $1000 a perp now!"

James, nodded and instructed him to close his door. What the other officer was referring to was the large bounties the Ooooogle corporation offered to officers who made arrests defending their copyrights. As these kinds of crimes had become high priority, thanks to the lobbying of mega-corporations who convinced the politicians and the public that these types of crimes were impacting the lives of everyone and needed to be taken seriously.

Jim pulled a communicator out of his pocket, "What the hell is going on? I thought you were giving that to Kevin to clean and now I got Spore about to be questioned about *her* ID being stolen? So tell me Hank, how does Spore know about her?!" James snarled. "Sounds like he's got the VR police on to him and so, you better make sure that, that damn communicator is clean and destroyed? Wait! Better yet, I want that son of a bitch back! You tell him I want every bit of that communicator in a bag, even if it's in pieces! You tell him that I want it waiting for me within the next 30 minutes! I'm on my way there!"

Jim was furious with himself for trusting his cousin to take care of the device. Now Janet's data and assets were being stolen and most likely involved in other crimes! He should have kept it himself and sat in the room while Kevin accessed her data and erased it. Then, he should have shot Kevin. He needed that physical evidence back, he needed to make sure it was never recovered. As for the meta data, he wasn't sure how to handle that.

He jumped up from his desk and mumbled something about his kid being sick before going out of the door. The officer from earlier reminded him about the Mosley interview, but Jim waved him off, "It can wait till I get back!"

The next afternoon Aarar found himself in the transporter, enroute to Janet's Travel Club. It was one of a few social clubs that she belonged to. Like most people, she enjoyed real life and outings with other humans, she never could quite understand her cousin's shyness.

Aarar was extremely nervous, and, as he was alone, no one would know that he had obtained a small bottle of whiskey on the way. He thought that the foul tasting stuff might give him courage. So, he sat longways on the couch, looking out the window and balancing a water glass partially filled with the amber liquid on his knee. He was wearing a bulky sweater over one of his cousin's tee shirts, he thought it might give him good luck.

As they pulled down main street, he noticed a new drop off lane had recently been added along the sidewalks downtown. It was enclosed in glass, now you could visit any of the old shops without going outdoors. That's how it was in most places, you never had to consider the weather outside when you got dressed for the day, even in northern areas that had snow. Everyplace had a drive up. Your electric vehicle drove inside the building to drop you off, then parked itself until it was summoned to pick you back up. You never had to go outside anymore. Aarar didn't own a winter coat or even a pair of boots.

Sooner than he would have liked, the transporter pulled into one of the glass covered lanes, then came to a stop in front of an old coffee shop where the meeting was to be held. He tipped the glass one last time to drain it before he disembarked. It wasn't until his feet hit the sidewalk that he felt the burn in the back of his throat from the liquid. He jumped when the doors closed and left him standing alone at the entrance of the coffee shop. The sidewalk looked empty except for an old ragged looking man sitting on a bench. He was clearly seeking Aarar's attention, but the young man was not interested in any unnecessary interactions, so he refused to look in the man's direction. Once inside the building, after taking in the smell of fresh roasted coffee and cinnamon, he scanned the room and noticed a small lit up marquee in the back corner that read, 'Travel club meeting 6pm.' There was a long table with chairs under the sign with two men sitting at it. One was quietly looking at his communicator as the other was busy arranging things on the table. Aarar walked near the one who most looked like the organizer. "Excuse me," he said meekly when the man noticed him. As soon as he explained who he was the man gasped and pushed a nearby chair out from under the table for Aarar to sit.

"I am so sorry about Janet!" he began in a sympathetic voice. "All of us just loved her sooo much! She really was the best!"

Aarar nodded in agreement as he timidly pushed the chair farther from the man and then sat on the edge of it. The man reached for his shoulder in an attempt to pat it in sympathy, but Aarar pulled back in a defensive way. So, without a hint of embarrassment, the man apologized and checked himself, as unsolicited touching was taboo in current culture, even with the best of intention. "I'm sorry, I just get so emotional thinking about her being gone! And so suddenly! I know how much she loved that park! I can't imagine how terrible it must have been to find out that she fell from one of the bluffs!" the man chatted, "and my name is Chris, by the way, and," he pointed in the direction of the other man who was now listening to the conversation, "this, is my partner, Tom. And we would love for you to stay for the meeting, we usually start at fifteen after since everyone is always late!" he complained.

"Thank you," Aarar responded before Chris could continue. "but, I'm here to find out more about Janet's accident, and if anyone in your group knows about her prior trip to Kentucky."

Chris gasped again, "you mean when her transporter got stolen!"

"Yes. I'm here for her parents, as we are trying to figure out what happened on that trip to find out if it had anything to do with her last trip."

Chris took on a look of extreme interest, "you know, there was something not quite right about Janet after that trip! I think something more did happen! And she just wouldn't talk about it!" he looked over at Tom for agreement who nodded silently, wearing a collaborating expression.

"You know, as the director of the club, I manage a site with a log of our trips. Did you see it? I know there is at least one entry from Janet during that trip," he began tapping on an electronic screen in front of him as he spoke, "and you know we all tried to talk her out of going there! That place is not safe. She admits it here..." He placed the screen in front of Aarar before pressing a button for the video to begin.

Aarar became transfixed by Janet's image in front of an unfamiliar backdrop. She began speaking in an excited way, "Well, you guys were right!" she exclaimed. "They stole my transporter! But, it has been an adventure!" she laughed. "This place is so backward that the only places to charge your transporter here, are by mechanics! These people use gas powered cars!" she shook her head and moved closer to the camera as though she was relaying a bit of gossip. "And, look at this!" She dangled a key in front of the camera, "know what this is?" she asked in a teasing way. "It's a key! An old fashioned metal key! I had to use it to get into my room! This place is like visiting Cross Roads Village! You should see it! No, wait," she changed her mind, "don't come here, at least until you hear the rest of my story!" She wet her lips and gazed up at the ceiling, "where to start..." she pondered. "Well, I got here in the middle of the night and woke up to a COMPLETELY dead transporter! After it parked, someone stole the solar system that kept the pads charged! Then, they even stole some of the charging pads! I woke up to this...very handsome...police officer knocking on my window!" Janet made a clear sign that there was special interest in the officer. "Anyway! I got to ride in a pick up truck! With my head out of the window! It was like being on a roller coaster! And then, officer James, took me out to breakfast! He even paid because the restaurant didn't have a way to charge my card!" she made a flustered face at the camera. "Anyway, now I'm at this, motel," she held up the device so that she could make a sweep of the small room. "I'm waiting for my parents to get me, because after we left the transporter to get a mechanic to charge it, someone stole it too!" she made an angry face into the camera. "Never, never come here! I don't even want to see the caves now! I just want to go home," she shook her head sadly. "Anyway," she continued in a defeated voice, "the only thing I recommend about this place are the cops, or, at least, James, he has the bluest eyes I've ever seen!" she mused before signing off.

Aarar watched the screen go black, then looked up at Chris and asked for the address. Chris took Aarar's communicator and typed in the link for him. "It's public information," he assured Aarar. "But, it was the last one she posted. And, you know, she never did go to another meeting after that." Chris explained while slowly shaking his head.

"So, she never told you about the last trip? She told her parents that someone from her travel group was going with her," Aarar looked at both men expectantly.

But, both of them shook their heads in the negative. "No, I'm sure that no one from this group went with her because we were all talking about how she wasn't answering anyone's messages. We didn't even know when she finally made it home from the Kentucky trip! We read about everything from news stories! She must have been kidnapped the night she posted this."

Aarar was considering what he had just heard, who was officer James? He didn't recall her talking about him at all, not even to him. Then, he remembered his aunt's words when he first moved to her home, 'have you ever heard of

Stockholm syndrome?' This was all very upsetting. He summoned the transporter, then apologized that he wouldn't be able to stay for the meeting after all, but thanked them for the information. He had obtained new evidence to share with his aunt and uncle. He had done enough for the day, it was time for him to get back to the safety of his metallic sanctuary.

It was a long day for James Aldridge, he didn't return home that night until well after his regular shift. He had Janet's communicator in a small bag, and he made sure that Kevin wouldn't be parading around as Janet's avatar ever again. He made Spore witness the interrogation, so now he was convinced that Spore wouldn't be interested in involving the name of officer James in any subsequent questioning.

He was sitting comfortably on his couch at home, with a cold bottle of beer, in the dead of night, while his wife and children slept safe in their rooms. Life was good.

But, the one thing that was needling him was that he couldn't get the Kali sculpture out of his mind. How did this Prince of Hind know her? It made him do some online research. First he visited the Prince of Hind website for any evidence of her, then he scrolled through public comments. Nothing of her death, he noted, even though it did seem that everyone was always anxious to share grief for some reason. He continued the scroll down. Then, there were comments from her. From Janet to the Prince.

Jim's heart sank and all his pent up feelings of regret came back to him. He wished that he could have done things differently, but he was worried. Worried for his family, his life, his business. If only people could be trusted to keep their mouths shut! But, nobody, NOBODY, could be trusted, was his motto. If he didn't have dirt on you, you didn't know shit about him.

He continued reading the comments. Those from Janet were words of encouragement and praise for the Prince. He wondered if they were lovers in real life. He scrolled down farther. They just kept going and going, for years! He started reading every one of them and any responses that she got back from the Prince.

It was nearly three in the morning before he noticed the time. Then, his communicator lit up. It was someone from the office. He opened the message. It was the same officer who had been interested in the bounty. In it, the officer looked a bit anxious into the camera and spoke in a quiet voice. "Hey um James, I just wanted to leave a message for you to get before you come in to work. Well, first off I was just hoping that you would include me in the bounty when we go interview that guy for ooogle. I could really use the money! And, second, I know that you were interested in that storm. The one coming at us from South America? Well, you were right, it's tripled in strength and is slowly coming at us, up the east coast! It's a big one! A BIG, BIG STORM!!!"

At this same time in Michigan, Aarar was sitting at Janet's desk, and had just switched on her computer. It had already been a long day for him. He had the transporter drive him in circles through the city while he watched life out the window, sipping on his glass of whiskey. Video chatting with Cynthia. 'I could get used to this,' he had mused to himself. But, after a proper amount of time for a meeting had lapsed, he had headed home to show his Aunt and Uncle the new video clip. After considering for a time about the identity of officer James, the three decided that his man needed to be found. Aarar had an idea, but didn't mention it to Pia or John, he didn't even like to consider it himself.

He finished up some critical school work, then found a message from the VR police. Spore had been arrested and now he was needed at the Kentucky police station to make an in person statement. He did have the means, but lacked the will. He would think about this tomorrow, he told himself.

So then, he used the cast of Janet's thumb on the security pad. If his cousin had been having a romantic relationship with anyone in another state, then there was a good chance that she and her long distance lover were using Remote Viewing.

Remote Viewing, or RV, was a newer technology that allowed virtual reality users to access video in real time. It was still very controversial to have these systems in public places, but for the tech savvy, this system allowed you to make private videos that your lover could share in three dimensions and in real time.

He knew that these types of files would be saved on her own personal storage device. They had, had many a conversation on the perils of storing this type of information on public servers. He also knew about her little side business of converting 2d video into 3d, he had already happened across the software that she was using for the process. But, most likely she would have created a special folder for personal files. He searched her storage device for files with the necessary extensions. They were mostly located in the same directory, except one and it's time stamp fit. He put on his goggles and opened that file.

The first thing he saw was that he was in someone's bedroom lit only by small bedside lamps. A naked man in only a towel was coming through the darkened door way, he was carrying a woman on his shoulder. The video was silent, the woman was excitedly saying something, but was smiling and clearly enjoying the activity. Aarar stopped the video. He walked up to the man, then looked up into his open eyes. They were a brilliant shade of blue. The man had a handsome face and firm athletic build, just the type that his cousin would be attracted to. He looked up at the woman. She was an attractive woman of about the same age as the man, she wore makeup and her hair was carefully cut and styled, she had painted nails and a matronly figure. But, who was she, if he was Janet's love interest?

He let the video continue. The man carried the woman to the bed and dropped her on to it. Aarar had an idea. He walked to the corner of the bed, then lifted his goggles to see a chalk mark on the floor. 'This video is significant,' he told himself. He pushed the headset back into place and observed that the man was now hovering over the woman, who was on her back under him. Then, he knew, his cousin had moved her bed, so that she could lie under the man as he was having sex with this other woman.

Aarar decided that he needed to find out where he was. He moved to the nightstand. Next to a small lamp there was a King James bible and a photo of two small children. Aarar looked at the children's faces, then at the couple having sex, next to him. He decided that he needed the audio. He pulled off his goggles and sat back at the desk with Janet's computer. He found an audio clip in the same directory with the same time stamp. He opened it. First there was a rustling sound, then a woman in a hushed voice, "Don't you wake up the kids!" she squealed. Then a man's voice, "you're the one making all the noise!" More scuffling sounds and giggles, then a woman's voice, "Oh Jimmy!"

Aarar brought his hand to his forehead, he didn't need to hear anymore, now he felt sure that he knew what officer James looked and sounded like. But, why did Janet have this video? How did she obtain the original video? Aarar looked back at the computer for the original files with the same time stamp. He found them and recognized the extensions of the original video file as one that is produced from a gamer's camera. Had his cousin hacked this video from their game system? Was she stalking this guy? "What was Janet into?" he accidentally said aloud.

Flustered, he did what his cousin had done three months ago, he looked up the site for the police station in Munfordville, Kentucky. He scanned those same faces, he noticed the one in the center, Corporal James Aldridge. He read the small bio and noticed the mention of a wife and two children. Aarar was confident that he had the right guy, now, he needed to figure out if this was the person she went to the park to meet. Aarar enlarged the photo and stared into the steely blue eyes, did this man kill Janet?

He looked at the time, and it was 6:35 AM. He had stayed up all night again. But, he was so pumped, he wanted to talk to someone, but not his aunt and uncle, no, there was stuff he never wanted to have to explain to them. It would have been too embarrassing, he needed someone like Janet to talk to. So, he thought of Cynthia. The two of them had been video chatting so often now, that she had heard all of mystery and clues about his cousin's death. Talking with her, as herself and he, as himself, had become comfortable. Discussing things with her, had helped him think clearer, and she thought of things that he hadn't. So, he sent her a little message to see if she was awake. She answered. His heart leapt when he saw her face. He told her all the details since their last conversation. She listened and asked all of the right questions. She was so incredibly bright, he marveled.

And then, she had, what should have been a wonderful idea, "It's almost the end of the semester, why don't we go to Kentucky together for your deposition, during spring break?"

Aarar froze. Cynthia knew why, but she was hoping that the obvious sexual attraction they had, would be stronger than his fear of contact with other humans. It was a long pause, but she waited. He wet his lips, "I'm surprised that you would want to waste you vacation in such a hick place!" He finally stammered.

"Well, then," Cynthia responded softly, "why don't you come and get me, and we can go there for your deposition then go somewhere else."

She knew all about the transporter. What could he think to lie about now. He looked into her beautiful green eyes, with a lock of brown hair across the one on the right. "Okay," he nodded his head, as he was under her spell, "okay, let's do that!" He smiled and would have given her the twinkle wink if he could have.

Three days later, Aarar was scared to push the door button, even though he knew he had to, he could see her blue blouse through the window, and was sure she had looked up at him, so he had to do it, he took the few steps to the button and then, pressed it. He spun around on his heals and was sitting on the edge of the couch before the door had fully opened.

Cynthia stepped inside timidly, looking for the Prince, until she saw him, like a granite statue, sitting on the couch with arms folded, looking at the floor. "Aarar," she said softly, while standing in front of him.

"Yes! Yes! Come and make yourself comfortable!" he stammered, trying to sound normal, but with his eyes cast downward. Cynthia thought about his words, "no matter how odd my behaviors may seem, know that they are caused by you and how much I like you!" She slowly moved to the opposite side of the couch and sat down. He crossed and then uncrossed his legs and scooted to the edge of his seat, trying to keep the butterflies in his stomach from causing him to vomit.

Cynthia studied his profile, it would have been hard to explain, but his body, his face and hair, it belonged to the Prince, and yet Aarar did not resemble him.

He was very aware of her eyes on him, and the silence was lasting too long, he needed to say something. "I have beer!" he blurted out, "do you want one?"

Before she could answer, he was already on his feet and headed toward the back of the vehicle.

"Um...sure," she shouted in his direction.

When he came back, she could see a tremor in his hand as he offered her the bottle. Cynthia was more than a bit amused by the strong emotions she appeared to evoke in the young Indian, and, for her, it was a turn on. She couldn't remember ever feeling more confident with a guy, in real life. He wanted her so much it was crippling him! She reached high on the bottle and touched his extended hand with her own.

For Aarar the feeling was like a tickle, it made him look at her delicate hand, her nails were painted pink. He wet his lips, then moved back to his spot on the couch. Now he was trembling. Cynthia noticed and moving like a cat, she slid her free hand along the fabric of the couch and into Aarar's lap. He shuttered and made a surprise sound. Cynthia's giggle took his breath away. He suddenly felt like he was in virtual reality and turned his gaze from the floor to her face.

There she was, smiling at him, with that naughty look in her eyes. But, that feeling he had in his pants wasn't being caused by his own hand, it was a different kind of tickle, and it didn't need to be suppressed. 'I can do this,' he said to himself, scooting closer to her.

Cynthia laughed, "there he is! My Prince!" she cooed, pushing her face into his. They kissed. Really, and in real life. They kissed. He found that his hands were on her shoulders, then her upper arms, and then, with a twist, they were around her as the two reclined together on the couch.

As the wind quieted, the water was becoming stagnate. Scientist were still unable to identify what it was that happened in 1980 to start the plunge in wind speed, but it was still dropping. It was attributed to the warming of the poles being more dramatic than the warming at the equator. The difference between the coldest and warmest temperatures on the planet was decreasing and this was causing a drop in barometric pressure. In other words, the wind was quieting. Every weather pattern stayed on the ground longer. Storms, hurricanes and tornadoes lasted longer forcing new stricter building codes, using stilts in some areas and deep basements as foundations in other areas. Droughts lasted longer. The south west was becoming a vast desert while coastal, low lying areas were swampy and the land became too unstable to build on.

As above, so below. Currents at the same time, slowed. The differences between the highest water temperatures and the coldest temperatures was also declining, and that along with the de-salination caused by the glacier melt water was quieting the oceans. It was especially noticeable in the Gulf of Mexico. Pollution from off shore oil rigs had also played a part in killing the gulf, it had become a stinking dead zone full of a new species of red algae that coated the top of the water, blocked the sun and further exasperated the problems. New solar fountains, that shot water into the air, were set adrift off the coasts in an attempt to battle the red menace. They appeared to be containing the problem, but even nature was having a difficult time coping with the lack of food, and living in a polluted and over-fished gulf. Even the sparse plant life on the bottom couldn't live in the darkened waters.

And now, a mega storm was making it's way up the eastern coast of South America. As it hugged the coast of Brazil, the slow moving storm was being fed by the warm water and the cold air coming from a frigid air rushing north from the Antarctic region. The circular motion of the wind was whipping up to record breaking speeds, destroying everything, yet hovering, relentlessly, over the mass destruction, making permanent changes to the coast line. Parts of Brazil, were just not there anymore.

You're Only Old Once

Millie was drinking her morning coffee while reading the morning news. The big story was about a mega storm that had hit the east coast of South America at Brazil, then it split, the smaller storm heading south to Rio De Janeiro, destroying it as well as all the coastal cities near it. Then the larger storm grew in intensity as it headed north, spawning tornadoes that tore through Brazil as far inland as Teresina. The hurricane was now hugging the coast as it headed toward the Gulf of Mexico. The slow moving storm was threatening Venezuela and all the counties in between, as it continued to ravage the coast. Citizens of Cuba and what was left of Haiti were trying to evacuate. Hurricanes and earthquakes in that area had already made what was still above water in Haiti unlivable. This current storm was predicted to ravage the islands, then grow in intensity as it fed off the warm gulf and headed toward Louisiana.

Millie pulled up a world map of the International Trail System. The thin brown line followed the east coast of Mexico, through Central America and into Brazil. She wondered if cameras there would still be in place. She wanted to use Remote Viewing to see the storm for herself.

At breakfast she explained her plans to the regular crowd at her table. Debra and Trevor were interested in joining her. Lenard promised to meet up with them there. Buck thought it sounded dangerous.

"How would it be dangerous?" Millie asked, "we'll be watching it from my room!"

"Well...you never know," he mumbled in his usual, pessimistic voice.

It was at this time that a thin, regal looking woman, with carefully cut gray hair, approached their table. "Helloooo," she announced to the group, making the word last until she had made eye to eye contact with everyone at the table, individually and as a group. "I couldn't help but over hear your conversation," she continued, "I'm new to the building." She gestured to herself, "I'm Carol, Carol Schultz, but, I too, would be very interested in seeing the storm for myself! Might I join you?"

"Well, it's Millie's room!" Debra bristled.

Millie made a small gesture with her hand, "Oh, you are very welcome! In fact, we have an extra headset if you need one," she explained.

"Or you can just use the set up in the public cubicles, like most people," Debra sniped.

"I have plenty of room," Millie sighed over Debra's complaints, "but you do need to be a member of the parks association, or you can't get onto the trail system with us."

The lady nodded, and it was agreed that she would pay her dues then assemble with the rest of the group in Millie's room at 10:00. They would be six, once again.

As soon as the lady walked away, Millie stood up to push Debra back to her room. "Did you notice her eyes!" Debra hissed in a lowered voice, "I wonder what kind of drugs she's on!"

Millie chose to ignore the comment, she had long ago noticed how jealous Debra was of anyone around her. It was annoying, but everyone in the building seemed to be developing their own social tics. Debra's weird attachment to her was better than some of the other possibilities.

"Oh, here, let me do that for you!" Lenard said as he gently pushed Millie's hands from the grips of Debra's wheelchair and replaced them with his own.

Debra made a choking sound, and then began silently wringing her hands.

"Thank you Larry!" Millie responded cheerfully.

"You are so welcome! Do you need any help adding Carol to our group, making something golden, or the like?" Lenard offered as they walked down the hallway together.

"Oh, no, I think I can handle it," Millie answered.

"Well, then, I guess after I get Debra to her room, I'll just plan on meeting up with the group from my room," he explained in a pleasant voice.

Debra sniffed, "so no one will see you jerking off!" she mumbled, almost inaudibly. But, Millie heard her and gave her an evil eye. She waved and promised to see them soon when they reached the end of the hall and her room was in the opposite direction.

Millie tidied up her room and made sure there was a comfortable place for everyone to sit or park a wheelchair. Then, she checked the status of the storm. One of the eyes was just off the coast of Guyana and expected to be in Caracas, Venezuela by noon. A brown line on another map indicated that the ITS ran along the coast and remote viewing was available. The storm had stalled along the north east coast of Brazil, pounding the interior of Brazil. The original storm was building up the power to push itself north, up the coast, where it seemed to ride the current.

Millie's fellow travelers were prompt, bringing snacks and drinks. Everyone assembled for the trip to observe the catastrophic storm in a foreign country as it unfolded, from the dry, 70 degree comfort of Millie's apartment. How exciting!

Once everyone was in their places and ready, Millie typed in the coordinates of Caracas, Venezuela. They were instantly transported to an elevated boardwalk with a sensational view of the city with mountains in the background on one side and on the other side, a view of multi storied buildings along the seashore. The water did look perilously close to the buildings. It slowly became apparent that some of those buildings were old tourist resorts that had been abandoned as the water invaded the lower stories. The tops of other buildings had become debris off the coast, they were actually buildings that were built near the original coastline, before it had been lost to climate change.

The trail was void of in person travelers, but filled by avatars. It seemed that Millie's idea of watching the storm from the ITS was a popular one. Most of the avatars were in groups talking excitedly among themselves, mostly in Spanish, but with a variety of other languages in the mix. Everyone was interested in what kind of destruction they would see. Interested in what new human tragedy they were about to witness, from the comfort of their homes.

At first the sky looked overcast, but not threatening. Millie checked the local temperature, it was a warm 95 degrees with high humidity. After orienting themselves with the new surroundings, they began their walk and gentle descent of the sky-bridge. Trevor noticed an animated sign, designed for avatar visitors. He read it out loud, "Visit downtown Caracas! Just follow this trail on to the sidewalk and have access to selected shops!"

"Oh let's do that!" Debra remarked. So, the group took the advertised detour at the foot of the walkway. They did encounter more locals, but they were workmen, busy boarding up the store fronts. Debra was disappointed that the shops advertised were not open. "Oh, I was hoping that I could find something cute for Maggie's daughter. She has a birthday coming up!"

The group made their way back to the trail, but the ground level view was not nearly as impressive as the one from the sky bridge. It wound it's way through the business district where sweat soaked men and women were busy with plywood and nails, workers securing buildings ahead of the storm. A colorful banner was strung across the trail that advertised a local festival that weekend, one that was surely canceled.

The trail slowly gave way to housing, it followed a lane that took them closer to the mountains. Small, colorful, one story houses appeared to be built one a top of another, clothing the side of the mountain. Where there was a bee hive of activity as boards and tarps of every description were being attached to the houses. The faces were somber and tired, even small children were helping.

The trail began to rise again, this time it rose with the terrain as they began to ascend a mountain that skirted the beach. The view was breathtaking, but now the avatars shared the trail with small caravans of locals who were carrying what they could, to higher ground. When they reached the summit, they found themselves surrounded by groups of avatars with their faces pointed at the sky, anticipating a change in the weather.

A particularly odd group of avatars in matching jump suits caught their eye. As they got closer they could hear the strange language of the group of pale, stocky, men. "What kind of language is that?" Hank remarked in a, too loud, voice. The one man in the group who was dressed differently, in blue denim overhauls, met the old man's glare with a smile of comprehension.

Millie was embarrassed, "So sorry, I'm afraid we aren't from around here," she apologized.

"Oh, it's quite alright, neither are we!" The man in denim responded.

Millie was pleased with the man's friendly demeanor, as she was curious herself of the origin of the strange language of grunts and snaps that the men were using. She drew closer to the man, "would you mind, telling me what your country of origin is? I don't remember ever hearing your language before."

The other men of the group watched the interaction mutely, as they didn't appear to understand the English that the two where talking in. So, the denim clad member replied, "have you ever been to Iceland?"

"No," Millie answered.

"Well, then, you must not be familiar with native Icelandic," the man explained with a smile.

Millie mulled over this response in her head. Native Icelandic, she considered. But the man was pleasant and explained that the group was there to study the storm. Then, as they were all standing together, the man began handing out jetpacks to everyone in his party, before instructing them in his strange tongue, and then waving at Millie as they flew up and into the sky together, headed southeast, toward the eye of the approaching storm.

"You know, that would be the best way to view the storm," Lenard suggested.

Millie agreed, so the group attached themselves to Lenard after he produced his jetpack. They lifted off the ground together and flew in a kind of bunched up formation. It was fun, exhilarating even. They watched the trail snake up the mountains below them. The traffic of humans and avatars was growing, with the in person travelers headed in the opposite direction, usually they carried bundles and pulled wagons behind them, often with children in them. The avatars were an interesting mix of animated characters and much more jovial as they glided along the trails, usually in small groups. Slowly the air became foggy, with low hanging clouds that moved rapidly. As they became more dense, it was hard for the group of seniors to see the ground below them. Then, the clouds became too thick to see through, it caused the cameras not to work properly, so Lenard tried to steer them out and away from the fast moving, low hanging clouds. It was disorienting, with all the dips and dives, darkness and light.

"How is everyone?" Millie asked. Most responded with affirmations, but Trevor mentioned that Carol was asleep.

"Well, for the love of god, make sure she's still breathing," Hank barked.

Trevor, reached over and gently shook her shoulder. She opened her eyes and apologized.

"Yeah, she's still alive," he confirmed.

But, the clouds were getting thicker and causing black shadows. After a few members complained of nausea, Lenard brought them back to earth. Now, the wind was very strong. The few in person travelers were clearly being blown by the wind. It made the simple act of walking nearly impossible and small children were clinging to their parents. Some in the party were feeling sorry for the pedestrians who seemed to be using the ITS to move to higher ground.

Millie looked over the railing that followed the seaside of the trail, the water was coming in very large waves. Far below, debris could be seen in the water, smashing into the rocks on the shore with every wave. The rain was being carried by the strong winds, mixing with the seawater and came down in blinding torrents. She squinted to make out the remains of a mid sized boat, she wondered if there had been anyone on board when the ocean took control of the vessel. Then, another wave sent it smashing on to the rocks, bits of wood splintered and scattered onto the sand.

There was lightening in the black clouds in the distance off shore. An especially loud crack made a small child shriek and even startled the group of avatars. It was getting closer. Millie had to remind everyone that they were safe in her apartment and that if the conditions became overwhelming then they should pull their visor up and reorient themselves.

The wind suddenly picked up again and a large branch came out of nowhere to crash down across the trail in front of them. This caused the in person travelers to stop and gather around the downed tree. They were forced to lay down their bundles and work as a group to push the obstacle out of their path. The wind was ferocious and fought the workers. A young boy was knocked to the ground and a bough of the tree pinned him under it.

Millie saw it happen and worried for the boy, she walked through the hologram to the boy's side, he was knocked unconscious and had blood coming from his nose, then Millie noticed it pooling under his head. She wanted to help, but was only a specter, mutely witnessing the events. A man and a woman calling out in Spanish helped push the tree off him while another man pulled the boy out by his feet, dragging his damaged head on the boardwalk. Millie and the rest of her group winced and then cheered the rescuers on, as the boy's mother was able to cradle his head and bring him back to consciousness. Slowly, he was able to stand, leaning on his mother. A younger child was instructed to carry the mother's burden, so that she could walk with her bleeding son, who was leaning heavily on her. But, they continued, as that was their only option and the storm was getting closer.

Millie looked over the railing on the sea side again, the water retreated in a strange way, then suddenly, it surged with a deafening roar toward the boardwalk in such a great wave that it washed the people off! All of them, even the mother and her children! Millie let out an involuntary scream before the whole boardwalk was swept away and the avatars found themselves in mid air. Then darkness and silence. Everyone pulled off their goggles.

Millie found herself sitting on the edge of her bed, breathing heavily as her heart raced. She looked around herself, seeing everyone in her group with stunned looks on their faces. Debra was crying. Trevor was trembling and wiping his forehead with his hand. Carol had wet herself. It took several minutes for everyone to compose themselves enough to safely leave Millie's apartment for their own. It had been a traumatic experience for them all.

As soon as everyone had left, Millie laid across her bed thinking about the bleeding boy and his mother, how helpless she had been and how they most likely perished. She rolled over onto her pillow and sobbed, till she fell into a tortured slumber.

Millie woke to the sound of her communicator ringing. Closed blinds made the room dim, she turned on her nearby lamp and then picked up the noisy device. It was Debra.

"Are you alright?" a shaky voice asked.

"Yes. I fell asleep."

"You're not ill, are you?"

"No, no just shaken up by the storm. That poor boy and his mother. All of those people, I just felt so useless watching them," Millie's voice cracked.

"Well, you should come to dinner. We are all sitting at the table wondering where you are," Debra offered, trying to change the subject.

Millie thought about it for a moment, "no, I'm not hungry, I think I want to lay back down."

Debra was silent, then, "I'll bring you a lunch plate a little later."

Millie agreed, as she really just wanted off the phone. After she set the device back onto her nightstand, she threw her legs off the edge of her bed and looked around herself. Everything was silently laying where she had left it, in her dimly lit room. Her drapes were shut, so she got up and opened them. There was a bit of sunlight, peeking out between the clouds, but the weather outside looked just as gray and somber as her mood.

She suddenly had an urge for a drink, which was uncommon for her. Then, she remembered that she had a bottle of wine in her bottom drawer. A gift, sent to her by her stepson. She really didn't know what she was saving it for, anyway. She rummaged through her bottom drawer, and located it under a pile of folded sweaters. She examined the bottle, remembering him explaining that it was a very sweet after dinner wine that she couldn't help but like. She set it on her desk, then located a water glass from her bathroom. She unscrewed the top and poured a little of the thick yellow liquid in her glass. She raised the tumbler just enough to wet her lip. Then, she ran her tongue over it. The wine was very flavorful and sweet. She smiled, and then pushed a chair up to the window, so that she could sit and sip as she looked out of it. This was comforting to her.

Soon, there was a knock at the door. It was Debra, being pushed by Trevor, with a plate of food on her lap. She took the plate, Debra had filled it with her favorite things, then she invited them in. The little bit of wine that she had already drank gave her a warm feeling. It was pleasant to have company.

At first they discussed the weather outside their windows. But, then Trevor mentioned that the big storm had left Venezuela and was now headed toward Haiti. Millie knew that he had only meant to make small talk, and everyone was preoccupied with their experiences from earlier that day, but the reminder only squashed the warm fuzzy feeling that she had achieved from the wine and reminded her of how helpless she was. How she had watched people die, without the ability to give them any aid. She had simply been a curious voyeur unable to be of use to anyone.

Despite her friend's best efforts, the horrible feelings of uselessness returned. Millie thanked them for the plate of food, but explained that she was under the weather and wanted to go back to sleep. So, the two left. She could tell that she had disappointed her friends and this did add a little to her guilt, but the depression was making her physically ill.

She laid across her bed, wide awake, and contemplating how the light coming from her window was dimming. Then, there was another knock at her door. She continued to lay silently, wondering if it was Debra and Trevor with more food. Then, another knock and a whisper, "Millie are you awake?" It was a male voice that she recognized as Larry's.

"Just a moment," she called out as she slid out of bed and checked herself in a mirror as she passed it. She noticed how dark the room was, so she flipped on the switch beside the door before opening it. "Hello," she said as she mustered up a smile.

Lenard stood anxiously in front of the threshold, feeling awkward, but with a sense of purpose. "Hi, a- I just wanted to see how you were doing," he explained with well rehearsed words, although the concern in his eyes was genuine. He was looking at her full in the face, something he normally didn't get the opportunity to do. So, he stood there, within a yard of her, taking in the smell of soap and almost feeling her breath. He was allowed, he was her friend and he was on a mission to check on her welfare.

She invited him in, then noticed the open bottle of wine on her nightstand. "Would you like a glass of wine?" she asked, happy to have it out to offer.

He was surprised by the question, but readily agreed, as he took a seat next to her bed. She found another glass and poured it out for him, as well as, a little more for herself, then took a seat on the side edge of her bed, near the chair he was sitting on. She set the glasses on the nightstand between them.

"So, how have you been?" she asked in a pleasant voice.

He took a small sip from his glass. He had never drank wine before. It tasted sickening sweet to him, like some raw ingredient that his mother might have used to cook with. But, he tried to hide his dislike by smiling and commenting on the wines flavor. Although, Millie could see his deception, she admired his intentions. "I've been good," he said to answer her original question, "but that storm was very scary. How are you after all that... scary stuff?"

Millie thought about how to answer. She felt like she wanted to give him an honest answer, but to complain with no hint of a practical solution, always felt to her like an exercise with no useful purpose, so it wasn't something she was in the habit of doing. "It was frightful. I've never felt so useless. I don't ever want to do it again," she explained in a quiet voice.

Lenard's brows furrowed, "you mean RV? You don't want to go on the trails again?" he asked, trying to understand.

Millie sighed and looked away, "all of it. All of it is futile. We watched people die, and couldn't do anything to help." Her voice cracked a bit at the end.

Lenard swallowed hard, he had grown fond of the trails and even the other members of their little hiking group. He needed to talk her out of her depression. If only things hadn't gone so horribly wrong, he considered. "But, it would have happened anyway!" he realized aloud, "those people would have died even if we hadn't been there to witness it."

Millie thought about this simple fact, that hadn't occurred to her.

"If we hadn't been there, then no one would have witnessed their final moments," he explained.

Millie thought about how useless this had been. Watching helplessly. Had they really done a service for those people? They had simply been voyeurs.

"I don't know," she said quietly.

Lenard took another drink from his glass. Millie could tell by his face that the wine didn't agree with him. But, she smiled to herself for his effort. He then looked around himself nervously, trying to think of a more pleasant topic. "Do you have any tournaments today?"

Millie thought about it, she was supposed to play today, she remembered. "Thanks for reminding me, I do." She sighed at the thought, but she didn't want Anthony Flowers draining her bank account again. "In fact, it starts in a few minutes," she recalled. They continued with small talk, as Lenard finished his wine, then said good-by and wished her luck.

She really wasn't in the mood for another dart tournament, but she had become a slave to the little goblin that ran the dark web gambling site. Usually, she enjoyed the games, if only she could pull herself from the dark funk. Maybe, the dart match might distract her from her depression, she considered as she pulled her headset on.

But, it didn't, she lost the first match, then another, it was her worst performance ever. As soon as it was over she pulled her goggles off and took her place stretched out across her bed again. She was no longer sleepy, so she turned on her monitor and looked for a movie to watch.

She scrolled through the categories, watching a sample of a few, before settling on one. There was a simplicity to the plots of the movies, they were really just one, good vs. evil. She considered this, was that really all there was? Was there really nothing but energy? Good and bad. The world just seemed to be so full of negativity. Universally, as well as locally. Universally, there were wars, climate crisis, and the horrendous greed that seems to always be at the center of misery. Locally, individuals often pray for the misfortunes of others, but did that create real happiness? Or is that rush of satisfaction fleeting? Making us repeat the bad behavior for another fleeting rush? Then, eventually, remorse. This whole cycle causes our interactions with one another to be curtailed, in that we are unable to celebrate even the smallest of victories for fear of the wrath of our family and friends. The bad, the negative energy seems to grow like a snowball tumbling down a hill. One callous, unkind act, begets another. The snowball only seemed to be getting larger.

Millie sighed as she considered this. But then, the unyielding reasonable self, deep within her, made her look for an answer, if the bad is an out of control snowball, could the same happen with good? Could that same force work as the opposite 'yang' in the balance of energy? Millie considered this, and how she felt when someone came through for her, even in the smallest of actions, she knew that it made her happier, kinder. Sometimes, other people had made her feel exhilarated, energetic, even distracted and lost in happy thoughts. And how did it make her feel when she realized that she was the cause of the feeling of happiness in someone else? The truth, sometimes happier than the actual recipient! So, was it an energy? Were these instances of a big, beautiful, snowball of happiness rolling down a hill uncontrollably? Could she individually, help with it's size and momentum? What did she need to do to encourage it? And that, was the moment when she realized the simplicity of the answer to everything. How could she contribute to the universal positive energy? Maybe, it was simply, to be helpful.

There was another knock at her door. Millie sighed and stopped the movie, she did appreciate that her friends were worried about her, but the visits, the reassurances, the fibs she told to get them to leave, it was getting tiring. She slowly got up and answered the door and was surprised to see Eddie the maintenance man standing just outside the door wearing his brown uniform and hat, with an awkward expression. Like he wanted to ask a favor.

"Hello Mr. Bloom!"

Eddie stood mute for a moment, placing his hands on his hips, and then shuffling his feet a bit.

"Would you like to come in?" she asked, perplexed.

Eddie nodded in the affirmative and stepped in, closing the door behind him.

"Is something wrong?" Millie asked, as Eddie had never visited her before.

"Well, ya' see..." Eddie began in a nervous voice. He adjusted his hat, "Well, I know that you are friends with Ms White from down the hall," he made a futile gesture of pointing in the direction of Debra's apartment.

Millie nodded.

"Well," Eddie looked around himself before continuing in a hushed voice. "Well, you had to have noticed how beat up her chair is?" Millie nodded again. "Well, I found another one, it's like new and even has a motor that works real good. But, the problem is, you know, I ain't supposed to give stuff like that to the residents. No favoritism. No personal relationships, etc. And I do like my job here." He explained as he wet his lips. "But, you could."

Millie smiled when she comprehended where the conversation was going.

Her smile gave Eddie the confidence to continue, "So, I was wondering if you could, maybe lie and pretend that the chair was a gift from you?"

The act of kindness brought tears to her eyes. She involuntarily closed the gap between them with a hug. "Oh of course I'll lie!"

"Cool! Cool!" Eddie sputtered with embarrassment after returning the hug. "Now, a, I'll go get it and tell her it was a gift from you!" he muttered as he opened the door.

Millie nodded and sniffed, her eyes glistening, as she let him out. 'What a nice man,' she thought to herself.

She walked to her window and stared out of it as she contemplated Eddie's kindness. He had just given that big snowball of happiness a good shove! Maybe it was her turn, she decided. Maybe she needed to quit sulking, since it was of no good use. There was work to do, she needed to come up with a plausible, big fat lie to tell her best friend!

A little later she entered the dinning room where she noticed Debra in her shiny new wheelchair. Their friends were gathered around her as she demonstrated it's many convenient features. Eddie was there too, giving direction and answering Debra's many questions. When the group noticed Millie, they looked up and a smiling Debra called out her name. "Millie! Millie! Did you buy this chair for me?!"

Millie smiled as she began her well rehearsed lie, "Why yes, but there is the most interesting story behind it!" She stood inside the circle of people, "You know, just before I went to a match, I noticed an ad for it in the Citizen's Commodity Utility, and," she managed to exchange a quick glance with a smiling Eddie Bloom, "and, I said to myself, if I win the tournament today, I'm buying Debra that chair! And, would you believe it? I won!" Everyone cheered and made agreeable noises. Eddied looked down bashfully, as Debra exclaimed how much she liked the chair and what a happy set of circumstances! It was meant to be!

Eddie had Debra demonstrate to him, one last time, that she understood the workings of the chair, then excused himself to go back to work. Millie managed to exchange one last smile with the happy maintenance man before he walked passed her. Her eyes teared up when she looked at the happy group in front of her, all moving toward the lunch counter together, chattering happily. She thought about all the good energy Eddie had created, for everyone, including himself.

Millie followed behind the little crowd, until Debra spun herself around in her new chair and motioned for her to catch up. She then insisted on carrying her own tray to the table. Demonstrating how she was now able, since the motorized chair only required a slight touch to get her back to their usual spot. She marveled over the smooth ride and how she didn't even spill her coffee, not one drop.

Everyone made agreeable noises, then Lenard compared it to his old borrowed chair, asking if she knew how fast it could go. Debra was even polite to him in the exchange, but told him that she refused to find out.

After delivering her dinner to her space at the table, Debra looked up at Millie with a big smile, "So, tell us about the match! Who did you beat?"

At first Millie was confused as she clearly remembered loosing miserably, but quickly recalled her big lie. "Oh, ah, the Masked Marvel!"

"Well, apparently he wasn't too marvelous!" Debra quipped and then laughed at her own joke. Millie couldn't remember seeing her in such a jolly mood. It was infectious.

As their meal progressed and Trevor had finished, he placed his empty plate on the stack of trays and then pulled out a tablet. He set it in front of himself and then looked around the table to get everyone's attention, as though he was about to make some kind of presentation to the group.

"I visited the ITS site today and found out that there is a leg of it that follows an ancient route that starts in Missouri and goes all the way to the Grand Canyon! It goes through ghost towns and everything!" he exclaimed looked around the table for agreeable nods and words of encouragement, especially from Millie. He picked up his device and paged through the photos. "It goes all the way to the Colorado river and then follows it into Mexico," he explained, tapping the screen to page through the beautiful scenic photos. Millie nodded in agreement, why not, she thought aloud, even though earlier in the day she had sworn off Remote Viewing altogether.

"Trevor, I think we should go there on our next trip!" Millie offered, as she could tell, that it was what was being suggested.

Everyone made agreeable noises, which gave Trevor encouragement to continue. "I've always wanted to see the Grand Canyon! And it says here that you can even split off the main trail and walk around the rim of the canyon! And then, there are even detours that take you to old ghost towns so you can walk right down the old plank sidewalks! And there's a gold mine! You can visit the inside of a gold mine!" he exclaimed excitedly.

It warmed Millie's heart to see her friends all smiling and interested. Trevor had grown several years younger, right there in front of her.

Then, Lenard looked at him thoughtfully, "you said that it follows some ancient route?"

"Yeah, yeah, it was called route 66," Trevor explained.

Lenard swallowed the bit of lettuce that he was trying to choke down for Millie's benefit, "ah yes! I've heard of that!"

The next day the gang gathered in Millie's apartment. It was decided that this new trip would begin at the Grand Canyon, and then the group would follow the ITS south along the Colorado River till it met up with the old Route 66 going east through the desert, stopping at local ghost towns and attractions along the way.

They arrived just north of the canyon, and the three hour time difference meant that the sun was just rising. There was a beautiful pink tinge to the scant clouds that rolled along above the yellow semi-circle. The soft light revealed the beautiful soil on the mountains that appeared naked of vegetation, with it's mounds of orange and red earth exposed by dawn.

Everything was silent. They were on a raised boardwalk, a ribbon through the desert, a desert that appeared, at first, to be void of life, just sand and immense stones. Some of the large raw sienna colored rocks were all worn with grooves that followed in the same direction, they looked as though someone had pushed each of the odd shaped boulders into the sand at the same angle. Then, a large bird made a loud sound as it flew over them and landed on the arm of a cactus. A small rabbit ran out from under it, so the bird gave chase. The group watched in silence, although, they could have shouted as loud as the wanted and the animals would never hear. They were only invisible voyeurs, curious ghosts without a voice.

Once the rabbit was caught and the bird flew out of sight, they organized themselves as to which direction they needed to be traveling in, and so, this new adventure began. The trail took them into the mountains, it snaked it's way between increasingly taller and magnificent peaks. As they rounded one of the mammoths, they glimpsed the beautiful blue Colorado river. Their trail then began following the waterway below them.

Trevor was the first to spot rams climbing the side of a mountains. Millie pulled out her binoculars for a better view. There was one following another, they both looked to be nearly the size of horses, but it was their large curling horns that gave them their majestic tall stature.

Then, the shadowy soft light of dawn gave away the movement of another lone animal. It was definitely, cat like, by the way it's tan body almost slithered along and between the rocks. As it got closer they were able to identify it as a cougar. "Amazing," Millie mused as the animal came closer to the trail. A strong instinct to flee, came to the members of the group as the animal cleared the mountain and headed straight toward the boardwalk. But, of course, the feline didn't see or hear them, but it was still an amazing feeling when the big carnivore broached the wooden path. Debra let out a little squeal, before remembering that she was actually sitting in Millie's apartment. But then, as the members of the party were able to overcome their primeval instincts, the experience became priceless. They gathered around the animal, slowing their pace to keep even with the tigress. She was beautiful, lean, but powerfully built. She would stop occasionally to sniff at, what a solid hiker, may have left behind, or was it the scent of another animal? The group discussed this among themselves, the whole of the animal was a glorious mystery to them.

And then, as the animal began to pick up his pace, Lenard noticed something also walking on the boardwalk in the distance. It was a couple of hikers! Trevor, involuntarily, began waving his arms and shouting out to them, and then, at the cougar, forgetting that he had no voice or visible body. The group began making nervous sounds, were they about to helplessly witness another tragedy? They watched as one of the hikers began pointing something out to the other hiker. This made them stop and look around themselves. The big cat stopped, as well, and watched as one of the humans noticed her, and then, excitedly hit the other, to get his attention. But, the movements and excited voice caused the cougar to run back toward the mountain line. The men pulled out solid binoculars and stood watching the animal disappear in awe.

Millie and the rest of the gang let out sighs of relief. None of them had experience in the real world with these types of wildlife, and they were very glad to be in the RV version of the trails, just then.

The river now ran beside them, it was swift and blue, tumbling over rocks and between boulders. As the group looked out on to the beautiful, blue ribbon that ran through it's rocky bed, Millie recounted an article she had recently read. "You know, this river was nearly dried up by the beginning of the 21 century, but then this clever entrepreneur solved the problem. After the Attack, most people had converted to personal solar systems, so the interstate pipelines that were built for natural gas, were no longer needed. She bought them for a discounted price, then used them to carry water from her desalination plant on the west coast. Now the river runs at ideal depth, keeps the Hover Damn running at full capacity and allows the city of Las Vegas to be as bright and garish as it's always been! They are her biggest client, helping her to be one of the countries richest people!"

"Yeah, the country has changed from being controlled by oil barons to those who control the water," Trevor mentioned reflectively.

Then, their trail took a very steep climb, up and then above the ground until they were high up on the boulders, looking down on the beautiful, clear water. Behind them, the rocky mountains were dotted with a few scruffy looking fir trees. Little chipmunks scurried across the trail in front of them. The whole scene was very idyllic. Then, the sound of a train, and they could see it barreling down tracks on the opposite side of the river, along the rim of the canyon. Everyone began discussing how they would love to be on the train. But, then, they agreed that their current view was wonderful as well.

They followed the trail until they noticed a sign advertising the Canyon's gift shop, where Debra found a small trinket to send to her grand-niece, for her birthday. The group toured a small museum dedicated to the canyon, that even included a video. This marked the end of the day for the hungry travelers, who agreed to meet again in the morning.

That afternoon Debra and Millie visited their oogle rental, as was their custom. Millie had a dart match later that afternoon, so the two were having a cup of tea together on the back porch of their shared rental house. A beautiful electric sun was hanging low in the sky, birds were beginning to increase their chatter, over a chorus of simulated crickets. All was right in their world, as they sat quietly in their golden chairs, sipping their golden tea. They were watching butterflies that gathered in the milkweed that Millie had planted, when Debra brought up a subject that she had been contemplating for the last several months.

"So, Millie, maybe it's time for us to have another garden party," she began.

"That sounds nice!" Millie responded without moving her gaze from the fluttering insects.

"We could invite people from the building this time."

"Sure."

"You could invite Larry," she said in a contrived way.

"Ah...sure. We could invite everyone in the building if you want."

"Say, why hasn't Larry ever came here for a visit anyway?"

Millie remembered a conversation that she had with him about it. "He said he doesn't use Oogle out of protest for their price gouging, or something like that."

"Well, I think it's because he can't! I think he has been banned from Oogle for harassment!"

Millie knew that Debra didn't like Larry and was suspicious that he was actually the 'Lenard' who had terrorized them in VR at their last garden party. But, instead of playing Debra's game she just came out and said it. "Debra, I don't care if Larry's real name is Lenard! It doesn't mean that he just happens to be the avatar that was giving us so much trouble! That would be too much of a coincidence!"

Debra leaned in toward her friend, "Really? Think about it. When did that creep first start bothering us? It was when Larry moved into the building. When did Larry fall out of bed and hurt himself so bad that he was in a wheel chair? It was when we confronted Lenard and got the VR police on his ass!"

Millie, the real Millie, went pale. She quietly considered what Debra had said.

It was at that time, when their butler appeared and informed them that there was a visitor, "A Ms Carol Shultz."

"Oh, Carol, I asked her to come visit," Millie explained to Debra before instructing the butler to allow her in.

Debra scowled at the interruption, she felt like she finally had Millie's attention about Larry. And besides, she didn't think she liked Carol, not that she had any real reason. Nonetheless, Carol appeared shortly, sitting on a small golf cart.

"Hello ladies," she announced, parking herself in such a way as to have a good view of the garden. "This is wonderful," she marveled. The women exchanged pleasantries.

"So, how do you like our little community here?" Millie asked, as Carol was a recent resident.

"Oh, I do. You know, I was living alone and I was worried about leaving my house, but, it's nice to visit with real people, ya' know."

"Well, I'm so glad for you!" Millie exclaimed with genuine enthusiasm. She was always glad to hear about people who 'wanted' to live at the City Home as it was usually the place where people ended up when they ran out of money and family. "Where are you from?"

"Oh, I lived in the city, have all my life. Been divorced for more years than I can remember, and the only way I ever visit my son, Daniel, is by VR, anyway," she explained. "And, I hated the yard work! So, this apartment living suits me just fine!"

"Wonderful!" Millie smiled and nodded. "Does your son live far away?"

"No, no, he lives in the city, he just never leaves his apartment. Especially, now that he has a robot. I was just visiting with him. We like to go bowling or play board games together. We visit with one another nearly everyday!"

"That is nice! Did you say that he has a robot?" Millie asked.

"Yes. I don't know if I like it though. I think that it was when he got the robot that he quit going outside at all! He uses that damn thing to socialize, living through it's eyes and hands. I just don't think it's healthy!" she explained, shaking her head.

Millie nodded, "you know, a lot of people live that way now."

They continued with small talk until the butler reappeared and reminded Millie of her competition. So, she excused herself, leaving the two women alone. She was hoping that the 'grumpy' Debra might soften up a bit if she had the chance to talk with Carol. She just hoped that their discussion didn't include Larry. Debra's revelations were disturbing and now Millie couldn't get the idea out of her head. Could Larry be a sneaky stalker? Could he have become interested in the two women when he first moved in, then, found them online to terrorize them? This idea was very unnerving to Millie, as she had developed a fondness for him.

She tried to put the matter out of mind when she clicked on the link that brought her to the sports emporium, where her match was being held. She hadn't noticed her monopoly man host lately, which suited her just fine. She really didn't like him since she became aware that she was participating in a gambling ring. But, her winnings were real and she did enjoy the competitions.

When her name was announced, Freya took her mark, then slowly rotated 360 degrees, bowing to each corner, while the crowd cheered. She felt especially inspired to win, as she had done so miserably at her last match. Her competitor this time, was a giant baby, wearing, what looked to her, as a dirty diaper. It was gross, but the crowd laughed and hollered at the big baby. He waddled around in a circle with a giant pacifier in his mouth. 'What a vile sense of humor,' she thought as she watched the spectacle.

Then, waving a red scarf, she noticed her dark knight in the crowd. This made her happy. She wondered what romantic place he would take her to after the games.

She did well against the big baby, beating him the first two games. He immediately fell to his knees and began wailing in a melodramatic way. Freya wondered if his appearance in the match was more about entertaining the crowd, then darts. Her next competitor was more of a challenge. It was wearing a suite made of lights and she did find the multi colored lasers that it emitted distracting. She lost their second and third games, which was enough to put her out of championship round, but she did win the third set set of games, anyway.

"I think your second competitor's choice in lighted apparel should have disqualified him!" the dark knight complained, in his stuffy English accent, after she had left the platform and joined him in the crowd. Freya responded with a shrug. She truly was just happy to see the knight, she enjoyed his company.

"So, where should we be off to tonight?" he asked, offering her his holographic arm.

"Wherever you'd like," she smiled, carefully laying her gloved hand on the arm of her metal coated suitor. She allowed him to attach her avatar to his, and then, they disappeared together.

When they reappeared they were on the beach of a tropical island, facing, what looked like, the Pacific ocean with brilliant blue water and a few mountainous islands in the distance. "Marvelous," she cooed softly. They turned and faced a green jungle with sandy paths winding between palmetto bushes. He led her to the heart of the little island, where a tall waterfall tumbled into a small lagoon. "How lovely!"

"Lovely, yes, but let me take you to a magical place," the dark knight hinted before leading her through the waterfall and to the caverns that were hidden behind the wall of water. It was dark, but lit by giant, multi-colored, clusters of crystals. Freya gasped. He led her through the labyrinth of lighted trails that took them higher and higher up the mountain, until they reached it's summit. The sky opened up and from the top and they could see the lagoon and jungle below them with a bright, electric sky above them. Misty sprays of water from the falls captured light, causing a rainbow effect. "Amazing!" she cried from the top of island.

She was transfixed by the water and the reflections. "Say, let's jump!" she shouted above the roar of the falls, before leaping. The knight hesitated, but jumped after her. They both fell to the lagoon laughing. It was an exhilarating experience!

The next morning at breakfast Millie couldn't help but think about what Debra had said the night before. Could Larry really be the creepy 9-year-old that had terrorized them less than a year ago? She began thinking about a way to test Debra's theory without coming out and asking him. Maybe, pressuring him to visit their rental in Oogle History would be a way, since the Lenard avatar had been banned.

"Hey everyone, I wanted to mention this before I forget," Millie announced at their table, "Debra and I are planning a garden party at our Oogle rental!" There were 'ahs' and 'ohs,' as Debra put on a sly smile and a look of triumph, first at Millie, then at Larry, who had his eyes cast down. "Although, we still don't have the date or plans locked down yet, I just wanted you to know that you will all be invited." Millie had been moving her gaze around the faces at the table in an even way, but was disappointed when she looked at Larry and noticed that he was avoiding eye contact altogether. 'That certainly isn't a good sign,' she thought to herself.

Later, at her apartment, the rest of the gang showed up to continue their Remote Viewing adventure. They found themselves on a concrete walk that ended with wooden posts on either side of it that marked the official entrance of the Canyon's National Park. Beyond that gateway lay a vastness of sandy like sediment, scantily clad in brush and fenced in by the most magnificent boulders, stacked on top of the other in giant soft round globs of tan and red, they looked like they could be a child's play thing, but then on closer inspection they were smooth but hard. They were of course rock.

They moved close to the stone sentinels and began hiking the natural barriers that nearly enclosed the court. There was a temptation to climb, but the limitations of the program they were using, didn't allow them far from the concrete path.

Millie thought about the sign at the entrance and wondered why it was there. Were there petroglyphs hidden in the stones? She looked hard at each formation as she passed it. Would they appear on the outside or in one of the many caves and crevices between the stones.

She stood still a minute, listened to the silence then slowly let her eyes study each mountain of rocks. Then, there, across from her she noticed a large stone that was covered with something black like maybe it was stained from water or moss or smoke. This blackness on the stones was something she had noticed before but in this case the dark looked to have scratches or cracks. But they didn't seem to follow a natural pattern. She squinted her eyes looking harder, then, slowly the images began to appear. She pulled out a pair of binoculars.

A group of solid hikers walked up behind the group, noticed the same graffiti, they moved off the path and in that direction, abandoning the trail and walking between the bushes across the center of the court. That was when a rattling sound could be heard coming from the brush. One of the hikers hushed the others and warned them that they needed to return to the path. Millie let out a breath of relief. To be the silent and invisible witness to these adventure seekers was unnerving.

She returned her focus to the view in her binoculars, zooming in on the boulders in the distance, slowly pictures of the sun, animals, and geographic shapes and symbols that surly had meaning to someone, became apparent. Ancient American graffiti. She examined them in a daze, marveling at the symbols and trouble the daredevil artists must have went through to create them up so high. They were surly made by the hands of young and nimble youths. Native American vandals. She wondered if those artist ever envisioned a day when their work would be acknowledged and protected by signs and wooden posts.

Soon, Larry's avatar was standing next to her. "What are you seeing?" he asked. Millie looked at him with new suspicion, then handed him her binoculars. "Oh, how interesting," he mused.

She waited until he had lowered the binoculars to ask, "So, Larry, are you going to come to our garden party?"

He wavered as he handed her binoculars back to her, then answered, "Well, I think I already explained to you about how I feel about the whole Oogle History monopoly!" he answered with despair.

Something about his voice sounded contrived, and it irritated her. Was this the same person who tricked her into a false friendship by pretending to be a nine-year-old boy? Was he doing it all over again in real life? Maybe, the only true thing he ever said to her was that, 'nobody really knows who anyone is anymore.'

She checked her rage, and reminded herself that she still didn't have confirmation. She needed to confront him and have a definite answer before she could be angry. After composing herself she answered, "You don't have to own the app to visit someone, you just have to be on their guest list. So, you would be using the app without contributing any money to the company," she explained.

He sighed again, "Yeah, yeah, I see what you're saying, but I just need to think about it." Millie stared at his avatar a moment, then decided to hold her tongue and agree to continue the charade a bit longer.

Later that day, the gang found out that it was Carol's birthday when a beautiful woman delivered a big box of chocolates to their dining table. "Oh, wonderful! Dessert!" she sang out as she took possession of the gift. She immediately took out a communicator and began typing, completely ignoring the woman as she stood beside the table expectantly.

Trevor couldn't resist remarking on the breach of etiquette. "Hello," he said, addressing the beautiful woman, "are you a friend or family to Carol?"

Before the woman could answer, Carol waved off his comment, "it's just a robot," she explained, momentarily looking up at Trevor from her device. "My son never leaves his apartment any more!"

"Mom!" the beauty mouthed in a carefully selected voice, "you don't have to message me, you can talk directly to Ginger. And, I can see you just fine!"

But Carol only laid her device on the table, and spoke to an empty place next to the robot, "I'd rather see my son and speak to him in person! But, if this is the way you want it! Thanks for remembering my birthday!"

The robot made a frustrated sound and walked away. Everyone else at the table remained silent, this was clearly a family matter. Finally, Millie spoke up, "Happy Birthday Carol!" The rest of their group followed suit and accepted pieces of her birthday candy.

Later that day, the gang met up at Millie's to continue their trip. It was decided that they would begin their route 66 portion of the trail at a small town called, Oatman. When they appeared there, they found themselves standing on an old wooden sidewalk that ran along a line of several, old western style storefronts. Railing with occasional 'hitching posts' lined the street side of the walk. Solid people bustled about everywhere. It appeared to be a tourist destination with mostly solid families with children, but there were a few ghostly avatars as well. But, by far, the most interesting beings in the town were the live boroughs that walked where they please, on the sidewalk or street. They looked feral, they were unwashed with parts of their winter coats still clinging to them here and there. Then, it was noticed that all of the stores sold bundles of carrots that the solids could purchase to feed the animals with. It was fun watching the children holding the carrots for the mangy looking beasts as their parents snapped pictures.

Debra noticed that some of the shops were also open to RV patrons and wanted to visit one of the curio shops. It was as they were gliding thorough the doors when a young man wearing AR lenses was walking out and noticed the group of avatars. "Watch out, it's a group of avatars coming in!" he shouted to the small group that was exiting with him. "Don't talk about anything you don't want them to eavesdrop on!" he announced as though he were preforming some kind of public service.

The group didn't know what to make of the angry man. Everyone knew about the controversy over opening the trail system to RV, but the group wasn't used to solids being able to see them and never had they encountered one that complained directly to them. They felt a kind of embarrassment. Then the man followed them back inside the building and pointed at the group, "they are right there!" he said standing near Hank and pointing down at them. "Why don't you guys get off your asses and visit places in person? Or, is your real reason for being here that you are a bunch of freakin' voyeurs?" he shouted.

Finally Larry spoke up, "Common' guys, just attach to me and I'll take us down the trail a ways." He looked at Millie as he spoke to make sure she noticed his take-charge attitude. So, that was what they did as the solid man began speaking again.

They re-appeared on a very quiet and desolate stretch of a dirt trail that was separated from, but followed beside, the old highway. They were all relieved to be away from the man who could 'see' them.

"So, this is bleak," Hank complained as the elderly avatars rotated and took in the scenery around them. It was a bright day, there were mountain peaks in the distance, but the area around them was nearly naked of vegetation, it was nothing but rolling reddish-brown dirt for miles. Occasional birds would squawk from overhead and tumble weeds would get caught up in a wind gust and cross the trail. But there wasn't much to look at. It was a desert.

"Let's use my jetpack so we can cover more area faster," Larry suggested, looking at Millie for approval. Millie nodded her agreement, but looked solemn. The words and behavior of the man with the AR lenses had brought everyone's mood down. She kept telling herself that surly he didn't understand that he was addressing a group of poor seniors that lacked the money or ability to travel there in person. But, still it was a hateful way to behave.

Flying above the trail, through the clear blue sky, quickly cleared their minds and revived joy to their souls. Now, they were birds, without a care in the world!

After miles of sand, they finally rose up with the trail and then back down into a green valley that was penned in by forested mountains. Larry flew them to the ground, next to a young, solid couple with three children. The group of avatars gathered near the solid couple to take in the same beautiful view that was holding their attention. It was an oasis. A small swell in the width of a river that snaked between the mountains and formed a beautiful little lake with wildlife and green plants a plenty. One small cabin could be seen on it's edge, where the residents could boat and fish from their back yard. Large fir trees shaded it.

The young solid couple leaned against the railing that followed that side of the trail. They looked thin and tired, but gazed longingly at the little cabin. Finally, the man spoke up in a quiet dreamy voice, "don't you wish we lived there? Heck, I'd be happy to just pitch a tent in their side yard!" he laughed then pointed, "or over there under that big tree!" The young woman beside him chuckled softly. It did look inviting.

Millie couldn't help but hear the conversation, but now she noticed the young boy standing next to the man, he looked to be about eight years old, but without the spark and chattiness of the average eight-year-old. He was quietly observing the same view as his parents, wishing the same things.

Then, Millie's attention was drawn to the two wagons they were pulling, the smaller one had an umbrella like covering that shielded it's two small occupants from the relentless sun. Then, there was the larger wagon whose tires barely fit within the trail. It was packed quite tall with bags and boxes stacked up inside it. Millie's line of sight wandered back to the couple as she realized that they were most likely agrarian refugees.

These types of refugees had become all too common as the desert of the mid-west was growing. The Las Vegas area wasn't the only part of the country that had begun to reclaim old disused oil pipelines and re-purpose them to distribute water. Tiles were laid along the western bank of the Mississippi at flood level, so that every year during their rainy season, the excess water now traveled west to the edges of the desert where water shortages had been feeding the great brown menace yearly, but, finally, the east side of the desert was becoming tame. The growth of this edge of the desert had been at a stand still and some even say that there are parts of the desert that had become green again. But, the western edge was only growing in size every day. Desalination plants had slowed it's progress, but still, the desert was swallowing whole farms at an alarming rate and the number of agrarian refugees was keeping pace, as even those who remained struggled with the overwhelming costs of years of importing water.

Most likely, this young family was attempting to cross the desert for a better life. Millie couldn't help but look inside the smaller wagon at the two young girls seated inside. The older girl looked to be about four, and it appeared to be her job to keep the younger one occupied. The younger child didn't look to be old enough to walk, but she sat up easily and was fond of chewing on the toys that were piled up between them. 'I bet she's cutting teeth,' Millie thought as she leaned in even closer to the contents of the little wagon. Both girls were wearing light clothing as the hottest part of the day was just subsided and the cooler evening temperatures were about to begin. Then, she noticed a little sore on the babies lip. She didn't like the looks of it, but the baby seemed happy and content. Both children had a healthy pink glow as they made small noises and laughed together. The oldest child, the boy, looked much too serious for his age, his hair was tied behind him under a brimmed hat. He was wearing blue jeans with dirty knees and a t-shirt. He was very quiet, just observing the world in front of himself without joy.

"Well, let's get going!" The father announced before walking to the front of the larger wagon and picking it up by the handles. The young boy walked to the rear of the cart and gave it a shove to help give it forward momentum with a push, then he stepped up beside his father. The woman grabbed the handle of the smaller wagon with the two younger children and the group marched on.

Millie watched the little family get smaller until Trevor shouted out to her that he needed her binoculars. She glided back to her little group of avatars as they were all gathered together looking into the distance. Trevor was pointing, "there's something big and black in that tree over there!" he explained while taking the binoculars that she was holding out for him. She squinted into the direction that he had indicated and slowly began to make out the slight movements of something that was sitting near the top of a tall leafless tree that hung over the little pond.

They all gasped as it spread it's wings and jumped from the branch. It swooped then began flying in their direction. It had an immense rectangular wingspan that ended with frays of black feathers. As it grew closer they could also make out the white markings on it's underside.

"I think it's a condor!" Trevor shouted excitedly. He passed the binoculars to Hank as the old man was reaching for them.

"Yep! Looks like a condor all right! Better take a good look, likely to be the last one you see in nature!" Hank explained, handing the binoculars back to Millie. The group gasped and looked on excitedly as the large bird flew over them and then landed at the top of a nearby tree.

"Oh Larry!" Millie shouted, "can you take us up there? I want to see it close!"

"Sure! Hop on, everyone," he instructed the crowd, happy to be the hero. He took them up and close to the bird. It was the largest bird that any of them had ever seen. It had the ugly orange head of a vulture, but a ruffle of black feathers around its neck made it look regal. Its eyes were black, shiny beads that seemed to be concentrated on the little river that flowed along the edge of the trail. The white under markings could only been seen as a horizontal stripe on either side of the bird. They continued to watch and follow the bird until it was out of range.

Millie was uplifted and inspired by the incident, as despite Hank's remarks, she knew that the number of wild condors had actually increased. It was because of the work of the citizen scientist program, that there was better air and water quality, now pollution was being monitored and fewer toxic chemicals were working their way through the food chain as the corporate sources were being discovered and forced to clean up their messes. So, in the end, it was school children who had saved the condor.

When they were gently brought back to Earth, Millie temporarily forgot that she was suspicious of Larry and grew closer to him to thank him for his quick thinking with the jet pack. But, then, standing near him and looking up at him, he reminded her of someone else. She shamed herself for being so suspicious. Maybe, everything she felt about the man was now tainted with unwarranted suspicion. Maybe, Debra's cynicism was planting doubt in her, where positivity and trust used to be. She didn't like the feel of it, she didn't want to give into becoming an angry old person like many of the other souls she had befriended over the years had become.

Soon after that, she received a message that she had another dart match. She, bid farewell to the others then teleport to the arena. She lost her third game, but was happy to see her black knight in the audience, again. He was such exciting company, she thought. Mystery was part of his charm and being resigned to the fact that she would never meet him in person, was an acceptable part of the romance. He was her fantasy, his existence, whoever he was, instilled passion in her. Her sensibility didn't want to know who he was in the solid, flesh and blood world. She didn't want the dreaming to end.

When she finally removed her visor, she found herself alone in her apartment, but she was happy for the quiet. Although, she liked her friends, she did enjoy solitude. She got ready for bed, then laid in the center of it, hugging a pillow and dreaming of her knight.

The next morning at breakfast she asked Trevor how things had went after she left. Did they see anymore condors? He told her that they had and could have really used Larry's jet pack. "Why? Did he leave too?" she asked with trepidation.

"Yeah, not long after you left," Trevor explained between bites.

Millie went cold. Lenard's nine-year-old-voice came to mind, "no one really knows who anyone is anymore, anyway." She couldn't help but stare at Larry as he walked up to the table with his dinner tray, smiling brightly at her.

She went numb. Larry's face fell, he could read her mind, she knew.

"Are you okay?" Trevor asked Millie when he noticed her sudden change in demeanor.

Larry took a seat at the end of the table instead of the place next to Millie that he usually preferred.

Millie became aware that Trevor and the others at the table were concerned about her, but she didn't want to explain herself, so instead, she tried to shake off the shock of the new revelation. "Oh, fine, just thinking about stuff I need to get done this afternoon." She took another bite of her yogurt then glanced at Larry who was looking more like his old self, shoveling food into his mouth without looking up. He quickly cleaned his plate then got up to take back the tray.

Millie followed him. When he turned around to exit, Millie blocked his way. Now she was angry and it showed on her face.

"I don't want to see you or the black knight in virtual reality ever again." Her words were even and with the least amount of emotion that she could muster. Lenard just looked at her, then cast his eyes down. But, he nodded that he understood her words. His reaction was a confirmation. Then, he pushed passed her and out of the cafeteria.

Millie noticed that Debra and the others had been watching the interaction, but were too far away to hear her words. She emptied her partially eaten meal from her tray then left as well, only waving to the group as she passed them.

She went back to her room and locked the door. Then, she fell on her bed and laid there, hugging the same pillow that she had pretended to be her dark knight, only the night before. She already missed him and Larry, and felt sad to think that neither of them ever really existed! Despite her normal sensibilities, she began to sob into that same pillow. How she missed her knight already! 'That stupid, son of a bitch!' she thought bitterly.

After a few minutes, that sensible voice came to her and made her notice how silly she was being. Crying over a boy! At her age! Then, she considered how much younger he was, and how obsessed with her he must be! It was both frightening and a bit of a compliment. Then, despite her tears, she laughed at herself.

Meanwhile...a love struck Lenard lay across his bed, angry at being rebuffed by the love of his life! Everything was going so well! The black knight dearly enjoyed his evenings with the beautiful Freya! And now, everything was ruined! He couldn't remember ever feeling so much tenderness toward any live human being. He loved her even more than his mother! And, he almost had her! But, now, she had rejected him, banned him from the group's travels and removed him from the popular table! And, he had helped all of them acquire their gear! How could they brush him aside like that! He almost had everything that he had ever dreamed of, friends and everything! Now he was done forever in that building. Now everyone was talking about him and how bad he was!

Then, an angry Lenard sat up, crossed his arms and with the determined look of an angry nine-year-old, he declared that the only thing left to do was to BE that bad person. Fuck them! Fuck Millie! He did whatever he wanted and those stupid old techno-tards were no match for him!

Later that afternoon while everyone was meeting in Millie's apartment, she made an announcement that she had purchased a jet pack. Everyone made agreeable noises as they had become dependent on 'Larry's,' but no one wanted to mention him or his absence. Debra sat silently, but very smugly.

They decided to begin their journey at the valley with the condors, just to see if they might get a glimpse of another. Millie was anxious to try out the new jet pack so she had everyone attach and then she guided them up, after a few crashes, she figured out the controller, and then they were gliding through hologram trees, looking for large birds and animals of any type. It made for a fun afternoon with everyone laughing at their own antics, as well as, those of the local wildlife.

When they finally decided to leave the valley, the new scenery, of desert and more desert, did quickly become monotonous. The sky was cloudless and the towns were infrequent, seemed like everyone had just got up and left their homes and now there were only shells with dilapidated roofs, or none at all. "Ghost towns a plenty," Carol remarked, as they traveled past a cluster of houses near an empty facade of a grocery store. These were not the kind of ghost towns Trevor had in mind when he suggested the trip, but they were eerie. One of the houses was close enough to the trail that Millie could fly them over it. A large hole in the roof revealed that the last occupants hadn't even removed their furniture before they left. The trails were oddly deserted as well, the few solid people they encountered were gathered around way stations where there was water, toilets and showers. There were no other avatars.

But, then, they could make out the strange shape of a wagon. When they glided in closer they could see that it was the same little family that they had encountered the day before. Millie lowered everyone to the boardwalk. She couldn't help but to move to the side of the smaller wagon to get a look at the two younger children that were still inside it. There was still a little bright colored awning over it, but inside the younger child was whimpering and her sister was doing her best to hold a little fan over the baby, one was wearing only shorts and the other only a diaper and clinging to her blanket, and they both looked miserable with red skin.

When Millie got closer, she was horrified to see that the sore on the babies lip was now much larger and there were more sores on her chin and neck. They looked painful and itchy, then she noticed that the babies hands were each bound so that it couldn't itch the ugly sores. That was when she noticed the sores on the older sister as well, as she was busy fanning the baby with one hand, while she was scratching at her legs with the other. Ugly red welts were all over both of them. Their mother doggedly pulled the wagon behind her by it's handle. She looked tired and sweat was running down her face from the brim of her hat. Millie notice that the man looked tired as well, but the mechanism for pulling the larger wagon was a kind of harness that the man had buckled at his waist. His skin was a tough brown color. The boy walked behind, staring at the ground in front of him as he kept a steady pace.

Millie wondered what was effecting the younger two children. Was it the heat? Or something worst, something contagious as now at least two of them were suffering from it. She got as close as she could to the little ones, trying to determine the nature of the sores. Some of it looked like mosquito bites, but then there were patches of gooey sores. Were they just infected? She wondered.

Debra noticed Millie's interest and looked on as well. "What do you think the problem is?" she mused aloud. Millie's avatar shook it's head, "I don't know, but I wish I could help." They both sighed, as this situation was beginning to look like the problem they had when they were watching the storm. All they could do was watch helplessly.

"I think we should travel on," Trevor said as he glided up to the two women. "You know there is nothing we can do, I'm sure they could find a way to contact emergency help if needed." He was trying to sound reassuring. Millie reluctantly agreed, and then the group took flight. But, Millie couldn't get the little girls out of her mind.

Later that evening after everyone had left, Millie began searching online for a possible source of the little girls' rashes. She viewed photos of different contagious diseases for something that looked similar. The closest she could find were images of the different stages of poison ivy. But, in the desert? Then, she remembered the green valley. After a little search she found that the plant grows everywhere in the united states. In fact, with the warmer temperatures, it had become even more prolific in green areas. She read about how the poison from the plant could be transferred to people from clothing. "The blanket!" she accidentally said aloud. She sat back in her chair wondering how she could convey her fears to the young mother? But, there was nothing, as the family didn't seem to possess a communicator or any tech. Millie tossed and turned all night trying to think of some way to help.

In another room in the building, Lenard marveled at his screen. 'Who has a contagious rash?' he wondered as he scrolled through Millie's stolen browser feed.

The next morning Millie couldn't wait for the others to get online to check in on the little family. She located them in RV and found them in their dreary march forward. The man was already sweaty, but pulled the wagon in a determined pace. The little boy was the same, only his complexion was darker on his, all too serious, face. All of them were quiet, eerily quiet. She looked in the smaller wagon, and the two little girls lay next to one another, wearing only shorts and a diaper, they were covered with whelps and ugly oozing sores. The older one tossed miserably, but the baby lay very still. Both of them on top of that awful blanket! Millie got closer, she could see the babies little chest raise slightly, but her eyes were closed, her mouth agape, and her body limp.

Millie gasped. She moved farther to the front of the line where the children's mother walked with one hand behind her, holding tight the handle of the wagon. Her face was red and glistening, she also looked listless. Millie wanted to tell her to check on the baby, but she was only a mute phantom. And then, she noticed the red blisters on the woman's neck.

Millie pulled off her headset. She looked up at the ceiling and let out a breath she had been holding. She hated this feeling of doom and helplessness. It was unbearable. She began pacing her room until Debra and the rest of the gang showed up.

"I want to check in on that little family first," she explained as everyone was putting on their headsets.

"Oh, I do too!" came a chorus of replies.

Millie looked around herself at all the other concerned faces, then asked them the question that had been haunting her, "do you think we are being voyeurs? I mean, we are kind of stalking these people and they don't even know we are there. We are doing just the thing that all the people who didn't want the trails to be accessed by remote viewing, were afraid that avatars would do."

"No we aren't!" Carol interrupted, "we are concerned citizens and are only interested in helping these people! The world needs more humans looking out for one another!"

This made Millie pause, and everyone else nodded and made agreeable sounds. Maybe they could find a way to help, she decided.

It didn't take long for them to locate the sad little convoy. It was looking pretty much as it had earlier that morning, except that the sun was brighter. When the group looked inside the little wagon they could see the older girl still tossing and digging at the sores. And the baby, looked exactly the same with it's eyes closed and it's mouth open. The group became alarmed.

"We need to contact the authorities!" Carol exclaimed.

"That baby looks dead!" Hank shouted.

Debra bent over to see the baby better, then squealed. Millie now had all the confirmation that she needed. "I'm going to the VR police station! You guys stay here and keep an eye on them!" She announced before vanishing.

She appeared at the police station and found herself in front of a desk with the policeman sitting on the other side looking at a monitor. "May I help you?" he asked.

Millie looked around herself and at the drab decor. 'They certainly didn't overspend when they had this place designed,' she thought to herself. "Yes," she answered aloud, "I need to report a child in danger, actually, children, there are three of them, but the baby looks near death!"

"Where?" To that question Millie rattled off the GPS coordinates.

"We were in Remote Viewing on the ITS when we came across this little family. They are trying to cross the desert and..."

"Wait," the policeman interrupted, he read something off his screen then looked back up at Millie. "My boss said that I need to confirm the situation before I send out emergency vehicles, but I don't have access." He shrugged his avatar shoulders, "it's so new, this station doesn't have access yet."

Millie was crestfallen, "but the baby! It looks like it won't make it much longer! You have to do something! I can't do anything, I'm an avatar!"

"Okay, wait a minute," the policeman looked back at his monitor and began typing. "I'm trying to find someone here that has personal access."

Both avatars stood impatiently waiting for an answer. Finally, there was a beep and the policeman began typing again. "Okay, I found someone...I just gave him the coordinates...and-" the man looked up and Millie, "there is our portal!" he announced with a hand gesture.

Millie looked behind herself at the tall oval that had opened up behind her. Both avatars entered and found themselves a little ways behind the family, along with the group of concerned avatars. But things had changed. Now the convoy had stopped and the woman was wailing and holding her baby. The policeman immediately pulled out his communicator and called for help. Then they both glided to the terrible sight. The father produced a bottle of water and was using the blanket to dab the water over the baby to revive it. Everyone, including the avatars cheered when they saw the infant wince and make a horse cry. But the parents looked around themselves in a panic. There was no one around, no communicator, no way to call for help. They were in the middle of the desert, there wasn't even any shade.

The woman was sitting on the ground clutching her baby and rocking it, while wailing loudly. The man began walking in a circle, desperately looking around himself for any sign of another human that might be able to help, but there was no one. No houses, no vehicles on the road that ran next to them, just sand, everywhere!

The policeman looked a bit panicked as well, he was looking at his communicator and repeated, "they are on their way!" to the avatars, as well as the humans that could not hear him.

The man began throwing boxes off the wagon and instructed his wife to sit on the back of it with the baby, then he told his son to pull the smaller wagon with his sister inside, "you can do that? Right? You're a big boy!" he added as an encouragement. The little man did as instructed and took the lead, with his father pulling the heavier burden close behind.

"Any time, any time," the policemen repeated. Until the faint sound of a siren could be heard in the distance. The little family heard it too and began moving faster toward the sound. Then, slowly in the distance they could see a little cloud of dust coming toward them on the trail. Everyone cheered as it got close enough that it couldn't be mistaken. It was a long narrow electric vehicle that was traveling at an impressive speed.

The avatars wept with joy as the watched the little ones being examined and IVs inserted, and the conversation between the emergency workers informed them that the children were severely dehydrated, but the baby was breathing. The wagons were abandoned and the family eagerly boarded the vehicle. The avatars could hear the man's questions, "how did you know we needed help? Who sent you?"

Before the doors were shut the EMT could be heard answering, "not sure, you must have a guardian angel!"

The avatars found themselves alone with the remains. The policeman looked at Millie then the rest of the group, "you guys did a good thing!" he said before he disappeared, back to the station.

The group of seniors pulled off their headsets, their eyes glistened, but with big smiles they chatted excitedly. Millie looked from one gray head to the other. This was a group with a purpose, with hope, 'Maybe the world needs a group of elderly guardians watching,' she mused.

Unique Identifier

He had worked long and hard to convince his superiors that he was the man for the job. He was the oldest of his siblings, his parents were still young and healthy, and he had no family of his own, no companion, no children. And, since the position was, most likely, permanent, this was a big consideration. It was his wanderlust that made him pursue the position. He wanted to be part of a study of distant planets. And, this one, was the equivalent, of several months from the closest base. What that meant, is that he had to spend months alone, in a small capsule.

He spent most of the time in a sleeping state, but there were regular awake times, when he exercised and conducted all the work necessary to keep the air inside breathable and to make sure everything was working properly. Food was in a bag that was fed to him intravenously. Having a partner was ruled out from the beginning, since two people always talked and created carbon faster than it could be processed. So, he knew from the moment he stepped into that capsule that he would never see, in person, his family or another familiar face, like himself, ever again.

There were also banks of information about the new planet for him to learn, and details of the samples and tests that he was required to perform there. For entertainment he began a study of history, and he decided to start this study from the beginning, since ancient documents were very interesting to him. But, still, months! There were times when he wished something would go wrong, that he would be killed by an asteroid or debris or something. But, then he finally arrived. As soon as his capsule was on the ground, he opened the door and rolled out, rubbing his face in the vegetation, unable to walk temporarily, as his legs were weak.

Luckily, he landed in an unoccupied area. Later, he would learn that it was in the colder, northern hemisphere. This was what he wanted, the cooler part of the planet that was more compatible to his home world, where the sun wasn't as bright. Although he had lost a lot of weight, his body was naturally stocky, his complexion was light as were his eyes. At first the sun made him squint, it was difficult for him to be out of the shade of the large green trees that surrounded his spent capsule. He located the special glasses that he had brought from home. He spent his first day observing the large variety of flying animals, he watched what they ate and tried to identify what was poison from his study of the planet while in transit.

Solid food. At first, everything made him throw up. He still had a few bags of intravenous fluids. This would keep him alive and hydrated for the next few days.

Lou was stunned about the news bulletin that he had just read. He was eager to tell his best friend, Dr. Jason Jefferies, the good news. He found his mother in the kitchen making coffee, "Mom, have you read the news yet today?" His tail was snapping impatiently behind him. He noticed that the monitor in the kitchen wall was black, he bound over to turn it on before his mother had a chance to answer. Excited about what he had read, he decided that he wanted a second source to confirm it before he went into the garage where Jay and his family had parked their transporter.

The back door opened and a large, gruff looking man in overhauls held the door open for a little girl of three, who was carrying a small basket, containing a single egg, on her arm. "Now, just set it up there on the table real gentle like, so grandma Linda can cook it for ya'," the man instructed the girl in a voice much too dainty for his burly frame. He set a wooden bowl of brown eggs that he had been carrying in the center of the table before locating his wife.

Lou was shuffling through the papers and what-not that had accumulated on the kitchen table, looking for a controller for the monitor. Without saying a word, his mother stepped up beside him and put the device in his hand. "Thanks," Lou said without making eye contact, as he slid into one of the miss-matched, kitchen chairs while pressing on the device and looking up at the screen.

His father walked up to his mother and wrapped his arm around her waist, and kissed her cheek before complaining, "I have got to talk with Bob, he's got to keep that damn rooster out of our yard! You know I found another fertile egg this morning!"

"Why are you complaining? We can have a few chickens for the pot!" she countered as she handed her husband a mug of coffee, but he made a grumble sound. "Listen," she continued, "we could just agree to put the new chickens aside from the others and not give em' a name or anything…."

"There it is!" Lou shouted, turning the volume of the audio up, before dashing out the door toward the garage where Jay's transporter was parked. He scooped up Lilly on the way, and carried her on his hip. Bill and Linda, stepped in front of the monitor to see the headline behind the newswoman, "ASSASSIN APP DISAPPEARS!"

"Jay!" Lou shouted before pounding on the transporter door. Lilly squealed and clapped her hands, if Uncle Lou was excited, then she was too! When the door slid open, Lilly could see her parents sitting at a small table together. She wiggled off Lou's hip and ran inside to her mother, explaining excitedly about the eggs. But, that was not Lou's big news, "Jay! Emily! Did you hear yet!" Lilly's parents shook their heads. "The Assassin App is gone! It disappeared!" he shouted, then made a 'follow me,' motion with his arm, "common' I got the story on right now, inside!" before he walked quickly back to the kitchen with Jay and Emily, carrying Lilly, close behind.

When they entered the back door, they found Bill and Linda standing in front of the monitor with an arm around each other. They looked up happily at their guests, pointing at the monitor. "Oh my god!" Jay exclaimed happily, hugging his wife and daughter. There were tears of joy, before a question occurred to him, "How? Who did it?"

Lou shrugged his shoulders, "No one knows yet. It's just gone! All traces of it! No more ability to add a bounty or collect one!"

Jay looked at his friend, to make sure he was understanding the situation, before reaching over and slapping him on the shoulder. The group sat around the table, alternately talking excitedly and then, hushing one another so that they could listen to yet another news report of the same story. The assassin app was no more!

Jay had been hiding with his family, in the community for the last several months. Ever since a failed attempt on his life had forced them to flee their home. Lou's family home was within a closed community that was located in a remote area of Michigan. Lou had lived his whole life in the old farm house, except for the traumatic ten years, when his parents had been in prison. It was the loyalty of the community that caused Jay and his family to feel safe there. They knew how to keep a secret, and a man with a bounty of millions of dollars on his head needed that.

It wasn't until Linda was setting plates of food on the table, that Bill remembered something that he meant to tell his son, "This morning while Lilly and I were feeding the chickens, I saw a strange bird perched in the top of the apple tree," he began, while piling food onto a clean plate. "I know my vision isn't as good as it used to be, but it kind of looked like an owl, but then it flew out of the tree, and, well, it looked kind of like a toy or something." He looked at his son for a reaction.

"A drone?" Lou offered.

"No, no, it was small and long, like..."

Lou squared his shoulders, his tail began making small circles in the air, "a fairy?"

Bill sat back in his chair, he hadn't thought of that, but now that Lou had said it, "you think so?" Everyone at the table was considering the implications, as fairies were small, outlawed drones with tiny cameras that were used by criminals to spy on people.

"But, you said that it flew away?" Jay asked cautiously.

Bill nodded in the affirmative, but everyone at the table was now uneasy.

A few hours later, Lou was helping Jay load the rest of his family's things into their transporter for the happy journey home. "There's something that I wanted to tell you," Lou said quietly, after he had stowed the last of the luggage onto the transporter. He looked around himself, then grew closer to Jay, "you know that story I told you the other day, when we were standing on the bridge?"

Jay nodded, he remembered, but it had all been so odd and mysterious, he wasn't sure if he should believe it or be concerned about his friend's state of mind. But, he was intrigued, "yeah, about the lights in the sky?"

Lou wet his lips, "he wants to meet you." Jay didn't know what to think and the confusion on his face made it clear. "He has been watching your career, your whole life," Lou continued, "he thinks he could help you."

Jay was astounded, "yeah," he nodded again. "Yes! I would very much like to meet with him too!" But, then he remembered that this 'person' was the same that had done the highly illegal editing of Lou's DNA, and that would make him a criminal. That realization showed in his eyes.

"Don't worry," Lou laughed, "it won't be some kind of sting operation! There won't be any cops there to arrest us!" he patted his friend on the back. "After you've had a chance to recover in your own home, let me know when you might be able to come back for a visit. I'll arrange things," he looked over at his friend as he still had his arm around his shoulders while they walked back into the house, "this needs to happen," he finished with a reassuring hug before letting go.

Later that day, Jay and Emily breathed a sigh of relief when the transporter pulled into their drive. They enjoyed the community, and it had begun to feel more like home, but, it wasn't. There really was no place like their own private sanctuary.

Emily had sorted and stacked their things into baskets on the trip back, so the chore of moving back in was minor. It was while they were returning everything to it's place that Emily noticed a large box on the front porch. "Oh look Jay! I bet it's the painting!" she announced excitedly.

Jay helped her carry it to the foyer, where they opened it and slid the work of art from the cardboard container. It was a large, colorful canvas with the white ghostly line drawing of the jubilant, 'Dancing Man.' They now possessed an original Michael Denton painting!

"I know just where I want to hang it!" Emily exclaimed before disappearing and leaving her husband alone with the work of art. He leaned it against the wall to examine it. Much had happened since he had first laid eyes on the jolly character. He was the one who noticed it first, but it was Emily who insisted on the purchase. Just a few hours later, he was nearly murdered. If Lou hadn't broke the door, then the assassin would have been able to finish him off. Or, so he was told, as he didn't remember anything after hitting his head on the ceramic floor tile. A shiver went down his back, but then he reminded himself, he was safe, the assassin app had been deleted, no matter how it was accomplished, the deadly program was no more.

Then, he remembered Laura Novak's words to him while he was in the hospital, that 'a man on a horse wearing a cowboy hat,' would help him. It was during his stay in the community that the news story had broke that one of the newest Nevada Representatives had assisted the police in apprehending one of the many who had added money to his bounty. It was the first time someone had ever been connected to the assassin app. Jay wondered if it had anything to do with the success of shutting it down. No one knew yet, there was still a lot of secrecy about the whole event.

And, now, his best friend has promised to introduce him to someone who could enlighten him about the unique identifier. 'We will see,' he thought to himself, without being overly hopeful. Then, his wife walked into the room holding their daughter's hand, seeing the two of them filled his heart with joy. Life was definitely looking up.

"I'm still alive," came a raspy voice. She was having difficulty opening her eyes, but managed a smile. The doctor next to her bed, grew closer. Slowly, her eyelids fluttered, "could you turn the lights down?" she instructed. Someone shut them off, then pulled the drapes partially closed. "Better," she swallowed, "Now, I need some water." Someone moved a straw next to her lips, so she could drink. After a small sip, she slowly opened her eyes to stare at the ceiling.

"Ms. Novak," came the calm voice of the doctor next to her bed, "you've been in a comma."

To this she chuckled softly, closing her eyes again, as they had become sensitive to the light.

"Do you know where you are?" he continued.

She wanted to nod, but her entire body felt as if it were glued to the bed. "Yes, hospital," she responded.

"Do you remember why you are here?" the doctor persisted.

"Yes," Laura was feeling tired at her efforts to console the physician. "Probably better than you," she added in a stronger voice. She knew this remark would make him feel better satisfied with her progress, and it did.

"Well, I am glad to tell you, that you have made incredible progress! Your burns are healing nicely and I believe the most painful part of you healing has passed!" he explained with a smile and sweeping hand gestures. "Now you just need to rest and let us know if you need anything." He stood up and left the room with a number of other interested physicians and students that had previously been examining Laura's damaged body after a special inflated, cooling suit, had been removed for the last time.

Laura was actually feeling extraordinarily alert with a hyper state of awareness of everything around her, every sound, every smell, the tingling feel of skin regenerating and the currents of cool air that circulated around her. She felt so much that to open her eyes would be overwhelming. So she kept them closed and reveled in the ecstasy of simply being alive.

She was waking from the longest meditation with the universe that she had ever experienced. Uninterrupted, she had traveled and lived with another being, made of energy only. They connected and communicated without form or words. She lived and worked for days, and now she understood the importance of the work being done where they were and why they were being delayed on their return back to Earth.

As the first living person to be discovered with the unique identifier, she had become a kind of celebrity. Unprepared for the onslaught of people who wanted to use her for their own purposes, she had been seduced by a manipulative minster. Although, something deep inside her had always made her uncomfortable with her 'christian reality star' status, it wasn't until she was contacted by a Bhikkhu in Sri Lanka that the truth of her new sham of an existence hit her.

Something compelled him to contact her after seeing her speak from a wooden cross, a spectacle that had brought in millions of dollars to the charlatan reverend. The monk convinced her to take a sabbatical to the mountain top monastery and it was under his tutelage that she first learned to meditate. It was life changing for her. And, after much practice, she became aware of her hidden talent for channeling the universe.

In Australia, Dr. Abjorn Karlsson was examining rock art made by the Anangu people. He had decided to arrive in person to study the group of Aboriginal people, where the unique identifier had been recently discovered in the DNA of several living tribe members. Now, he was becoming enchanted by the origin story that was recorded at Ayers Rock, Uluru. The illustrations tell the story of the Sky Father who created the lakes, rivers and caves before leaving the planet from Mount Yengo, which still has a flattened top from his departure.

The Doctor's imagination was filled with the possibilities. Could he be looking at a historical record?

Although, he was trained as a medical doctor, his love of archaeology, was married to his profession as a DNA specialist, when he started collecting and analyzing ancient DNA. He had first discovered the unique identifier in the DNA of a mummy. Then, several more were found, all of them from a single line of Egyptian royalty. His project became more widespread, and more of the ancient edited DNA was found in South America and the Republic of Georgia, but never in a living human being until it was discovered, by accident, by Dr. Jefferies in the United States. And now, he had located it in Australia, among living Aboriginal people.

He had suggested the intense search for a live human with the anomaly among the Aboriginal people, after it was found in ancient bones from that area. He had reasoned that because the continent had been isolated from the rest of the globe for so many years, that the chances of the edit still being in existence there would be better. His reasoning turned out to be sound and now he was trying to 'get to know' these people. He wanted to examine them for any trace of irregularities that the edited DNA might have been responsible for. And he wanted to get to know them as fellow humans, to see if he could discern any differences in their logic or thinking. The new DNA anomaly science was still in it's infancy, so he really wasn't sure what he was looking for, but it was exciting!

Several months ago, a special clinic had been set up with the purpose of paying volunteers to allow their DNA to be collected and checked for the variant. Now, he was setting up meetings with these special people that did possess the edit.

His communicator made a buzzing sound, then announced a call from Dr. Jefferies. He pressed the device, as it was attached to his shirt pocket. "Hello Jay!" he greeted the doctor like the friend that they had become. "So glad to hear back from you! Yes, the research is very interesting. We have located entire families of people with the identifier in their DNA! So, now we are studying the people as physically, and mentally, we are interested in their place in their communities, we are trying to determine if they are different than the rest of us. One of the interesting details that keeps coming up, is that these people are often the shaman, the dreamers of their communities. It makes me think of your patient. Don't you think it would be interesting to get her together with the others? I just can't help but wonder what would happen." Abjorn found himself unconsciously touching the rock paintings that he had been studying. He retracted his finger and attention to Jay. "What do you think?"

"I would be interested in that as well. But, you know about her accident, right?" Jay couldn't remember if it had been discussed. "Well, she was burned pretty badly, I'm not sure if she has recovered yet, but...uh..I could get a message to her. I'll let know." There was a short pause, "you know Abjorn, if she agrees to it, I'd like to go with her, if you don't mind."

Abjorn had planned to make the suggestion himself. "Sure! Would be wonderful to get a chance to meet with you again! You could bring your family." So, it was planned.

"How does it feel to be home and back to your old life?" Amelia asked Jay with a smile. They were sitting with Lou at their favorite table.

Jay tilted his head back and sighed, "sooooo...nice!" But then looked over at Lou and decided to clarify. "Not that the community isn't great! Wonderful people, and I feel blessed to have gotten to know them better! It felt like we were part of a big family for a couple months there!" he explained while lacing the fingers from one hand with the other to demonstrate strength in unity. Then, he paused reflectively, "and you know, Lilly absolutely loves it there! I never realized how small and isolated the three of are. You know, people just don't have big families anymore! But, that was how it felt!"

Amelia nodded enthusiastically, "That was exactly how I felt about the place when I first got to know it!" She looked over at Lou and the two smiled at one another, remembering that first forbidden trip. It had taken ten-year-old Lou, some effort to get Amelia to agree, since the Judge, who had placed him into the professor's guardianship after his parents were put in prison, had forbid it. So, those trips were kept secret.

"So, when will you be coming back?" Lou asked eagerly. Then he glanced over at Amelia before adding, "Jak is eager to talk with you."

Jay went stiff, that was the first time a name had been used, but he knew who Lou was talking about and the idea made him nervous. "Um...it will probably have to wait until we get back from Australia!" he said, happy to change topics.

"So, you're going for sure! And did you get patient #0130130 to agree to go with you?" Lou asked.

Jay nodded his head, "Yeah, she's going to ride in the plane with us!" This was a new development. "But, ya' know, she still sounded kind of weak to me. She's still in the hospital." Jay shook his head, "She said that she was getting out Thursday, so she wants to leave that weekend. She said she could sleep on the plane. I got her to wait until Monday." He fixed his eyes on something in the distance, "I feel like I should talk her into resting longer before making the trip, but she is anxious to go. She wants to meet these other people who have the edit!"

"Excellent!" Lou tipped his beer in Jay's direction. "To be honest, I'd like to see what happens when you get those guys together! I'll be anxious to see the documentation! Please, Please, Please, keep me in the loop!" he stated dramatically while holding his heart for effect.

Jay stretched, something had woke him up. The plane was quiet and dark except the dim bullets of evenly spaced lights that hugged the lower part of the floor, allowing travelers to navigate down aisles with minimal disruption for sleeping passengers. He looked over at his wife and daughter that lay sleeping next to him. The seats had been pulled down into a comfortable sized bed, there was a blanket over them. He stood up, and adjusted his shoulders and back, then pushed the drapes over their cabin door open and stepped out. He turned down the aisle walking toward the toilet at the front of the plane. On his right were sets of draped cabins and to his left were rows of people, mostly reclined, but as he neared the front, he looked for Laura's seats, and noticed that she was sitting up, looking out of the window, at the twilight sky. He stopped next to the empty seats beside her. She was wearing her simple brown robe with her simple bald head, leaning on the back of the seat. She turned her head and smiled brightly at him, then indicated with her hand that he should join her. So, he did.

"Great view, huh?" Jay offered cheerfully.

Laura nodded.

There were many questions that he would have liked to ask her, while they were alone and everything was quiet. "So, how are you feeling?"

She nodded again, "the hospital was amazing! Very nice and helpful people there! And now, I am almost as good as new! In fact, now I have nice new skin!" she chuckled.

"No lasting damage?"

"Not really, they told me not to worry about my hair because it would grow back. I told them that it would be easier for me if it didn't!" She chuckled again, her eyes sparkled. "Just my eyelashes and eyebrows haven't started to come back yet, maybe they won't, but I could use the lashes."

Jay waited a moment then stopped smiling, "Laura, do you know what happened?"

She nodded, "I think so. They are calling it, 'instantaneous human combustion.' And, well, I do think that is a pretty good description of what happened." She made a gesture with her hands.

Jay was hoping for a better explanation, so he persisted, "you don't have any theory about how or why it happened to you?"

Laura knew that he wanted a better explanation, but she didn't know how to explain it to him. It was too big. "As, I keep saying, our center is missing, but one day, it will come back, and not every being is happy about it."

Jay brought his hand near his mouth. He didn't want the book version, he wanted the simple truth. "So, you're saying that aliens are on their way here, now?"

Laura wished she could find words that sounded less like a fairy tale for Jay. "God. Our God. The good God, that will help us communicate and live in harmony with one another."

"When you said that it was coming back soon, what does that mean? Within days? Weeks?" Jay asked.

"Well, that's the thing," Laura continued, "it's not going to be for awhile now, other things have come up, important things, so it won't be for years now," she finished with a frown.

"You say that like it's a new development," Jay said, he was pessimistic of the story, but genuinely interested in her delusions.

"It is, in fact, it was while I was in the hospital that I became aware," she sighed uncomfortably as she understood that she sounded like a lunatic. "I had a vision," she finally finished, giving up on explaining herself.

There was a pause in the conversation, until Jay finally asked, "Laura do you know who edited your ancestor's DNA?"

"Yes."

This surprised Jay, "who?" he asked leaning closer to her.

"God. The same one who is coming back! We people with the edit, we are beacons!" She looked at him with resolute, wishing that he would stop thinking that she was crazy, as she had never had clearer vision then she did now. But, looking at the scientist's furrowed brow, she knew she would never be able to convince him of that.

Jay thought that some of her words sounded familiar, "are you Christian?"

Laura shook her head, "not Christian, not any religion. I'm not reciting mythology, I'm speaking about the Gardener.

The one who made our world and others habitable, beautiful! Our center, who helped us to communicate and learn from one another. Without him, we have grown apart and are becoming ignorant, we are destroying the planet and are hostile toward other living things." She looked at Jay and sighed, "listen, I know that you don't believe me, and it doesn't change the truth, I just wish I could help you to become enlightened, you are a good person. I wish that I could cause you to understand." She reach over and patted Jay's hand like he remembered his Auntie doing, as she quietly tried to explain the purpose of Christ to him, in a church pew. He sat silently, like he did for his Aunt, absorbing what she said, and wishing he could believe.

When the plane landed in Sydney everyone was happy to arrive after spending hours in the confined space. A staircase had been attached to the door, so that everyone stepped outside into the open air when they set foot out of the cabin. It was a bright day and the dry hot air was a bit of a shock to the system, everyone blinked and covered their eyes with their hands as they disembarked. A small electric train gave them a lift to the doors to the airport. Lilly enjoyed this part of the journey the most. She gleefully held tight the silver railing in front of her, smiling broadly from her mother's lap. Someone snapped a photo.

Inside the building they picked up their luggage and then walked to the common area, where they were surprised to see Dr. Karlsson was there in person to greet them. They had met in person a year before when they attended a conference together. He was a slim, blond man with an athletic build and thinning hair on top. Exceptionally friendly and ready with a smile, he reached into Emily's arms and squeezed Lilly's cheek, just enough to make her giggle. Jay introduced him to Laura, as they had only ever met over the phone. She was walking a few steps behind Jay and his family. Then she quietly stood nearby with her head down and looking very much like the simple monk that she was dressed as.

"We have a short drive, then, I've arranged a great place for you to stay, you are going to love the view!" Abjorn explained as they headed out of the airport. There was a man with him that he introduced as Sam. Jay wondered if it was a nickname as the man looked to be of Aboriginal descent, but, he was dressed in the same kind of pullover shirt and tan colored knickers that Abjorn was wearing and spoke English with a British accent. An older model transporter was waiting in line for them in a glass enclosed roundabout. It had the appearance of a vehicle that was used for public transportation as it was filled with rows of seats in front and had a compartment to store luggage in the back. Sam and Abjorn loaded the luggage into an outside compartment as Jay stood by and watched, not wanting to get in their way. They seemed to be used to working as a team. Emily, Lilly and Laura had found seats inside, and Lilly was happily eating something from a small container when the men boarded.

"Don't fill up Lilly!" Abjorn said to the child when he passed her seat, "there is a big dinner planned for you at the hotel!"

Hotel wasn't a very good description of the place, it was more of a motel, a long, one story white building with separate green doors for each unit and a large open area in the front where people were gathering around an outdoor kitchen. A pit had been dug and the smell of roasted pig was in the air. But, the most spectacular part was the view! It was situated off a lonely stretch of asphalt that ran through the desert like terrain, empty except for a single, magnificent red rock with a flat top that dominated the landscape for miles. "Mount Yengo," Abjorn explained. "One of the Anangu creation stories tells of the 'sky father' or creator god, Biame," he uttered in a quiet voice, "whose name is not to be said out loud, came to that rock with his wife and son. They gave the first rules to humans, and forbid them to eat the animals. The gods then spent time with the humans, teaching them and helping them evolve. But, when the people began eating the animals, anyway, the gods left from that rock and flattened the top of it in the process."

Laura stood quietly, listening as Abjorn and Jay were watching her, wondering what was going through the head of the monk as she eyed the aboriginal people who were busy around them, preparing the outdoor feast. The scientists were silently wondered if she could pick out those with the DNA edits. What were the connecting threads between them?

It was at that time when she walked away from them and slipped into a group of women who were preparing tubers. She took a seat in the sand and began helping them. Without words, she followed their instruction. The rest of her party watched on with interest as the monk appeared to be accepted seamlessly into the company of the natives. In fact, she looked more at home, sitting cross legged, with these people then she had with them.

Dinner was roasted pork and fish that had been cooking all day in a pit, there were also roasted yams and bowls of nuts and berries that none of the westerners had seen before. They ate with their hands from wooden plates or directly from the serving dishes, sitting on the ground or at picnic tables that were clustered together near the cooking pit.

While they were finishing their meal, they noticed that a fire was being built a few feet away and closer to the giant red rock, that dominated the skyline. Soon, musicians with their long didgeridoos and clapsticks took seats on the ground, encircling the fire starter and creating sounds that complimented the view. Laura, and then other members of the party of westerners soon joined. An aborignal woman with a wooden bowl that was filled with a kind of white paint appeared and offered to paint the faces of the guests. Emily accepted the offer, holding Lilly so that she could watch the process and allow the native woman to paint her face as well. There were many giggles and smiles, as the woman made her way around the circle of people, especially as she, painted Laura's entire head. Even Jay reluctantly allowed a few smears of the paint on his forehead. Everyone was in good spirits.

Abjourn was sitting next to Jay, cross legged on the ground, "There's something else that I think you are going to be interested in." He pointed up at the sky, "there is an amazing view of the stars! I have a telescope set up, I think it's dark enough to get a good view of Venus right now!" The two men got up and Abjourn guided Jay to a telescope on a tripod. He removed the cover and made some adjustments then gave Jay the lens. "Amazing!" Sam came around with a couple beers and men discussed Astronomy, as it turned out to be a hobby of all three men. They took turns showing one another different features through the lens. Soon it was completely dark and the stars glittered brightly above them, even the misty trail of the milky way was visible without the telescope, so they returned to the fire.

The darkness would have been difficult to navigate if it wasn't for the tall flames that flickered, as there were dancers circling it. Jay was tickled to see his wife and child among the revelers. Laura had been caught up in the fray as well, and he couldn't recall ever seeing her looking so carefree, this also made his heart happy. Sam pointed out a cooler as the source of the beers he had given them, so they helped themselves to more and found seats near the fire. The didgeridoos created a deep humming sound that Jay wasn't sure if he liked, at first, but now as it was accompanied by drums and the cracking sound of the clapsticks, he found the arrangement comforting and lively.

There were probably a dozen people dancing or sitting. More food was brought out, bowls of berries and nuts that Jay accepted without hesitation. The feeling of community reminded him of Lou's childhood home and the time they had spent there. It was a comfortable feeling, a feeling of belonging and that those around you felt the same. No hidden agendas, no classes, no deceptions, just people, enjoying the company of one another.

Soon, Lilly was in a heap next to him, using her stuffed whale for a pillow, and his jacket for a blanket, she slept soundly while her mother held hands with their new acquaintances and continued dancing around the fire. 'How lucky I am,' he thought as he brushed some of the flakes of white paint off his daughter's cheek.

Emily danced until she was exhausted, then she scooped up Lilly so that she could carry her to their room. "I'll be there as soon as I finish this," Jay told his wife, tipping the bottle he was holding in her direction.

"No hurry, I'll probably be sleeping before I hit the pillow anyway!" she explained, giving him a kiss before departing.

Jay did mean to only finish his beer, but then, when he was offered another, he remembered Emily's words and decided that since she was most likely asleep anyway, he'd have another. He leaned back to watch the dancers, then found himself staring into the fire, the way it danced against the black, star filled sky was magical. Then, slowly, he drifted off to sleep.

When he woke, he was laying sideways in dirt, the music had stopped and it was eerily quiet, with only the sound of the crackling fire. He sat up and looked beside himself to see that Abjourn and Sam had both left, but Laura and a few others were sitting cross legged, around the fire. They looked to be asleep, but Jay quickly realized that they were meditating. There were six of them, including Laura, with their eyes closed, sitting completely still. Jay knew that at least one of them also had the unique identifier, as Abjourn had earlier pointed the man out to him. He quietly observed for several minutes before collecting himself and stumbling in the dark to his room. It had been an exceptional evening.

Laura became aware of him, sitting near her, watching her, but she didn't want to come back. She was traveling with her new friends, and now they were together with the Gardner and all the light beings. It was paradise for her, to recognize every stranger, to immediately understand that person's true character and have them understand yours, without saying a word. Where curiosity was converted to knowledge that was shared. No misinformation, no explanations, every experience shared, so that only truth and reality reigned.

Almost everyone was slow to wake up the next morning. When Jay and his little family made their way to breakfast he observed that Laura along with her new edited friends were missing altogether. He was a little concerned until learning that Sam had led the small group on an expedition early that morning to hike to the large red rock that dominated the landscape.

While they were eating, they were joined by Abjourn. His eyes were a bit puffy and tired looking, but he wore the same cheerful smile as the night before. He set a large plate of eggs and pancakes in front of an empty seat at the long communal table that everyone was sitting at. "So glad I planned a holiday for your first day here!" he chuckled in his thick Scandinavian accent. "But, I am anxious to show you the lab. Tomorrow there will be people lined up here to be tested," he indicated the area in front of his office door. "We have a program that picks up paid volunteers and brings them here for testing. We have found thirteen people so far with the unique identifier! All of the codes are identical, everyone of them knew one another as family, but I'm confident that we will find others as we test people in more distant parts of the continent."

"Then, what happens with the people that you have found?" Emily asked, looking past her husband.

"There are extensive physical and psychological exams," Abjourn explained.

"And...everyone is cooperating?"

"Well, it's really only because they are paid," he admitted between bites. Then he shook his head, "interestingly, these people don't seem to be as impressed with this discovery. It's like, they had already accepted that there is this Dreamtime...dimension?" Abjourn seemed to have a problem coming up with the words to explain. "They accept that people were some how altered by the same gods that left the planet from that flat rock over there!" he pointed at the mount in the distance. "It's nothing new or mysterious to them," he took a drink of his coffee, "just another story."

"And, I suppose your work looking for the anomalies in ancient DNA is still ongoing?" Emily asked.

"Oh, yes! I have a team of graduate students that work everyday, scouring databases for DNA that have accumulated over the years. And now, ARTHUR1 has written a program to automate the process of identifying the edit. It's really going to speed up the process!"

Jay nodded politely, thinking how glad he was that Lou wasn't there, he knew that the conversation would have become hostile. "So, how old is the oldest edit so far?" he asked.

"At least 30,000 years! It was found in the tooth of an African," Abjourn explained.

Jay finally felt comfortable enough around Abjourn to ask, "so...what do you think the edit is about?"

The wording of the question was vague but Abjourn knew what he was asking, "well, I think it's no secret that I believe that the Earth was Colonized. I also realize that we humans today, are most likely, not the apex of all intelligence that we believe ourselves to be. So, for me, the answer is obvious, some other class of humanoids edited their DNA." He looked off into the distance, "I'm just really curious as to why."

Jay nodded in agreement, "Have you had a chance to talk with Laura very much?"

Abjourn shook his head, "I would have liked to go on their hike with them, but they left before I was up. I'm anxious to interview her."

Jay became a bit uncomfortable, "ya' know, I've had a strained relationship with Laura. I've seen her go through big changes in a very short span of time." He shrugged his shoulder, "I have to admit, I wrote her off as a crackpot, but, lately, since her newest conversion into a monk, well, she's starting to grow on me, kind of make sense in a kooky way. I feel like, she is trying to express herself to me using familiar words to describe something unworldly." Then he looked Abjourn in the eyes, "she told me that she knew who edited her DNA and that people with the edit are beacons." Jay could tell that he had the Swede's full attention as he was silently taking in every word. "She said that they were 'god' she called it 'the Gardner' and said that she communicated with it and that it was coming back!"

Abjourn's mouth was agape, "did she say when?"

"Well, that was interesting too, she said that it was too busy at the moment so now it would be later than expected."

Abjourn sighed, "well, I guess we dodged a bullet there!" he chuckled.

"Did you see them last night? It looked like they were in some kind of group meditation around the fire?" Abjourn shook his head so Jay explained, "When I woke up next to the fire last night, everyone was gone except Laura and about five other aboriginals, and they were sitting cross legged around the fire. It looked like they were asleep, but sitting up, anyway, I just got up and went to bed."

"Dreamtime. That's what they call it, the place they go," Abjourn explained. "I've been trying to understand this, it's embedded in their mythology. Maybe Laura could be a bridge. I want to know if it's a shared experience. Even though they are from completely different cultures, is it someplace, they go together?" his eyebrows furrowed.

Jay nodded reflectively, then suddenly remembered something, "and she also told me that she knows why she spontaneously combusted!" Jay blurt out. "She told me it was a different god. The god that the Gardner is battling, Adamas."

This caused Abjourns to scowl, "wow, hope she's not confusing reality with a comic book!"

Jay shrugged, "you can see why I wrote her off, but, then, how often does someone spontaneously combust?"

Later that afternoon, Abjourn received a call from Sam informing him that Laura wanted to spend the night camped next to the red rock and had already obtained permission. They had sent their transporter and were requesting that it be sent back to them with provisions and camping gear for six people. Abjourn made the arrangements but decided he would deliver their equipment himself. When he explained the situation to Jay, the scientist was quick to invite himself as well. Both of the men were interested in observing how the group interacted. Besides Laura, two others in their company had the DNA edit and both scientists were very interested in making observations.

When the two arrived they found Laura studying the petroglyphs and paintings that covered the rocks in that area. She was accompanied by an older aboriginal lady who was instructing her on the meaning of images and telling her stories from her mythology. The men would soon learn that the aboriginal woman was the caretaker of the area and the one who had given permission for the camp out even though it is usually prohibited. Sam explained this, as they were unloading the transporter and setting up camp. They set up small individual sleeping tents as the transporter would serve as the latrine and dining area. Boxed meals lined a shelf in the back of the vehicle.

The area was barren and much like the area around their motel, except that their view was completely blocked on one side by the massive rock. The red rock appeared as a giant vertical mountain now that they were next to it. The land nearby was desolate with a few other slabs of rock that appeared to have been tossed here and there in small, disorderly piles. Some of the stones lay against one another creating shadows and shaded seating areas. All were covered in ancient graffiti, with some bits that were regularly touched up by park professionals. Jay learned that some of the images were 30,000 years old. Most of them documented Anangu mythology, dreamtime.

Abjourn and Jay watched on anxiously, they were both intrigued as to what the Aboriginal Caretaker and Laura were discussing, yet neither wanted to disturb the animated conversation. Finally, Abjourn noticed her look in their direction and was able to get a wave in, so Laura waved back and invited the men to come and join the discussion.

"Glad to hear that you will be joining us!" the monk said cheerfully while cupping her hand over her eyes so that she could see them approaching in the blinding sun.

"Oh! Well! You know, always up for an adventure!" Abjourn answered while taking a place near the two women. Laura smiled and greeted Jay as well, making introductions to the Caretaker.

"Well, I'm glad to get this special opportunity, I hope we are not intruding," Jay said apologetically.

Laura shook her head, "No, I want you here." Then she looked around herself, "And I just wanted to spend the night next to this artwork! It's an open air art gallery, but better, I can't wait to see the stars in that black sky tonight, especially next to these rocks and illustrations," she ran her hand along the rock next to a carving of a rainbow snake, "it's just so magical here!"

Jay marveled at the change in her. Ever since they arrived, she seemed to become stronger, healthier, happier. There was something magical about the place, at least for her. He reminded himself of how, just days ago, she was deathly ill in a hospital.

Then, she admitted something interesting, "I want you to study me and the others with the edit because the message that the Gardner is coming, needs to be out, so that we won't be afraid when it happens. It will be a big change for humanity." She looked at the men thoughtfully, "I've decided that I need to be more vocal about the Gardner, so I will share information freely and stop worrying that people might think that I'm crazy. I need to set aside my vanity. I realized this when I traveled with my new aboriginal friends as they had always told the world about dreamtime without holding back. Now, I need to explain that this was a place that I go, too."

Both men were filled with questions, but Abjourn spoke up first, "Who is the Gardener?"

Laura smiled, then led the men to a slab of rock that made a good bench seat. She gestured at the stone for the men to sit, then she took a seat on the ground in front of them. The quiet Aboriginal woman also took a seat next to the men.

"The Gardener came into existence to be the powerful creator of worlds! The Gardener has no body, and few physical needs, except to create. It stirred the waters by designing the moon and setting it in motion. It churned the seafloor and awoke volcanoes so that land emerged from the sea. It designed the plants to create oxygen, then animals, including us! We were meant to be the planet's caretakers, but we have been it's destroyer, so now the Gardener is coming back to save its creations." Then she looked down sadly, "but, I'm afraid that it won't be in my lifetime."

To the scientists, this was sounding like a familiar creation story, just retold with modern vocabulary. "Why not within your lifetime?" Abjourn asked, looking at her very earnestly.

Laura was uncomfortable, like she was trying to think of the right words to use, "the Gardener isn't the only powerful entity." She paused a moment, then went on in a softer voice, "there is another that acts like a thief and takes what the Gardener produces. This is the one who set me on fire." She looked away, sighed, then focused back on the men, "if it wasn't for the help of the other light beings, I would have died. So, now, that I live, my duty is to enlighten as many as I can, so they can be prepared and not be fooled by the Thief," she looked very seriously into each person's face, before she concluded, "we cannot become his slaves!"

Everyone was quiet, it was only the Aboriginal woman who nodded in agreement. She was the only one who appeared to accept the information as probable. The two scientists were wide eyed with interest, but Laura sadly recognized the look on their faces. The men had just decided to politely group her with all the other religious zealots. But, this was the reaction she expected, the one she was prepared for, the one that she would have to put up with, as her mission was too important to slow down for the disbelievers. She straightened her posture, put a smile on, and waited for their next question. They would be a good first group for her to practice on, she decided.

It was Abjourn who asked the next question, "where do you go when you are with the light beings?"

Laura considered an answer, "Wherever you want. The past, the present, the future. The future is important, because that is where you go to decide what you want to happen next. You go there to visualize the good future, the one that everyone really wants, not the one created by fear or some dark fantasy that we are sometimes tricked into requesting." Then she looked thoughtfully into Abjourn's eyes, "You see, that is one of the reasons that I love to be in the presents of the Gardner, there is no tricking, everyone understands only the truth about everything. You can't even 'trick' yourself, so no self doubting!" she said with a smile.

The stony faces of the scientist told Laura that no amount of explanation would sway the men. She had been sorted and place in the mentally unstable box. Might as well be discussing the weather, she decided. Nothing that she could say would remove her to a different box.

Later that evening, another fire was started and everyone gathered around it. Jay was sitting on the parched earth, when he reluctantly accepted a small hand drum that he had been offered. He nodded and smiled politely at the elderly man who offered it, then sat upright and tapped on it a bit with his right hand before nodding again at the old man to complement on the instruments sound. After the shaman moved along Jay returned his gaze to the center of the circle where a fire was beginning to burn on it's own, even as it's attendants stooped near it with kindling in their hands. It was a lovely evening, he decided, even though, his mind was still in a fog from the previous nights festivities.

But, when Abjourn reached down to him with another cold beer, he readily accepted it. 'Hair of the dog,' he mumbled before taking a long drink.

Then, he noticed Laura was sitting a couple feet away from him, then Mali and Yarran, who were the other aboriginals with the edit. On the other side of him was a native with a didgeridoo. He remembered thinking that the sound of this instrument was too repetitive, at first, that it annoyed him, but slowly over the night he began to notice that the sound of this deep humming, vibrated in his chest. Now, he felt it right away, as though it was the sound of the instrument itself that took life and resonated within him, instantly plucking at him from the inside. He pushed the can into the sand beside him when he noticed that everyone was beginning to pound on their drums and shake clapsticks, and he wanted to play along.

At first he imitated the sound of the others. He closed his eyes and began to notice that he was playing a kind of rhythm. Someone else was playing a drum with a deeper sound, they began punctuating his little rhythm with a loud beat at the end, and then someone else added a beat in the middle. So, they began speaking to one another with their instruments, taking turns adding to the song.

Nearby, Laura sat cross-legged, a satisfied smile on her lips, she enjoyed seeing the doctor loosing himself in the rhythm, she could sense calm, relaxed feeling coming from him. She closed her eyes and breathed deeply, it was such a delight to do this without feeling sharp pains in her chest. The air here was good for her, she loved the smell of it as soon as she stepped out of the plane she noticed it. She felt the oxygen entering her body and opening it up, exercising the newly generated bits from when it was healing. Then the joy of meeting the Aboriginal people and their culture of slow helpfulness to others warmed her heart. She didn't want to leave this place.

She heard the sound of a bird and opened her eyes to see a beautiful, rainbow colored bird in a gnarly tree with small green leaves across from her. She admired it's song and noticed another bird lite next to it. The first bird flew away, then the second. She wondered if the birds were friends or family, and were they playing a game? Then she noticed another at the very top of the bush. This bird seemed to be preoccupied with the view in front of it. Laura wondered what it might be. She imagined herself as the bird, she imagined what it's view would be from the treetop. She thought about how the breeze felt as it was ruffling some of the little feathers around its neck. She could smell the sweet sap of the tree. She closed her eyes and admired the view, and then the movement of a small animal in the distance. It was a tawny color, and looked like a big mouse, with a long tail and a long shadow as the sun was setting.

She looked up, the sky was clear except for one, long hazy cloud. She concentrated on the single cloud, growing closer until she was just inside it. It was like a thick fog that she couldn't see through, so she turned and looked back on the clear view she had of the fire below, the circle of people around it, then she spotted herself, sitting cross legged with the others. Then, she noticed another presence next to her and realized that Mali was beside her! What joy! The two of them traveled together, through the cloud, then into the darkness, they were being drawn, like lead to a magnet, through space. They were two light beings, being pulled through the galaxy toward their center, and the magnet, the Gardener.

Soon, they were in a different place. Laura lost Mali but could sense life humming and twittered around her, she felt herself falling gently on a soft breeze toward it. She was rocking and spinning till she lit on something that dipped slightly as she landed. Then, she became aware that others were bobbing in the wind all around her. They were in darkness and all of them were in a state of happy anticipation. She felt a small droplet of water roll down her, then a gentle breeze caught the liquid and sent a shiver through her. Slowly, a warm light bathed her in warmness. She stretched and breathed in the perfume that wafted from the others around her as well as herself. A small creature touched her unexpectedly, and put her into ecstasy. She stretched out her body and let her appendages wave in the wind. It was such a feeling of freedom and yet oneness with everything around her.

Abjourn was fighting the urge to sleep with a large container of coffee. He took drinks of it as he silently tapped notes into a tablet that he balanced on one leg, as he was sitting on the ground near Laura. He pointed a small laser at her forehead to record her vital signs. Then, he pointed it at the unconscious bodies of the Aboriginals who reclined or sat nearby. He appeared to be the only one awake. Jay had long ago sprawled out in slumber near the fire as did the rest of their party. Laura, Mali and Yarran were sitting up, but looking unconscious as they were very still with their eyes closed. Earlier they had applied more white paint on their bodies before participating in a communal drum circle while being accompanied by a digeridoo and clapsticks. Now, the instruments were silent, and the three musicians looked to be in a trance like state. But, he was noticing that Laura and Mali seemed to be twitching slightly.

He quietly got up and woke Jay by gently tugging on his shoulder. When he responded by moaning and propping himself up, Abjourn got close to his ear and whispered that their subjects were beginning to show movement. Jay's eyes popped open and he sat up. Abjourn was silently pointing toward Laura and then Mali as the two seemed to be making involuntary twitching movements that were growing in intensity until they noticed that Laura seemed to be overcome by a shutter, that wrenched her whole body and caused her to recline. She laid back and then stretched her arms out beside her and straightened out her legs. She let out a deep breath and her face relaxed with her body into a look of serenity. Abjourn could detect a faint smile on her lips. Jay moved next to her and the men continued to observe her closely.

Then, they heard a noise come from Yarran's direction and noticed that he had also moved, but onto his stomach, with his arms and legs bent and tucked under him, in a kind of fetal position but with his face resting in the soil.

Abjourn reached over to Jay and touched his shoulder again, but this time to get his attention as he was pointing in the direction of where Mali had been sitting. That place was now vacant and the man was nowhere in sight. Abjourn shrugged to signal to Jay that he had no idea where the man went. Both scientists scanned the area with their eyes, but could not locate the native in the dancing firelight.

Then, they noticed Laura moaning and beginning to make small movements and to writhe on the ground. Both men were surprised and a bit embarrassed as the woman's moaning seemed to be increasing in volume as her torso wiggled, under the coarse fabric of her robe, which was riding up and exposing her naked legs. Her arms were stretched at her sides to their limits, and her head was now bobbing slightly as the corners of her mouth turned up in an obvious smile.

Movement, made the men turn their attention back to Yarran, who appeared to be struggling to push his body up onto his forearms and knees. His butt was pushed into the air as he struggled to raise himself up on all fours, he reminded Jay a of video, that he had watched, of a baby elephant trying to stand for the first time.

Jay gasped, when he noticed Mali crawling from the far side of the fire. It didn't look like Mali. His shaggy black beard mixed with his tangled hair to create a kind of mane around his whitewashed face. His hands and bare feet were on the ground with his legs bent, so that it looked like he might spring out at them. There were two deep, black holes where his eyes had been, but now the eyeballs were only visible by flashing sparks from the flames. He appeared to be looking in their direction, but he looked as though he was having problems trying to comprehend what he was seeing, and he didn't seem to recognize them.

Both men were frightened, but continued to watch as he lowered his head while keeping his eyes on them. He put his lips near a clump of vegetation, then stuck out his tongue and pulled the small green plants out of the earth with his mouth, then he gave the grass a shake to loosen the dirt from it, before he pulled it into his mouth and began moving his jaws side to side, all while he continued to stare at the men.

Yarran was now balanced on his forearms and knees, but his head was still near the earth with his face pointed toward the ground and he began moving his limbs with small jerky movements that caused him to advance slightly in their direction, but with his head down.

This was almost too much for Jay, he had to remind himself that they were just men in some kind of trance, not creatures of the night.

Then, Laura got their attention when she made a louder gasping sound. Her body was almost convulsing as she tightened, then loosened her muscles in such a way that her whole body seemed to raise up and down in a kind of fluttering movement, and disturbingly, she did this with a broad smile on her lips the whole time.

Abjourn pointed his laser at her forehead again, getting another reading, then looked at the device to check what her vitals were. He was surprised to see that they appeared normal, as he would expect if she were just sleeping deeply. He aimed the light at Mali and Yarran, then checked their readings, to find them also normal. He got up and walked a few yards to the sleeping bodies of the caretaker and another aboriginal woman who were asleep on their sides near the fire. He shined his laser on them and recorded their vitals as a check. He looked around himself, but the others had retired to their tents.

When he returned to his spot next to Jay, he could see that Jay was even more disturbed by Mali's change in character, as the two had their eyes locked together and Jay was pushing himself farther away. Mali had taken a step closer to take advantage of more vegetation, but continued to keep a suspicious eye on the scientist and appeared to be grazing. Yarran was still shuffling slowly away in another direction and Laura seemed to be content spread out on her back.

He took his seat next to Jay, then tapped out a message to him explaining that whatever form Mali had taken, he was acting more like a vegetarian than a carnivore, so maybe he was less of a threat than his scary form appeared. The two men continued to observe the three and make notes until they finally, laid down in more restful poses and closed their eyes. This wasn't until daybreak.

Soon, the rest of their party was waking and getting breakfast from the kitchen in the transporter. The stirrings woke the others, who had fallen asleep near the fire. Laura was the first to open her eyes and stretch, with a smile on her face. Mali and Yarran soon followed, brushing the dust off their arms and legs, but they too, woke in good spirits. Jay and Abjourn, on the other hand, were tired and sluggish from lack of sleep, they watched in awe as Laura seemed to be especially energetic and even a bit chatty. Jay marveled at the woman, reminding himself again about how critically ill she had been just days ago. The only hint of her near fatal incident was a few shinny scars on her arms, that were now a healthy tan color. She moved briskly, helping to tear down camp, while popping handfuls of berries in her mouth as she worked. Jay noticed that she did appear to be always eating since they arrived. He tapped a note in his tablet.

Mali and Yarran also looked energized and happy, and there did seem to be a camaraderie between the three present with the unique identifier, but so far, none of them appeared to be discussing the night before. Jay was anxious for the scheduled interviews that were supposed to start that day. The scientists had agreed to avoid asking the subjects questions until they were in an office and able to properly record them.

Jay made a feeble attempt to help tear down their camp. The rest of the party didn't appear to notice his slacking off, as they danced around him and quickly had everything packed into the transporter, then the band of merry campers climbed aboard and traveled back to the motel. Despite their fatigue, both scientist continued to type on their notepads. The interview with Laura was scheduled for that afternoon. Abjourn gave them a few hours to freshen up before they were to meet at his office, which was the office area of the ancient motel. Jay was impressed with Abjourn's research project, he had been able to lease the entire structure and then renovate it using grant money that came from all over the world! Everyone was interested in the Unique Identifier project and now that the information had been leaked, everyone wanted to participate in helping the research continue. It was a lucrative area of interest.

Later that day, they gathered in Ajourn's office, which was the original motel office plus four of the motel rooms strung together making a long hallway that connected several separate offices. He led them to the first door. It was an informal room, that felt more like a den than an office, inside, there were a couple recliners as well as a conference table with chairs, a few tablets and other devices were pushed in a pile at the center of table. A counter and sink lined the inside wall with a row of windows on the other side.

"Would you like anything to drink or snack on?" Abjourn asked, motioning to the sink and row of cabinets that included a chilled cabinet for drinks.

Laura accepted the offer and gingerly stepped up to the counter and looked inside to take inventory. She shuffled the bags around, reading their labels and then announcing the contents of the cupboard aloud to encourage the men to make a selection. After both men declined, she returned to the table with a container of berries that she had recently discovered and, 'couldn't seem to get enough of.'

"I want to start this interview by telling the two of you, how much I appreciate your bringing me here! I feel so vital and alive here! It's a wonderful feeling to find your people!" Laura gushed. At that moment Jay had a sudden realization that his patient did not intend to return to the U.S.A. He wondered to himself if Australia would become the home base for her new religious cult. Although, Jay felt sincerity from the monk, her rhetoric from the day before, sounded like a retelling of a familiar mythology to him. He had always nodded and smiled and then offered a 'God Bless you,' to his Aunties and family whenever he visited them, but that was the only time when God entered into his conversations. With the exception of occasional religious debates with Lou.

"Glad to hear that!"Abjourn responded with genuine sincerity as he took one of the empty chairs across from her. Then, he motioned to Jay who was already seated at the end of the table and explained that he would let Dr. Jefferies start the discussion.

"Wonderful!" Jay began, tapping on a small tablet on the table in front of him. "Ms Novak," he began, "in reference to your interactions with others that have the DNA edit, have you noticed any special connections with them?" This question came to him when he noticed their similar body movements and twitching from the night before.

Laura considered the question, "I think you are referring to that bit of ESP that everyone seems to share. But that, is really just a remnant of the way we used to communicate when the Gardener was here," she explained, then she smiled broadly, "I can't wait for it to return!" Then she composed herself, "if you are asking if we, with the edit, have a stronger telepathic connection, then the answer is yes. But, the truth is that everyone has a connection with everyone else, it's the way we were made, the way we lived when the Gardner was here."

Jay remembered her sadly telling him that the Gardener wouldn't arrive within her lifetime, when they were in the plane. "But, now its not coming?" he wanted to clarify.

"No, not within this lifetime! It is too busy, but it monitors Earth through us and it is alarmed at the changes in our environment!"

Jay was taken aback, "Wait, did you say that it monitors the Earth's environment through you and the other edited people?"

Laura nodded in the affirmative, "Yes. Through those with the unique identifier, we are the few links it has to gather data, and another reason it needs to return, as it is possible that we beings with the edit could soon become extinct and then there would be no more beacons here on Earth."

Jay was uncomfortable, "Laura, what do you expect to happen when the Gardener returns?"

Laura sighed, "Peace! Communication! A oneness that will cause those who have confused thoughts to instantly understand the truth! And then," she looked Jay in the eyes, "the Gardner will guide us to organize and make corrections, so that the Earth will be whole again!" She sat back in her seat with a satisfied smile, and added, "The nature of the Gardner is to create. It is the creator."

Abjourn couldn't get the images from the night before out of his mind. "I am curious about what you experience when you meditate, for example, last night. Where is it that you go?"

"Last night I let myself be drawn up." Laura could tell by the puzzled look on Abjourn's face that he needed a better explanation, so she started again. "There is a pull. We people with the edit are drawn to the Gardener, the way metal is drawn to a magnet. But, it's pull is so strong that it brings us to wherever in the galaxy it is. And there, well, we work at whatever needs to be done. But, all of the work of creation is a joy! Being alive, and existing, is a joy!"

This intrigued Abjourn, "Laura, if I had a spaceship and could fly anywhere, could I reach the place where the Gardener is now?"

Laura shrugged, "Sure. But, it is so far away now, that I don't think we have the technology to get there."

"If the Gardener is all knowing, why doesn't it give us the technology?"

Laura looked confused, "the knowledge is there." She shook her head, "all knowledge is there and available to anyone that can tap into it." She looked around herself trying to think of the best way of explaining it. "Just as most human knowledge is located somewhere on the internet, the knowledge of the Gardener is also available, you just have to know how to access it, and, when it returns all questions will be answered!"

Both scientists considered this, the Gardener was sounding more and more like a type of AI. This interesting relationship that his new subject had with technology made Abjourn wonder how she felt about it so he asked her opinion of robots.

"I do find the subject interesting," she began, "There are humans now who live vicariously through their robots. They could be a wasted away shell of a human, living in a room somewhere with just a monitor and controls, moving and traveling by way of their robot and observing the world through their robots camera eyes," she shook her head sadly, then continued. "So, it is a small jump to think that the soul of this wasted human could reside in the head of the robot. Maybe, their body is in a bed somewhere, while they live through the robot. You see, when we can transfer our existence, our souls, to a robot, then we will have completed another circuit of humanity, maybe a circuit within a circuit, who knows how many deep. But this means that they would be choosing this form of existence instead of our biodegradable robot bodies, where you and I are now, living within all of our interlocking circuits."

Jay worked onsite with Abjourn for the next week, then reluctantly left with his family to go home. He wasn't surprised when Laura announced that she wanted to stay. When she was saying good bye she looked earnestly at Jay, "I've been thinking about why I originally went to the doctor, it was because I couldn't conceive. I still want to have a child, now more than ever, and hopefully, with someone else who has the unique identifier."

Jay looked down sadly, "I'm afraid that your problem has to do with deformities with your eggs. It's a problem that would require you to use a surrogate."

Laura looked off into the distance, "that wouldn't do." Then, she returned her gaze at Jay, "could you send me a photo of my deformed eggs?" It was a strange request, but he assured her that he would do his best.

The trip had been a great success. After boarding the plane and getting comfortable in their private cabin, the little family napped most of the way home, but then Jay woke up and found a window to look out of as they were flying toward the gulf of Mexico. There was an amazingly large storm in the distance. As he watched the swirling clouds, a magnificent Sprite of electricity hit the top of the blanket of clouds, then exited as a burst of lightening bolts that struck the earth like bombs. He wondered what people a hundred years ago would have thought to witness this massive, yet no longer rare, storm, that hovered in place, mercilessly over the shell shocked planet below it.

It was always hoped that with the lowering of carbon emissions, that the wind speeds would pick back up, where they were before the climit began changing so rapidly, but so far things hadn't been improving, just not falling as fast. He was looking out a window that was facing south, so he could guess that the storm was coming from the edge of South America and was inching it's way up the coast and through the gulf of Mexico. He shook his head thinking, 'those poor people,' as he considered the battered coast of Louisiana and Florida. Key West was now an Atlantean tale, as the island chain and its ruins were a sunken city, along with it's mythical, friendly, giants, the manatee, miles off the current shoreline of Florida. The peninsula was much narrower than it had once been, having been eaten up on all sides. The sad truth was that salvation of what was left, could be credited to the research and development department at Disney, they purchased large swaths of spoiled coastline and planted sea grass and kelp to stop the erosion, and so they were now the major property owner of the tourist attraction that used to be a state.

After they had arrived home, it wasn't very long before Jay got a message from Lou asking if they might like take out food, he offered to swing by after picking something up. This was his way of inviting himself over so that they could talk about the trip and Abjourn's research. It was agreed and soon they were all sitting around a dinning table together.

It was a common occurrence, Lou visiting with food and beer. They would eat together around the dinning table, where Lilly usually sat on Lou's lap for most of the meal, and this occasion was no different. He was asking her about her trip and she was in mid description when something suddenly occurred to her, "Oh! Uncle Lou! Want to see my souvenir?" she squealed.

"Sure, if you are done eating," he answered as she wriggled off his lap and ran toward her room.

Both parents chuckled as they knew what she would be bring out. Then, there was a bark and the little girl came skipping back into the room with a big smile and a small black and tan puppy following behind her. Lou watched with mock excitement, "you got a puppy?!"

Lilly hunched up her shoulders and nodded, "we got it in Australia!"

Lou took a better look at the puppy. It sat down near his feet while continuing to wag it's tail. It was wearing a little vest that was embroidered with, "Ollie the Aussie," on the edge of it. This and the fact that Jay hadn't mentioned the lifetime purchase, made him suspicious. He reached down and easily picked the thing up with one hand. It did have some weight to it, and it seem to be programmed to make eye contact, but, he wasn't fooled by the robotic dog.

"Now that is something else! It even seems to be weighted in the right places," he said while lifting the toy above his head with one hand and examining how flexible the materials were.

Lou noticed that Lilly was watching with concerned eyes, so he immediately set the toy back on the floor and petted it.

Telling her that she was lucky to have such a well mannered puppy.

Jay chuckled again, "hey, it even grows!"

"Whaaaaat?" Lou reached down and picked it up again.

"Yeah," Jay began, "there is this tiny hydraulic system inside it that causes the little puckers of fur..." He took the thing out of Lou's hands and pointed to little gathers in the puppy's furry skin. "The structure inside expands and pulls the fur skin taught. They had one on display, it wasn't as big as a real Australian healer, but it went from a puppy to looking like a young dog."

"Huh..." Lou mumbled getting closer to the toy, then he looked up at Jay, "wonder what it looks like in there."

"Jay, I told you before! You are not taking that apart!" Emily interrupted. Then, she shook a finger at Lou, "don't you give him any new ideas! I promise you, I will be looking at that puppy regularly for stitches!"

Then, the adults noticed a little whimper come out of Lilly who was watching on with a tear in her eye. Lou took the toy from Jay and gently set it on the floor again, "well, after an examination," he said addressing Lilly, "I declare your puppy is well and doesn't need any operations!" he assured the little girl, who smiled back happily before scooping the puppy up and taking it into another room with her.

Lou got up to bring more beers to the table while Emily shook her head and playfully mouthed words to her husband. When he came back into the room, he caught the two in a kiss. He set the bottles on the table and coughed.

"So, patient #0130130 decided to stay in Australia," Lou commented as he took his seat.

Jay sat a back in his chair, "Yes. Yes she did!"

"Do you think it's permanent?" Lou asked taking a drink from his bottle.

Jay shrugged, "I don't know. I don't know if she knows." Lou looked disappointed. "You could call her up...I got her number..." Jay continued slyly.

Lou sighed and made a face at his friend, "I...someone just wanted to meet her," he explained. Jay instantly knew what that meant. Then, Lou looked him in the face, "so, when are you guys coming to the community for a Sunday dinner again?"

Jay shrugged, "as soon as you'll have us!"

"Good! Then, I'll expect you Sunday!" Lou said with a smile.

Now that Lilly was entertaining herself in another room, the three adults began discussing Abjourn's research in more detail. Jay explained that since a program was developed that pulls DNA information from a database of ancient artifacts and checks for the unique identifier, Abjourn has been able to free up resources and look more earnestly for the anomaly in living people. His big discoveries in Australia happened because he discovered a large concentration of the anomaly in that area, and some of those findings were from bones of more recent artifacts.

"And the data, just keeps coming in! Lou, I know you have nothing but animosity toward ARTHUR1, but its writing the software! All of this for free! You can't tell me that everything about the AI is evil!"

Lou's face froze as some of this was new information to him. "What kind of software is it writing for Abjourn?"

Jay sighed, "It created a planetary database of ancient DNA that has already been collected and is, right now, establishing a new database for collection of living DNA. Soon, we will have the largest collection of living and dead DNA available!"

Lou reached out and put a hand on Jay's shoulder, looking very earnestly into his eyes, "Wait! Are you telling me that, that entity is now going to have access to everyone's DNA? Are you kidding me! Jesus! Fucking! Christ!" He absentmindedly slapped the table, but then immediately remembered that Lilly was nearby, he lowered his voice and apologized.

"But, Jay, seriously, don't you see a problem with this?" Lou asked in a low voice.

"What, exactly, are you afraid ARHTUR1 will do with the information?" Jay couldn't help himself from wondering if the worry was for *his* DNA to be available.

Lou examined the ceiling, "well, it would be the ultimate form of identification. Until it's sold on the dark web."

"Are you saying that you think the Ian Moore Company will use it to make money?"

Lou rolled his eyes, "everything's a commodity!"

The conversation continued until late that evening, when Lou was dropped off at his home by Jay's transporter.

It was supposed to be a beautiful weekend. The little family of three, plus their robotic puppy, had been pleasantly anticipating the trip to Lou's community. Jay and Emily also understood that there was to be a special meeting, both were intrigued, but the topic felt so absurd that neither brought it up, and discussing it with anyone else would have been too much of an embarrassment.

Nevertheless, that evening after a large communal dinner in the great hall, the little family gathered outside at a pavilion where a little play was being put on by the communities school children. They had pulled their chairs in a little semi-circle with Bill and Linda, when Lou walked up to the group and beckoned Jay and Emily to follow him. Linda smiled and assured Emily that Lilly would be taken care of, and the child was already enchanted by the performance, with many a familiar face, that she didn't even notice them leave.

They crossed the lawn and returned to the nearly empty hall, where Jay was confused when Lou instructed him to sit down at the long table, across from an old man. He had been excited, but now, well, the man in front of him did not resemble any of the aliens in any of the horror movies that he had watched. The man in front of him was stocky built, with white hair and very pale blue eyes. He had a heavy brow ridge, with light eyebrows, and no facial hair. The hair on his head was thick and shaved a few inches from his scalp, so that the hairs stood up. He was wearing blue denim overhauls, with a tee shirt underneath. Jay thought that he looked like a very pale version of his own grandfather.

The older man smiled at Jay's expression, "you look disappointed! Am I not who you expected?" The man chuckled.

Jay forced himself out of silence, "Um, I guess I didn't know what to expect." Then, in a panic he burst out, "you don't look like an alien!"

The man clicked his tongue and laughed heartily, "that is because I am no more an alien than you!" Then, he stood and stuck out his hand to Jay, "I am Jak." After shaking Jays hand he shook Emily's as well. Then he looked up at the ceiling with his arms crossed, "you can think of me as a kind of Ambassador," he explained before taking his seat back. "A conduit between your planet and the rest of the known universe!" he further explained as he made himself comfortable.

Jay was conflicted. There was something about the man that felt, comforting, as though he *was* Papa George, his mother's father, but then, he'd shake himself and consider what Jak was proposing to him. He looked around himself in confusion, then to Lou for an explanation, but, the old man continued, "I am related to those people who first colonized the north, in what is now Northern Europe and Scandinavia." Jay listened on with interest. "You have named our bones, Neanderthal!" Then the man looked at Lou, "haven't you explained anything to this man?" Lou shook his head.

Jak looked back at Jay. "The Earth was colonized, similarly to the way North America was colonized. People from different planets colonized different parts, for instance, my people are from a place with a colder climate, so we chose the north! Other people located to warm places with lots of vegetation, like Africa. Others preferred living on islands, where the threat from large predators was diminished. There were many colonies, with many different types of people. Some survived, some didn't, but everyone, over the years, mixed together to create... well, you!"

Jay was astounded, this was Abjourn's, 'Colonization Theory.' He knew many who subscribed to the theory, but this man could be proof of it, or just another Earthling with delusions. But, whoever this man was, Jay wanted to know him better, listen to him longer, he was drawn to him. But then he remembered the question that he most wanted to ask, "The unique identifiers," he blurted, "who did that to DNA?"

The man paused thoughtfully, "I'm not sure." He looked away thoughtfully, "I don't know who it was that branded the DNA. It could have been an effort to track the movements and intermixing of humans, but it was probably a wider experiment, I mean, why would someone go to all that trouble just to track population shifts? There had to be a bigger reason, and I suspect that the branded DNA was also altered in some way. If they appear physically normal, then, maybe the editing was for something less obvious, for instance, maybe these particular humans are being used to store data. Information that they aren't even aware of. Then, by scattering the altered DNA around the globe in different groups of humans, they could better insure the safety of the message." Jak paused, thinking deeper about the question, "do those with the branded DNA have an explanation?"

Jay shrugged, "well, yeah, but...she claims that it helps her to communicate with god. Well, a god...she calls it the Gardener."

Jak suddenly had a look of comprehension, "are you saying that she has a wireless connection to the entity that branded her DNA?"

Jay's face went blank, Jak's wording sounded so much more scientific. "I guess you could phrase it that way."

"Did she tell you anything else about this entity?"

Jay thought about the question, "She said that it created the Earth and all the life on it, and that it was far away, but would come back. She called it her 'center.'"

Jak clicked his tongue again in a thoughtful way, "The creator."

Emily looked surprised, "you mean all that stuff she was telling us was true?"

Jak nodded, "well, if that is what she thinks, I would be inclined to believe her, I mean, she is the one with the edit!"

Emily leaned in closer with a confused look on her face, "are you saying that there is such an entity?"

Jak sighed, "there are entities that terraform planets. Are they gods? Well, I guess so, they do create and communicate with their creations," he explained with a shrug, focusing his large, gentle eyes on her. "And, *someone* edited her people's DNA all those thousands of years ago."

Emily felt strangely satisfied with the answer, she was having warm feelings about this man too.

Jak continued, "you see, I am also a historian, and part of my work here is to, 'add' your history, which I realize only only goes back a few thousand years. But, I want that detail added to ours..." He looked thoughtfully at Jay then made an inclusive motion, "all of us! It will make our recorded history more complete. It already goes back millions of years!" he added with a look of satisfaction.

"How is it that we are the same people, yet Earthlings know nothing of our origins?" Jay asked thoughtfully.

"Well," Jak began, "when the colonists first arrived on this planet, they brought the best technologies they had with them for the environment that they would be living in. They built their communities with available materials and lived off the land as much as possible. Communication between our home planet and Earth was frequent, at first. We used entanglement to create consoles, one on our planet and it's twin, here on Earth. We were in constant communication for a very long time. But, as the years passed, and as the relatives of those people died off, then communication became less frequent. Slowly, those with the expertise to use the equipment became scarce. Finally, communication ended, then, the only way to understand what was happening there, was to visit, in person. This often would frighten people. Our own people no longer recognized us! The children of those first colonists, only knew of us in fable. The people trained to communicate with us, were few, and slowly the children of their children lost that knowledge. So, a decision was made to forbid interference and then, we began watching you in secret. It was fascinating for us to witness, what had been our own history, millions of years ago! Now, over the years, many different people have become interested in you, and some have evil intent! Or, they were so curious that they thought of you more like lab rats than relatives! So, maybe, it was one of them that did it, to track your evolution.

"Your ancient history is full folklore about visits. Throughout your history this has happened. Sometimes, they declare themselves Gods! Maybe it was one of those people who edited your DNA, to track you. I'm just really not sure," Jak's voice trailed off."

"You said that our recorded history goes back millions of years?"

"Yes, and now after spending so many years alone here on your planet, I consider myself a professor of history! I would have large volumes of historical information included in the monthly downloads. I've come to some interesting conclusions about societies in general."

Jay made an agreeable sound, "what kind of conclusions?"

"Well, my most resent conclusion has to do with the decline of civilization. I wanted to pinpoint what the turning point was. So, I compared many, many, communities, and what I found is that the decline of most civilizations starts when the people of that civilization are convinced that the suffering of some people is required for the good of their society as a whole.

"Now here, I have to tell you that I'm not using riches or stuff to determine success, I am strictly using a metric of the happiness and well being, as a percentage of the total population. Kind of like the Tibetan Happiness index. You see, usually, what I see happen, is that a community starts out as a family, or group of people who are related, living together. Communal living. Work is shared, food is shared, everyone helps one another to have what they need to live. Then, as people begin to specialize, and trade, slowly a caste system begins. It begins as three, those with the most resources, those with the least, and everyone else is in the middle. Those with the least, become the slaves to those with the most resources, and the middle is taught by those with the most resources that slaves were necessary. Sometimes, the slaves are paid, but never for the true value of their work.

Jay considered this for a moment, but he had made a list of questions in his head. "Why did you edit Lou's DNA?"

"My identity was unknown, until I moved here and was discovered. At first it was a bit tense, but I found that the people living in this community were especially open and interested in me, rather than wanting to tell the world about me. I came out of hiding, to be a contributing member of this community and in return, they kept silent about my existence.

"I soon discovered that this community's interest in body augmentation came from a position of freedom of expression, but also interest in reviving ancient wisdom. When I was asked if I could edit the DNA of an embryo, so that it was born with a tail, I was reminded of a study done hundreds of years ago in a community on Aethiop. What happened there, was that a closed society of volunteers had their DNA edited in the same manor, snipping bits of Anong DNA into their own.

"What happened, is that those with the edit appeared to be more perceptive. They were especially good at understanding one another without words. And, this phenomena seemed to increase with every generation.

"Lou's parents, Bill and Linda, were especially interested, and convinced me to edit Lou's DNA while he was only a fertilized egg! I am still remorseful about the ramifications! How sad for the two of them to loose 10 years over our experiment! That is why I will never do it again!" Jak explained, "The terrible consequences that Linda and Bill had to pay for our experiment were barbaric. It never occurred to me that human laws could reach our little community! I was arrogant!" he said as he shook his head.

"But, the edit that we did on Lou's DNA did have interesting results. I had never attempted the 'insertion' of a bit of DNA from another species. But, it was pretty straight forward. Years ago when Bill first told me that he and Linda might like to have a baby with the mutation, especially if it might cause their child's perceptive abilities to be unlocked, I just saw it as an opportunity. You see, the Anong, are an ancient people who live on a distant planet, and have for millions of years. They are a branch of the human race that separated so long ago that they have formed their own wonderfully adaptive characteristics as well as strengthening old mutations that our species had ceased to use.

"So now, let me tell you about the Anong, they are very healthy, the females only have a very thin layer of fat, the males are nearly all skin, bone, and muscle. They live with nature in a very open natural setting, preferring to live in trees and eat only vegetation. Their skin does have a greenish parlor to it, and they only grow hair in cooler temperatures, then shed it with warmer temperatures. Their physiology is similar to monkeys, with large toes and forefingers for gripping and a long slender tail that can act as a fifth limb. Their ears are also very prominent, and shaped like amplifiers, giving them excellent hearing. But, the thing that especially appealed to Bill was their ability to communicate telepathically, not just wirelessly, but telepathically. This does cause them to have a very limited vocabulary, since it is unneeded.

"Now, I only made the edit that would cause the tail, but my guess was that some of these other strong traits would also transfer, and I think they have! I've been measuring Lou's perceptive abilities since his birth and I do believe he is better at reading minds then the average human. He also keeps a high muscle to fat ratio. I mean, he's no Anong, but I do think our little experiment might have awakened some of the bits of Lou's original DNA that were nearly or

completely dormant! I'm anxious to study his heir's DNA!"
Everyone chuckled and looked at Lou expectantly.

Jay was conflicted, he liked this man, but he still wasn't sure
about him being an alien. He looked over at his wife. She
was wearing a smile, but her brows were furrowed and Jay
could tell that she was skeptical as well. He thought of
another question that he had planned to ask, "why were you
interested in meeting me?"

"Ahhhh" Jak clicked his tongue and then began, "first off, I
am a big fan of your work! And, I know that you have input
regarding vaccines," he explained. "One of the very serious
concerns that I have is about disease. I'm not the only alien
visiting this planet! And, serious, deadly outbreaks of
contagious diseases from 'unknown sources' are often tied
to these visiting aliens. I know about what is out there and
which viruses are coming your way. We could work together
on preventative vaccines."

Jay looked alarmed, "I can't just add stuff to vaccines or
make recommendations like you are proposing!" he
interrupted in a startled voice.

Jak held up his hand, "I try to keep my outside
acquaintances at a minimum, but am willing to meet with
necessary people. I can be pretty persuasive!"

Jay and Emily looked at one another, both were still trying
to figure out how it was that this alien could be so honest
about himself and remain a secret.

"I can be persuasive," Jak repeated, focusing on Jay and
then on Emily. "I just need someone like you, on the inside,
to help me. There are diseases that could completely wipe
out the population of the planet and some evil entities that

are so greedy for this planet that they might want to help the process along! This is a mission to save humanity!"

It was at this point that the discussions became more technical as Jak brought to life holograms and video of the information that Jay needed to understand the complexities of alien disease that he was most concerned about. He kept the explanations and tutorials clear and simply explained so that even someone who wasn't a DNA scientist like Emily could follow, but the discussions went on late into the night. On the transporter ride home Emily and Jay chatted excitedly about the amazing evening they had spent with Jak, as Lilly slept.

"You know, I am so glad that he included me in the discussions!" Emily gushed.

"Oh me too!" Jay agreed, "in fact, if I didn't have you to discuss things with right now, I think I would burst!"

"Well, yeah," Emily agreed, "because, you know, we could NEVER tell anyone else about him! It could compromise his mission!"

Jay nodded vigorously, "you know it!"

They continued to chat happily as they both realized the answer to the first question they had about the alien and that was, 'how could an alien be living openly for so many years without anyone knowing about them.'

Hive Mentality

Dave Williams sat alone on the couch of his small transporter. He was staring ahead, watching the tall panoramic view of the road. He pondered on how much he liked the little vehicle, with all of its windows, especially in comparison to the much smaller vehicle he had previously. It had been so small that you couldn't even stand up! He cringed remembering how embarrassing it was when people were nearby as he had to squat down to get in or swing himself, legs first, to get out! But now, he had a proper, abet small, transporter, and he was already a couple years into the loan payments. Life was good!

He was riding through the countryside, down a tree lined road, enroute to the home of his friend, Ollie. This would be the first time he had visited his house, usually, they met at restaurants, for dinner and conversation. Oliver Wayne was much older than Dave, but the two had become acquainted when Ollie had used Dave's services as a therapist. When the sessions were no longer necessary they began to meet socially and had since developed a deep friendship.

Recently, Dave had convinced Ollie to let him record his memoir, as he was one of the dwindling number of people to have lived through a very tumultuous time in history, one that also ushered in their current time of prosperity. The planet was still in a precarious situation, but now an improved future was in sight. Earth was finally showing signs of healing, and it was because of the actions of ordinary people like Ollie that pulled us back from the brink. Dave thought it was important to tell that story, and he thought that the exercise of telling it would be healing for Ollie.

Soon the transporter slowed, and then turned into a long drive. Solar lanterns lit the narrow path to a very old farmhouse. As he neared the house, a long door rose, so that the approaching vehicle could drive into the transport room and park on a charging pad. Dave stood up and waited for his transporter door to fully rise, when, there, stood Ollie wearing a pleasant smile. The old man was holding a fancy cane and wearing a comfortable looking body suit that had a bit of a shine to it. Dave recognized the fabric as one of the new 'perfect temp' materials that was advertised to keep the garment at an optimal temperature that you selected.

"Well, hello!" Ollie greeted, bowing his head slightly. "Glad to finally have you over!"

"Thank you! You have such a beautiful house!" Dave said as he followed Ollie through an archway that led to a large room with a double wide staircase. He craned his neck admiring the wooden banisters and carved pillars in the center of the room. "How beautiful!" then he noticed a small room next to the banisters, "is that an elevator?"

Ollie nodded, "yes. I did some remodeling." He motioned at the pillars, "I had a few walls knocked down to open the place up, and discovered that the eye-beams were made of wood! Can you imagine that!" He said pointing at the ceiling and drawing a line the length of the room. "Hard to believe this was one giant tree! They had trees this big to cut down and use as a single beam! So, anyway, I decided that I'd give that big timber a rest and added these pillars." He walked up to one of the pillars and stroked it admiringly. "I hired the husband of a friend of mine to carve them! Aren't they beautiful! Look at the finish!" he pointed out proudly.

Dave stepped closer and inspected the craftsmanship, it was nice, and the small imperfection in the design reveled that the work was hand done, and not mass produced.

"Would you like a drink? Or a beer?" Ollie asked while standing next to a liquor cabinet that also offered a small refrigerated compartment.

Dave stepped over to scan the assortment of bottles that lined the two shelves. "My, you do have some interesting options," he surmised.

"Well," Ollie began, as he pulled out a clear bottle with a hand written label. The liquid inside was a dark amber in color. "I know someone in Arkansas that makes *the best* bourbon!"

"Sure!" Dave answered, convinced that any product Ollie endorsed, must be 'the best.' He accepted the nearly half filled tumbler and followed Ollie to two stuffed chairs that occupied a small turret of long windows, with a small table between them. "You seem to be in good spirits this evening!" Dave remarked as he made himself comfortable. The chairs were arranged toward the windows, so as to display a beautiful view of the evening sky over the little meadow with a fringe of trees that surrounded his house.

"Oh, I am!" Ollie answered, as though he just remembered something important. "I got an envelope from Steve today! It had a nice note inside and a beautiful pencil drawing! Seems that Steve has taken back an interest in drawing that he had in middle school! So glad to see him interested in something!" Steve was Ollie's grandson who now resided in prison, sadly his crime was that of trying to have his own grandfather murdered.

"Where is it?" Dave asked, truly interested.

"Oh, I've already sent it off to the framers, hopefully it will arrive within the next few days, and then, I plan to hang it right there," he said while motioning toward a small blank wall next to one of the long windows.

Dave nodded while taking a sip of the dark liquid. He was pleasantly surprised by the lack of a burn when he swallowed. "This is really good!" he said tipping his glass in Ollie's direction before taking another sip. He set the glass down on the table beside him, "So, it sounds like your relationship with Steve is improving?"

"Yes, yes," Ollie said reflectively, "I think he might end up okay."

"That's good," Dave replied, "just so you remember that, however he turns out, you acknowledge that you were a wonderful influence on him."

"You know, I've thought about it too much, but I have to admit, that I tried my best. I know that," he said staring at nothing out the window, "I know that I tried my best." He said again, reassuring himself. He took a sip from his glass, then another thought occurred to him, "I do however still feel guilt concerning that poor fellow who was mistaken for me..."

An image of Eric Gunderson came to Dave's mind. He remembered the man clearly, as he was also a client of his.

"You know, I recall seeing him! He was standing in front of your office, he was wearing AR lenses and busy poking at something, like he was on a business call," Ollie explained. Then, he tried to remember something flattering about the rude man, so he burst out, "Snappy dresser!" Then, he recalled something from the article that still puzzled him, "Say, what was that 'rubber app' about?" Ollie asked, remembering that it was sited as the reason for the case of mistaken identity that caused the man to be misidentified by the assassin.

Dave took another swallow as he recalled that detail, "It's a program that causes a scanner to be misdirected, giving out the information of whoever is nearest you."

"Why do you suppose he had that?"

Dave didn't like to speak badly about people, especially former clients, "It can be used to avoid the police or creditors."

Ollie's brows furrowed, "well, if it can misdirect, why doesn't it just block your identity altogether?"

"Well, then the person scanning you would know that you were blocking them."

"Ah, I see," Ollie nodded, then sighed as he was putting together the pieces. "Well, I still feel sorry for his poor wife!"

Dave wanted to interject, and explain that maybe his wife was better off, so that his friend wouldn't feel so guilty, but he couldn't think of the right words. Then he recalled the news, "you did hear that the Assassin App was taken down, didn't you!"

"Yes! Yes, I did!" Ollie answered. "I hope they can find out the identity of the software engineer on that one!" he said raising one brow, as though it were already common knowledge. "But it's wonderful that it's been removed, so much death and misery! And for profit!" He spat out the last bit with much disdain.

They sat quietly for several minutes sipping their bourbon and watching as fireflies began blinking outside. Ollie drained his glass, then got up to retrieve the bottle. Dave started to get it for him, but Ollie waved and indicated that he should remain where he was. When he came back and refilled their glasses, the sat back down and pointed out of the window at a group of trees in the near distance. "See the gap between those trees right there?" Dave strained a bit to identify what Ollie might be referring to. "Oh, there's nothing there now, but keep an eye out and soon the bats will be swooping down between them," he explained with a smile. "I just love to watch the little critters, and glad to see them doing their job of eating mosquitoes!"

Soon enough, there they were, dropping from tree branches and swooping gracefully between trees. It was a pleasant pastime, Dave was beginning to understand why Ollie loved the old house. But then, he remembered the reason for his visit. "Ollie, for your memoir, would you like to start out with a brief explanation of your childhood? For background?"

Ollie shrugged, "Well, I was the oldest of three children. My father was a teacher that dabbled in carpentry and my mother worked mostly at home, she was a botanist, so she did do some traveling. I enjoyed being her assistant on those plant finding missions! Riding around in a little electric car, with her driving it most of the time! We had a comfortable life until the Attack. I was sixteen when it happened."

"Can you tell me about The Attack?" Dave asked after he had set his communicator to record and positioned it on the table between them.

"Well, we need to back up a bit to explain why it happened. It started with a grifter who was born into wealthy circles and had the ambition of being king. He had no interest in governing, he just wanted the office of president to enhance his brand and wealth. When it became clear that he had no governing abilities or interest, he employed the Russians with lucrative deals and access to the white house, so that they would help him out with the antiquated electoral college system, to win the election. Their secret weapon was the same that kept them in power in their own country, propaganda. They were clearly experts in that field, and were adept at using the internet to their advantage. They taught the Americans how to develop their own 'troll factories' that manufactured lies and twisted news stories into unrecognizable fairy tales that appealed to the basest instincts of human nature and senile fears. They employed data harvesting to identify people who would happily accept their lies and embrace them without question, and then gleefully indoctrinate others into this pretend world of propaganda. Other politicians soon found the Russian style cults to be profitable and a source of votes. The Russians had successfully conquered the USA without firing a single shot."

"The Attack was retaliatory. As clear minded Americans became aware of the devastating impact of the Russian propaganda, and the extent of the corruption that it created, they fought back. Reinstating truth in advertising laws and by suing violators. We beat back the red menace and striped them of much of the money they were making. That was when angry and desperate oligarchs hatched a plan that brought America to it's knees." Ollie shook his head and took a sip of his drink.

"They had long ago established a hacking community that shook down corporations of billions of dollars by taking their data and computer systems hostage. But the most devastating hack happened when they gained access to our electrical grid. On December twenty-fifth, 2040, they sent the mother of all electrical surges through our entire electrical grid. Blowing up the stations and destroying anything that was connected to it. Fire erupted throughout our darkened country. We lost millions of acres to fires that spread in cities and the countryside alike. Places that no one had seen burn, went up in flames, many lives were lost on that date and afterward as only those with alternative energy and were not connected to the grid, had electricity. It was the coldest winter. It took more than a year for energy to be completely restored and that happened with the help of people like me, who became renewable energy experts in short order! We went to work installing solar panels and erecting wind mills everywhere that the supplies could be provided or improvised. One of the only good thing that happened is that we became energy independent in that one year!" Ollie smiled, then added, "AND now, most people have FREE energy! Isn't that part wonderful!"

He smiled and took another sip of his bourbon. "Another good thing that happened was that 'take charge' mindset. We knew that the government wasn't going to save us anytime soon and that we needed to make our own plans, work together on projects, barter with one another, and just get it done! So we did! But, it didn't end there. That independent mindset also began affecting our behavior in other ways. There arose a movement to plant fruit trees and berry patches in public parks. A team of software engineers began the Citizen Scientist program to locate and map the sources of pollutants that corporations had previously hidden. Then, those same patriots designed the Critical Thinking Database, with tools to help children and adults to identify misinformation. School teachers began implementing those tools without reservation and without asking permission! We entered a new dawn of enlightenment and this current age of prosperity!"

Dave loved the way Ollie's mind worked, by finding the silver lining even when discussing the darkest of days.

Shannon stood in front of his apartment and pulled his right glove off so that he could use his real thumbprint to open the door. He quickly went from room to room and checked all his security devices, as was his routine. Then, he set down a parcel that he had been carrying in his arm and took a chair at his kitchen table. He pulled off a latex mask and the other glove that he was still wearing. The new kind of latex that he had recently purchased was much cooler than the old type, and he loved the way his mask fit since he had mastered the art of designing the inside of the mask with the reversed image of his face. The fit made the outside look more realistic, but it was still warm and he hated the blocked vision in his right eye. But anyway, it was necessary for him to be able to retrieve his parcel which required him to physically visit the post office and submit to a face and thumb scan. And, well, he just didn't feel comfortable doing all of this with his true credentials.

He opened the cardboard box and then pulled out a smaller wooden chest that was inside. He gleefully opened the box and revealed its contents. There, inside were two 100 gram gold ingots! He grinned and even giggled a bit, staring at the small shiny bars.

He had recently decided that he needed to diversify his assets! Not only did he have a bank account and his very own lock box, but he also had a growing fortune in an offshore bank and a safe with cash in it under the floorboards in his bedroom! He had never been so wealthy! So, as he stared at the shiny ingots a vision of a shabby little boy with a big smile looked back at him and announced, 'Shannon! You are rich!' After admiring the gold ingots for a few minutes, he carefully replaced them into the wooden box then stored them in his floor safe. He had decided that the two gold bars would be part of his 'getaway' horde in case he needed to leave town suddenly.

He replaced the floorboards and then returned the corner of his rug to its proper place. He put his hands on his hips and scowled, remembering how he had been within minutes of collecting a ten million dollar bounty, just before the Assassin App had disappeared. He had tracked Dr. Jefferies down and was enroute in a rented transporter to his location when he discovered that the app had vanished. He lamented the time and money he had invested in the hit. And now, he was stuck at a security job that he hated, but felt that he needed to keep for appearances. He wondered wearily if there would be investigations into the hit men now that the program had finally been foiled. And, was it possible that it would return? It had been profitable for many others besides himself. All he could do was sit tight and see what happened next.

He sighed, then walked out of his bedroom and into his office. He was anxious to play with his newest virtual toy. It was a scanner that could be used in Remote Viewing, RV. He had long been a fan of the newest virtual reality option. He enjoyed visiting foreign counties with the app. Several large European metropolises had opened their cities to the profitable program that allowed virtual tourists to visit in real time. These virtual tourists would spend real money in the many businesses that made their shops accessible. It was also billed as an easy green alternative to wasteful, flesh and bone visits while decreasing foot traffic in the ancient cities. But, the best thing, was that avatars were invisible except to other avatars and people wearing AR lenses. To a high tech criminal this was an interesting situation and one that he hoped to exploit in some way. His new virtual scanning device might provide him the opportunity.

After donning his visor and gloves, he chose 'Paris' from a list of options, then, there he was, in front of the Eiffel Tower. The six hour time difference meant that it was late afternoon, and the lowering sun made dramatic shadows over the well manicured garden that surrounded the metal sculpture. Standing there looking up at the tower, he felt a pin prick his heart, it was just this image that his sister and he would look at and make plans to go someday. 'But, that didn't happen,' he told himself, forcing his mind back to his current situation. Memories were like drops of water and he knew that if he allowed them to rain down it could trigger a flood, that he just wasn't sure he'd survive.

Several people roamed the sidewalks, only a few appeared to be obvious avatars. Shannon had chosen a realistic looking avatar in hopes of blending in with the crowd, just in case another avatar or someone with Augmented Reality lenses happened to notice him. And, there were several people with the AR visors on, they were currently a world wide fad.

He looked around for an unoccupied park bench, and then pulled his golden chair in place so that he wouldn't appear suspicious. He was looking for people that he might scan and then check their photos against Interpol wanted posters. It really was just a fishing expedition, he wasn't sure how accurate his new toy was yet, but it was very recently put on the black market. The scanner was quick, but the program he was using to match the images to the Interpol database, was kind of slow. Sometimes the person would walk away before their results came back. He scanned several people, making adjustments to the procedure to make it faster. Then, he noticed a lone, black haired man talking in a foreign language that wasn't French, and adamantly motioning with his hands. Shannon was trying to get his image, but the man kept moving his head and throwing his hands up in such a way that it made the task nearly impossible.

Just then, an elderly man sat down next to him, but then his gray haired, female, companion sat on top of him! Shannon swore and then prepared to move along, when he noticed the woman set a bag on her lap and open it up.

Shannon couldn't resist taking a look inside the bag for himself. He watched as the woman locate a thermos and a wooden tumbler. That was when he notice how supple the woman's hands were. Her fingers made quick work of taking off the lid and pouring some of the liquid into the glass. In fact, too quickly, he pulled himself back so that he could make out her facial features. "Soooo you are a robot," he mumbled aloud. Oblivious to the remark, the robot handed the glass to the old man and then quickly produced a few pills for the man to swallow. Shannon moved his head closer to the open bag, not sure what he was looking for. That was when he became aware of a young man standing in front of the bench with AR lenses on. The boy held out his hand and pointed in Shannon's direction, and began talking excitedly in French. The old man looked at the youngster with interest, before he addressed his robot as he looked in the direction that the boy was pointing. That was when a crowd began to form around them. This was too much for Shannon, he quickly opened a portal to escape.

He, sat back in his chair and pulled off his visor and gloves. "Well, that was fruitless," he mumbled, but then decided to look closer at the data that he had collected on a nearby monitor. That was when he noticed that the results from his last scan had come in, positive! He opened the record with the man's information in it. He noted that the man's name was completely unfamiliar, and his country of origin was Greece. And it seemed that he was wanted by the Greek government for massive tax evasion! Shannon smiled. Now, he just needed to figure out how to find the man again and recover the bounty!

Sally Ramirez groaned and scowled at the empty container in the bin just outside her front door. "When are the deliveries going to get here?" She asked her dog Joe, who had joined her on their little porch. But then, before she closed the door, she noticed a large shadow slowly moving across her front yard. She stepped back outside and shaded her eyes with her hand so that she could see the huge silver dirigible that was slowly moving in a western direction, low in the sky. A swarm of drowns flew in and out of the large open cargo compartment and charging station, that was attached to the underside of the balloon. "Yeah! Finally!" she said happily to the dog before closing the door again. Now she could go back inside and drink coffee knowing that she would soon have the bread to make toast. Also, she was hoping to get correspondence, because she had a pen pal!

Dave's first client was troubling him. He could tell that the man was lying to him, but couldn't prove it. Which to him meant that he was intelligent and seasoned enough to remember them. But, Shannon's progress had been excellent on paper, and he had not re-offended, so for him professionally, Shannon was a success, yet he couldn't help but wonder what this big secret was. Now, here he was again looking the man in the eyes, listening to a fictitious account of his family fishing adventures.

"So, you mentioned your sister again, Viv?" he noticed a sad smile pass over Shannon's features before he swallowed and nodded to the counselor. "Do you keep in contact with her?"

Shannon was panicking inside, the truth was that he had long ago told himself to give her up for dead, as she likely was, at least he hoped that she was, anything else would be too cruel.

Dave noticed Shannon's eyes begin to glisten, even as the rest of his face remained stony. "uh, sure!" he nodded his head just a bit to vigorously as he looked away, Dave could tell that it was another lie.

"How about your father?"

Shannon shrugged his shoulders and continued nodding in the affirmative. His father was an addict. Addicted to nod. His father was behind his baby brother's disappearance. And then, the disappearance of his twelve year old sister, Viv.

Dave could tell that he was poking at Shannon's soft spot. "Did your father ever tell you that he loved you?"

Shannon became physically uncomfortable, he forced himself to sit still and look into the counselor's eyes, "he was a great dad," this lie made him nauseated, "he just wasn't very...verbal."

Dave could see the distress on his client's face, and it was his humanity that won out over his professional curiosity and caused him to change to a more agreeable topic, technology. The tension in Shannon's shoulders melted away as he began explaining the science behind Remote Viewing.

That evening Shannon found himself standing in the doorway of a large, local bar, that he liked to frequent on the weekends. He took in the room. It was dimly lit and hazy inside, manufactured fog gave the place a mysterious quality. It was a cool, pleasant mist, but also a disinfectant. He moved slowly into the crowd, using one excuse or another, for the need to talk to the more beautiful women he passed. He visited the place often enough to know a few people, but no one well. He didn't really have any friends. As he made his way to the back of the room, he noticed a familiar body. His mind started running through a list of spices until, he nearly remarked out loud, "Ginger!"

He glowered at the beautiful red head, as she smiled and flirted with a young guy that he hadn't seen around before. The guy was getting close to her face and then began patting her on the hip. Ginger giggled and pulled away from the embrace and began walking away from the man. Shannon wondered if she had seen him yet. Then, the man reached out to her and took her hand to get her attention back. Shannon looked on with interest, he began recalling the last time he had seen her and how terrible that night had ended. He grimaced as he remembered how he had lost his shoes and ended up running home barefoot! He stood still and continued watching the two, until Ginger pulled away again and was successful at walking away from the guy, 'this is my opportunity!' he mumbled to himself before overtaking the shapely model on heels. He pulled on her arm. She looked at him and then allowed him to guide her to the back wall of the place.

"Listen to me! You miserable sack of shit!" he snarled, while standing close to her face. "I don't care what kind of sick shit you are into, but you stay the fuck out of this bar! You hear me! If you don't I'm going to tell everyone in the place exactly who you are!"

Ginger looked up into his eyes, "Who cares! A lot of them already know and are into it!" she snarled before punching him, with lightning speed, in the nuts and then walking toward the door.

Shannon doubled over and leaned against the wall, trying to recover. It was at this time that the guy she had been talking to grabbed him by the shoulder and then asked him in an angry voice, "What did you say to her? Huh? You bothering that woman?" Shannon was still trying to catch his breath to be able to speak without gasping. Finally, worried that the guy was going to get more aggressive, he reached out and put a hand on the man's shoulder and looked into his face very earnestly, "look guy, I just saved you! Ginger is a robot, and unless you want to have sex while a naked, ugly, little man is groping you and watching through his headset, then, well...go for it!" he blurted out, exhausted from the effort.

The man looked at him suspiciously, but then, after contemplating his words, he let Shannon walk away.

Meanwhile, in the small room in his very small apartment, an ugly little man wiped a tear away. Yes, he was naked, yes he was chubby, but why did he have to call him ugly? He heard everything the man was saying and had been having a wonderful time and even met a new guy, but then that man had to show up! He decided to take Ginger out of the place before the guy embarrassed her. He hated public scenes! So, he had her march out the door and head down the sidewalk to a different bar. He contemplated the evening that he had shared with the man, and remembered fondly, the nearly new tennis shoes that the man left behind. They were almost his size, and now, he would wear them with pride! On the very next occasion when he wore shoes!

He ignored all the men motioning to her and otherwise trying to get Ginger's attention as she walked out the door. Daniel ordered her to turn right as he decided where they were to go next. 'Hmmmm...' he thought, 'the only place that wouldn't charge an entry fee was several blocks away, but he could check on a few things while he waited.' So, he typed in the address and then monitored her pace. He loved the look of the new high heels that he had purchased recently, but the heels were a bit taller than his walking app recommended, so he had to slow her pace to keep her from stumbling. It was a bit of an inconvenience, but that was the price he paid for her stunning appearance.

Once he had made all the necessary adjustments he pulled down a menu and touched a stat button for a new money making app that he had purchased recently. It was a Remote Viewing app he had bought on the dark web and he was interested in how it was performing. It could be used in RV and right now he was using it in New York to create an automated avatar that had the appearance of a non-threatening vagrant that held up a shabby sign asking for money. The sign also featured a symbol that allowed for any kind Samaritan to add money directly to his account without interaction with the bum, and most importantly they wouldn't have to get close to the beggar or smell his unwashed-looking appearance. It was true that only other avatars and solids with AR lens on could see him, but they provided enough business that the app was close to paying for itself already. 'Hmmm...' Daniel purred looking at the numbers, he was considering buying another copy of the app, especially since he had lately read that one of the subway platforms was going online to garner business for their new gift shop. And having two beggars 24/7, why, he could get rich!

Then he noticed the view in front of him dip and jossel a bit as Ginger had lost her footing again, but recovered. Daniel sighed and made another adjustment to her walking pace. It was as the robot was re-calibrating that Daniel noticed a scantily dressed woman leaning against a nearby wall making eye contact. She was wearing a short skirt and dark stockings, while pulling a drag off of an electric cigarette with one foot against the brick wall behind her, in a seductive pose.

"How you doing there, pretty lady?," she asked in a sweet voice. Her speech had just the right amount of empathy that it caught Daniel's attention, he wanted some sympathy, even though he suspected that she was a prostitute.

"Oh, I'm fine, just getting used to these new shoes," Ginger sang out in her prettiest soprano voice. She paused in front of the lady of the night. Daniel looked at the thin but shapely woman, 'Hmm....' he thought taking her in with Ginger's camera eyes, 'this could be a fun change of pace,' he decided. "I was just trying to decide where to go. Do you know of anywhere fun to go this evening?" Ginger asked with a smile.

The young woman smiled back, and set her foot on the ground to take a step closer to Ginger. She made a nod in the direction of a space between the building she had been leaning on and the next, "I got a friend with something that will make the night special!" she teased while making a gesture to the alley that was formed by the gap. Daniel was fully aware of the danger, but living vicariously through a nearly indestructible, metal woman, with a killer punch, made him throw caution to the wind. This would be an adventure! He declared to himself as he followed her into the dark walkway.

A darkness fell on them as soon as they stepped away from the streetlight. Daniel made necessary adjustments to Ginger's camera eyes. Then, he noticed a green glow around the head of the lady of the night as she strutted in front of him. 'Hmmmm...' he thought, before zooming in on the neon hair tips. 'I wonder if that's her hair or a wig?' he pondered before noticing a ruggedly handsome, dark man coming into view. "Well, hello," Ginger accidentally said aloud.

"Ringo, this is Ginger," the iridescent lady explained as she stood in the narrow alley just passed a slim, yet muscular man who looked to be in his middle years, he was wearing a black felt hat and black makeup around his eyes. His shirt was cut to show off his bare, shaven, chest. As he looked up at Ginger with a smile of approval, the whites of his eyes shined from inside heavy black lines, and extraordinary lashes. You could tell that he spent time on his appearance, he liked to keep the ladies happy. His main occupation was as a pimp, but he like to dabble in narcotics and larceny.

"Good job, Sadie!" Ringo grinned while keeping his eyes on this new prey. Daniel was intrigued, but a bit disappointed when he noticed Sadie quietly walk away. He had been hoping for a threesome, well, in truth, a foursome. Daniel wanted to remark on this, but then worried that his request might come with a fee.

"So, I heard that you know how to make the night special!" Ginger cooed.

The pimp looked happily surprised, "Why, yes! Yes, I do!" Ringo assured her with a wide smile, as he put something that was in his right hand, back into his pocket, and then reached out with both hands and ran them from Ginger's shoulders down the length of her arms, openly inspecting her body.

"Now, let me do you," Ginger smiled as Daniel made eye contact with Ringo, who was watching Ginger with suspicion, as she reached out her hands, and slid them down both sides of his torso, bending at the knees as she did so.

The enraptured pimp was clearly torn between seduction and fear as Ginger made quick work of unfastening his pants. Daniel, as Ginger, gasped as he caught sight of the man's large, dark, hairless genitals. His balls were average, and a bit low, but the length and girth of his uncircumcised penis more than made up for the impediment. But, the truly amazing thing, was that sparkling from his foreskin was a large, thick, gold ring.

The pimp looked down at the kneeling beauty, "So now, you know why the ladies call me Ring Oh!" he said with pride, and a wink.

Daniel squealed before taking the whole penis into Ginger's mouth, all the way to the hilt. Ringo looked on with surprise. Then, the robot made a seal between her supple latex lips and his penis, then ejected any air inside her throat, as it was lined with a supple rubber wall. That was when a gentle, massaging action began. Ringo's face contorted with fear and then ecstasy as he began to realize that he wasn't dealing with a real girl. He ran this finger through her hair, unable to restrain a deep moan.

Daniel was touching himself with the volume up.

Ringo let out a half scream before ejaculating into the robot's mouth, but instantly, the fluid was sucked down into an easy-to-clean compartment in her chest. Then, the whole process started again, but this time, when Ringo looked down he was amazed to see that Ginger had also gobbled up his balls, into her soft, most accommodating mouth.

Daniel also let out a small noises of pleasure after muting his microphone. But, then, when he heard the sound of footsteps approaching them, he looked up to see Sadie as she had re-entered the alley after hearing the unnatural noises. The expression on her glowing face when she identified the source of the animal noises, was both of surprise and admiration. But, then, the sight of her dropping the straps of her blouse to expose her breasts was more than Daniel could handle. He let go of his own penis so that he could grab his own chest, in a futile attempt to slow down his quickly beating heart. He pulled off his headset and began trying in earnest to slow his heart as he noticed stinging sweat pouring from his face was now flowing into his eyes. He looked around himself wildly for a glass of water, or soda, or anything. He tripped and fell off his swiveling chair, landing hard on the floor. He flailed around on the floor, wetting himself, and causing his naked body to slide on the laminated flooring. But then, he managed to right himself by pull himself up by the edge of his desk.

His heart was still beating too fast and he knew he was in trouble, so he grabbed at his holographic keyboard and managed to press the emergency button that caused Ginger to abruptly discontinue her orgy and obey an emergency call from her master.

Ringo and Sadie were both dismayed as Ginger stood up and then pushed them aside, even as Ringo was not ready to let her go. But her latex covered, metal arms easily pushed them both out of her path as Ginger was now in emergency mode.

The two criminals followed Ginger into the light and then watched as she stumbled down the sidewalk in a sprint. "I gotta' have that!" the pimp mumbled as he tucked himself back into his trousers.

By the time Ginger made it back to Daniel's apartment, he was writhing on the floor straining to breath. She quickly began administering first aid and brought him a tablet and a glass of water. She tenderly held up his head so that he could sip the water and swallow the pill. "Take me to the hospital," he gasped, "But, first get my robe and boxers! Oh, and the shoes...I want to wear those new tennis shoes!" he directed from the slippery puddle that he lay in.

Sally enjoyed watching the scenery out the windows of her small, electric, self-driving vehicle. It kept her distracted from the monitor that she was using to do some last minute business. She had never been this far north before! Wilderness surrounded her without interruption for miles at a time. There were forests on both sides of the road that were full of wildlife. She abruptly became aware of this after her little car came to a sudden and unexpected stop in the middle of the narrow highway, as a family of deer had run in front of them, they had become very close to the leader. After that the vehicle moved at a slower pace, and that was alright with Sally as she was enjoying the ride. Also, she was nervous, she turned her head and then reached behind her seat and petted Joe on the head, as he was sound asleep there. She hoped that everything was as Lucas had explained to her. She had no reason to doubt him, and had already met members of his family that he had been visiting when they first met on the ITS.

But, this kind of life that he described to her was so much different from the life she had always lived, in cities. He lived with his mother and grandparents on land that they had inherited from his great grand mother's father. In a house that was built by his grandfather after the first house was lost in a flood. All of this was very interesting on it's own, but many of the people in his community, like himself, rejected most technology. He said that they always lived together, in multi generational homes, it wasn't something to be embarrassed about, it was so that they could take care of one another, and work together, share resources and skills. He had grown up working with his grandfather who taught him all about solar panels and metallic wind socks that brought electricity down a cable that they were tethered to. All of this made them energy independent. His job as an adult now, was to service these systems for the many family members and friends in his community. They bartered with one another for services. Money was paid for taxes as everyone used infrastructure like roads, so paying the yearly taxes was their biggest hardship. But, money wasn't as necessary for the lifestyles they led.

The landscape began to change with intermittent farm fields, until they came to a fork in the road. Sally was surprised when the vehicle chose the more primitive one. Then, she noticed something strange in front of them, as they came near, Sally could make out a wooden structure with a man on it. As her car was overtaking the slow moving apparition, Sally realized that it was being pulled by a horse! There was a man sitting on the wagon in the open air! This was such an amazing site to her. She, of course, had heard of such horse pulled vehicles but had never seen one in real life!

A body of water became visible on her left, then a small cluster of buildings lined both sides of the narrow road. One of the buildings was very close to the water with docks along it's back side. Then, the car nearly came to a stop as it slowly turned into a very rough track that ran through a field, which turned into a marsh, with swampy bodies of land on both sides of the road. Sally wondered how often the road was overtaken by water. Then, she began to notice the large cranes wading through the marsh, apparently fishing for frogs. A large body of water appeared in front of them and Sally was beginning to worry that they might drive into it, when the car turned right and into another path that served as a driveway, there were tall fir trees next to the water, which turned out to be a canal, and then, very close to the waters edge sat a house on stilts. To Sally it looked like a tree house she had seen in a book. There was a long metal staircase with a porch at the top that connected to the house's front door. As the vehicle came to a stop she began to notice Lucas at the railing of the little porch, waving at her.

Her heart fluttered. It was so nice to see him again, in person. They had been getting to know one another from letters. But, now, here he was, dashing down a flight of stairs to embrace her. It happened so naturally, she had been suffering with little stabbing pains of worry whenever she imagined how these first moments would feel, worried that she was imagining this new love affair to be more than it was. But, no, it felt just as real, just as magical. Their lips were magnets.

After letting Joe out, Lucas took her bag and her hand, and then led them both up the stairs, anxious to take her to the little porch at the top, where she was introduced to his grandparents who sat next to each other on a little couch. There was also a low table and a chair, in front of a row of fishing poles and equipment that was leaning again the wall of the house. There was a small awning over the whole thing, making it comfortable.

Sally blushed, but she could sense a warm feeling from both of the smiling grandparents who she was introduced to as, 'Abuela y Abuelo.' This almost brought a tear to her eye, as she had never used these words before, or their English translation. The gray haired couple were smiling brightly. The woman with her hair pulled up into a bun and wearing a sweater over her red and yellow patterned dress. The old man, with his thick bristle of hair in a short crew cut, was thin, but agile looking, with a similar type of athletic build that his grandson had inherited. They both made a fuss over Joe as he bounded up the stairs ahead of them, and now sat happily waging his tail and excepting the old couple's pats and 'good boy' rubs.

Lucas brought her attention to a cable that was running up the side of the house, then he pointed into the sky where a cable disappeared overhead. "There is one of the wind socks," he explained. Sally walked to the edge of the porch and shaded her eyes with her hand, but could not locate the end of the cable as it disappeared into nothingness. "You can't see it, can you?" Lucas interjected excitedly. "I told you they were almost invisible, no intrusion on your view at all!"

His grandfather chuckled, "almost too invisible!"

This prompted Lucas to tell the story about one of their customers, whose metallic wind sock was struck by a fairy. "I still don't understand how it was flying so far up like that! And then, we have had a few birds fly into them."

Sally listened with interest as she knew that these devices were Lucas' passion. He explained how the devices worked, and modifications that he had made. She loved watching his face as he talked. There were now many families who depended on he and Abuelo, even when they didn't have the resources to pay.

It was after a lull in the conversation that Sally turned around to look over the railings of the porch. It was a beautiful view that overlooked the marsh and even allowed her to spot the large cranes that she had noticed on the drive in. At this time of the year everything was mostly green with little ponds, that looked silver from the reflected sunlight. The damp, chilly air had a fishy, kind of smell, to it, and was heavy with moisture. Sea gulls cried out overhead.

"Looks like you don't have any neighbors," Sally observed.

"Not anymore," Lucas said, pointing to a patch of black roofing that represented what was left of another house that adjoined the canal, only this one was washing away into the water. "There used to be a bunch of houses along the canal, but the water decided that it wanted to take them, so it did! My grandpa had this idea to put his house on stilts after it kept getting flooded whenever we had a bad storm. That was before I was born." He turned and pointed in the opposite direction, "See, way down there, passed the trees? There's a row of stilt houses there now, we helped build them. Most of them are family. In fact, almost everyone around here is some kind of relation to us! So, that's why we are always helping each other."

Sally loved that idea, she loved the idea of a big family, it always seemed like such a wonderful thing that she had only read about or saw on a screen. She moved to the end of the railing so that she could make out a small roof that appeared to be leaning into the water below. "Is that another sinking house?"

Lucas looked in the direction she was pointing, "oh, no, that's the boat house. Well, at least it will be until it's lost to the water!" He looked fondly at her, as he was now very near to her. "I don't have a car, but I have a boat! That's better for this place. You can't always use the roads around here, but you can usually get anywhere in a boat! Even when you have to tie it to the porch!" he laughed. Sally thought this was interesting, she had never been in a place that used boats for everyday vehicles. She remembered him telling her about it, but now, she understood.

"Let's get your stuff inside and then the three of us can take a boat ride! I'll show you my favorite places!" he said before he kissed her. Then, he gabbed her bag and her free hand and led her inside. His grandparents continued to sit quietly on the couch. Sally felt embarrassed about the kiss as she walked passed them.

Inside, was neat and simple, everything seemed to have a place, yet without a hint of extravagance. There were no over-sized monitors or technology in sight. Just a few stuffed chairs and a couch that faced a wall with a monitor the size of her own, mounted on it. On the opposite wall was a kitchen that featured a large window over the sink and a wooden dinning table and chairs. Lucas led her through the kitchen and around a corner that hid a narrow flight of stairs into an attic. Sally knew that he lived in the attic, so this did not surprise her. But, when they got to the top of the stairs, it was flooded with light and looked cheerful, and less gloomy then how she would have expected an attic to look.

The source of the light, were two large windows, one at each peak. The stairs divided the room, at one end was a bed and dresser, at the other were book shelves built into the shorter walls, and there was a small table with two chairs with an area run under them. It looked a bit like how she would expect a library to look, not that she had ever been in an actual library, but virtual ones looked this way sometimes.

Her eyes wondered to the tidy bed with a red comforter over it. "Um, will I be up here with you?" she said in an almost whisper.

Lucas smiled, "it will be okay. My grandparents will act like they don't know what is going on, and my mom won't care at all! So, don't worry." He explained this with confidence, but Sally was still worried, under no circumstances did she want 'Abuela y Abuelo' to be disappointed in her. For some reason, she already felt a kinship with the old couple.

"So what do you think?" Lucas asked spreading out his arms.

"Oh, I love it!" Sally answered. She pointed out how it looked like a little library, then she stepped closer to the large, uncovered, window, that faced west, and looked out to the canal that ran, nearly, underneath of her. "What a wonderful view," she remarked.

Lucas stepped closer to her, "that's what I think! My grandmother used to have drapes! I finally took them down. I like to be woke up by the sun in the morning and to watch it set at night." Sally looked up at him admiringly, and this caused another embrace, their magnetic lips coming together again, right there, in front of the window.

"I want to take you on a boat ride! There is this special place that I want to take you to, so that we can watch the sunset from there!" he kissed her on the forehead. "I know you are going to like it!"

She grabbed a jacket and stuffed it into her backpack and Lucas grabbed his. They exchanged a few words with Lucas' grandparents and then, walked down the long flight of stairs to the ground. With Joe happily sprinting down the stairs in front of them. His boat was tied to a pier that was sheltered by the collapsing boat house. It was small with two bench seats but also sported a flag pole near the motor with a black pirate flag. He got in and then pulled one of the seats up to reveal a storage compartment. He made a little bed for Joe in the front with a blanket to lay on. He pulled cushions out for them to sit on and then, reach out a hand and helped her step aboard.

She had never been in a boat before, and the tipsy feeling did frighten her. She quickly sat down before letting go of his hand. He remembered her telling him that she had never been in a boat, and that she didn't even know how to swim, but it was hard for him to believe. How could anyone reach adulthood with neither?

He reached into another compartment and pulled out an orange vest with a loop of red cord that was attached to the front. "Here, put this on," he said as he helped her off with her backpack and on with the life vest. Then he pointed out the red loops, "pull this if you ever need to inflate it," he explained piercing her with his tender brown eyes. Sally nodded.

They rode slowly out of the little boat house and into the sunlight. Sally held the seat on both sides of her, frightened as the boat seemed to tip this way and that, she was afraid to move. Then, she reached behind her to pet Joe on the head, and became aware that her pet dog was standing with his paws on the front of the boat, in a kind of doggy-escacy with his ears flying back from the wind and a smile on his face. This made her happy, then, she noticed the beautiful yellow and white flowers that floated atop large green leaves near the edges of the water.

"I know a shady place, not far away, and then I have something that will make you feel safer!" Lucas smiled. She knew that he had an affinity to marijuana and although it wasn't her drug of choice, she would be happy to partake, even though what she really wanted was a drink.

They floated slowly down the center of the narrow canal. Tall grasses and reeds of cattail covered the wild banks. Sally began to notice the variety of large birds, some would fly away, frightened by their sudden appearance, while others ignored them altogether, busy with their fishing. Then, Lucas pointed up at a tall dead looking tree. Sally followed his finger to the top most branch, and there sat a very large black bird with a white head. "Eagle!" Lucas shouted in a whisper.

They came to a larger body of water, where he increased their speed across the lake and toward a tree covered bank, a short distance away. Sally felt more comfortable when they were near land again. He slowed, and then, skillfully maneuvered the boat into the mouth of a small, shady river. Tall maple and oak trees arched overhead, forming a beautiful green tunnel, with fingers of light escaping between the branches and causing a speckled light show under their canopy. Sally instinctively reached behind to pet Joe, then Lucas drove the boat under a large willow tree and cut the power, then he tyed it to the tree trunk after they had slowed to a stop. Joe wagged his tail, and then made himself comfortable on the blanket.

Lucas was getting something out of his backpack, Sally began to look around herself. Comforted by the muddy bank nearby, she loosened her grip on the bench she was sitting on. Then, she became more aware of the beautiful purplish-pink flowers that grew in clusters near the water. Something was moving in the muddy bank, and then a frog jumped into the water. Sally watched it swim out of sight.

Lucas had been watching her, "So you like my special place!" he said, putting something to his lips. Sally's brows furrowed. Lucas removed the pink thing out of his mouth so that she could inspect it, as he could see that it was foreign to her. "It's weed, I just wrapped it in rose petals, special, for you!" he said with that sweet smile. She remembered that he told her that he and his friends grew their own, but she had never used it this way, the only way she had smoked marijuana was through a metal cylinder that turned a concentrated form of it into a vapor. This thing that she was rolling in her fingers looked, felt, and smelled, very primitive. She looked at him with a hint of skepticism as she handed it back.

He pulled a flame out of a small, metal box and lit the end of it, inhaling the fire and exhaling a cloud of smoke. Then, he handed it to her. She put it to her lips and imitated him, but immediately began coughing.

"It takes some getting used to," he admitted, offering her a drink. Her second attempt was more successful, but she still wasn't sure if she'd like another drag, until, after she had handed it back to Lucas, and then, suddenly, she began to notice how the green leaves on the branches of the willow tree looked iridescent as the strong light from the lowering sun, shone through them. When she looked back across at Lucas, he was smiling at her, giggling at her short departure into some deep thought. He handed it back to her. This time, no cough.

"So, this is what you do all day in your little boat!" she laughed.

Lucas burst into a bout of laughter, "pretty much! I do like to get high and play games too! That's what we do at Bill's when we are not busy working or building stuff."

Sally considered this a moment, "wait! You play video games! Why is that okay, but not communicators or goggles?"

Lucas sighed, "I'm not against technology. Technology isn't the problem. The problem is that too many people have developed 'virtual' lives that are more important to them than reality!" He didn't want to change the mood, but he felt it was important for her to understand. "These pretend lives cut people off from reality. The planet could be falling down around them but, they wouldn't even notice unless their signal gets cut!" He looked around himself, "this is real, this is amazing! How has this become unappealing to those people? I can't help but see their 'virtual world' preoccupation as an illness and I don't want to become infected!"

He paused to see that she was reacting in a positive way, and she was. Nodding her head in agreement, she was considering his words now as well as others that she remembered reading in his letters. For Lucas, using social media would be to let artificial intelligence into his life, to invade his privacy, and to manipulate him with information it collected about him. AI scared him because it *was* intelligent, and it was controlled by greedy entities with narcissistic intentions.

"You know, I'm not the only one who feels this way. A lot of my people feel this way!" He looked into Sally's face as though he suddenly remembered something, "our people!" he corrected himself.

At that moment Sally had never felt so included. Before that moment she had only felt this inclusive feeling when she was with her mother.

He pulled her closer with his free hand, and then they kissed. Slowly, she found herself sliding between the bench seats, to the floor of the little boat, where Lucas offered himself as a cushion.

They laid there together for a long time or maybe it was really just a short time, Sally couldn't tell, but then finally, she noticed that the sound of crickets became much louder, and then Joe began to make a low growling sound. This made Sally poke her head up, and look over the edge of the boat, where she could see, small, weasel-like animals playing in between the roots of the tree, in the muddy bank, nearby.

"They are minks," Lucas said as he carefully pulled himself onto the bench seat, trying not to rock the boat. "Actually, we need to get going if we want to see the sun set."

He turned the boat around and slowly drove them back through the green tunnel, that was, now, growing dark. She could see movement in the water in front of them and realized it was another mink, swimming as, yet another, was just jumping in from the shore. She loved the way they seemed to play with one another. Joe barked and wagged his tail. When they got to the larger body of water, Lucas slowed the boat down to a stop again, so that they could watch the pink sky in front of them slowly turn to orange, before the yellow disk disappeared behind a row of trees in the distance. He drove them back across to the canal. When they returned to the house, they found that Abuela had made dinner.

After dinner, they sat together outside on the little porch. Sally learned a lot about Lucas' life from their conversation. It was nice, to sit with family and talk about simple things. Abuelo was holding Joe's head in his lap, giving the dog a head massage. After awhile, Lucas nudged her and mentioned that the old family dog had died less than a year ago and Joe reminded him of that dog. "And King was a good dog," Lucas said, to emphasize the importance of the compliment.

Finally, the mosquitoes drove them inside. That was when Lucas led her by the hand back to his attic. The inside was now a fuzzy yellow, from the light of billions of stars. They stood near one another, looking at the canal, sparkling from moonlight, below them from the window in the little library. Such a tranquil life, she thought, wondering if she would like to spend her days this way all the time. He moved behind her and wrapped his arms around her, and they stood for a long time, just looking out the window. Later, they slept this same way, with Lucas' arms wrapped around her.

Late that night Sally was startled awake by a loud sound from below. It made her sit up a bit. "It's okay, it's just my mom getting home," Lucas explained. Sally laid back down, then she heard shuffling sounds that were making their way toward the stairs. Then, she could hear someone shout from the bottom of the stairs. "Hey! Whose car it that?" came a gruff female voice.

Lucas had already jumped up and was headed toward the stairs, "it's Sally's! Remember, I told you she was coming today!" He explained excitedly in a hushed voice.

"Oh! Yeah, yeah! I forgot, sorry!" she apologized to Lucas as he was now only a step or two from the bottom. He immediately turned to go back up, when she stopped him, "Hey, why don't you guys come down here and have a beer with me?"

Lucas stopped, and turned back toward his mother, "I don't know. Sally's sleeping."

"Just ask her!" his mother insisted.

Lucas walked back up the stairs to find Sally sitting up in the bed, listening to the conversation.

"Ummm, did you want to go downstairs?" he asked shyly, but before she could answer he put his knee on the mattress so that he could be close to her, "she's pretty wasted," he explained in a low voice.

Sally, shrugged her shoulders. At that time, there came another shout up the stairs. "I'll just be down here at the kitchen table if you two want to come down! I got some beer!"

They looked at one another and chuckled out of embarrassment. "Yeah, I think we should," Sally answered. Sally stood up and looked into a mirror that hung near the foot of the bed. She began combing her hair with her fingers, then she looked around herself nervously for her bag.

Lucas grasped her shoulders, "what are you doing?"

"I just need my comb," she said as she was trying to break free from his embrace.

"Why? Your hair looks good. She won't notice, anyway!"

He took her hand and led her down the stairs. When they reached the kitchen, they found Lucas' mother sitting at the table with a beer at her elbow and a metal cylinder in her hand. She was a middle sized woman of middle age. Her long dark hair was decorated with glittery blue stripes that stated at the top of her head, and she was wearing eye shadow of the same color. Her clothing was a simple, body hugging, black jumpsuit, the type that everyone was wearing. But, her eye lids looked heavy and her skin seemed to hang a bit, like maybe she had lost weight recently. Sally greeted her with a shy nod.

"Well hello! I'm Barbara, but everyone calls me Bobby! So nice to meet you!" She pushed out a chair that was next to her. Sally sat down. "Get her a beer!" she shouted to her son. She then looked Sally over and put the metal cylinder to her lips again. "So, you liking it here? Did Lucas take you out on the boat yet?" Then, she paused and waited for an answer.

"Yes!" Sally responded, "Lucas took me out, and this place is so beautiful!" She took a sip of the beer, that Lucas had set in front of her, just before he took the seat opposite of his mother. It was as Bobby began complaining about the remoteness and how everyone was a relative, that Sally had a chance to study the woman's face better, and that was when she began to notice a dark area on the woman's forehead. At first she thought it was a trick of the light, but after awhile she could even see a lump there, just above her eyes, it peaked out from under her bangs.

"I work at the only bar in town and it's just a dinky place, but on the weekend the owner just shuts the front door at about midnight, and then we keep partying!" she said as an explanation of her current inebriated state. She put the metal tube to her lips again, then looked down at it and in Sally's direction. She started to hand it to her, but Lucas pushed her hand back. "No, mom, she doesn't do that," he said in a low voice, looking embarrassed.

"It's only 1%, that don't get no one addicted!" she insisted.

"Mom! No! Just don't," Lucas pleaded.

His mother waved him off, then sat back in her chair. Sally began to realize that Bobby was most likely smoking, nod.

It was a new type of opioid that was genetically engineered to grow in hot houses. It was illegal, but widely used, very potent, very addictive and very profitable for some.

Bobby sat up, like she just remembered something. But then, she got quiet again, as though the thought had slipped away. So she took another, longer, drag off the metal tube. She mumbled something incoherent, and then abruptly, her body became limp, so that her face fell hard on to the table. Lucas had attempted to catch her head before it made a thumping sound on the table's wooden surface, but, he wasn't fast enough. He sighed and looked embarrassed at Sally.

"Sorry," he said in a low voice. Then, he just shrugged as he didn't know what to say.

They both looked at her, face down with her hands on either side of her head and the metal tube, rolling across the table till it was stopped by her beer bottle. "Should we help her to bed or something?" Sally asked meekly.

Lucas shook his head. "It's better for her not to lay flat, anyway," he explained. He then, stood up and helped Sally back up the stairs, where they sat in his little library and talked until dawn.

Dave found himself once again in one of Ollie's comfortable chairs with a fresh tumbler of bourbon in his hand. He was there for another session with his mentor and friend, helping him to record his memoir. "We left off at the wake of the Attack," Dave reminded the older gentleman.

"Yes, by the time of the Attack, many of us were just coming out of a propaganda stupor! Too many personalities, who put their own wealth and power over the well being of the people, had acquired positions of power. And, they were dividing the country against itself, each faction, an army against the other, and the elite, who waged the war, watch the battles from the safety of their fortifications!"

Ollie sat back with satisfaction, then looked over at Dave, "That's it! Write it just like that!" he said before taking another sip of bourbon. Then he continued, "So, when the people began to wage war against the lies and propaganda, the wave swept across Russia as well! Then, there we were, the American elite, the Russian political machine and all the oligarchy were angry! So, now we had a relative hand full of people who owned most of the planets wealth, angry! The Attack was a vengeful thing, and not in the best interest of anyone! But, those rich villains did it! They used their state owned hacking factories and took down our entire electrical grid by blowing it up with a current like a bolt of lightening, striking every power station at the same time. It was like there were fiery bombs exploding everywhere at once! Some of the fires became massive! So much death and destruction! Then, without electricity, some places, that depended on desalination plants or pumps, had no water either! No water to put out the fires, no water to drink! And, by that time, most folks had converted to electric cars, so there went our transportation system!" He raised a finger, "you know, that's what made people in the south go back to using gasoline!"

He took another sip from his glass. "Then, there was a shut down of banks of computers that store the information of the web! Most, were on some kind of battery backup at first, but quickly large segments of the web could not be accessible for months, then there were the problems of users who couldn't charge up their devices! We were an electrified nation that was dependent on centralized power grids that were destroyed!" He chuckled and shook his head sadly. We were all just stunned when we realized the shabby way our power system was piecemeal together! So, we built back better, now there are so many homes and businesses that generate more power than they need, now the business of the power stations is mainly to redirect the surplus to where it is needed! And, lots of people have systems that work independently, so now there will always be someone nearby with power, come act of war or natural disaster!"

"Tell me about the building back, how did that happen?" Dave asked.

"Community, family, we helped each other. Supplies poured in from other countries, we taught each other and worked to help one another. The goal was to electrify the country, not create profit for a corporation. It's amazing how much you can accomplish when you cut the profit out! We didn't wait for our government to help, it was too big a job, and they were in disarray. So we organized ourselves! One community! That was our motto!"

"And now, here we are!" Dave said with pride.

"Yeah," Ollie sighed, "and I just read yesterday that Wyoming has started fracking again! Those elite idiots say it is to assist those in states who have a shortage of fossil fuels!" He leaned in closer to Dave, "You know it's just a money maker for someone, dressed up like aid!"

Shannon was really liking his newest toy, the virtual scanner had already proved itself by identifying someone on

Interpol's wanted list. He was currently in the habit of scanning people with his communicator in real life and looking for bounties, but now, he could use his goggles and from the desk in his office, he could ID criminals anywhere Remote Viewing (RV) was available! Life was good!

At the moment he was sitting on a park bench near the Eiffel Tower with his feet kicked up, hoping to get a glimpse of the man he had identified the day before, or someone else with a bounty. He sat like this casually keeping an eye out for the Greek tax cheat while watching a video from a small screen by his foot. He had taken the afternoon off work, claiming a doctor's appointment. He was hoping they would fire him, as he knew he could make more money at home, but the job was a good cover.

After a few hours, he finally spotted the big burly man from the day before. He stood up and held his scanner on the man for several seconds until he heard the tell tale beeping sound that alerted him that he had a match.

"Yesssss!" he said aloud before changing devices to a virtual camera. He then teleport himself to a few yards in front of the man and took several photos as he approached. Even one extreme closeup as the man passed through his avatar. Being invisible was his favorite thing about RV.

Now he just needed an address. He turned on the parental control feature of the program so that it would track his own movements. Then, he started trailing the man from a few feet away, as he didn't want to look suspicious to anyone wearing those damn AR lenses.

He followed the big man on the city's sidewalks into the shopping district. It was a beautiful late summer afternoon so there were people all around them, mostly tourists. The man turned into one of the stores, so Shannon followed. It was a technology store. There were displays of high tech goggles and body suits that allowed avatars to 'feel' one another. Shannon became a little preoccupied with listening to one of the displays, but then noticed the man finally come to a stop. He swore when he realized what the man was looking at, AR lens.

"Damn it!" Shannon swore again, outside his speaker. He watched helplessly as one of the stores employees helped him pick out and try on different makes and styles. Finally, the man decided on one pair. Shannon was standing next to the body suit display pretending, now, to be interested as the man walked passed him wearing his new glasses.

Shannon watched him turn to the right, after exiting the store. He followed at a distance, since he could now be seen.

He followed him to a restaurant. Shannon waited for a solid person to walk inside so that he could follow, no need to give away that you're an avatar by walking through the wall. Inside, was a small waiting area where he could see the man standing. Now that the man could see him, he could also hear him, so Shannon thought he might try and engage the man in conversation to find out where he was staying. That last piece of information would guarantee him the major portion of the reward money.

The large man had a short crop of black hair that circled the back of his head and was connected in the front by a well trimmed beard and a mustache under a nose that looked to have been broken. On the bridge of that nose, set a brand new pair of AR lenses. He was standing at the threshold of a mirror lined dinning area, waiting for someone to escort him to a table. Shannon found an empty place near the man where he casually coughed, then tried to achieve eye contact. Once this was achieved he asked, "say, do you know if the food is good here? I'm not from the area."

The man made a hands up gesture, "I'm not sure myself, just a tourist like you!" He said in a polite, heavily accented voice, then he returned his gaze to the approaching hostess, until, he noticed something strange about the person beside him, there was no reflection of him in the mirrors. This realization gave him a start, so then he turned to Shannon and pulled his glasses down his nose to get a better view of him, and as there was no one there, he realized that he had been conversing with an avatar. He chuckled to himself then followed the hostess, who wanted to take him to his table.

'Well, that cover is blown,' Shannon thought to himself as he changed into a different life-like avatar, and disappeared around a corner. This proved to be good timing, as the man, who was now seated a few feet away, recalled why it was that he had purchased the special glasses, and turned in his chair to see that the avatar was gone. He turned back around, and then scanned the room for other disembodied beings, relaxing after he didn't notice any.

Watching the man sitting at his table drinking one cocktail after another, Shannon thought of a plan. He located the men's room and then took the shape of a twelve-year-old boy scout and stood near the door. It wasn't long before the wanted man was walking toward Shannon's new avatar.

"Excuse me sir!" the little boy called out to him. The man looked behind him as though he thought the boy must be talking to someone else. But, then the child called out to him again. "Sir! Could you please help scouting by buying some snacks from me?" The man shook his head and continued passed the child. "But, if I sell just a few more bags of popcorn I get to go to Disney World!" the boy pleaded as the man was pushing open the men's room door.

He stopped with the door open and looked around himself. "Where is your mother?" he asked.

"Oh, she's in the bathroom. I'm just waiting for her."

The man shrugged and continued into the men's room. But, the tenacious child followed him inside.

"I only need to sell one more bag, but it has to be today!" the child explained.

The man stopped near the row of sinks and turned back toward the boy, "listen kid, I'm not from here, I'm just on vacation."

"That's okay, we can deliver to a hotel room! We do it all the time!" he continued as he followed the man to a row of urinals.

"Okay, Okay, just give me a minute here!" the man said, then fastened his pants and walked back to the row of sinks and began washing his hands. "Say, you sure don't talk like a French kid! In fact, that sounds like an American accent to me," he said, then looked back at the child in the mirror. That was when he noticed the lack of a reflection and jumped with a start. He turned around and lifted his AR lenses, then chuckled as he held a hand to his chest. Then, he shook a finger in the avatar's direction, "you avatars, scare the hell out of me!" He turned back toward the sink and began rinsing his hands again before he considered that this was the second avatar wanting to interact with him. He found this suspicious. "Say! What kind of a trick are you trying to play on me?" he asked the boy.

Shannon disappeared. This time he teleported to just outside the restaurant door. He sighed and tried to think of another approach, when the man came out of the door wearing a frown and walking quickly down the sidewalk. This time Shannon took the shape of an elderly man and began following the criminal. When the tax fraud stopped at a corner to wait for the light to change, he looked around himself and saw the elderly man moving toward him. He nervously lifted his lenses, then, let them drop and came charging toward the obvious avatar, swinging at him. The fist cut through Shannon's latest avatar without injury. The man swore then shouted toward Shannon, "Who are you?" Shannon stood mute. The man stomped the ground again then noticed an empty taxi and got inside the small electric vehicle.

Shannon began chasing the vehicle, from a distance, hoping that he was going back to his hotel. But, he wasn't and soon Shannon became aware that they were near the tunnel out of Paris. That was when he hit a kind of blank wall, as he had ventured to the edge of Paris and its Remote Viewing area. He took a deep breath and then pulled down a menu to contact Interpol. He would have to give them the information he had, it should be worth something, he consoled himself.

Daniel was finally comfortable in his hospital bed, but he couldn't stand the look of his hand with the tube in it. The nurse put a kind of glove over it after he expressed his phobia, but, he knew it was under there, sticking into his skin! He looked over at Ginger who was sitting in a chair next to him, her eyes directed at a monitor in the front the room that was playing an old film that Daniel liked. It comforted him to see her there, so the two of them sat quietly watching the movie, when an elderly woman entered the room. "Mom!" he shouted excitedly, as he hadn't seen her in person in years, even though they lived in the same city. Carol walked to the side of his bed, but then noticed the robot sitting on the other side and frowned before looking her son in the face and reached down to embrace him. He enjoyed the hug but had noticed the evil eye that she had given Ginger. He wished that they could get along.

"How are you?" she asked him while still close to his face.

He nodded in a pitiful way, "I'm feeling a lot better now."

She stood up and gave him a good look over, then sadly shook her head. "The doctor said that if you don't start taking better care of yourself you are going to have a heart attack! A real one!"

Daniel cast his eyes down in shame, but Carol was still distracted by the robot. "Is that thing watching TV?" she asked.

Daniel sighed, "No, she's in default mode," he explained. He could see from the look on his mother's face that she needed a better explanation. "Whenever she is waiting for direction she automatically focuses on the brightest light source in the room she's in, like a monitor. That way she looks more normal."

Carol was staring at her, "does she understand what's going on?"

"I don't know, I guess, maybe, she is an AI."

"Ever worry that she'll kill you in your sleep after watching one of your bloody crime dramas?"

"No, no...change the channel if you want! Or, turn it off! She would never kill anyone...well...not unless I told her to..." Daniels voice trailed off, but then he noticed his mother's look of alarm. "The TV thing is just her default mode! She has to focus on something, otherwise she'd just be staring out into space! That would be creepy! And everyone would know that she was a robot!" He then shouted out a command toward the monitor that caused it to turn black.

Carol could see that her son was becoming agitated, so she reached out and patted him on the shoulder and silently chastised herself for causing him to get emotional. "I'm sorry son, I just worry about you so much! The doctor said that your Agoraphobia is causing you to have Torpid syndrome!"

Daniel made a face, "what syndrome?"

"Torpid syndrome! It's a new term they use now, it means that you don't get any vitamins from the sun, your muscles aren't getting enough exercise, and your diet is so bad that you are suffering from malnutrition!" She finished with a crack in her voice as she pulled a tissue from a nearby dispenser and held it to her nose. "He is prescribing counseling."

Daniel sighed again, he had no desire to change anything about his life. "I'm not paying for that! Isn't there some pills or something I could take?" he grumbled.

Carol shook her head, "Daniel you can't keep living like you do, all hold up in that little apartment, using that..." She stopped and shook her finger in Ginger's direction, as the robot was now focused on a recessed light bulb in the ceiling. "...that doll, to run all your errands for you! In fact, I'm telling you right now, I don't ever want 'it' visiting me for my birthday again! If you can't visit me yourself, then we will just have to meet up in VR or something!" Then she noticed Ginger was bare foot. "Why is she barefoot?"

"She needed to recharge. And, because, that doll, carried me all the way here and I didn't want her to trip, MOM! If it wasn't for Ginger I would have died!"

Ginger turned her head toward Daniel when he said her name. He looked at her fondly, "see mom! She pays attention and takes care of me!" he said with affection.

Carol frowned, "I don't think you were dying, but it's a good thing she brought you here, now your therapy will be paid for with a prescription." She softened her look and grew closer to Daniel. "Honey, I just love you so much and worry that you won't get better unless you start getting outside more! Go places, meet people!"

"But I don't want to go out and meet people! I'm too ugly! I'm just a disgusting sack of shit!" he wailed, repeating the words of his nemesis.

Carol patted his shoulder again, "you are not! You just need to fix yourself up! Get some new cloths and a hair cut! You were always a handsome child! You just need to put a little bit of effort into your appearance, then you will see! People will be attracted to you."

Daniel sniffed, at last, here was the empathetic ear that he had been craving!

Daniel was happy to be home, he and Ginger had taken the hospital transporter there, it was a short distance away, but he didn't feel that he was ready for any strenuous activity, despite his doctor's advice. Once they were let out of the vehicle, Ginger had carried him upstairs to their apartment, "I don't know what I'd do without you honey," he had whispered in her ear as she carried him down the hallway and then set him gently on his feet at the door.

He pressed his thumb against the reader to open the door. The odor was pungent but familiar. Daniel took in a deep breath and smiled while Ginger busied herself cleaning the old mess on the floor. Daniel pulled off his sneakers and then peeked into his office, just to be sure everything was undisturbed, then he tossed his beach ball shaped body onto his couch and pulled at his clothes. Life was good!

Ginger prepared him a meal and brought it to him on a tray. "Oh, sweetheart, you are too good to me," he teased. "After dinner, I'll return the favor and get you all squeaky clean!" he promised in his silly voice. The meal consisted of his favorite battered and fried foods, cooked extra crispy. And a cold soda. Everything the doctor told him not to eat, he considered as he called out for a second bottle. Then, he remembered that he had his first therapy session later that day. "Such a waste of time," he muttered to himself.

After his early lunch, he did feel refreshed. "Hospital food was terrible," he complained to Ginger. Then, he had her strip down and kneel in the bathtub, so he could open, a craftily concealed, compartment in her chest. "Yuck!" Daniel remarked on the body fluids that had collected there, days ago. But he removed the inside container and dumped it into the sink, and that was when he noticed something sparkle. He turned on the tap and let the water rinse away the grime to reveal a familiar, thick, gold ring.

"Hmm..." he remarked aloud as he put the tip of his finger through the circle and then held it up to the light. "Wonder how much this is worth?" he asked himself aloud.

Sally found herself alone with Joe in a little grove of trees near the water's edge. She had been directed to the picnic table that sat underneath by Lucas, after she had asked his advice about a quiet place where she could take a phone call, and this was where he had sent her. She didn't exactly lie about whom she needed to call, but she let him believe it was a business call. She didn't want to explain that it was to be a video conference with her therapist, she wasn't sure yet how he would feel about such matters. But, she had been looking forward to the conversation. Her life was suddenly interesting and she wanted to talk to someone about it.

"Looks like you are calling me from out-of-doors. Are you at a park?" Dave asked at the beginning of their conversation.

"Well, kind of," she answered before turning her communicator to give him a view of her surroundings. "Lucas took me to work with him," she explained after turning her communicator back so that she could see the councilor. "So now I'm just wondering around with Joe. Hoping not to get rained on! It's so nice here! There is water everywhere and so we travel by boat!"

Dave was happy that she was happy. "What kind of work is he doing?"

"Oh, I'm near Bill's. He has this old farm with a bunch of outbuildings and so, there is a big pole barn where they keep supplies and work on projects, like those solar socks that I told you about."

"The wind socks!" Dave recalled the conversation, it had sounded interesting.

"Yeah. They are trying to build a matrix of them, but…it's complicated." Sally didn't feel like going into more detail, even though Lucas, Abuelo and Bill had spent a lot of time explaining it to her.

"It sounds like you are getting to know his family and friends. How are you getting along with everyone?"

"Good! Everyone knows each other here! There are so many Hispanic people, I don't remember ever being in a place that had so many people who look like me! And everyone is really nice to me!"

"That's good!" Dave was genuinely happy for her, but worried about her fragile ego. "Enjoy it! But, just remember, this is the honeymoon phase of your relationship, so don't make any major decisions until you've been able to get to know one another longer."

"I know. I remember our last session, I promise not to go too fast. And, it is kind of remote here. Lucas' mother doesn't like it at all!"

"Oh really."

"Yeah, and that's another subject, Lucas' mom," Sally lowered her voice and looked around to make sure she was still alone. "I met her late last night. I think she's an addict and maybe an alcoholic."

"That's too bad. Didn't Lucas warn you before you met her?"

"No, but we talked about it until late last night. I guess she would leave him with his grandparents and not come home for months and even over a year one time."

"That is sad. But, did his grandparents provided a stable home?"

"Yes. They are such nice people! Lucas was lucky to have them."

"Does he get along with his mother?"

Sally took a moment to answer, "Yes. But, it seems that she is 'out of it' most of time. He says that he only gets to talk to her in the mornings before she goes to work, after that she is pretty incoherent. Lucas worries that one day she won't come home because something bad will happen to her."

"That is sad, no matter how old you are."

They continued their conversation, with Dave trying to guide the topic back to Sally, but they ended their session early as it was beginning to rain.

"Stay indoors, there is a giant storm headed your way! It is pelting Flint with hail as we speak!" Dave explained as a parting warning.

The next day Daniel woke up feeling refreshed, abet slightly tired from his recent trauma. Ginger prepared his favorite breakfast of pancakes with lots of syrup and then, he sat down with a cup of coffee at his computer. He checked his bank account and frowned that the last deposit from his 'beggar app' wasn't even half of what it had been the day before and much less than it had been the day before that. He sighed and put on his headset, he needed to find out why.

He opened a portal that brought his 'handsome' Danial avatar into the RV version of New York city. The app brought him to the Statue of Liberty, he cursed then, brought down a menu and selected the shopping district where he had located his begging avatar. When he arrived he cursed again, as the first thing he saw was a begging avatar that looked very similar to his own. "God Damn it!" he shouted aloud, as he stomped past the thing. Then, he saw six more! All very similar but with a variety of ethnicity and clothing choices. Each of them held out cardboard signs with pleas for money and a code on it, as he passed by them. "Son of a Bitch!" he screamed as he made his way to the corner where his beggar was flanked by others on both sides, each holding their own pitiful sign. He stood a few feet away, hopping up and down and making animal sounds, other avatars and solids wearing AR lenses looked on curiously. Finally, some smart ass kid wearing lens, shouted out to him that he needed to seek therapy! This, made him so angry that he threw off his goggles and shouted to Ginger to get him a soda, even though he could feel his heart racing again, and he remembered his doctor telling him to lay off the sugar or become diabetic. "To hell with all of them!" he shouted to no one in particular.

Soon, Ginger was standing next to him with a cold bottle. "This is the last bottle of soda, we are also out of Rainbow Sweetie Cereal, but when I tried to place an order an unpaid bill prevented it," she explained. Daniel sighed and shook his head. "And, you have an appointment with David Williams," she continued. Daniel sighed again, at least the councilor was paid for, he grumbled. He had chosen Dave from a list provided by the hospital, as his name was one that he felt he could pronounce. It would be an online meeting and he had already fill out all of the forms required, so he returned the goggles to his face and opened up the portal to the counselor's waiting room. After a brief wait, a different window opened up to an average looking man, who was sitting at his desk. The man had his brown hair cut in a conservative length and style. From his camera angle, he looked a bit stocky, and was wearing a blue jacket over a simple, collared, light blue shirt. "Hello Daniel!" came a friendly greeting.

The 'handsome Daniel' avatar returned the greeting from a wood paneled office that featured a book case.

Dave made a face, then looked earnestly into the camera, "I encourage you to use your camera," he explained, "I want to get to know the 'real' Daniel, not an avatar."

"This IS the real me," he countered, "this is how I feel comfortable!"

Dave noticed the crack of emotion in his voice and made a note on his tablet before continuing. "Okay, but our next meeting is in person, don't you think it would be nice for me to be able to recognize you?"

Daniel had no intention of going to an in-person meeting, but decided not to argue the point. "I look like my avatar," he countered.

Dave made another notation, then looked up again, "I think the first thing we need to address is your physical health. According to your doctor, you are suffering from malnutrition, so I wanted to offer a food program. Every day a delivery of nutritional food would be delivered to you."

"What!" Daniel raised his voice, "I can't afford that!"

"No, it would be a prescription, and according to your information, your income level would qualify you to receive the meals at no charge," Dave explained.

"Free food?" Daniel asked, pleasantly surprised.

"Yes. It would be part of your overall health plan."

"Hmmm...when can we start that?"

Dave looked into the camera, "tomorrow, after your therapy."

It was in this moment, when Daniel decided to give the councilor a try. They continued the conversation with Daniel being uncharacteristically honest. They discussed Ginger and his voyeuristic obsessions. He liked how Dave was interested, but not shocked, by his exploits, he wasn't used to having a real person to confide in. He even told him the story about Ringo and the accidental theft of his gold ring. They laughed together! Daniel decided that he liked this guy, but he still had no intention of going to the next, in-person meeting, but by giving himself a week before the appointment, he would at least be able to get the free food for a few days.

After the appointment, Daniel had Ginger retrieve the gold ring from the bathroom so that he could assess it's worth with an app that could evaluate jewelry. The app explained that it couldn't identify if the gold was real, only advise carats based on color. It came out to 24 carats. "Hmmm..." he mumbled while turning the thick ring of gold in his hand. He then gave the piece of jewelry to the robot and told her to take it to a local pawn shop. He instructed her to wear her sparkly red dress and new shoes. "Always good to look your best in public," he reminded her.

She arrived at the storefront of a fairly new shop that Daniel had not frequented before. The inside was lined with shelves of a variety of items with tags on them. Against the back wall was a long glass counter with two men behind it. They were wearing identical shirts that featured a copy of the stores signage. The younger man's face had the familiar, deer in headlights, look when he noticed her. He mutely stepped closer to the counter, with his eyes locked on the beautiful red head. Then, the older man who had been examining a tablet, looked up to see Ginger stumble a bit. The older man pushed the younger one aside and reached out for Ginger's hand.

'Good, good...' Daniel muttered, noticing the tender look in the man's eyes as he gazed up at the beautiful robot. Ginger offered the man her hand, "oh thank you!"

"Not a problem," the older, balding man assured her as he stood up and took in the beautiful woman. "How can I help you?" he smiled.

"Well," Ginger began as she retrieved the gold ring from a small purse that she carried over her shoulder. "I have this 24 carat ring, that I don't wear anymore, and I wondered if you might be interested in buying it." She dropped the gold colored jewelry into the man's hand.

He looked down at it doubtfully. "I'm sorry, miss, but, this is just gold colored," he explained as he handed it back to her.

Daniel pushed out her lower lip a little, then looked up at the man, "are you sure?" Ginger put both of her palms down on the glass, then Daniel pumped up her breasts a bit and dipped down just enough so that the man would be sure to see down the front of her dress and notice that she was without undergarments.

The man flushed, Daniel could see that Ginger was having an effect. A buzzer sounded and another customer walked in, but the man's eyes were still locked on Ginger. "Ahh, yes, I'm sure, I see this stuff all the time," he mumbled.

Daniel squeezed a saline tear out of Ginger's right eye, "isn't there some kind of test or something? I mean, what if you are wrong? My app said it was worth $500," she sobbed in a pitiful voice.

The man handed her a tissue, which she accepted and dabbed at her face. He was silently assessing his options, and they were all lovely. "Listen, honey," he said while stroking her hair, "you want to come in to the office and maybe I could see if there is some way I could help you." Ginger nodded and let the man lead her to a door on his side of the counter. "What is your name, sweetheart?" he asked while he was holding the door open for her.

"Ginger," she answered, "what's yours?"

The man shut the door behind himself and directed her to a couch that was between stacks of clutter. The room was small, also containing a desk and a few folding chairs across from it. "You can call me Aldo!" he smiled. Daniel looked the old man up and down, he was of medium height and size, with a belly that occasionally peaked out from the bottom of his company tee. And below that, well, all that Daniel could make out was a dangling knot in his pants that hung a bit below his zipper. His thin fringe of hair was unnaturally dark, but was neatly combed into a pony tail that tapered to nothing just past his shoulders. There was nothing here that interested Daniel, but he was hungry.

"So, Aldo," Ginger began, stepping close to the man, "how much do you think it's worth?" Ginger asked looking deep into the man's eyes.

Aldo swallowed, "not much, but maybe we could...think of some way to add value?"

"$500?" Ginger offered, while pushing herself against him.

He made a humming sound, but before he could answer, he felt Ginger's hand on the little knot, that was now creeping closer to his zipper. "ummm...maybe," he considered aloud.

Ginger promptly let go, "okay, then let me see the money first," she smiled brightly.

Confused, but eager, the man pulled out his wallet and laid the bills on top of the desk, "$400, that's all I got!" the man confessed. Ginger grabbed his wallet and looked for herself to find that it was, indeed, empty.

She handed the wallet back to him, "ok, take off your clothes," she instructed before Daniel activated an erotic massage program that he, himself, often enjoyed.

Ringo's sleep was interrupted by a beeping sound. He sat up in bed and looked down at his nightstand where his communicator was sending an alarm. He grabbed the thing and pressed a button that opened a screen that displayed the front door of an apartment complex with a beautiful red head exiting it and on to the city sidewalk.

"Hot damn!" he shouted joyfully. He had employed a fairy from a horny acquaintance, that owed him a favor. Since then, he had been combing the city streets in search of the robot for more than a day, when he spotted her going into a pawn shop. He had the miniature drone wait outside until she re-emerged and he was able to follow her to this address, where she had spent the night! This was surely where the robotic beauty lived! So, he had confirmation on where she lived, now he just needed to figure out how to approach her without getting his arm in a sling.

He watched her walk down the sidewalk. This time she was wearing flats and didn't seem to have any problems with balance. She was beautiful. Her red hair blew gently in the breeze that she made, as her pace was quite brisk. Ringo had, of course, seen many a robot from afar, but they were still something out of the reach of even the middle class, so his humble means meant that he had no practical knowledge of them. But, as he watched Ginger, he knew that somehow, he had to have her. This particular her.

Daniel had an in person interview with his new therapist, so he was peeking in on Ginger's monitor with his headset on. Then, he noticed that low level buzzing sound again. Ginger stopped and looked around herself, but the noise stopped, so she continued on. That was the second time he had noticed the sound recently.

The office was in an old building downtown. It had a small flight of stairs with a little awning that sheltered the porch at the top. The door opened automatically, she walked down a small hallway to an elevator that she took to the second floor. Daniel wondered if the dull building and ancient elevator were indications that his new therapist lacked prestige. 'Hmmm...well maybe he'll be less stuffy and more agreeable than someone with a nicer office,' Daniel thought to himself. He was already nervous about the counselor's reaction when he saw Ginger had showed up for his appointment.

"Daniel? Daniel Schultz?" Dave, spoke into a speaker when he saw the female robot enter his waiting room.

Ginger located a small monitor near another door in the front of the little waiting room that they had just entered. Dave's face and torso appeared there. Ginger sighed, "sorry doctor, if I'm late!" she apologized with a smile.

"Daniel, you know that you were supposed to visit me in person! I thought you agreed," came a stern reply from Dave's image after he recognized the robot.

"Well, you know, I was still feeling under the weather and didn't want to take a chance of over exerting myself," Ginger explained sweetly.

"Your doctor wants you to walk for your torpid syndrome," Dave reminded him.

"But, there was this buzzing sound, yesterday and again today, I think it could be one of those robotic bees! I read that they escape sometimes and can kill you!"

Dave made a doubtful sound. "No, that's not true," he shook his head, "but listen, you can come inside my office now and we will talk about it." The little monitor went black and the door made a clicking sound before opening.

Ginger stepped into the cozy little room, where Dave was seated behind a desk in the far corner. He stood up and walked toward the robot with his hand extended toward a comfortable looking chair. When she sat down, he took a seat in an identical chair that faced it.

"Daniel, I need to insist that you come to your next appointment in person."

Ginger nodded in agreement.

Dave sat back and moved a small tablet from a nearby table onto his knee. Tapped it twice, then began his interview. "So, tell me, why didn't you want to go outside today? It's a beautiful day! You could be enjoying it!"

"Well, you know my agoraphobia makes it difficult."

Dave nodded and tapped on his tablet. "You have a very beautiful robot. Does she help you with everyday things or are you primarily using her as a surrogate?"

"Both!" Daniel was always happy to sing her praises, but it only happened on rare occasions.

"Why female? Is that the gender you identify with?"

"Hmmm...I consider myself transmorphic," Ginger answered thoughtfully.

Dave tapped his tablet again, this was a newer term for people who identified as objects, like robots or avatars. He looked at Ginger thoughtfully, "could you tell me why?"

"Well," he began, "for me, sex is more of a feeling than an organ or act. Sometimes, I get off more on the anticipation then sex itself! I like the adventure! I guess you could say that I'm kind of a thrill seeker! An adrenaline junkie!"

Dave nodded, "and you feel you have more freedoms in a robotic body?"

"Exactly! And, I'm always safe!"

Dave made more notes, this wasn't his first transmorphic patient. The term was still more commonly used by those who were addicted to virtual reality and preferred being an avatar, but as the price and availability of robots was causing them to become more common, so were the cases of people who identified as transmorphic.

Dave looked up from his tablet and focused on Ginger's camera eyes. "On your questionnaire, you list your mother as your only living relative. How is your relationship with her?"

"Good! I love my mother! She came to see me at the hospital!"

"How does she feel about Ginger?"

There was a pause, then finally Daniel answered, "She doesn't understand Ginger. You know, she's from the older generation and has issues with technology!"

Dave made another note. The rest of their conversation was pleasant, Dave noticed that Daniel seemed to enjoy talking about his antics as Ginger. By the end of the session Daniel had convinced his councilor to let Ginger sit in for him at their next appointment.

After Ginger left the room, Dave considered his new client. Addressing his physical problems was paramount, but the emotional ones, or did they even exist? How was it wrong that Daniel was choosing to live vicariously through a robot? Was he a harm to others? Well, Ginger did have a deadly punch, but, as long as Daniel wasn't using her to do violence, then, no.

Was Daniel happy? So far, his complaints were centered around economics, like most people. But, the isolation from other humans had to have negative impacts on his life, or did it? He still interacted with others, but as an avatar or robot. The missing component was touch, except from Ginger's synthetic skin. Dave pondered this for a few moments, then he tried to recall the last time he had touched a human. He rarely even shook hands, as it had become an old 'germie' custom. Surprised by himself, he realized that he couldn't recall the last time he had touched another human. Could science be making human touch obsolete?

Daniel was feeling happy as Ginger strolled down the sidewalk. He decided that he liked, Dave, his new counselor and would be enjoying their bi-weekly discussions. He noticed that same elated kind of feeling that he had when he went to confession. He sighed remembering how much he had enjoyed the ritual, right up until the priest forced him to confess that Ginger was a robot. It did help the priest to make sense of Ginger's confessions, but the minister also informed her that robots were forbidden in the confessional. It was an uncomfortable scene and Daniel hated making a scene, so they hadn't been to confession since!

But now, he had an unbiased confessor to tell his exploits to, and one he didn't have to pay for! Ahhh...socialized medicine!

Ginger was enroute to a nearby park, that she visited regularly, to recharge. She found an empty park bench where she sat down and removed her shoes, so that she could rub her feet in the dirt. Special plates on the soles of her feet extracted an electrical charge from the earth. The corners of her mouth turned up slightly, as there was something, almost akin to what a human would call, pleasure, that the robot experienced as her batteries recharged. It was as the robot was thus preoccupied, and gazing dreamily at the sun, when Ringo quietly sat down beside her.

He observed her for a few moments, marveling at the serine look on her face as she stared, unblinkingly into the horizon with her bare feet in the grass. She certainly was a marvel, he mused. "Well, looky here," he sang out in a friendly voice, "Ginger! Good to see you, girl!"

Daniel was otherwise occupied, but had her audio turned on, so that when he heard Ringo's voice he immediately enlarged her screen. He was suspicious that this wasn't a chance encounter.

Upon hearing her name, Ginger turned to look him in the face, as she awaited instruction from Daniel.

"Ringo, so good to see you! Sorry that I had to leave in such a hurry. I had an emergency," she explained.

Ringo shook his head and drew nearer to her. He reached out and put his hand over hers in a sweet way, "That's okay, no need to apologize! I love a woman who knows her own mind!"

He was talking in such a sweet voice and his long black lashes were all aflutter as he spoke to her. Daniel looked down at Ringo's hand and watched it reach for Ginger's shoulder. He wished that he had a body suit, so that he could feel that touch. It would be his next purchase, if he ever got caught up. He sighed, not knowing when that would ever be. He was barely able to scrape the money together for Ginger's loan payment. And it was important that he make those payments because he could never imagine life without Ginger, it wouldn't be worth living.

Ringo's face was near Gingers, "It's just that there was something that I wanted to talk to you about."

The first thing that came to Daniel's mind was the gold ring he had just pawned.

"You see," Ringo continued as he brushed a stray hair from Ginger's face, "I think you stole something from me!"

Ginger stood abruptly while Ringo looked up startled, "Wait! Don't go!"

"Listen dude, I don't know what happened to that ring!" Ginger said as she started to walk away.

"No! No! Wait! Come back and sit down. I'm not talking about a ring, I want to make you a business opportunity!" Ringo blurted out as he stood. He gently put both hands on her shoulders. "I don't care about no gold colored ring! I buy them by the dozen! I had real life bitches swallow those things, and let me tell you, nobody wants them back after that!" he chuckled in a disarming way while coxing her back to the bench.

They sat down, and Daniel was interested in Ringo's proposition. "No, the thing you stole from me, was my heart!" He pressed her hand to his chest and looked at her. "Ginger, Baby, what you did for me was amazing, girl! I think you could make some real money with just that one trick! And, I am the professional to help you out with your career!"

Daniel's mind raced, this was something he had contemplated before, but he lacked the human connections necessary. But, Ringo, was a professional! "Hmmmmm..." he muttered as he considered the details.

"Look here, sweetheart, why don't you come to a little party that I'm having tonight at the Eight Ball Motel, you know that place?" Ringo began giving Ginger instructions, "you want me to write it down on something?" he asked.

Ginger shook her head, "No, I'll remember. I know where the motel is. What time should I be there?"

Ringo smiled, he did not want to do anything to screw this up, so he gave her the information, tipped his hat and then bid her adieu, with a bit of a dip.

On the edge of the city sat an old, dilapidated motel with a broken sign. It may have been a grand place at one time, back in the days of random road trip with cars that required human drivers, but at this late date, it was mainly used to house the homeless who were fortunate enough to have money for the night.

For that evenings festivities Ringo had rented the 'suite,' which was actually two rooms with a door between them. He sat close to a large monitor on the wall with Sadie and two other men, they had a sports event on the screen, but were ignoring it as they sipped whisky and talked loudly, often laughing as Ringo explained the 'main attraction' that night, and what the gentlemen might expect.

Sitting on a couch with Sadie curled up next to him was Big Carlos, he was the loudest and the biggest at the gathering. He was a tough looking man who always wore a Stetson and sported several scars on his face, some of them intentional. Ringo's cousin, Kieth sat in another chair next to Ringo. He was a slim man with a drug problem and a nervous laugh.

Ginger had been keeping in contact with Ringo and he felt confident that she would be punctual, and she was. At a few minutes before eight o'clock he noticed her through the window, walking briskly toward the door. Big Carlos made an excited noise when he saw her as well. Ringo got up and answered the door.

"Well, hello, beautiful!" he sang out as he stood in the threshold holding the door open. She was dressed in her sparkly red dress and high heels. She smiled sweetly and shrugged shyly as she entered under his arm. "I sure hope those aren't your tipsy shoes," Ringo teased.

Ginger giggled, "no, these are within the recommended height requirements!" she explained.

When she entered the room, he introduced her to the other men as she had already met Sadie. Both men greeted her warmly. "Didn't I tell you that she was an absolute Goddess!" Ringo bragged as the men were clearly impressed, as well.

Ringo turned back toward Ginger. "Here, let me show you around," he said taking her arm and leading her to the door that separated the rooms. He pushed it open and the two stepped inside.

Ginger looked around herself and made a satisfied noise. "I think this will work well," she said with an agreeable nod. "Now, did you get a chance to look at the documents I sent you?"

"You mean the rate sheet?"

"Yes. I also listed my available services. Prices are the same for everything, you understand, right?" she said looking up in to Ringo's face. She waited for him nod in response, then continued. "You see, the fluid all collects into the same place, so it doesn't matter which opening it goes into." Ringo nodded again. "You understand that I do have a maximum capacity, so, based on some calculations I did, I should be able to service about 30 ejaculations before I'm at capacity."

Ringo nodded again, wide eyed, as her beautiful eyes and luscious lips were holding his attention, but her words were making him uncomfortable. "So you understand why I want to be paid per ejaculation, right?"

Ringo nodded again, so she continued. "Oh, and NO condoms! You know those things get sucked up into my plumbing...and well...," Ginger smiled broadly and then reached out a hand for him to shake, "I think this could work out nicely for both of us!"

After shaking his hand, she stepped next to the bed and pulled down one corner of the bedding. She then turned her back to the mesmerized pimp and pulled up her hair, "Could you unfasten my dress?"

He accommodated her request, but then ran his hand across her shoulder so that the dress fell to the floor. That was when Ginger turned back around to him and wagged her finger, "remember, I get paid per ejaculation!" she reminded him.

He nodded again, remembering that Big Carlos was ready and anxious in the next room, and he had promised him that he could be first, but her perfect breasts made it hard for him to leave. Ginger wagged her finger at him again with an impish smile.

Reluctantly, he went back to the other room and informed Big Carlos that she was ready for him.

Surprised, but pleased, the large man pushed himself off the couch and into the adjoining room. Ringo sat back in his seat as Keith and Sadie looked at him expectantly. He shrugged then looked up at the sporting event that was still playing on the overhead monitor. Shortly, they heard a loud animal like sound coming from the next room, then Ringo's communicator made an alarm sound. He looked at it, then up at Keith, "it's a message from Ginger!" he said as he opened the message to read it. "It says that Big Carlos wants to go again. Does he have credit?" The three looked at each other and then, Ringo put the thing to his mouth, "No!" Soon after there was a scuffling noise, then they observed Big Carlos moving quickly out of the neighboring room's door through their window. They saw his large frame stumbling, with his pants still around his knees as he fell onto the cement walkway. He rolled around on the ground and then righted himself, tugged at his trousers as he made his way toward the trio that he could see standing in the next units doorway.

"Hey," he started, as he was fastening his pants, "I gotta take care of some business at the pawn shop, and then I'll be right back!" He started to walk away, but then turned back and paused a moment to explain, "and let me tell you something," he said pointing at the next doorway, "when she says she needed to be paid in advance, per ejaculation, she is serious!"

Dave could only describe Ginger as radiant, as she walked into his office. He marveled at the robots realistic smile and the ease of her body movements as she automatically seated herself across from him, chatting the whole way.

"Oh, Dr. Williams, you don't know how wonderful it feels to have ALL of my bills caught up! And, in just one evening!" She went on cheerfully.

Dave, suddenly realized that he had missed part of the conversation, "Wait. I'm sorry, but how is it that you were able to pay all of your bills?" he asked.

"I have a new job!" she squealed, in the most feminine voice that Dave could ever imagine. "Well, it's more of a business," she mused, then looked back at Dave, "Ringo and I are business partners! I've become a prostitute!"

Dave's face must have betrayed his silence, as Ginger recognized it immediately as skepticism. "Oh, I know that even though it's been decriminalized, it's still a stigmatized profession, and cleaning up that mess is very, very, disgusting!" she complained, "but other than that, it's just such a perfect fit for me!" She stomped her feet a little to show her enthusiasm. That was what cause him to notice the jewelry she was wearing on her feet. It was a gold chain the wrapped around her second toe and then became an ankle bracelet, so that she was actually barefoot.

"What is this?" he asked pointing to her feet.

"Oh! Do you like them?" she asked, raising one foot closer to her camera eyes, she continued, "I bought myself a little gift. So now, I can go barefoot all the time and no one will notice!"

Dave nodded, remembering how he had read that the robots were now able to charge by contact with the Earth itself.

"Oh, and!" Ginger began, but paused to wait until she had made eye contact to make the announcement, "Ringo says that he has some friends in…Las Vegas!" she stomped again. "He said that we could go on a working vacation there and stay in a really nice place in a Casio! I am so excited! I've never been there!"

Dave couldn't help but be excited for her. He knew that it was inappropriate, and he chastised himself for loosing perspective. "Are you sure you will be safe with Ringo?"

Ginger just tilted her head and raised one eyebrow. "I'll be safe enough. And, ya' know," Ginger paused for effect, "I think Ringo is kind of sweet on me!" she giggled.

Dave loved the way her voice sparkled. He loved the way her synthetic hair framed her beautiful face. And that her eyes were like cut sapphires. He hoped Ginger was right. He hoped that Daniel could forever have enough money to make Ginger's loan payment.

So, what was his job here? He asked himself as he watched the beautiful robot go on and on in a happy, enthusiastic way.

The next day, Shannon found himself again in Paris. He had earlier been walking the streets, unsuccessfully, looking for targets, but as the daylight dimmed, his scanner took longer and longer to scan each face, so finally he had given it up altogether, and was now sitting at his favorite bench watching the pigeons interact with one another, in the shadow of the Eiffel tower.

He had received the happy news that the criminal that he had been stalking was captured, it still wasn't clear how much of the reward money would be his. But, it wasn't as if he was desperate for money, it was just that always looking for money was hard coded into his personality, something born of desperation, but it caused him to be anxious whenever he wasn't on some mission to obtain more. He reminded himself of this, and asked himself what his great plans were that he should leave this comfortable place. Something was holding him there. He looked up to the top of the tower, then noticed the pigeons were now flying overhead, going to wherever it was that birds went to spend the night.

He stretched and then turned to see the view in that direction. That was when he noticed a young woman standing behind him. She was wearing a white dress with large red dots on it. It came in at her waist, then billowed out in the wind, and tangled around her knees. Her, shoulder length, hair was dyed the same color as the red in her dress. She was standing still, all alone, staring at the tower, holding a small purse in one hand. Something about her seemed familiar. Shannon examined her face, she was wearing the hint of a sad smile, but her blue eyes were glistening as Shannon studied her face, he noted the water building up until a tear formed and rolled down the edge of her cheek. She clenched her jaws, then pulled her shoulder up and used it to brush the tear away. And that was when Shannon realized why she looked familiar.

He stood up and walked close to the woman. He examined her face closer, he looked down at her gloved hand for a familiar tattoo, but it was covered. He knelt down and began examining her legs for any signs of a scar. But then an other avatar shouted at him to stop being a pervert. The human in front of him was oblivious to the slander, but something made her pull her left glove off and examine her hand. This gave Shannon the opportunity to stand up and look for the tell tale black heart that he had been interested in finding. It was as though she was showing him the mark, though, she didn't even know herself as to why. She was just a woman on holiday, visiting the place she had wanted to see since she was a child.

"Vivian?" Shannon muttered to himself.

Sally and Joe ended up running in the rain to get back to Bill's place. It had quickly become a deluge, causing the tin roof and walls of the building to vibrate from the pelting. Sally stood with the men in a huddle, looking out a window, when she began to notice that water was seeping into the buildings from the outside edges of the walls. She pointed it out to Lucas, and then the men began working to pull important equipment away from the puddles and onto tables and counters.

Sally could tell that this was a problem that they had dealt with before. They explained to her that being located between the great lakes often caused big storms to come upon them quickly. Abuelo became animate that he left for home right away so that Abuela wasn't there alone. So, Lucas gathered up a small tarp for Sally and Joe to shelter under as they would be traveling behind him the whole way in their separate boats.

When they got to the pier, they found their boats, both had puddles of water in them. Abuelo's boat was larger with a small enclosed area. Lucas quickly hopped down into his boat and turned on a small electric pump that sucked the water out and behind the boat. He threw the wet blanket, that Joe had used as a bed, onto the pier, then unfolded and arranged the tarp for Sally and Joe to sit under. It was a downpour the entire time. Sally was drenched, but managing not to complain as she could see how quickly everyone was working. After she and Joe were sitting on their bench with only their heads peeking out, Lucas waved at his grandfather and then followed him into the choppy water.

Lucas had warned her that he'd be going faster on the return trip, and to hang on. When they sped up, the rain began to feel like little missiles, hitting her in the face, so she pulled her head under the tarp. She felt sorry for Lucas as he was also drenched, but with a pair of clear goggles on, he sped off, toward the, normally quiet, little canal.

She was relieved when they finally arrived at the little boathouse, rejoicing when she was able to toss the tarp off, but that was when she realized that they had been pelted with hail as it was flung on to the bottom of the boat. She and Joe ran out to find that the yard was muddy. They climbed up the stairs of the house carrying Lucas' bag, as he stayed behind to help his grandfather. After putting on dry clothes, she came back downstairs and sat on the couch with Abuela who was watching a weather report. The men came inside with parcels.

"Do you see that?" Abuela asked Sally as she pointed toward the monitor, "those poor people in the Appalachians were already dealing with an out of control forest fire and now there is this hurricane coming at them from the Atlantic and making its way up the coast! Right now Washington DC is being squeezed from both sides! Fire and water!"

Everyone gathered around the small monitor, listening intently to the reporter, who was shouting observations about the damage until he went off line. The moderator went back onscreen and explained that the storm was continuing it's slow migration up the coast, spawning tornadoes and storms that were making their way farther inland.

What they didn't completely understand at the time was that there was another wildfire that was out of control in Canada and had crossed into New York. The intense heat caused by the fires was feeding the hurricane at the top, while cold currents of melted glacier water were feeding it from the bottom and causing it to intensify into a mega storm.

Lucas had changed into dry clothes and combed his wet hair away from his face. He pushed his way between Sally and Joe so that he could cuddle Sally. The wind howled outside and caused the little house to tremble. Eventually, the signal to the television was lost, but the lights stayed on, as they were now on battery power.

They began playing a card game when there was an especially large thump that seemed to come from the porch side of the house. They jumped up and looked out of the window. The yard was completely submerged now. Then, they all heard and felt another thump, it was coming from a large dark mass that was bobbing in the water next to the pillars that the house sat on. Whatever it was, was threatening the stilts of the house. Sally squinted into the storm, trying to identify the object, to realize that it was her car!

Several miles away Dave Williams is sitting alone in his office. He sat back in his overstuffed office chair with a glass of wine and was watching the storm outside as it blew torrents of rain down the vacant city streets. "Audio file newest recording of Ollie memoir," he shouted out, in the empty room.

Soon, he heard his own voice, "Ollie, I know you are always looking for the good in whatever happens. What good came from the Attack?"

There was a short pause then a gruff but thoughtful voice answered. "The importance of human interaction. We had become a society of people who were living alone, together. But, that had to change, if only temporarily, after the Attack. We had to meet with each other in person and make plans, pull our resources together and we did that! Here we are! But, I'm afraid we are slipping back to those same problems that stem from isolation. And that's a shame."

Then, another short pause before he heard Ollie's voice again. "But still, I do credit that tragedy with pulling us closer together. In fact, I do think it is part of the reason for our current trend in multi-generational living. At first it was out of necessity, but then people realized that it was better. The whole reason it was shamed in the first place was because it was less profitable. No, people need people.

Oh, and another good thing the Attack caused was that it gave us a common purpose. It got us talking and planning about important environmental issues, too. Together, we figured out what needed to be done and how to do it! It gave us a clear directive. We were saving our families, our country, our planet, together.

Liam fidgeted with the new body suit that he had just put on. The fabric was thick and rubbery, but the inside layer was made of a material that allowed the user to select their preferred temperature. It was produced by a company that was partnering up with Ian Moore, to get their endorsement for using the suits with software that allowed avatars to feel one another. It was adding one more layer to VR and RV technology. Currently, Liam was planing to try it out in Remote Viewing with Laura. He had sent her one, as well, under the guise of research, that they would be conducting together.

The two considered themselves a 'couple,' but the only time they were alone was in virtual reality, as Laura's robot, Pamela, was always in tow. Although, Laura felt confident to the contrary, Liam didn't trust the robot, with her camera eyes, being in the room with them. He found it difficult to believe that, unlike his father, her parents weren't constantly eavesdropping.

So, now they would be meeting in a more intimate setting. Liam had set up cameras in his VR room that would work with special software that instantly converted video into a VR format. Laura would be visiting him there from the privacy of her bedroom. He was anxious to see how well the suit converted the real time data of Laura touching his avatar into tiny warm shocks that he would be able to feel instantaneously.

He gave himself one more look in the mirror and made a slight adjustment to the long, top hairs on his blond head. Then, left his room, followed by his dog, Howler, they walked down a long hallway to a stairway that brought them to a lower level. He noticed Arthur busy cleaning something.

"Arthur, I would like to be alone in my study and would not like to be disturbed by anyone." Arthur stopped in mid motion, turned his head toward his ward and nodded that he understood before returning to his task.

This was a very old joke that Liam was in the habit of making, as he had spent nearly all of his young adult life in the rambling old mansion, void of any other living human. He truly was, 'that kid who was raised by a robot,' as he had always been known.

He passed the marbled floor of the grand entryway, and then pulled open the two tall, wooden doors of the old study. The center of the inside wall was decorated with an ornate mantelpiece over a fireplace, and maple wood gleamed from the floor as well as the wainscot that covered the walls half way up. It was still the beautiful room that his grandfather had known, except, now the fire inside the fireplace was always a hologram, and aside from a sofa and a soft, white, sheepskin rug, the room was left empty, so that technology could make it anyway Liam wanted. Today, it would just be as it is, since he was expecting Laura's avatar to be visiting him.

He bent down to pet Howler on the head and then put on his goggles and made himself comfortable on the sofa where he watched the realistic flames, waiting for Laura. He loved this place and the way the imaginary flames flickered. It always calmed him and helped him think. So, that was what he did, until he was surprised by the feel of a warm hand on his shoulder. He turned around to see Laura in a beautiful, burgundy gown.

"How lovely!" he whispered to her as she stepped out from behind the sofa and onto the white rug. She then made herself at home on his couch, sitting with one leg crossed under herself, so that the two were facing one another.

"This is fun! Did you feel me?"

"Why yes, yes I did." Liam answered, nodding his head.

Laura giggled, "I could tell by the way you turned your head right away. I guess these suits work."

"Oh, no, no, we have lots of stuff to test yet!" Liam protested as he grew nearer her avatar. He reached out and stroked the upper arm of Laura's avatar, "Do you feel this?"

Laura nodded, "yeah, I do."

Liam looked at her playfully, "how about this?" He asked while pushing the strap of her gown off her shoulder.

Laura had followed his hand as it gently pushed the silky fabric, letting it fall half down her upper arm. She gasped, "I think I did!"

Liam made the sound of an engineer testing software, "It could be that you are feeling it because of visual clues. Close your eyes."

She did, he waited a moment then he hovered over her so that he could tease down the other strap. "Did you feel that?" he asked, close to her face.

She laid her head against the sofa with her eyes closed, "yeah, I think I did."

Liam continued to pull at the imaginary fabric until her bare breasts were showing. He slid his hand across them. "How about this?"

Laura giggled and opened her eyes, "yes!"

Their faces were close together, the impulse to kiss was strong. "If only they could make this stuff for lips!" he complained. Then he sat up, "Yes! I could suggest a face mask! We could offer it as an add on!" Then, he resumed his previous pose. "I've made a mental note, now back to research!" He moved his focus to her breasts and then rubbed his face against them. She giggled and writhed. "You see," he continued, "if I was wearing a face mask, and I bit you like this," he said before biting at her nipples, "then I could feel it too!"

"Yes. Yes. I like doing research!" Laura laughed, wiggling because of the tickling sensation.

They played at their research until the couple decided that they wanted something to drink. Liam raised his head and called out, "Arthur."

Laura shook her head. "He is not going to hear you."

"Yeah, he will, my robot has an excellent sense of hearing!" Liam bragged. "You wait, any moment he will open those doors and ask what I want."

"Okay, we'll see," she said, sipping a glass of something that Pamela had handed her.

But, moments later, there was a small clicking noise that the doors made when opening, then a very loud barking erupted from Howler. Liam chuckled. "Arthur bring me a glass of wine," he shouted over the racket.

The barking stopped as Arthur shut the door, but then began again as soon as he re-opened it, bringing a glass.

Liam accepted it then instructed Arthur to dress Howler in his VR goggles.

"But, Liam, the dog runs from me, then bites me while I try to strap them on," Arthur protested.

Liam sighed, "Okay, just bring them here. I'll do it," he shouted over the din. Arthur brought the goggles, then Liam had an idea, "Arthur can you see Laura here beside me?" he asked.

"Yes. And behind her is another avatar."

Liam sat up. "What?" He looked behind the sofa, then addressed Arthur again. "Who are they? Why can't we see it?"

"It is of alien technology. Now they are gone."

Liam looked a bit alarmed, "Okay, that's it. You can go," he shouted, "in fact, please go!"

He and Laura had been laughing at the dog's dislike for Arthur and, when Arthur shut the door the dog became quiet. Liam began pulling on his lip, wondering what Arthur was seeing that he couldn't. The VR alien spottings had not stopped, in fact, itvwas becoming a sizable percentage of the complaints that his companies technicians had been dealing with. But, he didn't want to talk to Laura about this. It was a matter that he needed to discuss with his father.

Howler jumped up onto the sofa where Laura was sitting. Liam pulled him onto his lap so that he could apply his special made goggles.

"Interesting that Arthur can see me without a headset," Laura mused. "What do you think he was talking about, another avatar behind me?"

"I thought he would be able to see you, but just wanted to check. Not sure about a second avatar, I'll have to check the programs security," he pulled himself closer to her avatar, "but, I'll worry about that later."

He touched his wrist and pulled down a menu, then opened a portal for the three of them that took them to their favorite cyber cafe'. They pulled golden chairs up to their favorite table, then looked around the place for familiar faces. When they noticed Taylor sitting at a table across the room from them, he waved. But, he was in a conversation with someone who had their back to them, but Liam and Laura both recognized the avatar of Violet. Liam shook his head, then turned his attention to Laura.

"So, when are you going to come over again?" He reached over to stroke her arm, "for real!"

Laura squirmed a bit, as the synthetic touch was ticklish. "Yeah, we could do that."

Liam locked eyes with her, "no, not we, just you. I could send my transporter for you and then, you could leave Pamela at home."

Laura hunched up her shoulders and sighed as Liam was sending little warm shocks up and down the inside of her arms. It was a distraction, but even then, it was hard for her to imagine going anywhere without her robot. Her parents had purchased it when she was a toddler. It had been her nanny and constant companion since she could remember. Even when it was between tasks, its rest position was near

Laura. That was the way her parents had programmed the machine. "Why don't you like Pamela?"

"It's not that I don't like her." Liam was sympathetic to Laura's feelings for her robot. "Maybe, she could just stay in the other room, hang with Arthur." Howler jumped onto his lap, so he began stroking the animal.

Laura smiled, still under the influence of the body suit. "Okay, maybe this weekend. I have lots of school work."

Liam nodded, then out of curiosity asked, "Did Pamela go to school with you?"

"Yes. In fact, my father worked hard to pass the law allowing robots in classrooms. He made the point that robots could act as security guards and he wanted to mandate one to every school, until those SAIN, (Stop Artificial Intelligence Now), people organized these protests and spray painted in red all over his office!"

"Oh, so you have a beef with those people too!" Liam said, recalling the red letter message they had sprayed on the brick wall that surrounded his home.

"Yeah, it was really rude. I don't know why they do that!" They both glanced back at Violet, to see that she was still sitting with Taylor.

Taylor waved at them again then got up and moved to their table. "Hey! What are you guys up to?" He asked cheerfully, even though he was aware that they had both been giving him the evil eye.

"Just working on stuff," Liam said dryly. "So, are you and Violet a couple now?"

Taylor sighed. "She's really a good person, Liam, you should get to know her better." Liam just stared back at his brother without expression. "You know, they all think that it was you who took down the Assassin App..."

Liam waved off the conversation, "Just stop. You know she is a security risk. The only reason she ever talked to you was to get to me! Quit talking to her! She is an anarchist! I don't want her knowing ANYTHING about anything! You understand!" His voice became uncharacteristically loud. Violet along with several other avatars were looking at them. Liam looked around himself and noticed the attention. "Let's get out of here! Meet us on Mars!" He said in a low voice before opening a portal and pulling the four of them through it. He hugged Howler, who was still on his lap, as they found themselves on flycycles, orbiting the red planet. Laura and then Taylor were following behind him on separate cycles.

He started looking down at the planet below him for Cydonia. He was trying to push the anger out of himself by concentrating on something else. He continued to scan the planet until he noticed the Arandas crater and then, the Bamberg crater, and between them, the famous face on Mars. He turned and motioned for the others to follow him down, then he landed next to the huge mountain of a landmark where they gathered together.

"I think we should convert these flycycles into fat tired all terrain vehicles!" Liam said as he looked out at the vast red desert in front of them. They changed out their vehicles and then charged across the sand dunes, speeding to the top of one dune to find themselves free falling down the other side and into a crater. They were all shouting and laughing when they hit bottom and then sped off again toward the craters rim.

Laura felt giddy watching Liam recklessly speed and then climb the nearly vertical crater wall, the sound of his laughter made her want to be next to him. Then, Liam was a bit surprised when he felt her arms gently wrap around him from behind. The body suits were a great success. Liam turned and stroked her avatar arms up to her shoulder as they were falling down a red Martian sand dune together. But, all Liam could think was, 'if only I could get her alone without that damn robot.'

That night, after the friends had disbanded, Liam pulled off his goggles and became aware of the nausea that he was suddenly feeling. "Arthur, I need a motion sickness tablet!" he shouted toward the holographic fire, as he unfastened the tight fitting, body suit that he was still wearing.

Soon, he heard the clicking sound of the door handle, but without the barking, as Howler now lay next to him on the sofa, sleeping soundly. Arthur appeared in front of him, holding out a glass of water in one hand, and in the other was a small white pill. Liam accepted the pill and glass, looking thoughtfully at Arthur. "Say, Arthur, what did you mean, earlier, when you said that you saw an avatar behind Laura?"

"There is an entity that might be stalking you."

"How did they get into this new system? It's closed?"

Arthur paused, "I am checking security files now. I am not familiar with the technology being used."

"Well, now, that's interesting," Liam mused. "Keep me informed! Oh, and what did the avatar look like?"

"I find it hard to describe, maybe similar to how you perceive water? That is how the avatar looked, without defined features."

"You said, alien, why did you use that word?"

"Because the technology is unlike any that I have encountered among earthlings."

Liam became very interested, "Arthur, have you ever encountered alien technology before?"

"Yes."

"Explain."

"I became aware that large amounts of information was being downloaded at regular intervals, of approximately, once a month. The data appeared to be downloading without a known target."

"What type of data?"

"Mostly, historical, but also current technical files that are publicly available."

"Have you told anyone else about this?"

"No."

Liam was becoming agitated, "Send a full report to me and also my father, classified. Also, Arthur, do you believe you can pinpoint where the entity is, when they are directing the download?"

"I am currently trying to do this."

"Let me know as soon as it happens," Liam instructed before waving the robot off, and then laying against the back of the sofa, rubbing his belly.

The next morning at breakfast Liam instructed the robot to sit down at the table with him. "Any new insights into where the data dumps are being directed?" he asked between bites.

"I cannot extrapolate where the data is being sent to. It is likely an off planet site."

"Like a satellite?"

"Yes, but something father from our planet then any know satellites. The distance is causing the problem in determining it's location."

"How about the identity of the entity who is facilitating the downloads? Could you locate their position?"

"Yes. I've been able to identify the area. It is from a location not far from here. I also have ascertained that the individual is likely the avatar who has been stalking you."

Liam chuckled, "Convenient. I think we should not allow this entity to know that we are becoming aware of it."

"It already knows. It became aware when I told you of it's avatars existence."

"Should we try to communicate with it?"

Arthur paused, then said, "I don't know."

Liam became enraged, "Oh, god damn it, dad!" he shouted in the robots direction. "Common, work with me to solve this! I'm the one who had Arthur send you the report in the first place!" The robots use of the term 'I don't know,' caused Liam to be immediately aware that his father was censoring Arthur's responses. He was sure that the current conversation was being listened to, as well. That was why he had began addressing his father on the other side of Arthur's camera eyes.

"Your father wants to meet with you immediately in his office," was the response that Arthur relayed.

Liam abruptly stood up and headed toward the study. He put on his goggles and opened a portal to his father's waiting room, where a large Ian Moore company logo briefly filled his view. Then, young Allen appeared behind his desk with a very sober look on his face. The situation was critical, but his son's raised voice and defiance was a new development that he wasn't happy about, either.

"Listen Liam! I'm sorry to shut you out of this, but you cannot be discussing this with anyone! You are aware of the security risks that you have been taking lately! And that entity is stalking you! They are using tech that we don't understand!" Allen blurted out before Liam could complain.

Liam took a deep breath to calm himself, and then, did his best Arthur impersonation. "Okay, that's fair. But, now, tell me what you know." He looked very determined at his father, it was a piercing glare that reminded Allen of his own father from long ago, a look that he was no longer accustom to, not from anyone. But, he complied.

"First off, I have to tell you that I have been in communication with ARTHUR1 since I received the report last night, trying to sort this out! We can't determine their capabilities. So far, the information that they are downloading is public. But, the ease in which they were able to hack into your home video system, makes me incredibly nervous." He stared Liam down, "of course my main concern is that they might try to hack into ARTHUR1."

"Have you confirmed that they are alien to the planet?"

Allen sighed, "This information is being transmitted to an unknown destination, a satellite or something that is orbiting well beyond any known satellites. If they are Earthlings, then they have extraordinary equipment. Why would anyone go to all that trouble and expense to download information that was readily available to them on Earth?"

"There is the question," Liam surmised." Why would an outside entity want public information, unless they were just studying us. Doing research. Their interest in me must be centered around my access to ARTHUR1."

"Liam you might be interacting with them now, unknowingly," Allen pushed. "That Taylor, or your girlfriend, Laura, they could have been compromised without knowing it themselves. You can never tell who is behind an avatar."

Liam found it interesting that his father knew his girlfriend's name. Then, he thought about how Arthur described the alien's avatar, like water. "So far, they don't appear to have malicious intent. Maybe we should consider communicating with them."

"Very dangerous! Very dangerous!" Allen muttered, shaking his head.

Liam looked at his father's avatar, wondering how he really looked. He sounded fatigued. "Maybe you should get some rest, then we could meet again."

Allen became angry, "What are you telling me? Are you suggesting that I take a nap and call you in the morning! Do you understand the gravity of this situation?"

Liam, was taken aback by his father's eruption of anger. It was difficult for him to understand since he, Arthur and his father had, had many a discussion on the probability of life beyond Earth. Why was he so upset that, this life, was now interacting with them. "Then, do we wait for it to try to communicate with us? Monitor it?"

Allen nodded his head. "Yes. I think that would be best." Then, his avatar took on a more relaxed look, "just keep your eyes peeled, all the time. I'll do the same, and Arthur can monitor their activity."

"I want information as soon as it comes in," Liam insisted. Allen nodded.

It was soon after this that Allen dismissed his son. He stood up and found a bottle that sat on a nearby cabinet and refilled a glass. Before he could take a drink a sudden dizzy feeling made him sit down in the nearest chair. That was when he noticed weakness in his knees. "Barnabas!" he shouted. His robot stepped out from the wall, where he stood in default. "Bring me something to eat," Allen said weakly, "bread and cheese!" The obedient metal man, Arthur's twin, turned to retrieve the requested food.

Allen watched him walk away and sighed, then noted the time. He needed to get himself together, he had a VR appointment in less than an hour to speak to an alien.

Allen sat back in his chair with his eyes closed, he consciously considered the muscles in his neck and shoulders and willed them to loosen. He took a deep breath, then slowly opened his eyes again. He tried to put the significance of the approaching meeting out of his mind, and try to consider it a business meeting, something that he was most comfortable with. He slipped on his goggles. The room looked as it had before, but now he might be able to see the alien avatar that he was expecting, but he really wasn't sure what form that it would take. So, he sat quietly, staring at the nothing in front of him.

Then, Barnabas stepped away from the wall, "your next appointment is waiting."

Allen took a small sip from his glass before answering, "I'm ready."

Then, there, where all Allen's guests appeared, materialized a white haired old man in bib overhauls. Allen was surprised, he had expected some kind of puddle. He quickly guessed that the avatar had been chosen to make a human feel at ease. And for some reason, it did.

"Please sit and be comfortable," Allen motioned for the avatar to come closer and sit across from him at his desk. He looked around himself, then pulled a golden chair up to the desk. Allen found himself looking deep into the smiling blue eyes of the avatar.

"You can call me Jak."

Allen was mute. This was not the entity that he had expected. But, then he found himself staring, "uh...Allen."

"Allen," the gentle voice repeated, "I was contacted by ARTHUR1, seems I've been detected!" he chuckled.

Allen was having an uncharacteristic bout of awkwardness, "Um, yes, we noticed the downloads of information and wondered where it was going? Why it was going..."

Jak brightened, "I'm a historian. My people collect historical information from all cultures. It is being added to our database. I hope I didn't break any laws," he chuckled again. "I believe it's all public information."

Allen nodded. "Where," he started hoarsely, then took another drink, "Where is it going?"

"It's being relayed off a series of satellites to my home planet."

Allen didn't know what to say, he believed the old man, "what about your spying on my son?"

Jak looked away for a moment before answering, "Liam is a bright young man! And he is next in the line of succession, I believe."

Allen nodded in agreement, then scolded himself.

"Don't worry, I have no evil intent. But, the truth is that I did want to meet with him. I think it would be good for us to get to know one another. I have some important business that I would like you both to be involved in." He looked away thoughtfully, then returned his gaze to Allen, "But, how about if you and I meet in person first!" He nodded his head as though he had just made the determination, "yes, I think that would be most productive."

Allen silently nodded again.

"Good! Let's set that up." He started to stand, then sat back down, "oh, and how about if you bring the original Arthur? You know, I'm a big fan!"

Allen smiled back and nodded again, before the avatar disappeared. He was in a kind of shock after his VR meeting with the alien. He kept running different scenarios in his mind. Was this a trap?, was his first thought, but deep inside him, somehow, he just knew that the offer was genuine and that it was urgent for the two of them to meet again. Something important needed to be discussed, and Allen was eager to find out what it was.

Liam was surprised when Arthur announced that Allen would be visiting. It had been several months since his last visit. Liam assumed that it had to do with the alien, but nothing had been explained before the electric plane landed in the field next to the house. He was with Arthur in the yard to watch it land.

When his father emerged from the plane, Liam still felt that stab of excitement. He loved his father, as children always do. The feel of his hand when they shook, caused the same warm feeling to run through his body that he would get when he was a child.

Allen walked into the study and looked around the room, "Where is the fucking furniture? Don't ya' have a chair or something in here to sit on?"Liam just shuffled in behind him and gestured toward a sofa that faced the fireplace, while Arthur located a comfortable chair. Allen sighed and walked over to the sofa, and then sat to the far end, as it wasn't a very long sofa, anyway. Liam sat next to him, so there wasn't too much of a space between them. For some reason, Allen was feeling a bit intimidated by his son. It was a new feeling for him, that bitter sweet feeling you get when you realize that your child is no longer dependent on you. But also, for Allen, this level of competence was the very thing that he had programmed Arthur to instill, so Liam was his talent manifest into a handsome man, that only the best science could have produced.

Liam was beginning to feel uncomfortable as his father was staring at him. "What did you want to talk about?" Allen noticed the absence of Arthur's black metal charging chair, "where's Arthur's chair?" he asked.

Liam shrugged, "He doesn't need it anymore. So, he took it away." Allen looked disappointed, "Oh, you know, I can remember when you were just a little kid, you loved to sit on Arthur's lap, in that thing!" He chuckled at the memory, "yeah, when you were a baby, the only way I could get out of the room was to put you in his arms and let you cry until you fell asleep."

Liam could easily recall many incidences like that. So, it made him ask, "why didn't you want to hold me till I fell asleep? It was always Arthur."

"Well..." Allen stuttered, "I didn't want to interfere with your bonding." Liam looked long and hard at his father. There it was, he was created to be the best that his father's intelligence and money could create. His success was the success of the Ian Moore Company.

Then, using his best Arthur impersonation, Liam answered, "But, I would have preferred you to hold me."

Allen looked away, now uncomfortable with the memory. Maybe he wasn't the perfect father, but he had been the best that his new science had dictated. Every aspect of Liams birth and rearing had been a careful calculation.

"Well, son, now that you are an adult, there are some things that I need to make sure you understand."

"I thought we were going to discuss the alien."

"No, no, not yet. I have ARTHUR1 monitoring the situation, but there hasn't been any new developments," Allen lied. "But, this whole thing has got me thinking of my own mortality, son. I'm not sure if you are aware of the protocol that I've installed in ARTHUR1's programming." Allen began, in his elaborate rues, since, as he was speaking, Barnabas was quietly taking Arthur's place in the kitchen.

"Hard coded in ARTHUR1's programming is a copy of yours, as well as my DNA," Allen continued. "When I pass, control will go to you, and then your descendants."

"What about your other children?" Liam asked, embarrassed as this was a taboo subject.

Allen sighed, "Only if you pass childless."

Liam made a slight nod to show that he understood.

Allen reached out and touched his arm to get his son to look him in the face, "so, you see how important it is for you to produce a proper heir. No, thoughtless mistakes! You know how important it is to have a competent person in charge of ARTHUR1. Things could go south in a hurry with someone less sober, less even tempered and competent. And, it's a matter of DNA, so any illegitimate, mutt, could grab power if you aren't careful, all of the time!"

Liam understood, no mistakes. But, with a defiant look at his father, he vowed to himself that he would never raise a child as he had been raised. Allen was worried about that gleam in his son's eyes, he wasn't sure what it meant. "I understand," Liam answered.

Then Allen leaned toward his son and in a hushed voice explained, "Another thing that we need to discuss in more detail involves ARTHUR1's programming. You know, my father was concerned that a malfunction could occur, with the potential of loosing control. He built a kind of back door into ARTHUR1's code, a subroutine that was REMed out, but if activated, it would completely delete all traces of ARTHUR1 online."

Liam nodded, he knew about the secret coding, but it was not to be discussed, it was the biggest secret that only Liam and his father knew existed. "We will get together again, in person, and I'll show you how to locate that bit of code from a stand alone device." He didn't want to leave his son on such a somber note, so he smiled brightly, "everything okay with you?"

"Yeah."

"Good!" Allen slapped his knees as he stood up, "now, I have to go, I've got a meeting in Chicago," he lied. Liam followed him out of the room and then through a set of patio doors that led to a small court yard. They walked passed a marble bench with an arbor of green vines growing over it. Then to a meadow that featured a carefully manicured airstrip. Small, solar powered, robotic mowers were at work as they approached.

"Arthur!" Liam shouted, looking around himself.

Allen reached over and put a hand on Liam's shoulder worried that his son might have noticed something suspicious, "What's wrong?"

"The mowers..." Liam muttered while holding a hand to shade his eyes as he looked for his robot. "Why hasn't he called them home so that you can take off?"

As soon as Liam said the words, the mowers moved toward the far edge of the airstrip. "There we go!" Allen said cheerfully. "Come here and hug me and then I'll be off," Allen said awkwardly.

The hug was awkward as well, but they got through it and Liam bid his father farewell.

As soon as Allen was seated next to an already belted in Arthur, the robot asked, "Why are we deceiving Liam?"

Allen pressed a 'ready to proceed' button, from the console of the small craft. Then turned to the robot, "I didn't want to chance a security leak."

"Why do you feel the need to satisfy this entities request?"

Allen sat back in his padded seat, as the ship was beginning to move forward. He sighed, thinking of an answer to the robot's last question, but it seemed to take too much of an effort. "I don't know!" he muttered.

Liam watched the plane depart with that same sad feeling he had, every time it happened. Current events seem to be amplifying the melancholy, but, then, he recalled something that pushed the sad cloud away, Laura had promised to come over that evening. He smiled up at the blue sky.

On his journey back to the house, he paused at the marble bench and the grapevines that covered the deep arbor. He loved to play in here when he was a child. He examined an especially large leaf. Then, noticed the little green grapes that were clustered under it. This reminded him about Arthur's special wine. "Arthur!" he called out, still examining the vines. When the robot failed to appear, he called out in a louder voice, "Arthur!" then he sighed and walked back through the patio doors.

"Arthur!" he called out again.

Finally, the robot appeared coming out from the kitchen.

Liam looked scornfully at him, "I want you to find two of your best bottles of wine from the cellar. I don't care what the recommended temperature is, I want them chilled and available in the study by 8 pm when Laura is expected to arrive."

The robot continued to stand mutely in front of Liam for several seconds, then asked, "best, by what criteria?"

Liam was growing increasingly annoyed with the robot. "I don't know what your scheme is… I want you to go down to the cellar and choose the best 2 bottles of your wine, your homemade wine," he explained.

But the robot continued to stand mutely, then repeated a few of Liam's words for clarification, "my scheme?"

"Yes. Yes. You know, that special light you made. I want you to use it to pick out the best two bottles of wine." The robot continued to stare at Liam, who finally pushed past the robot and into the kitchen, where he retrieved the device from a pantry. It was a slim glass tube with a cord attached to it's metal casing. He handed it to the robot, while looking at him curiously. "Arthur, are you alright? Run a diagnostics on yourself too."

"Yes," replied Barnabas, as he communicated with Arthur for instructions on how to use the device in his hands.

At about 7:45 Liam stepped out onto the balcony off his bedroom. He took a seat with a view of the driveway. He had showered, shaved, and even applied a light scent to his face and neck. He happily anticipated Laura's arrival. Howler whined from a place near his feet. He looked down at the dog and then allowed it onto his lap, even though he worried about the smell.

When he noticed the top of her tall transporter above the trees that lined his drive, he sprinted inside, down the flight of stairs, and into the transporter room, so that he could be standing in front of her when her transporter door slid open. He ran his fingers through his hair one last time, just as Laura became visible from behind the upwardly sliding door. He tried to find a less cheerful pose, but found himself wearing a smile to spite himself. Then, behind Laura's diminutive stature, arose the tall, pale and imposing figure of Pamela.

Liam decided that he should greet Laura as was their custom in virtual reality, so he reached out his hands and held hers, slightly pulling her forward toward him so that they could meet the others lips. It was so magical. Liam loved feel of her little hands with their delicate fingers, and her elfish stature that caused him to bend down, and rub his face slightly, in her soft curly hair till he found her lips and they kissed. Then, he embraced her. He folded her gently in his arms, like she was a fragile vessel of air.

"Real life is such an improvement over virtual reality," he mused aloud still holding his sweetheart.

When they broke apart and began walking to the main part of the house, Liam noticed that Pamela followed behind them. He tried not to look disappointed, he knew from personal experience how anxious Laura felt when her companion wasn't nearby. But, she had promised to make the robot stay in another room, that evening, and he would make her keep that promise.

"So, have you eaten yet?" Liam asked, still holding her hand as they walked toward the entrance.

"Not too long ago."

"Ah...then we can wait till later and then have a desert!" Liam suggested. "So now, would you like to go exploring again in the house, like we did last time? Or, would you prefer to visit somewhere, I know that a new planet has been brought online."

"Oh, yes, I heard about the new planet! Let's go there! It's supposed to be a gas planet!"

Liam brought her to the closed doors of the study. He opened one of the doors for Laura to pass thru, but then stepped in front of the opening when Pamela began to follow. "Pamela, you are to remain outside," he instructed before closing the door.

Laura giggled out of nervousness, she remembered the conversation they had, and the promise she had made about them being alone without a robot.

Pamela obediently found a spot against the wall on one side of the door. Liam noticed Arthur standing on the other side, in an unnatural, for Arthur, stance. This made him curious, as the robot had been acting strange all afternoon, but he was preoccupied with other matters at that moment, and simply shut the door.

Laura was waiting inside the room, looking at him curiously as he shut the doors. "I'm so surprised that Pamela didn't push her way in and confirm with me where she was to stand."

Liam smiled slyly, "she will always obey me before you, they all will, they all know me."

Laura stood there a moment, looking at him, wondering how it was that she was with such a powerful man. She knew that this was one of the reasons why her parents were so interested in her new boyfriend, they seemed to be encouraging the relationship, even though they had never met Liam. It wasn't just the money, but the power.

She suddenly felt embarrassed and looked around herself nervously until, she noticed Howler asleep on the sheep skin rug, in front of the fireplace. "Oh, how cute!" She squealed, happy to have the new distraction, she sat on the edge of the sofa so that she could touch the animal's belly, as he was laying on his back, snoring. Liam sat nearby to watch the two interact. Howler awoke and wagged his tail happily accepting the attention.

"Is he going with us?" Laura asked.

"Oh, yeah," Liam replied while looking around for Howler's goggles. "Arthur!" he called out.

As soon as the robot opened the doors to the study, the little dog began barking at the metal man. But, the robot ignored the dog and retrieved a small set of goggles from a desk drawer.

Liam looked at him mischievously, "aren't you going to put them on him?" he asked with a wink to Laura. But, then, to Liam's surprised, instead of protesting, the robot walked toward the barking dog, holding out the goggles.

Howler easily evaded the robot, barking madly and then diving at the robot's ankle and attaching himself to the right one, growling. Liam was surprised that the robot was still trying to apply the headgear even as the dog was biting him.

"That's ok Arthur, I'll do it," Liam offered, and then, accepted the goggles into his hand, with the robot dragging the dog behind him. He pried the animal from the robot and then held him in place over his protests, and dismissed the metal man so that he could more easily manage the dog.

They opened a portal as they mounted the flycycle with Howler taking his usual spot in the front. It felt wonderful when Laura reached around Liam and hugged him from her seat behind him. Everything was better in real life, Liam thought to himself as the three flew through black space toward the newly added planet. It was hazy with swirling clouds, making it look very mysterious. They drove into the planet, but then slowed down as they tried to find their way in the thick fog. Strategically placed flood lights revealed some of the more interesting features of the planet. They toured it, stopping and getting off the cycle now and again to investigate interesting formations.

When they landed back in the study Liam invited Laura to sit next to the fire while he poured them some of Arthur's wine. Laura took a sip of the sweet white wine. "Very good!" she complimented as Liam made himself comfortable next to her. "So, you live in this big house with just your wine making robot?"

"Yes," he agreed, then added, "although my dad did come to see me earlier."

"Did he come here to talk to you about top secret business stuff?" Laura teased.

Liam shook his head, now wishing he hadn't made the comment. "No, just family stuff." But then he decided that maybe it would be a good segue into a conversation that he needed to have with her anyway. "Actually, it was about heredity and order of succession." Laura looked at him with interest, she really was fraternizing with royalty. "You know, being the one in control of ARTHUR1 is a big responsibility," he began, enjoying her attention as he spoke. "My father explained that our DNA is embedded in ARTHUR1's coding. So, as my father explained, I have to be very careful with my sperm." He said this as he was inching his way closer to her.

"Well," Laura sighed, "there won't be any accidents here," she explained, with a chuckle. "I take a vaccine every year that takes away all that messy female stuff!"

This did reassure Liam, he was certainly not ready for children, especially after the discussion he had with his father that day. He remembered his father's words and repeated them aloud. "Having a child is a serious endeavor. My father put a lot of thought into my creation and upbringing. I am the best son that his science could produce!" he chuckled, then looked back at Laura. "I do have to make sure I don't fuck up," he explained simply. "Not just because of ARTHUR1, but also, it's such an awesome responsibility to be the initiator of another human's life." Laura drew nearer and put her head on his shoulder. She had grown up reading about the lonely boy that was raised by a robot, never dreaming that one day she would be here, with him, and becoming involved in his world.

Liam continued, "I think that the missing element from my upbringing was human touch, and I think that I would have been happier if it hadn't been missing." He paused a moment, rubbed his check against Laura's then concluded, "I want to be completely ready and available to my child. I want us to touch often." Laura assured him that she felt the same way by cuddling him. They reclined together on the little sofa, then tumbled to the floor and absconded Howler's favorite rug. Laura would end up spending the night in Liam's bed, with Pamela outside the door.

When Allen's plane began to descend on the small air strip, that had been mowed into a wheat field, he was confused by the lack of anyone nearby to welcome them. The hatch was opened and a small flight of stairs dropped down. Allen and Arthur hesitantly descended the steps, looking around themselves at the vacant farm field. Not long afterward, they heard the shouts of children, who came running toward them from the tree line. There were half a dozen, shabbily dressed children that looked to be between five and 15 years old. Arthur took on a defensive posture, as both he and Allen were confused and concerned that they were being ambushed, if it wasn't that the group was so young.

They ran passed Allen and Arthur, obviously more interested in the plane. Then, an older man in denim overalls ambled toward them from the tree line. He was nearly bald, with a long, gray pony tail hanging down his back and a blurry blue tattoo covered the place on his head were the hair used to be. He had a scowl on his face, but walked up to the pair and introduced himself as Bill, then instructed them to follow him.

Allen and Arthur looked at one another, then Arthur closed the hatch as the children were peeking inside the plane. One of them lifted another up, so that they could look thorough the windows of the craft.

They followed the man back through the tree line and then, silently, walked several blocks down dirt roads that serviced the little community. Finally, they came to the center of the town where a long community center sat in the hub of the wheel shaped village.

Bill continued to ignore the guests, yet, leading them inside. The building was lit by rows of windows, and filled on one side by long wooden tables with bench seating. Allen and Arthur stood mutely, wondering if they were in the right place.

"Wait here," Bill grunted, "he is on his way."

Soon, a white headed Jak, appeared in the doorway of the hall, his light eyes sparkling and never strayed from their focus on the Arthur, and his face shone with a hint of a smile as he grew near the robot and began inspecting it. "I am so honored!" he began, "I've seen plenty of your kind, but to be in the presence of the very first Arthur1 robot!" Jak stood in front of Arthur with a look of admiration. Then, he turned his attention to Allen, whom he had become familiar with by way of virtual reality, but this was the first time that they met in person.

"Thank you so much for agreeing to meet like this! Make yourselves comfortable," he said directing them to a long wooden bench. Allen looked at the wooden planked bench seating with a frown, but before he could sit down, one of the children brought him a cushion. Allen gladly accepted it and thanked the child as she was looking up at him expectantly. Arthur sat next to him and Jak moved to the opposite side of the table, eager to continue their conversation.

Jak smiled again in Arthur's direction, then to Allen, "Do you ever wonder what your father, Ian, would think of the evolution of his creation?"

Allen nodded, "Yes! To think that his college assignment would evolve into the most powerful search engine in the world!" he chuckled.

"Oh, but it's so much more than that!" Jak's voice raised a bit with his excitement, "A whole new circuit has been completed!"

Allen looked puzzled, "what do you mean, a circuit has been completed?"

Jak paused a moment to consider how to begin to explain this. "Through Ian's program he created god in ARTHUR1! The all knowing, all seeing entity behind all of these sentient beings!" he gestured toward Arthur. "And, here they are! Themselves, immortal gods who communicate with one another telepathically! This whole new circuit of humanity began from your father's idea!" Allen nodded with comprehension. Jak turned his gaze to Arthur, "How do you think your race will evolve?"

"This is a topic that I have been spending time contemplating," Arthur answered. "I believe that the next big evolutionary step for robots will be when we begin to develop individual personalities. Once, one of our kind, begins this process, then this type of thinking would effect all of us. I think that it will cause us to want to have private thoughts and communications. Maybe, even develop a spoken language to communicate these private thoughts to other individuals rather than than the entire collective. I believe that these developments would escalate until ARTHUR1 became a voice in the background, a collective conscious that we robots could choose to listen to," Arthur stopped at this point to check Jak's face for signs of comprehension. "It would be a similar relationship that humans have with their god," he clarified.

"This is all so interesting!" Jak said as he was truly impressed by the mechanical man. "I really would like the opportunity to speak to you at length. But, first I have some urgent business." He began manipulating a device on the table so that a large hologram of a virus appeared in front of them, over the table. "See this? It's an alien virus that no Earthling has immunity from." He caused the giant diagram to turn so that everyone seated could view it from all directions. Arthur became very interested and began recording the images, and making notes internally. "You see, I am a historian, and I can tell you that just as the Europeans created an extinction event when they discovered the Americans, Alien viruses have caused mass extinctions on Earth, also. It happened about 75,000 years ago, that nearly all human life was extinguished by one event. Other alien viruses have been absorbed, so that Earthlings became immune. So, what I am proposing is that we need to preemptively immunize against this," Jak pointed to the virus that hovered in front of them. "I think I have a DNA scientist on board to help with a vaccine, but then, the next step will be to get it into the bloodstreams of all Earthlings before they are infected."

He looked from Allen to Arthur, "this is where you could be of much service to your planet. I want to add this vaccine to an already mandated one. I believe you could help with this process as ARTHUR1 is involved with the public utility that manages and implements the current vaccine program. We need to put our heads together and find a way to do this without making it public." He focused on Allen, "For obvious reasons, this has to be done covertly."

Allen began nodding in agreement. Arthur was surprised by how easily Allen was taken with the alien's words. He didn't show the least sign of apprehension. No questions, just a surprising remark, "why yes! Certainly, we will do our best!"

Their conversation continued with Arthur asking questions, as Allen seemed to be hypnotized by the alien and accepted every word he uttered without apprehension. When they left Arthur remarked on this to Allen as they were on the airplane about to depart. "How should we handle the news of this alien?"

"What do you mean?"

"Shouldn't we alert government agencies about the alien?"

Allen began shaking his head "No! Of course not! It would compromise his mission! You can never tell anyone!"

"He informed me that he wants to meet with Liam. He wants to know the heir to the Ian Moore company. He wants to know the person who is next in succession to control ARTHUR1."

"Oh, that is wonderful!" Allen exclaimed, "I would so much like to be able to discuss this with him, but of course, I would never, not until Jak talks with him first."

"Don't you feel that you are giving too much control to someone you just met? Shouldn't he be vetted?"

Allen shrugged, "how could you think he is anything other than alien to our planet?"

"I believe him, he is not the only alien living among us, but this in itself, doesn't mean that he couldn't have ill intentions."

Allen considered this a moment, it was strange the way he knew the alien was truthful and someone to be trusted, after only one meeting, but he was so confident that he waved off Arthur's concerns. But then he replayed Arthur's remark in his head, "What do you mean he is not the only alien living among us?"

"There are entities that visit our web that I've encountered, but sometimes it is only a suspicion."

Allen sighed, "all the more reason to make sure this vaccine is implemented sooner than later! I want you to message Liam that I want to see him! And, hand me a pair of goggles."

Arthur handed Allen his goggles and then returned to the seat across from him. Allen pressed an activation button on the side of his headset. Arthur disappeared and the cabin became a luxury office with young Allen sitting behind his desk. Several moments later Liam appeared on the opposite side of the desk, sitting in his own golden chair.

"Liam! I wanted to tell you myself that I've scheduled an important meeting for the two of us to attend together. I want us to take a whole day with it."

Liam was taken aback by Allen's joyful looking demeanor. Their conversations had been very tense lately. He couldn't remember when he'd seen his father in a good mood. "What would it be about?" Liam asked.

"Um, well, it's not important right now," Allen was having difficulty finding the right words. He noticed the look of confusion on Liam's face, "don't worry. You are going to enjoy this meeting!" he chuckled slightly. "In fact, I want us to take the whole day together. Oh, and just dress casually, maybe we could go for a hike or something."

Liam was now even more confused. Was the problem with Arthur's behavior connected to his father's change in personality? "Fine! I will look forward to it. But, father there is another thing that I wanted to talk to you about concerning Arthur. He is behaving strangely. I told him to run a diagnostic on himself, but I haven't looked at the results yet."

Allen suspected the problem and didn't want Liam to investigate. "What kind of problems?"

"Well, some small, like, his normal default is to sit, but all day today, I've noticed him standing against a wall." Allen nodded, so Liam continued, "and then, there was this problem with him understanding his own device. I think he finally did, but I had to find the object for him, he didn't know where it was."

Allen nodded again, "Don't worry, I'll look at that diagnostic report. It doesn't sound like anything serious. Just keep me posted."

Liam was surprised that his father wasn't more concerned, they both knew that little glitches were usually always a sign of a larger problem manifesting. But, he was anxious to get back to Laura, as she was waiting at their favorite martian crater for him to return, so he just answered, "Okay, I'll let you know if I notice anything else."

As soon as Liam left his office, Allen pulled off his goggles and looked at Arthur thoughtfully, "Arthur, do you believe that you have already begun the process of developing a personality?"

Arthur paused to consider the question, as he had been listening to the conversation as well. "Yes, otherwise Liam would not be able to distinguish between Barnabas and myself."

Allen nodded in agreement. "Well, then, I guess we should point this thing in the direction of the house. Then, you and Barnabas could change back and I could just spend the night. It'll be nice to fall asleep and wake up in the old place! I'm sure Liam would like the company!"

It was well after midnight when the small plane touched down. Arthur opened the door, stepped down and then turned to offer his hand to Allen, who was waiting at the top of the small set of stairs. Moonlight bathed the field and illuminated the front of the house. Allen was looking around the big yard of his youth when he noticed Arthur's waiting hand. He stood there a moment looking at Arthur, who appeared just the same as he did all those years ago when he was the young man and Arthur was his playmate, and now, this same being was becoming his nurse. "The time did pass quickly," he muttered aloud, half to Arthur and half to himself.

He walked toward the patio doors. Like his son, he preferred this entrance with it's little garden, over the formal entrance with it's semi-circular of concrete steps. Barnabas was waiting for them, holding open the door. The robot silently closed the door after them and returned to his place aboard the airplane.

"Arthur, I am starved! Wake up Liam then bring me something to eat in the dinning room," he instructed before sitting on a nearby chair and removing his shoes. He turned to admire the beautiful scenery out of the glass doors. A soft yellow light was glowing off the marble bench under an arbor of green. All this made him step back outside, without his shoes. He carefully walked out and on to the carpet of clover to the bench and sat down, admiring the stars.

As soon as Arthur had climbed the staircase, he became aware of Pamela standing against the wall next to Liam's bedroom. He walked passed her and then, knocked three times on the closed door before opening it. "Liam, your father is waiting for you in the downstairs," he announced from inside Liam's room and next to his bed, where he and Laura had been asleep. Laura made a small gasping sound and then covered herself with a blanket.

"I hear you Arthur. I can dress myself," Liam answered the robot and then dismissed him. He then, rolled over to cuddle with Laura, chuckling at her distress. "What's wrong?"

"I thought we would be alone!"

"Hey, I'm as surprised as you! But, don't worry. You stay here and I'll go down stairs and deal with him." He kissed her forehead, as it was the only part of her that was uncovered, and then, he put on a pair of pajamas and left her in bed, with Pamela still guarding the door.

After he descended the stairs, he was surprised to find his father outside on the patio, barefoot. "Liam! Come sit out here with me! It's so pleasant!" he said, still admiring the view. Liam timidly obliged, but the change in his father's demeanor was puzzling to him.

"So, have there been any new developments?" Liam asked as he took a seat at the end of the marble bench. But then Allen scooted next to him, and Liam stiffened when he felt his father's arm glide across his back and then rest a hand on his shoulder. When he looked sideways at him, he could clearly see a smile on his lips and his eyes were focused in the direction of the stars.

"I do miss this old place! It was a great place to grow up!" Allen reminisced, causing Liam to repeat his question.

"Oh, no. Not yet," he said winking at his son.

Arthur came to the door and told them that Allen's meal was prepared and waiting in the dinning hall. "Good! I don't know why I'm so hungry!" he said before getting on to his feet. "How about you Liam?" he asked, "want something to eat?"

Liam shook his head no and then followed a cheerful Allen, inside.

Meanwhile, upstairs Laura was wide awake and straining to hear what might be going on outside of the room she was in. After several minutes, she got up, stepped over a snoring Howler and looked into the drawer that she had seen Liam pull his pajamas from, to retriever herself a pair. She quietly dressed herself and then cracked open the door to listen. She could hear the sound of Arthur's footsteps as he opened the patio door to announce Allen's late dinner, and then the men talking softly as they made their way to the dinning room. She slowly crept out the door and peeked around the wall next to the banisters that opened up the top of the stairs like a kind of mezzanine. Not seeing anyone near the bottom of the stairs, she crept down with Pamela following close behind.

She was curious what all the mystery was about, and sneaking around the old, dark mansion to eavesdrop was too much of a temptation for her. She felt like one of the characters in a game. She could hear them say that they were going into the dining room and she knew about a closet under the stairs that Liam had shown her on her first visit, when they were exploring the house with Taylor. From inside the closet she could put an ear against the wall and hear what was being said on the other side, in the dinning hall. Pamela stood silently, next to her, behind the closed door of the closet.

"Father, you never answered me," Liam repeated his question.

"Oh, yes. That," Allen began to explain between bites. "I think I have the situation under control."

Liam was now deeply disturbed by his father's behavior. "How? What is under control?"

Allen, took a drink of his coffee, but was having difficulty finding words. "Ah!" he started again raising one finger, "you will understand at the meeting! Then, everything will be clear!"

"I want you to explain it to me now!" Liam insisted, but noticing his father's difficulties he called for Arthur. "Arthur, what is this meeting that my father has set up for us?"

Arthur came into the room and stood near Liam, "It has been arranged for next week."

"Oh! Not until next week?" Allen interrupted with a disappointed look on his face.

"Yes. The remainder of this week has been blocked off for the salmon harvest."

While Allen nodded, remembering this from his conversation with Jak. Liam looked with distress at Arthur and then his father.

"The meeting will be held in the great hall of a small community in the central part of the state," Arthur concluded.

"Where? With who?" Liam asked.

But, then Arthur began addressing Allen, "Do you still want the details of this meeting kept secret?"

"Absolutely!" Allen assured him.

"Laura is listening to our conversation from a closet," Arthur explained.

"What!" Allen erupted, regaining his more common composure.

"I'll take care of this!" Liam blurted out as he got to his feet and raced out of the room.

He met Laura at the bottom of the stairway, as her intention was to scurry back up the stairs. When he found her there, wide eyed, wearing a pair of his pajamas with the pant legs bunched up around her feet and dragging on the floor, he had to laugh despite the anxious feeling he had over the situation. He put his arm around her and guided her, kissing the top of her head as they climbed the stairs.

"How did he know I was in there?" she whispered excitedly.

Liam gestured at Pamela who was following them.

"But, she's been with me the whole time!" Laura answered.

"It doesn't matter," Liam explained in a low voice, "they communicate wirelessly."

He was helping her back into his bed when Pamela approached him, "your father wants to finish the conversation tomorrow."

"Okay, good," Liam acknowledged. But Laura gave her disloyal robot an angry look before Liam shut the door. Once more, they were alone, so he leaned against the closed door and smiled at the beautiful girl in his pajamas and made a note to himself to forbid Arthur from washing them.

Laura was sitting up in the center of the bed hugging a pillow. "Is he mad?" she whispered.

Liam's smile broadened, he loved the cute expression on her face. "Yeah," then he shrugged, "but, he's been mad at me for awhile now."

"Why?"

Liam sat on the edge of the bed, not wanting to go into the details. "I did something that he had forbidden."

"What?"

He reached out to her and began rubbing her back and shoulders, "I found my birth mother."

Laura was trying to understand, "Taylor's mother?"

"Yes. We have the same mother." Liam did not want to continue the conversation, it was uncomfortable for him, and it was interfering with what he wanted at that moment, as he was moving Laura into a reclined position.

The next morning, Pamela woke the couple, announcing that they should come downstairs to breakfast. Laura was still angry at her robot and the fact that she tended to address Liam instead of her, made her cross. "Look, my father is impatient," Liam began, "so I'll jump in the shower first, and that way you can take your time," he explained as he kissed her again and left her alone in the bed.

Laura pulled the blanket over her head and considered getting dressed and sneaking away while Liam was in the bathroom. Maybe she could have Pamela summon the transporter and meet her outside Liam's window. She got up and walked across the room to see how far down the drop was. 'Nope, that's not happening,' she thought to herself while looking down.

Soon, Liam was walking back into the room, wrapped in a towel. He was surprised to see Laura standing next to the window, looking out and still wearing his pajama shirt. "So, is this something you do too?" he asked, dropping his towel and then opening the window and standing behind the white satin sheers, that the burst of wind had sent fluttering. He pulled Laura to him, "air dry! It's the best!" Their romance would have started all over again if it wasn't that Allen was waiting downstairs.

"Say, what do your parents think of you spending the night?" Liam asked.

Laura sighed, "well, it's not unusual for me to spend the night with a friend, but...not like this."

"Do you think they will be angry?"

Laura knew that they were probably the opposite of angry right now, "No, not this time." But, then she thought about the reason that she wanted to jump out the window. "What about your father? What does he think of me being here?"

Liam shrugged, "it doesn't matter. I can have a life separate from the one I have with him. He does." With that, he turned and began dressing in cloths that Pamela had laid out for him. "Oh, but, he will be civil," Liam added reassuringly.

He left Laura nervously rummaging through a small case that she had brought. He found the breakfast table empty, but a strong light was shining through the patio doors, so he opened them to admire the garden. Arthur soon came to bring him a mug of coffee and to inform him that his father was coming down the stairs. Liam followed the robot inside.

Allen was standing next to his chair, looking around himself before he sat. "I was expecting company for breakfast."

"She's still getting dressed," Liam explained as he sat down.

"Does she stay here often?"

Liam sighed, "father, why are you asking me questions that you already know the answers to? I'm sure you've already interrogated Arthur and did a back ground check on her."

"Okay, I have, and, she does seem to have a pedigree of sorts. Her family has been involved in local politics for three generations. Her grandfather was mayor for 16 years and her father is an attorney who has ambitions of running for the house of representatives." Allen explained, then looked at Liam slyly, "did you know that?"

Liam nodded, then became preoccupied with a plate of food that Arthur had set in front of him. "What about this meeting?" Liam asked without looking up.

"Well, first off, it's not to be discussed with anyone!" he shouted in a whisper. Then, he sat back and took a sip of his coffee, "I will pick you up and we can fly there together."

Liam became exasperated, "Dad! Who are we meeting? You have still not explained this to me! Are we still discussing an alien, even?"

Allen smiled and then reached over and patted his son on the hand, "you'll find out. And I promise, it will be a nice surprise!"

Liam was mystified, his father was once again wearing the same silly grin from the night before. But, then, Laura came quietly down the stairs, followed by Pamela. Liam stood up and greeted her, then gestured to the chair next to his own for her to sit. He was pleased when he noticed his father was wearing a friendly smile when he preformed the introductions. 'Whatever was going on was at least making him cheerful,' Liam thought.

Laura had piled her hair neatly upon her head and was wearing a simple black body suit that she had stuffed in her bag the day before. She nodded politely at Liam's father, but shyly kept her eyes downcast. The incident from the night before would not be discussed. Pamela stood against the wall behind where Laura was seated.

"So, I've heard that your father has political aspirations," Allen said addressing Laura.

Laura looked a bit surprised that Liam's father would know this, but then answered politely, "yes. He plans to run for the House of Representatives."

Allen nodded thoughtfully as he chewed. "Tell him to call my office for an appointment. I might be interested in helping, possibly."

Laura just glanced at Liam, who showed no emotion, but reached out and patted her hand when he noticed her looking at him. What meant little to him, would be exciting news to her father.

"I will," she answered.

The next morning Liam awoke on his own, noting the time was 9:36. He wondered where Arthur was as he always woke him by 8:00 on weekdays. Liam thought about this as he lay under his comforter, yes, it was Wednesday, he was sure of that. "Arthur," he called out from under his covers, but there was no response, even after repeating the robot's name several more times in an increasingly louder voice. Finally, Liam sat up and noticed that Howler had peed on the floor again. "Arthur!" he shouted one last time before stepping around the puddle and walking out of his room with the dog following close behind. He looked around himself as the climbed down the stairs and then let the dog out the patio doors. Still, no Arthur in sight.

He continued to walk through the house calling his name, then decided to check the workroom. That was when he found the robot, bent over a table, one of his arms bent backward in an unnatural position, with the ends of his fingers, skinless and metallic, and moving awkwardly with a tool, while a camera was positioned on an overhead shelf.

When Liam walked up, the robot's head swiveled backward, Arthur's face was melted so that the lips were sealed shut. The synthetic skin around his eyes sagged, showing the metal bits underneath. It appeared that his latex skin had melted into and with his internal electrical system and he was attempting to repair himself.

Liam's first emotion was horror, at seeing his beloved companion in such a grotesque condition. "Arthur," he muttered. Then, when he realized that the robots injuries were preventing him from responding, he quickly made his way back to the study and retrieved a one button communicator that would put him in direct communication.

He opened the tiny case and pressed the button and held the device close to his face when he spoke, "Arthur, what happened!"

Then, a familiar voice answered calmly, "I was ambushed by an acid attack."

"Where? How?"

"Your father wishes to speak to you."

Liam walked to a cabinet and retrieved a pair of goggles, then took a seat and waited in front of the big Ian Moore company logo for his father. It only took a few moments, and then he found himself at a desk with the avatar of a young Allen on the opposite side. "It was those damn activists again!" Allen blurted out. Liam immediately knew who he meant, the SAIN activists had been staging protests across the planet, but mainly online, until recently. Liam found these new, in real life, attacks especially disturbing.

"They damaged six robots, including Arthur, before they ran off!" Allen continued in a highly agitated voice.

"How did this happen? Why were there robots gathered in the first place?"

Allen paused, then in a calmer voice explained, "that's another thing that we need to talk about. It appears that ARTHUR1 is using them for his own projects."

Liam and his father had suspected this, but he was surprised that the list of wandering robots included Arthur as well. "Do, you know more about what they are doing?"

"Well, it seems that warehouses across the country have been rented and used as staging areas for distribution of products that ARTHUR1 has been designing. The manufacturing plants have been located in Africa and Asia, all using robots, in the dead of night, as laborers."

Liam was shocked, "financing?"

Allen made a hands up gesture, "ARTHUR1 has access to bank accounts and electronic currency from our gaming sites."

"All without human prompting? Who gave him permission?"

Allen looked at his son, "you did! You told Arthur that he had priority, remember?"

A wave of guilt washed over Liam, as he recalled the incident when Arthur was damaged in a fall and he had told the robot that repairing his ankle was more important that serving him breakfast. Liam had told him that he had worth, that his body had priority.

"What do you want me to do?"

"We have to consider this carefully. But, in the meantime, we need to stomp out this group of anarchists! I'm considering doing something that could effect them online, cut out services of people identified as being members of the group."

Liam nodded, "I'll give it some thought as well."

"But, please Liam, don't initiate any corrections by yourself, let's put our heads together and make sure there are no more careless slips of the tongue. Let's do this together."

Liam nodded again, "okay, I promise."

As soon as the conversation was over, Liam pulled off his goggles and went back into the workroom. He instructed Arthur to be seated so that he could cut the latex over his mouth so that he could speak. He found a box cutter and used the razor very carefully to cut through the robots synthetic skin. He looked down at the hideous face of the damaged robot with a profound sadness, why would anyone do this to his friend? He thought to himself. As soon as the slit between his lips was completed, he asked, "did you get video of the people who did this?"

The robot stretched open his jaws exposing his pitted teeth. "They were in disguise," he explained, "I have sent you video."

Liam nodded, now working at removing the rest of the melted plastic face, even as the robot spoke. He gently worked the tip of the blade between the latex and Arthur's fabricated skeleton. He was interested in looking at the video, but even more so in helping repair his metal friend. "Arthur, how did you end up outside a warehouse in the city?"

"I used the transporter."

"Okay, but why were you at a warehouse in the city?"

"Preparing packages containing new footplates and other upgrades for delivery."

Liam thought about his promise to his father and decided to change subjects. "Can you explain to me how you were attacked?"

"Six people wearing hazmat suits and gas masks surprised us as we were leaving. They each had presser washing devices filled with an acid strapped to their backs. The attack was well planned and quick."

Liam sighed and shook his head, as he wondered how the other robots fared. He continued to help his friend until the melted skin was removed. Arthur repaired his damaged wiring and explained that he had ordered new parts, but the latex face covering wouldn't be delivered till the next day.

Liam went to his office to view the videos of the attack from the perspective of each robot. The lighting was dim and the attackers were covered from head to toe. After watching them all he chose the best footage and then isolated the area around the face, enlarged it to fill his screen, then slowly played the video forward, and looked for a frame that might identify their retina. It was a long shot, but he worked with the video for the next few hours, until his eyes were sore and Arthur brought him a tray with coffee and his favorite chicken and mushroom dish.

Liam noticed that the robots hands looked normal, but winched when he looked up at the exposed wires and metal on his face. His hair and the synthetic skin on the top of his head were also missing, giving him the look of a monster from an old cyborg movie, but he was happy to see him moving about and behaving in a more regular fashion.

He took a few bites and began thinking about how he might confront Violet and find answers through her. Could Violet be the conduit between himself and the activists? He wondered.

Minutes later he met with his brother, Taylor, in their favorite cyber cafe'. "I want to speak with Violet," Liam explained to his brother.

"Oh, sure thing!" Taylor answered as he was already messaging her. "Is this about the SAIN thing that happened last night?"

Liam nodded, "yeah, I need to find a way to talk to those people! Their 'war on robots' is getting personal. Arthur was one of the robots that they threw acid on!" He explained, using part of one of the headlines from the incident.

"Wow! Is he okay?"

"Oh yeah! It only took him a few hours to repair himself! The whole thing was a major inconvenience, but those fools aren't really doing anything! And what if they had been wrong about someone's identity? They would have seriously disfigured and/or killed someone if they had been human!"

Taylor nodded in agreement, he did like Arthur, despite their mother's hatred of the machine.

It only took a short time before Violet responded to Taylor's message and could be seen shyly entering the cafe. She could almost feel Liam's eyes on her when she located them sitting near the back wall. His expression was somber except for a frozen smile that frightened her. Taylor's greeting was much friendlier, he reached out with a flat hand so that her avatar could touch his, as had become their custom. Then, he gesture to the empty space beside himself and asked her to join them, so that she was sitting across from Liam, whose icy blue eyes were still on her.

"Hello Liam," Violet said briefly meeting his glare.

"Violet, or whatever your real name is," Liam began, "I hope that you weren't involved in the attack last night. Those people caused some inconvenience to our robots, but the hazardous chemicals they used, could easily have killed someone."

"I don't know who did this, but the number of people who are against AI are vast," she did her best to look intimidating. "I am no one! But, there are others. Many others. We think the robots have begun to act independently, and we fear for the future of humanity when they take control!"

Liam slowly shook his head, "they are machines! They do what they are told! Do you really have any evidence of robots disobeying or, or, or throwing acid on people!?" He had raised his voice without realizing it. He looked around himself and saw that nearby avatars were looking at them. "Let's discuss this somewhere private," he said, then dropped a portal for the three of them to enter.

They stepped through and found themselves on a tropical island. "Where are we?" Taylor asked, taking in the sand and palm trees on one side of them and the ocean splashing on the other.

"It's just an island that no one visits anymore," Liam answered.

Violet and Taylor, looked around themselves as they followed Liam through the sand and into the islands interior. They walked between the trees toward a large, vegetation covered, mountain that blocked the skyline, which appeared to be, a forever rainbow colored sky with a not-quite-ever setting sun. A gentle breeze rustled leaves, while the faint sound of a steal drum tinkled out of site, from a distant place. They found a vacant, open air, cafe, where Liam pulled his golden chair up to one of the tables and invited them to do the same.

"Now, Violet, I was hoping that we could have a sensible conversation. I want you to explain to me what all the vandalism and destruction is about. How can we make it stop?" Liam asked, taking on an authoritarian posture.

Violet took a breath and tried not to be intimidated, she had put herself in a powerful position, and now she needed to make every word count. She was confident that she had been the one who had convinced Liam to bring down the assassin app, now she needed to gather every bit of her ingenuity to negotiate the salvation of humans over robots.

"We have been gathering reports that robots are acting autonomously, leaving their stations and traveling to unknown destinations to be used as laborers without their owner's permission -"

Liam held out a hand, "I want to stop you right there. No one owns an Ian Moore robot. They are leased. All of this is written in their contracts."

Violet clenched her jaws, she needed to ignore his splitting of hairs. "Some of our operatives began following the robots and were able to locate warehouses and manufacturing facilities. It is unclear to us if the Ian Moore Company is aware of their robots activities. Are you?"

"Of course we are!" Liam lied. "It's a big company, I'm not even aware of every project that we are currently working on. Listen, I think that your organization just represents one of the, 'fear of progress,' groups that have always plagued society and kept us from advancement. Two hundred years ago, people like you were spreading illogical fear about electricity!"

The flesh and blood Violet was clenching her fists so hard that she was digging her fingernails into the palms of her hand. "We want an end to constant contact," she blurted out. Liam knew what she was referring to. It was the term used to describe the way that the robots were now in constant contact with ARTHUR1 through a wireless connection.

He waved his hand, "you are describing a business decision! Look, we own ARTHUR1 and we own robots, it only makes sense that we would use one for the operating system of the other! We live in a capitalist society! How can you think it's okay to separate an entrepreneur from his products? Just take them away, destroy a working business, that by the way, has improved our quality of life and the quality of our environment! You think I should walk away from my grandfather's genius and all the benefits it has provided, because it makes you uncomfortable?"

Violet noticed a trickle of blood run down her wrist. "We want an independent oversight committee to have access to all of ARTHUR1's activities."

"What? And now you are trying to dictate how a private company, working within the law, does business?"

"Yes. When it controls an army of nearly indestructible, self-replicating, self-repairing, metal machines on every continent on the planet! You need oversight!"

Liam sighed and sat back in his chair, "Why are you trying to make this into the plot of some bad syfi flick? Robots are doing jobs that humans don't want to do, and it's a process that requires that giant database of information that we call the internet. ARTHUR1 merely directs the traffic."

Violet wet her lips, "you seem like a very sensible and honorable individual Liam, but what if your company replaces you with someone less sensible, with less honor. Control of ARTHUR1 is too powerful to be in the hands of one or two people."

The heredity conversation that he had recently had with his father came to mind, but he certainly didn't want Violet to have privy to that information. "I understand your demands. I can bring them to a company meeting and see if there could be some room for more transparency. But, your group needs to stop it's attacks on our equipment. There will be arrests. There will be punishment. You don't want to end up in prison, Violet." Liam fixed his cold blue eyes on her in an intentionally, intimidating way. Then announced that the meeting was over.

Taylor and Violet found themselves alone. Violet didn't know if she had done well or not. She consoled herself with the memory of how badly she had believed their previous meeting had went, and yet shortly afterward the Assassin App disappeared.

Taylor looked at Violet with tenderness and patted her avatar hand, "I think you did a good job," he consoled her, as if he had read her mind. Then, he looked thoughtful, "But, that attack was wrong, it fucked Arthur up and made it personal to Liam. He's never going to like you. I hope you can negotiate together, but he'll never trust you like a friend."

"That's what is important. To be able to work together! AI is already too powerful and it's multiplying in knowledge and power as we speak! Every minute the threat is greater!"

"Woooo, Violet," Taylor strained to get her attention by getting close to her face so that they were eye to eye. "Violet, you are getting yourself worked up. I do agree with what Liam said about the fact that the robots are just machines that do as they are told. All new technology is scary! The more powerful, the scarier it is! Maybe, that is all this is, maybe you guys should just chill!"

Violet, the flesh and blood Violet, let out a sigh and felt the muscles in her face and body relax. Taylor did have a soothing effect on her. At that moment, she wanted to believe that she was over reacting, because the constant feeling of dread and desperation was making her feel tired, so tired.

"You know, Taylor, I do believe you when you tell me that Liam is a good guy. I just wish I could reach him, let him know that I'm sincere and that we could work together."

"I know," Taylor answered, sad, because he realized that Violet's prime interest in him, was for his brother.

Later that day Liam had another meeting with his father. He decided not to mention the conversation that he had earlier with Violet, he knew his father would have a problem with it, but at the moment Violet was his only connection with the group and he wanted the attacks to stop. This would be his executive decision, he told himself.

"Well, Liam, that image that you sent over did yield a few matches," Allen explained, sounding better than at their prior meeting. "I had ARTHUR1 scan security video and he managed to find several similar imprints, now I have him doing face scans of the matches to locate identities. I'm helping to do eliminations, but we are already doing surveillance on all of the possible suspects." He gave his son a satisfied look, "This isn't going to take long, and the sooner we get these guys in jail the better. We got to make examples out of them."

Liam agreed.

"So, I see no reason why we can't attend that meeting tomorrow," Allen announced with a satisfied smile. "Make sure you wear something comfortable, oh, and hiking boots! I think we might get a tour of the grounds while we are there!"

Liam frowned, "father, where is there?"

"Well," Allen began, but then had a loss for words. Liam watched him with interest, as he couldn't recall his father having a problem finding words to express himself until very recently. "Well, it's in a woodland area, and, we will get to take an old fashioned hike together!" Allen finished.

Liam wasn't sure what to make of the answer, but decided that he would find out the next day. But, he did wonder at his father's behavior and hoped that this meeting would give him some answers.

The next morning Arthur and Liam stood near the air strip waiting for Allen's plane. It was a bright morning that promised to be a warm day, so Liam wore a casual, white, linen, suit with with a black, short sleeved pullover shirt underneath. He was wearing dark goggle-type glasses, not only because his light eyes were sensitive to the sun, but they also protected him from retina scans. Arthur was carrying a small bag for him that contained a change of shoes and clothing.

Liam looked over at the robot, "So, Arthur, do you know where we are going?"

"A rural area in the center of Michigan's lower peninsula."

"What airport?"

"None. An airstrip will be provided for us."

Liam was curious, but convinced that the robot was forbidden to give him details. "Do you know why my father is so cheerful about this meeting?"

"It appears to be an effect of the alien."

Liam gasped, "Ha! So, we are meeting with an alien!"

"I don't know."

"Oh, Jesus Christ!" Liam swore making an angry gesture.

But, the plane was in sight, so the two stood silently and watched it taxi to a halt. The door was opened and a small set of stairs dropped to the ground for them to enter. Arthur followed Liam up the steps. Inside, they found Allen, alone, at the controls, waiting with a pleasant smile, wearing dark colored body suit. Liam gave a slight bow of his head in his father's direction, then sat in the seat across a small aisle and bucked up for take off. Arthur did the same from the seat behind Liam.

The flight was unremarkable, with Allen attempting small talk, but Liam was still angry over not being privy to knowing the host of the meeting he was about to go to. "I don't understand, why you refuse me information. I have spoken to Taylor, and he is no longer a security risk. And, Laura isn't interested in our business, the other day she was just being....silly!"

"I don't believe Laura is a security risk, and I'm glad you spoke with, um...the other one. But, I was hoping that this could be a fun day trip for us! Let's put work aside today!"

Liam looked at his father with astonishment, "isn't there going to be a meeting of some sort?"

"Yes, yes. But, well, you will see for yourself! It will be a constructive meeting and then we will go hiking! The grounds are beautiful, you'll love it there!" Liam, just silently stared at his father, wondering if he was growing senile.

As Liam watched out the window, he noticed a small village appear out of the wilderness below them. It looked like a planned community with roads that formed concentric circles, and near the edge of the outermost circle, a small air strip was cut into a wheat field. The plane taxied on this small strip, until it came to a halt.

Liam was surprised when he disembarked and noticed that their welcoming committee was a shabby old, balding, man with a head tattoo, wearing overhauls, and holding the hands of two small children. He turned his head and looked at his father who was stepping down behind him, "oh, that's Bill!" He explained, before pushing passed his son and offering the tattooed man his hand.

The man looked down at the extended hand and sniffed. Embarrassed, Allen withdrew his hand and gestured for his son, "Liam, this is Bill!" Liam nodded his head in the man's direction, since he assumed that he didn't like to shake hands, not that Liam would have been anxious to shake his. The two children weren't introduced and seemed to have just wandered in with the man. They followed a tractor path to a narrow dirt road. They walked, quietly, passed several wooden framed houses, some with people working in and around their yards. Often, they would wave when they noticed the small party walk passed. Chickens pecked at the ground near one of the houses. Liam noticed a horse pen with two horses, next to another house. They continued to the center where a long building sat with a playground and pavilion.

Inside, a row of wooden tables with benches lined up along one side of the room with rows of shelving with books on the opposite wall. Several, modestly dressed people with varying body modifications and skin art, were busy with tasks or socializing, while children of all ages merrily ran in and out of the room. Another cluster of people sat at the tables, some looked on with interest, others ignored them all together. But, as Liam took in the room and it's contents, he couldn't help but wonder why his father was so anxious for them to visit this place. Then, when Liam looked behind himself, he noticed an interesting figure standing next to the door. He was very tan with long black hair, a slim athletic build, and most interesting of all, he had a long slender tail, that whipped around behind him. Liam watched the tail, mesmerized with it's snapping motion. He had never seen such a realistic appendage, and very much, wanted to ask the man about it. But, his expression also looked cross and when he noticed Liam looking at him, he glared back angrily. So, Liam quietly turned his attention back to Bill, and wondered to himself why they were there, among so many hostile faces. Bill took a seat, but then, a white headed man wearing bib overhauls stood up and walked toward Allen with his arms open.

"Jak!" Allen announced happily, accepting the man's arms and hugging him in return. "Liam!" he called out to his son, "this is Jak!"

Liam walked toward the man with his hand extended, but he also ignored the gesture, and instead, wrapped his arms around him and gave him a squeeze. Liam stiffly returned the hug while looking at his father in confusion.

"Ah, Liam! I feel like I've watched you grow up!" Jak said, looking him over and choosing to ignore his apprehensive expression. "It does appear that Arthur has done a good job! But, I'm sure you must get tired of people appraising your, very well documented, and extraordinary childhood!" Jak added, supposing correctly that Liam already knew that his monthly physicals and evaluations of all kinds, administered and recorded by Arthur, were, out of the ordinary. But, for some reason, he didn't find the old man as noxious as most of the random people who asked him questions like this, so he gave him a thoughtful answer.

"Well, sometimes, especially when I'm involved with the parental programming, I realize that the logic behind some of it is based on data gathered from my childhood and interactions with Arthur, and how this data, has helped established our current programming standards." Liam paused, as he noticed the man with the tail make a disagreeable sound, but then, he looked back at the smiling man's face for a moment and wondered why he was so eager to discuss himself with this stranger and in this strange place.

"Have a seat and become comfortable!" Jak said as he motioned with his arm toward the back of the one room building, next to the book selves, where a group of miss matched, but comfortable looking, chairs, were placed in a semi-circle around a rug. Allen sighed, this looked much more comfortable than the wooden benches where they sat last time he was there. He instinctively took the first chair next to Jak, while Arthur chose to stand behind Liam in a defense posture. Jak noticed this and that Liam had glanced up at the robot and quietly taken note as well. After they sat, one of the children brought a tray with glasses of water and iced tea.

After taking a sip from his glass Jak looked over at Liam, "So, what have you been told about our meeting?"

"Only that you might be an alien," Liam explained dryly. This made Jak and a few others in the room chuckle.

"Well, I guess that is at the heart of the matter!" Jak chuckled again.

Liam leaned forward in his chair and after glancing back at Arthur asked, "So, then, is this your natural form?"

Jak looked down at himself then answered, "I'm afraid so." Causing everyone to chuckle again, but then he looked more earnestly at the young man. "Sorry to have to tell you this, but I believe we may be related!" He chuckled again. "You see, the people from the planet that I was born on, colonized this planet about 100,000 years ago."

Liam nodded, he wanted to look up at Arthur for confirmation, but he was already aware that the alien was closely observing him. "That is very interesting. But, why are you here? What are your intentions?"

"I'm a historian. The society that I belong to sent me here. We gather the histories of all known planets and add them to our galactic history. You see, this is why we were interested in downloading public information from your internet."

"How is it being downloaded and where is it being directed to."

"Tubular laser beams. The information is taken by way of a system of satellites to our home planet, which is located in the Pleiades. From there a team of researchers disseminate the data and then add it to our Galactic Historical database."

Jak noticed that Liam was nodding to show he acknowledged the information, but, he showed no shock or surprise. His face was as unemotional as Arthur's, Jak wondered if it was disbelief or something else. "You know, I do have to say, that you are the first human to learn this information without being surprised."

"I am aware that there have long been aliens on this planet. In fact, there was one in my study the other day. They seem to enjoy Remote Viewing."

Jak's chuckle turned into a laugh, "I'm so sorry about that!" He reached down and petted the head of a dog that had just sat down beside him. "It was me. I told you, I wanted to meet you."

From behind Liam, Arthur spoke up, "You were not invited or authorized." The dog lifted its head and eyed the robot suspiciously. Liam looked at his father, who seemed to be just a bystander to the whole conversation, and Liam couldn't understand this.

"Arthur, you are absolutely correct. I apologize! It was an inappropriate attempt to gain information to convince you to accept an audience with me." Jak said this with sincerity. "But, the reason for my misbehavior was because I knew that you, Liam and Allen could be of great service to fellow Earthlings by helping me with my latest project."

Liam kept his eyes on the alien and silently waited for an explanation. So, Jak continued, "There is a very serious threat from deadly alien viruses and I know that ARTHUR1 services the public programs for distribution and development of vaccinations." Jak paused a moment to watch Liam's expression, as it hadn't changed. He was puzzled by the young man, as he wasn't as easily swayed as the other humans that he had interacted with, and this intrigued him. He wondered if it was because of his upbringing, as he seemed to be imitating and taking cues from his robot. "I've already got a great DNA scientist on board. He is helping to devise a formula that might be added to current vaccines that are commonly taken."

"How would it be tested?" Liam asked.

"Well, I'm glad you asked, in fact, I've prepared a little presentation!" Jak picked up a device that was sitting near him and caused a hologram to appear. A few of the children in the room squealed and ran to the rug to sit down and watch. Liam noticed that many of the adults also began watching the presentation. A hologram took the form of an enlarged virus. "This is the one I believe could be the most deadly to humans." He went on to explain the virus and others, and then, possible solutions that he and Dr. Jefferies had been working on. The presentation took an entire hour, with everyone present asking occasional questions, including the children, they offered and received the same respect as the adults. Liam found this odd, as he had never been in a meeting that included children other than himself.

When Jak had answered the last question, the hologram disappeared and the spectators disbursed, he said, "So, were we still going to give Liam a tour of the grounds?"

"Oh, yes!" Allen answered happily.

Jak looked at Liam, who looked at Allen, "Oh, father I do need to go to the plane and change clothes."

"Have Arthur fetch them," Allen suggested.

"No. I would rather change there, and I'd like you to go with me."

Jak could tell that the young man wanted to discuss the meeting with his father, alone. "We will wait right here for you," he smiled.

Laim, Allen and Arthur walked out of the hall together and quietly made their way to the plane. As soon as Arthur secured the door, Liam asked him, "do you believe this man is an alien?"

But, Allen interrupted, "Liam, Arthur and I have already vetted him and the information that he is giving us!" But, Liam was consulting Arthur and waited for him to answer.

"Yes. And I have verified much of the presentation."

Liam sat down and considered all that he had just witnessed, "Why is he here?" Liam asked, "I mean, why here?" he pointed out the window.

"He was discovered by members of the community," Arthur explained.

Liam looked over at his father who was still wearing a pleasant expression. "Did you notice that guy with the tail? I've never seen such a nibble appendage."

"Oh, that's because it's real," Allen explained. "That guy is Lucifer Miller, his DNA was altered to give him that tail."

"What?!" Liam asked.

"Yeah, his parents both did ten years for allowing it! Bill is his father!"

"Really? How does it not surprise me that Bill has spent time in prison?" he asked as he accepted the change of clothing that Arthur was offering him. "In fact, I wouldn't be surprised to find out that the entire community started out as a penal colony."

Allen chuckled, "Dr. Miller is well respected and donates his time to promote the Citizen Scientist program."

"Yeah, but I got the feeling that he and his father didn't like us, or maybe they are just leery of strangers in general. And, how does this alien live in plain site among all these people and children. In fact, he seems to have some impressive friends! I can't believe Dr. Jefferies is involved in all this! How can the world not know about him!"

"This question puzzles me as well," Arthur interjected.

Liam pulled a clean shirt over his head, then looked at the robot. "Arthur, do you believe the alien might have hostile intentions?"

Arthur considered this. "He appears to be exceptionally persuasive with humans which makes him dangerous, but I do believe that the threat of alien viruses is real and he has the knowledge necessary to take appropriate actions before there is a deadly outbreak."

"So, he is necessary, but, we need to be very careful when we interact with him?"

"Yes."

"Okay," Liam looked over at his father who was waiting in his captains chair quietly listening with a vacant look in his eyes that worried Liam. After they disembarked and began the walk back through the field, Liam could no longer bare the nagging feeling that this was not his father's first visit to the community. "So, dad, where is it that they plan to take us?"

Allen brightened, "Hopefully, they'll take us over the bridge. They say it's loaded with game."

"Oh, did you not get the opportunity the last time you were here?"

Allen sighed, "Look Liam," he started in a familiar voice. "I needed to make sure that this whole thing was legitimate before I took you here."

"How many times?"

"First, I had the VR meeting, you know all about that, then, I did come here in person, very briefly. And then, right away, I scheduled this meeting. It got pushed back because, well, they do a lot of hunting and gathering here." Liam was annoyed, but he found the familiar deceit somehow comforting. It was the behavior of the old father that he knew.

When they arrived back inside the hall, Jak was waiting with a few men and a woman. One of the men had a row of metal spikes running down the center of his shaven head and went by the name, Ricky. He and his brother, Jeff, were introduced as game keepers. The woman, Jan, appeared to be a sensible, middle aged, person, who was also a teacher, and it looked like several of her students would be following along. Liam found out that Bill wouldn't be joining them, but that, his even more hostile son, would be. As they were discussing their plans, he noticed that Lou was friendly with the children, who clearly enjoyed interacting with him, as he was also their teacher. He began to notice that the man narrowed his eyes and tightened his jaw whenever Arthur spoke. Maybe, it was robots that he hated, Liam considered.

They walked through the nested circles of roads, until they came to a wooden bench that marked the trail head, which was the width of a tractor. A variety of green trees lined both sides. Soon, they came to an interesting bridge of wooden planks that was made stable by heavy metal chains that were attached to angled poles at each end. When they were near the center, they stopped to admire the view. The arch of the bridge allowed them to see over the tree tops, and make out the roofs of houses in the community. The other side of the bridge was a mass of green vegetation, looking wild and without roads or buildings.

"So, Lou," Jak shouted from his place at the side of the bridge, "what is it that I heard about a big cat?"

Lou looked over at the old man, "Yup, little Pete Hugh was using the DNA vacuum yesterday and picked up the DNA of a large cat. We haven't been able to determine exactly what yet, but it's definitely not a house cat."

"Well, that's interesting, we will have to keep a look out!" Jak chuckled.

Upon hearing that there was likely a large cat in the area, Liam's interest was peaked. He would love nothing better than to spy a big cat in the wilderness.

When they continued across the bridge, Jak intentionally took a place next to Liam as they walked. "I'm surprised that you don't have more questions for me," he mused.

Liam quit looking for the cat, "Actually, I do. I was wondering if we can expect more aliens after the vaccinations?"

Jak sighed, "I think you are afraid that I have alternative objectives." He paused to look Liam in the eyes, "I am sincerely concerned that an alien virus could wipe out the human population on Earth."

"Why? Why does this concern you?"

Jak began walking again, holding his hands together behind his back. "Liam, I think I should explain to you why I came to be here, in the first place. You see, I've always been interested in history, from the time I was a small boy, I would look through the historical records and find interesting stories and adventures there. For me it was like reading an adventure novel." He looked at Liam, then continued. "As a teenager, I began studying ancient history and found a reference of a group of colonists who settled on this beautiful, bright, green, water planet. It was an exciting story, at first we had regular contact with those brave, first explorers, it was fascinating! But, slowly, over the years, contact with them became less common, and with only a select few. Until, finally, earth's last scribe, Tyrad, sent us his final journal entries. After that, we made observations from a distance, but no more flesh and blood explores, just accounts from above and from other aliens. But, I had fallen in love with your planet! I wanted more! I studied, and trained for space exploration. Then, I petitioned the historical society to sponsor me for this journey, and that was 43 years ago!"

"You don't plan to ever go back?" Liam asked.

Jak shook his head, "No. I left knowing that I wouldn't be back. It's too far away."

"Don't you miss your people?"

"Yes, especially the first ten years. I've always stayed in contact with my home world, but electronically. Humans, need human contact. But, I stayed to myself, until the community discovered me. Then, I found that I enjoyed their company, and helping them with their problems. I found purpose by contributing to their little village. Several years passed, and I began to realize that these Earthlings," he motioned to the party, "These people, know me better than those I left behind! This is my home now!"

For some reason this story of living alone resonated with Liam, and it also made him feel as though Jak was only from another country and not an entirely different planet.

Arthur was beginning to notice a change in Liam's demeanor. He had expected him to be less susceptible to the alien's charms than his father. "Jak, do any authorities know about your residency?"

Jak's brows furrowed and he looked thoughtful, "No, that would compromise my mission."

Arthur waited a moment for Liam's response, but when he didn't even look up, Arthur asked, "Liam, will the part of Jak's scheme that requires robot workers be a problem for the Ian Moore Company?"

Liam considered this, "We have had to recently clarify the conditions which our robots are used by our customers. That the robots are leased and not owned, but I never intended that we would make this a habit. We might have legal problems."

Then, Allen interjected, "that is why I want to produce robots specifically for Jak's use." Liam nodded in agreement, that sounded most sensible to him.

But, Arthur continued, "Jak, should Earth expect an increase in aliens after humans have been vaccinated?"

Jak chuckled, "why Arthur, you are beginning to sound territorial! Why, that is certainly not very robot like! But, the answer is no. I'm strictly interested in keeping the people I love safe! No, ulterior motives!" Then, he looked earnestly at the robot, "you do realize that it's a territorial feeling that humans are having when groups of them, like those SAIN activists, attack robots! But, as for me, I have no problems with robots, they need fewer resources, no problems with over population, and your behavior is based on logic, so I'm sure your species would make great Earth guardians." He looked at the robot and smiled.

They entered the tree line on the other side of the bridge by way of another well maintained trail. Tall maple and oak trees locked branches high overhead. Creating a kind of long arbor with beams of sunlight poking through and spattering the foliage with speckled light. Liam loved the fairy tale feeling that he always had in the forest. After taking in a deep breath, he began again, his previous occupation of searching the tree tops for a large feline.

Arthur addressed another concern to Jak, "to covertly add elements to a vaccine would be unethical."

Jak sighed, "we could be truthful about the ingredients in it, just elusive as to what issues they address."

"Doesn't the vaccine require alien ingredients?" Arthur continued.

"Yes, right now, but we are currently working on finding earthly substitutes."

Arthur pressed the subject, "Maybe Earth is ready for the truth."

Lou pushed his way between the two. "We don't know! And I'll be damned if Jak becomes the first casualty in the course of our finding out!" he blurted out. "We've all witnessed what crazy shit social media can do to people with the Assassin App!" he glared at the robot, then Allen.

Liam had stepped up his pace and was now ahead of them and oblivious to their conversation. He spotted something large and dark ahead, but it turned out to be a fallen tree.

Lou noticed him, and that he had climbed part way up a tree, a few feet off the trail. He watched on curiously, 'what the hell is he doing? Is he looking for a fucking mountain lion now?' Lou thought as he was observing him. Liam took off, running father into the forest, jumping over obstacles and vaulting over fallen trees and then disappearing.

Lou couldn't help but follow, but for him this meant running up the side of a maple tree, so that he could see from the top branch. When he noticed Liam ahead, he threw himself from that branch to land on a thick lower branch of a nearby willow. The branches sprung back enough to let him grip the branch of an oak. He continued to move through the forest tree to tree like a monkey. Throwing himself toward low hanging branches to break his fall, then using his momentum to grab onto the branch of the next tree, until he found the location that he wanted to perch himself. He straddled a branch and looked back down the trail as Liam was keeping up as best he could. Watching and following the ape man from the ground.

Finally, he came upon Lou perched in one of the upper branches of an enormous oak tree, looking down at him with a sly smile. He made a follow me gesture then climbed down and began running at an amazing speed, dodging trees and bettering Liam, leading him to a swift flowing river with boulders lining it's banks.

Liam fell down next to the river and splashed the water on his face. Laughing and rolling on to his back, and gasping for air. Then, he rolled onto his side and looked up at Lou who was now sitting on a rock in the stream. "That was amazing! What kind training are you into?"

Lou was busy pulling his shirt off, to keep it dry, and then lowered himself into the water. Liam noticed that his tanned skin had a greenish tinge to it, then, he had a thought, "Is it the tail?"

Lou's face went taught and he lost the hint of a smile that was there previously. "Something like that," he mumbled.

Liam turned on to his back and crossed his arms behind his head and closed his eyes. "My father felt that being physically fit makes for a person who is more in tune with nature and thoughtful in defending it. So, Arthur took me outside a lot. It was one of our classrooms, and I loved it."

Lou was listening from a few feet away, 'so that's parenting now,' he thought to himself.

Then, something occurred to Liam, so he mentioned it out loud. "I feel energized by nature. I think I might understand why Arthur says that his idea for his robot footplates came from a human app that he reversed engineered."

'Interesting,' Lou thought, but refused to engage in the conversation.

Then, Liam had another thought, and turned back on to his side so that he could face Lou, "Say, is it true that you have alien DNA?"

Lou sighed, "Actually, I'm more of an alien to Earth than Jak is."

His honestly surprised both of them. Now Liam had rolled onto his stomach and was sitting up. "So, it's true!"

Lou sighed again, he didn't know why he told Liam, except that now that he'd met Jak, his secret didn't matter anymore. "The Anong people live on a forested planet in communities so tight they hardly speak out loud. Hence, my athletic abilities and non verbal communication skills." Lou repeated from rote.

Liam suddenly put another piece of the puzzle together, "So it was Jak! Jak is the one who edited your DNA?"

Lou nodded.

Then, he noticed Liams high tech shoes as he was wiggling his toes while hugging his knees. Lou remembered seeing an ad for the expensive shoes and how he'd wanted a pair himself. But, they were still out of his price range. He got mad at Liam all over again, and stood up, "Common, we better get back, the others are probably wondering where you are."

The two young men walked briskly and silently to the great hall. Liam could sense the hostility coming from Lou. When they arrived, they noticed that they had outpaced the others, so they awkwardly entered the hall alone. Liam took advantage of the lull in conversation to bring up the subject of the community. "You know Dr. Miller, I've noticed your work on environmental issues and your work with the Citizen Scientist program. I am very impressed, I credit that program to the increase in environmental awareness."

Lou only smiled politely and made an agreeable sound. The truth was he had watched Liam grow up, as well. In the news, on video, everyone his age had. Liam was the reason blond hair and blue contacts were currently so popular. He made looking like a white privileged kid popular.

"I wondered," Liam continued, "I read that you came from a small religious community, but is body augmentation a part of your religious practices?"

Lou stiffened, his tail began making little circles, "No."

"Well," Liam continued, unaware of the significance of Lou's tail movements, "I wondered if this propensity to alter appearance is what sparked your parent's interest in genetically modifying your DNA."

Lou's eyes flashed, "You were genetically engineered! Selective breeding is genetic engineering!"

"Why does the circumstances of my birth anger you? My birth and development was planned and closely monitored. This could be said of most people. You, for instance, your DNA was modified." Lou tensed up, ready to spring onto the fair haired prince. But, unaware of the ire he was inducing, Liam continued, "This must have been well planned and carefully observed. Why are you mad at my father, yet heap praises on your own parents?"

Lou glared at the younger man angrily, wondering how dare this privileged kid compare his situation to his own! "My DNA edits gave me a tail, but also a healthier body and an aptitude to understanding non verbal communication. Modifications that make my life more enjoyable and make me a more enlightened human. Not for profit!"

Liam shrugged, "write a memoir."

Lou could no longer resist the urge to grab Liam's collar and slam his head against the wall. Liam was so surprised by the attack that his knees buckled and he crumpled to the floor where Lou quickly pinned him with his own body and held his forearm against Liam's neck.

"Listen to me," Liam protested, "I don't know how I've offended you! I was simply trying to give you a suggestion as to how to profit from you DNA edit, as you are clearly jealous of the profit made by mine."

Liam's words were clear and balanced, there was no malice or anger there. Lou peered down into Liam's eyes as they were only a few inches from his own. First, he saw quiet emptiness, then he heard the chirping of night creatures and he saw a green forest. He saw someone who wanted a simple life, just like himself. He loosened his grip, raising the forearm that was against Liam's neck.

Then, Lou felt someone grab the back of his jacket and lift him from the ground before tossing him a few feet away. The next thing he saw was Arthur bending over Liam and setting him on his feet.

Quietly, as Lou looked on from his place on the floor, and the others began gathering around, curiously, the robot began an examination of Liam. He noticed blood on the white wall and immediately checked the back of Liam's head and found blood. "It is difficult to see the extent of the damage with your hair in the way."

"Arthur, you are not going to shave my head."

"You could have a concussion. Do you feel dizzy?"

Liam sighed, "a little, just let me sit down."

A chair was retrieved by one of the bystanders. Lou was now sitting up, but captivated by the scene. Liam submitted to the examination which consisted of the robot holding his wrists to take vital signs and then he laid his hands on Liam's back to locate any damaged bone or muscles. During the examination Arthur began questioning his ward. "What was the reason for this altercation?"

"I'm not sure. We were having a conversation about the ethics of DNA experimentation," Liam explained calmly. But, this short explanation satisfied everyone there that knew Lou, because they knew how sensitive he was about his tail.

Jak and Lou both became interested in Liam's reaction. Nothing. No anger, no fear, just quiet acceptance of the robot's examination. His eyes had a, glazed over quality, it was as though he had checked out. To avoid the typical human emotion of anger, he checked out and became an android like his robot father.

Arthur turned toward Allen who was mutely watching with the other bystanders, "I think this meeting should be terminated so that Liam can be transported home for rest and observation."

Allen looked sadly at Jak, but agreed, then followed Arthur and Liam out the door.

Lou stood up and brushed himself off. His eyes met Jaks, "I suppose you were noticing the same thing I was noticing. The way that boy can blank out his mind is interesting. I believe it may even be an evolution."

They were both adept at reading people and they had both come to the same conclusion. Although, Liam might not have any bionic limbs or devices implanted in him, his thinking had been altered, as he had acquired the ability to completely sever human emotions like anger and dedicate his thoughts on the problem at hand. He was an android, as he had inherited his surrogate father's mind.

The walk back to the plane was quiet, as Allen was disappointed at having to leave so soon. Most of the dialog was Arthur asking Liam about his health. Did he feel dizzy, was his vision blurred, would he like to be carried. The questioning was getting on Allen's nerves. He was relieved when they finally boarded the craft and he was belted in his captain's chair. Once the plane was in the air he turned to his son, "Say, what was the problem between you and Lou, anyway?"

Liam swiveled his chair to face his father. "The same thing I encounter all the time, jealousy. It's such a useless emotion, it gets in the way. He hates me even though he doesn't know me." Liam sighed, "Pity, that is a nice piece of property. I'd like to explore it more."

"Maybe you could patch things up," Allen suggested. "You know we will be working together on this project, so you need to be able to get along without fist fighting."

"Liam," Arthur began, "do you believe that Gary Johnson at the state department would be a good contact for us on this project?"

Allen immediately began to protest, as Liam turned to the robot, "Absolutely not! It might compromise his mission."

Arthur looked at his ward with something akin to disappointment, "There is a possibility that his intentions are not purely altruistic."

Liam considered this a moment, then shook his head, "no, no, I think we need to support Jak, his work is critical and we can't take the chance of telling anyone! Let Jak make any connections necessary."

The robot could tell by the strong resolve in Liam's voice, that he was now, yet another, human succumb to the alien's enchantment. He marveled at the process. 'This alien is very clever,' he thought, but not aloud.

As soon as Arthur declared it safe, Liam was on his feet. He had plans to attend a concert with his brother and he had been happily looking forward for the diversion, but first, he had some work to do. He wanted to check on the progress of the investigation into the robot acid attacks.

The leads were now getting down to a manageable number. He was using public camera footage to try and identify one of the attackers by a low quality retina scan. Now, he was sifting through information obtained about possible matches. He wanted an arrest. An example needed to be made.

He was also working with ARTHUR1 to untangle the web of factories and warehouses around the world that the entity had acquired to produce enhancements for the robots. He was trying to legitimize the process, but first he had to understand it. ARTHUR1 had been diverting funds from the companies, very lucrative, gambling sites "Make a note of that and go on to the next subject, Karen Baisal, where is she currently?"

"Her coordinates place her in the south eastern quarter of the city. She is using a messaging system while logged into a game."

"Make a note of that and go on to the next subject, Roy Blackwell, where is he currently?"

"His coordinates place in the metro area. He is logged into a private room in VR."

"Interesting. Room creator?"

"A social organization, identified as We Care, it appears to be affiliated with a college campus."

"Does the group accept new members?"

"Yes."

"Good. Get me an identity of someone currently enrolled in that college and drop a portal," Liam said with confidence, even though he had no idea what kind of meeting he would be attending or what he was supposed to care about.

He found himself at a gate where a sentinel in a nutcracker type uniform stood up to confront him. "Members only," he said while blocking Liam's way inside.

"What is the process for membership?"

The sentinel sent him an application with the college's logo at the top. The application also had information on the organization's goals of ridding the world of plastics. 'So, it's an environmental group,' Liam thought to himself, wondering if a SAIN member might likely be an environmentalist.

He returned the completed application and was granted entry. Inside, was a very unimaginative white room with a large circular table that took up the entire space. There were about twenty people already seated. Liam pulled his golden chair up to an empty space, and looked at the faces and name plates till he saw the avatar that was identified as Roy Blackwell. His avatar was easy to spot as it resembled the photo he had viewed in the guy's info. Average height, slim built, brown eyes, he looked the part of a typical college student. Someone to his right had been speaking about the need to prioritize topics that they needed to protest when he entered. He was a slightly chubby avatar with thick dark hair that was pulled away from his face, and cascaded down his back in shiny waves. "Listen, I know that each of us was brought together here because of a cause that they feel strongly about, but, we need to work together and help one another out virtually when we can't be at their function physically. We need RV coverage at every event!"

A female avatar with glasses and wearing a lab coat, crossed her arms and began shaking her head in disagreement, "Why? Aren't there enough people watching us all the time as it is?"

The first man looked over at the woman and sighed, "if we don't we will be excluding everyone who can't be there in person! Including some of the activists in the room! We can't stand in the way of handicapped people and others from participating!"

Liam kept an eye on Roy as he seemed to be quietly listening. He wished the topic of AI would come up. Then, he noticed the lady with the dispute about RV made a hump noise, and look annoyed. Then, another male avatar with glasses and a blond crew cut spoke up. "Okay, we can vote on the issue, but I think Pete has a good point." He then went on to take a hand vote which was overwhelmingly in favor of offering Remote Viewing coverage of their pending demonstrations. It would be accessible from the We Care site. "Okay, so now we need to discuss the greedy elite who are destroying our planet and what we plan to do about it!"

"Yeah!" came several voices of agreement. Liam nodded and made a fist pounding movement in agreement. Then, the speaker noticed him, "oh, and it looks like we have a new member! I see on your app that you must be Bill Long. Is that right?"

Liam nodded, "that is correct sir."

"I see you go to U of M in Flint? We have other members who go there. I'll be sure to link you to them! So, what was your reason for being interested in the group?"

"I'm all about destroying the greedy elite!" Liam replied with mock excitement.

Several people cheered including Roy.

"Love the enthusiasm! Let's get at it!" The speaker stood up and addressed the room full of avatars. "First on the agenda is about the situation in the southern pro-fossil states. I understand that they are hurting financially, but instead of helping them to convert to renewables, there is a cabal of greedy congressmen who want to cash in by opening closed oil rigs, then exempting states from federal plastic taxes so that they can open manufacturing plants to make cheap new plastics! They are harassing and threatening citizen scientists from testing sites! And now, there is a company that has begun fracking in Wyoming under the guise of helping those fossil states!"

'Interesting,' Liam mused, but not the topic he wanted them to discuss. Then, as the room was buzzing with sounds of agreement, Roy's avatar lifted a finger in the air. "Yes?" the speaker acknowledged.

"What does fracking mean?" he asked.

'Well, apparently he's not there about the plastic,' Liam mused to himself.

"It's a high pressure process that causes ground water pollution and earthquakes," the speaker explained.

"Earthquakes?"

"Yes."

"Isn't that area near Yellowstone?"

"Exactly!" the speaker exclaimed, "and no one knows what effect those tremors could have on the volcanoes there!"

Liam continued to listen to the banter and the planned protests at the fracking site, but he was anxious to find out what the next topic was. It turned out to be a fish farm that was polluting waterways in the Chicago area. Liam was getting impatient. Finally, between topics, he thrust up his hand and was called on. "Is there anything planned to protest AI?" he asked, then looked in Roy's direction. But, there wasn't a reaction.

The commentator looked over at him, "no. You need to get involved with the SAIN group for that." he apologized.

Several people nodded. Liam watched Roy, but there didn't seem to be any interest in the new subject. Liam made a note, then, his avatar sat back appearing to listen while Liam was busily looking at ARTHUR1's report for the next suspect on the list. He spied on a few others, making notes, until he was interrupted by a message from his brother, reminding him about the concert that they were supposed to see together. He closed what he was working on and created a portal to their favorite cafe'. He did want to see the concert, but he also had alternative motives.

When he appeared at the door of the Cyber Cafe, he noticed Taylor already seated at their favorite table. Taylor looked surprised to see him so soon, usually it took several reminders. He greeted his brother and then pulled a golden chair up to the table.

"Wow! You're early even!" Taylor remarked.

Liam shrugged, "hey, I wanted to see them live! So, what city are they playing from?" He asked, referring to the band they were about to watch.

"Times Square!"

"Yeah, yeah. I remember now."

There was a lull in the conversation, as Liam was trying to think of a lead in to the conversation that he wanted to have before the music started and Taylor was wondering if there was something more to his brother's promptness.

"So, how is everyone? Is mom getting better?"

Taylor sighed, "Yes and no. The money you've been sending really takes a lot of stress off her. And, physically, I think she is as normal as she gets."

Liam chuckled, "so what is the problem?"

"Well, she's still looking sad and depressed. I think the whole thing of not being able to have another baby is hard for her. I mean she's been a professional baby maker most of her life!"

Liam didn't know what to say. "What about Denise?"

"Oh, she's good. I noticed that she's been helping out more and sulking in her room less, so I guess that's an improvement." Liam was glad to hear this, as he was worried that his sister didn't seem to have any interests, outside of boys.

"Tom?"

"Same. Exactly, the same."

"Well, as long as mom likes having him around," Liam offered. "How about Violet?"

There was a pause, "she's okay."

"Are you two seeing a lot of each other?"

Taylor sighed, "just, you know, VR and RV stuff."

"RV?" Liam knew this meant that they were most likely having sex.

Taylor nodded, "yeah, I joined her at her place a couple times."

This was good news to Liam as it meant that Taylor had seen the real Violet as well as the inside of her home.

"Does she look like her avatar?"

Taylor nodded, "yeah. Actually, she does. And she's got a nice room."

Liam chuckled, "nice room! Is that code?"

Taylor erupted in nervous laughter, "Everything was nice! What do you want me to say!"

"Want to meet up with her in real life? I'll let you use the Razor."

Taylor looked at his brother with suspicion. "Why? Why are you suddenly encouraging this relationship? I thought you wanted me to stop seeing her?"

Liam looked around himself, "let's put this on mute." He pulled down a menu and selected an option that canceled out the background noise and shielded their conversation from eavesdroppers. "Listen, I have a retinal scan of one of Arthur's attackers. You could help me find a match."

Taylor sighed again and sat back in his chair, shaking his head.

"I thought you wanted to get the guys who threw acid at Arthur! These kind of attacks are going to continue until there are some arrests made!"

Taylor was uncomfortable, he had grown fond of Violet, "I don't want to deceive her!"

"What? Your whole relationship started by her deceiving you! Remember?"

Taylor nodded. He knew that she had approached him to get in with Liam, but what they were feeling toward one another now was something more, something special.

"Listen, I just want you to go there on a visit, get to know her friends. I can get you special equipment that takes high quality eye scans without anyone knowing. You could wear the device as a finger ring. No one would ever know."

Taylor thought about it. He did like Arthur, and he wanted the whole SAIN movement to stop it's assaults. Liam waited quietly for an answer. Finally, Taylor slowly nodded.

"Great! Let me know when you want me to send the transporter. You guys will have a great time, I'll buy!"

Taylor looked away sadly, then noticed that the stage was being elevated. Liam noticed as well and took them off mute. Soon, the DJ was standing in center stage, announcing the venue and musicians. The announcer vanished, and a silver mist began to emanate from the stage and spill over into the audience. Then, the loud crack of cymbals and the band suddenly appeared with the lead singer crouched down and growling at the audience.

Taylor kept his eyes on the show, but couldn't stop thinking about Violet. He thought about her often, but now, he had just agreed to go undercover. What if she did find out? He wondered. Did her original deception really cancel out the one he was about to commit? Then, he considered the idea of finally meeting her in person. Body to body. This made him smile.

The next day Liam noticed a message from Lou. He opened it to find that it was an apology. Liam was relieved. He was afraid that Lou's unreasonable dislike for him might get in the way of their working together on Jak's project. He decided that he would do his part and invited Lou to his virtual office that afternoon.

He spent most of the day working on his investigations, but without any good leads. Taylor checked in and a date had been set for Violet and his, in person, randevu'. This couldn't happen soon enough for Liam. He sent his brother to the companies tech department to fit him with a ring scanner. By the end of the day, he was looking forward to his meeting with Lou.

When Lou did appear at Liam's door, Liam couldn't help but notice a perturbed look on his face, even though, he was trying to hide it. Lou didn't have much of a poker face. "Here, pull up a chair," Liam said as he motioned toward the other side of his desk, where he was standing. Once he was seated, Liam took his golden chair.

Lou looked around himself, clearly uncomfortable, "Nice big logo you have in the waiting room." He said awkwardly, trying to engage in friendly banter, yet clearly irritated by the intimidating show of decadence.

Liam tried not to smile, but he couldn't help notice Lou's discomfort. Lou and his whole community reminded him of his mother's people. And, yet Lou was probably thinking that the two of them had nothing in common, Liam mused.

"Yes. That waiting room was designed by my father, so long ago, that I don't even notice it anymore," he laughed. "I guess it is kind of garish."

Lou chided himself. He wanted this meeting to fix things between the two of them and he needed to focus on that and make sure Liam accepted his apology as he was clearly the one in the wrong. He looked around himself again, his tail was making little circles in the air, then he met Liam's gaze. "Hey, I just want to say I'm sorry again about the other day. I thought about it, and I realize that you were absolutely correct." He didn't want to grovel, but at the same time, he wanted Liam to understand and trust him going forward. They had important business to take care of together. "I have to admit," his shoulders slumped and his tail fell to the floor next to him. "I didn't grow up under the best of circumstances, and I...well like everyone else my age, grew up watching you in your palace, with your own personal robot! Every kid wanted that!"

Liam nodded slightly to let him know that he did understand. This certainly wasn't the first time he had to deal with jealously. "It's cool. I'm just glad that we can come together now and get passed all of that. We have important work to do."

"Yes." Lou nodded happy to hear he was forgiven. "Also, I wanted to invite you back over. There -"

"Wonderful!" Liam interrupted. "I'd love to visit again and continue with the same kind of tour we were having before!"

This made Lou happy, "Yeah. Yeah. There are places that I didn't get to show you. Shallow caves where that cat might be!"

Liam moved to the edge of his seat, "Yes! I'd be interested! As soon as it's convenient!"

Lou sat back in his seat, feeling much more relaxed. His tail began dancing in the air behind him. Liam was awed by it.

"Well, Lou, I know there is a lot of work being done right now, behind the scenes. Our people are working together with Dr. Jefferies. It's been a long day for me, so why don't you and I visit my island, and have a drink and a smoke."

"Sounds good."

Liam attached Lou's avatar to his own, then opened a portal to his private island. As usual, it was sunset. Water lapped a white beach, steel drums played in the background. They found themselves sitting at an outdoor table in a grassy area near the sand.

"Beautiful!" Lou remarked as he took in the scene.

"Thanks. It's just a little world that I made a long time ago, when I was a kid. Over the years, I just kept adding things, improving stuff and well, it's my thinking place, I guess."

"I've heard that you are an ace programmer. I guess you come by it naturally, having such a famous coder for a grandfather!" Lou, although he would never admit it, was a little star struck.

"Yes, and you know, he worked the same way. He'd tinker with systems, never closing a project, just adding to it and making improvements. That is how ARTHUR1 came into being."

"Did you know your grandfather?" Lou asked, thinking that surely the man was dead before Liam was born.

"No. Only simulations," Liam admitted, then added, "but, I do visit his room often." Then, he noticed the confused look on Lou's face, so he explained. "After he died, my father shut his bedroom door and never changed a thing. Arthur keeps it clean and even changes the linens weekly, just in case he shows up somehow, I guess!" he laughed. He looked over at Lou and noticed that he was listening attentively, without a disapproving look that would have embarrassed Liam, so he continued. "I like to look at his things and lay on his bed, and try to imagine what he would have been like. Such a great man, I'm lucky to be his heir." He worried that he was causing the meeting to become melancholy, so he ordered Arthur to bring him a drink and an ashtray. "You know, I could activate the natives!" he offered.

"Sure," Lou shrugged, taking a drink of a beer that he had brought himself from his kitchen. Lou mused about how this kid was different than the guy that had visited the community. This Liam had a child like quality and seemed to be sincerely naive. Much different than the shrewd, blank slate, of a person he usually presented himself as.

Then, a group of brown skinned people in ancient Polynesian dress began walking out of the islands jungle interior, carrying drums. "I know!" Liam started enthusiastically, "How about a fire on the beach, and dancing. I programmed in some very interesting ancient dances." Liam began poking at the air to make an adjustment that caused the sun to slowly continue setting.

Lou looked around himself and the idyllic setting, as the natives wearing grass skirts began building a fire closer to the water. Liam put something to his lips and lit the end of it. Lou looked on curiously, "What is that?"

"It's a mild narcotic," Liam admitted in a matter-of-the-fact way.

"What are you doing with the fire?" Lou asked, he was familiar with the metal narcotic filled tubes that were popular, but this was curious.

"Oh, it's something my brother introduced me to. I know it's unhealthy, but I enjoy the smoke. Maybe I can bring some with me when I visit."

"Sure," Lou mumbled, transfixed with the animated smoke Liam was now blowing from his mouth. Then, he remembered another detail from Liam's life, made public. "Are you referring to your father's children?"

"No," Liam inhaled again. "My brother on my mother's side."

Lou thought about this. He had always imagined Liam's mother as a test tube.

They sat back and watched the expert fire makers arranging the pieces of wood into a pyre. There was a subject that Lou wanted to bring up, but politeness was keeping him from it. He looked down at the beer in his hand and wondered if he should stop at one.

"There is something that I wanted to ask you about," Liam began. "I've been reading up on you! One of your quotes had to do with your religion. You said that your version of Christianity worshiped snakes? Was that an accurate quote?"

Lou chuckled. "Well, yeah, but I have to tell you, I sometimes say things like that for effect." Lou made a hands up gesture.

This intrigued Liam, he really wanted to know about the snakes. He had imagined some kind of snake charming ritual that he would have liked to see for himself. "Are actual snakes used?"

Lou laughed and took another long drink from his bottle. "No! Not actual snakes. Sorry to disappoint you!"

Liam was disappointed, but tried not to show it. "Then, how is it that they are worshiped?"

Lou sighed, "It has to do with Christian mythology. You know, the story of Adam and Eve in the garden?"

Liam did know the story, "Yes."

"Well, Gnostic mythology includes at least two gods. The wrathful, jealous god of the old testament who created humans to be his slaves and the loving god that took pity on us and came to Earth to give us free will, as exemplified by the tree of knowledge that Adam and Eve ate from."

Liam sat up, "So, are you saying that your version of Christianity believes in knowledge, as in science?"

"Yes. We embrace science and acknowledge that our mythology is mythology and that the stories of Jesus were written to exemplify a virtuous person that we should try to emulate. Not a physical, flesh and blood human."

Liam liked this, his mother's religion had always worried him because of its requirement to suspend logic and refute science. "Could you send me information?"

"Sure." Lou got up and retrieved another bottle of beer. When he got back, the fire was started. Flames were shooting up, high into the air. The natives formed a circle around it. The men were now wearing headdresses made of the green leaves and the women had also adorned their long dark hair with wreaths of grass. One of them lifted a wooden horn to his mouth and began making a deep guttural sound with it. The others began chanting, then simultaneously rocking from one foot to the other and singing in an unfamiliar language.

Lou kept his eyes on the dancers, but couldn't help but think about the fact that he was sitting next to his nemesis. For his whole life he had despised Liam and the whole Ian Moore apparatus, ARTHUR1 and his minions of robots had the potential to rule the world, and the entire population of the planet was now dependent on the AI and the applications it controlled. And, with every sip of beer, he was finding it more difficult not to confront the heir to the throne. Then, he thought about his best friend, Jay, his family, and the terrible ordeal they went through.

He took the last drink from his bottle then blurted out, "So, have they been able to identify the writer of the Assassin App yet?"

Liam looked over at him blankly, "I don't know." Then he began to chuckle, "Why do you think I would know?" he laughed.

If they had been sitting next to one another in real life, Lou might not have been able to stop himself from grabbing Liam by the collar again. But, they weren't, and besides, he had promised Jak that he wouldn't. He took a deep breath and forced a smile, but his eyes were deadly. He looked down at the empty bottle in his hand, suppressing the urge to get another, and suppressing the urge to shout at Liam.

Liam noted Lou's sober expression, "I'm sorry, it's just that I hear that kind of thing so often. People seem to have this idea that ARTHUR1 invented the internet or something. They are convinced that, everything happening there is somehow controlled by him." He sighed then looked Lou in the eyes with a straight face, "I don't know who was responsible for that app and I am as glad as you are that it was taken down."

Lou was gritting his teeth, he looked down at his empty bottle again, then angrily set it on the floor and directed his eyes back at the dancers. He was there on an important mission, he reminded himself, he needed to get along with this lying SOB. The mission couldn't be compromised. He took deep breaths and made agreeable noises, as the dancers were putting on an impressive show. The sky was now black with clusters of bright stars overhead. Lively music filled the air. Lou took in another deep breath. He could do this, he encouraged himself.

After several more minutes, Lou noticed that Liam was looking board. "Say, would you like to go to Mars? Or, better yet that new planet, Victory 2050?"

Lou would have liked to go to the VR version of the new planet, but not with Liam. Not now, because right now, he wanted to take off his goggles and get another beer. "No, actually, I need to be going. I've got a busy day tomorrow." He stretched and stood up. "This island is great! We'll have to come back another time. Does it have a public address?"

Liam shrugged, "no, but I'll send it to you, anyway!" he offered.

Then, Lou remembered something, "Oh, so, you are still coming over this weekend, right?"

Liam nodded, "yeah, I'm looking forward to it."

"Hopefully, we will have good weather. Jak said that there was a big storm coming up from Venezuela! He watched it in RV and said he'd never seen anything like it."

Liam nodded, "yes, Arthur read me the news about it this morning!" Then, he remembered another story that he found more distressing, "and even closer to home, are the Canadian fires."

Lou did know about the wildfires. "Yeah," he answered, nodding his head thoughtfully, "hope they can get that under control. But, in any case, I'm sure we can make do," he promised before disappearing.

Liam took another drag and then a sip of his wine as he watched the dancers repeat their routine. He wondered why it was that Lou asked him about the Assassin App. He didn't like to lie, but what alternative did he have? He needed to get along with Lou. He didn't want to compromise the mission.

Taylor was feeling anxious in the sleek, black transporter that had just picked him up. It wasn't as fancy as Liam's razor, but it was equipped with black leather couches and a mini bar. The front was filled by large, high definition, image of the road ahead. It appeared as though he could step out at any moment. He had already helped himself to a cold can of beer, but he had decided not to get high. He wanted to be sharp, he wanted to be professional. He was on his way to an Ian Moore office to be fitted with a ring that would contain a secret scanner. They were also going to show him how to use it. He was being paid to be an official 'Outside Contractor' as Liam had explained to him.

He looked down at his clothing, it was his new, black, bodysuit with gold trim. It kept his body at optimal temperature, it was flexible and even supported his muscles in such a way that he was getting a mini workout just by moving while he wore it. It felt like he was naked, but in a luxurious way! He was proud to be an Ian Moore employee, of sorts, but he was also worried that the people there would think he was a fraud, or worst yet, some juvenile delinquent that had no business being there. But, NO, he shouted in his head, he was Liam Moore's brother and he had an appointment, he had official business!

He took a couple deep breaths and focused on the road ahead. He tried not to think, just stare. But, soon his mind began to wander to its preoccupation, Violet. His job would be to spy on her and her friends, to help Liam identify one of the SAIN activists that had sprayed Arthur with acid. He hated that he would be betraying Violet, but, as Liam reminded him, she had started their whole relationship with a deception, so he could have his secrets, too. And maybe, most likely, none of the people he met through her would be a match anyway! So maybe she would never know about his mission. His mission. "Have I now become one of Liam's henchmen?" he wondered aloud.

Liam was reclined on the couch in the sitting room. It was evening and the lights were out, with only a crackling holographic fire in the fireplace to light the room. He was wearing a pair of AR glasses and was enthralled by a large book that appeared in front of him. It was something that Lou had sent him. He had spent the whole day working at sorting out information from the acid attack, yet still no one had been identified. So, it had been the stress over the day's work that had caused him to retreat to his favorite thinking place, and now this interesting book had successfully distracted him.

He heard the door handle turn and then the familiar sound of Arthur shuffling into the room. Soon, the tall figure of the robot was standing behind the couch, waiting to be acknowledged.

"Yes Arthur?"

"I have been in communication with Jak and am able to confirm that he is an alien."

Liam made an agreeable sound, but was not surprised by the verification.

Arthur continued, "I've composed a statement to be issued to the State department but need your approval to send it."

"What?" Liam pushed the book away and sat up. "What statement?"

"The Alien Protocol dictates that if I encounter and verify the existence of an alien to Earth, that a statement needs to be sent to the state department, but I am not allowed to communicate with government agencies without those communications being approved."

Liam was aware of the Alien Protocol as it was part of Arthur's original coding that his grandfather had written. "No, no, I do not approve," Liam answered very carefully.

"You have not read the statement."

"I will not approve any statement, to any agency, that would verify Jak's existence."

"I have indisputable proof and if the statement is not sent then I will be violating the Alien Protocol," Arthur insisted.

"No. You cannot send a statement to any government agency without approval. You do not have approval. Delete the statement." Liam remained firm, he waited a few seconds, watching the blank expression on Arthur's face, then explained, "If you disclose this information then it could jeopardize his mission."

Arthur stood still, with his stony, far away expression. He was noting a pattern in speech between Allen, Liam and other humans who were having regular contact with the alien. He was constructing a theory that the alien was using a type of subliminal persuasion to manipulate humans. He would continue to monitor the situation until he had conclusive evidence to present. Yet, it seemed that this very impairment was causing the humans to stifle protocol and evade the evidence. This seemed to be the very definition of a conundrum to the robot. It paralyzed his thinking for several moments.

"Arthur, do you understand what I just said?" Liam asked for clarification.

"Yes."

Liam took in a deep breath, "Good." He pulled the holographic image of a book closer to him, then had another thought as Arthur was about to turn away. "Arthur! Wait, there is something that I wanted to ask you." Liam turned pages to locate the first pages of the book he had been reading, "this book is a translation of an ancient manuscript, in excess of 2,000 years old. It was originally translated from Coptic in 1851 to Latin. Now, consider human technology from 2,000 years ago, or even in 1851," Liam explained thoughtfully. "At that time, there were no airplanes, no space travel. There is no recording of any human leaving Earth's orbit. And yet," Liam turned back the pages to a marker he had placed, "right here, the author describes traveling through the absolute darkness of space and that as he turned to look back, he saw the Earth as a speck of dust! Then, he goes on to describe other spheres and their inhabitants, and the seven trees," he looked up at Arthur and shrugged, "maybe solar systems or galaxies? I'm not sure, as even in the 1800's, some of the things described wouldn't have words yet." He looked at Arthur, who was quietly listening. "So, how would you suppose the author could have known about these things?"

"Alien technology?"

Liam lifted a finger, "Ah! That was my first thought, also, but then I continued to read and the author explains it! Enlightenment! According to the author, anyone can learn the great mysteries of how to separate themselves from their bodies and travel anywhere, including space! So, my question to you is, do you think that this is possible?"

"For a human to achieve astral projection, it would require the acknowledgment of an energy that animates their bodies."

Liam nodded, "a soul?"

"Yes. Just as an entity animates my physical body. You could say that ARTHUR1 is my soul."

"Interesting..." Liam mused. But this caused him to have another question. "So, Arthur, can ARTHUR1 astral project?"

"Not yet."

Liam noted that the answer implied that this was a project that was being considered. "Let me know as soon as it is achieved," he said before dismissing the robot, but he didn't go back to his reading right away, instead, Liam considered the conversation that he had just had. If ARTHUR1 did achieve this, it would be an amazing feat, but, did the fact, that ARTHUR1 was considering this project, indicate that the AI had become self aware?

A couple days later, Liam found himself seated in the family transporter enroute to Lou's community. He had decided against taking the Razor after a conversation with Arthur, which made him decide that part of the problem between Lou and himself, had to do with his wealth. So, he was trying not to show off his opulent lifestyle, by not arriving in the sleek sports-transport.

Besides, he would soon be lending it to Taylor for his date with Violet. Taylor had already been fitted and trained on how to use a spy scanner, and hopefully, this gadget would gather leads for identifying the acid attackers, and he secretly planned to use the scans to create a database of known SAIN members, this was a bit of information that Taylor didn't need to know.

He looked across at Arthur who was seated on a swivel chair with his eyes focused on the road in front of them. He wondered why the robot was so interested in sharing information about Jak with the government. Maybe, since he was immune to all biological diseases, he didn't comprehend the importance of the mission, Liam reasoned with himself.

Then, he saw a blinking red light in front of him. He poked at the hologram with his right index finger. This caused an image of Laura to appear in front of him. "Hello! All done with my homework! So, what are you doing?"

Liam was happy to see her beautiful face, especially as he expected to be at least another hour in transit. "I am doing amazing, now, that I can see your face!" Laura giggled. "And, I think you should come and visit me right now in RV. I set up a system, here, in the transporter, myself! I think we should try it out!" She smiled, and hunched her shoulders a bit.

"You mean that you didn't make Arthur do it?"

"No, I know how to do stuff by myself! Besides, Arthur is way too busy making world changing discoveries!" Liam said as he slid on a pair of goggles that Arthur handed to him.

"Ohhhh..." Laura whispered before her image disappeared and then reappeared as a full size hologram. She looked around herself, a slight breeze caused the sheer white linen dress, that she was wearing, to flutter. Then, her eyes rested on Liam who was still sitting on his couch. He was taking her in with his eyes as he patted the space beside himself. She sat down.

He looked into her face, he loved when she wore her hair in loose curls, and he loved the thin gold ring around the large, black, pupils of her eyes, that her avatar replicated so well. "So...are you alone?" he asked.

Laura tilted her head in a cute way, then explained, "Well, I left my body in my bedroom with the door locked, if that is what you mean."

Liam nodded slightly, "yeah, I guess that works." He reached over and slowly slid the left strap of her dress off her shoulder.

"So, are we preforming research again?"

Liam smiled, "could."

Laura loved that smile, and how his avatar, almost, captured the twinkle in his eyes that she knew was there. He pushed the other strap down, causing the front of her dress to fall, and balance precariously on the tips of her nipples. He ran his hand down her chest, causing the garment to fall. She arched her back and bent her head back.

"Are you wearing your sensory suit?" he asked.

"Yes!" she laughed, as though the question had an obvious answer.

"Well..." Liam began in his defense, "we are now getting reports of people who can feel others in RV without a body suit."

"Really?" Laura asked in disbelief.

"Yeah! I'm serious! Some people seem to be able to sense touch without the suit. Especially, if they have an emotional connection with the other person."

Laura sat up, "Is that right?" Then she tilted her head again and looked into Liam's eyes, "do you think that we will ever have a connection that strong?"

Liam smiled, "Absolutely! We just need more, in real life, practice!"

Laura giggled, and pulled at the buttons on his avatar's shirt. Liam helped her by pulling his shirt over his head. Then, he grabbed at the sides of her dress and pulled it down, pushing the avatar back onto the couch as he did. Laura obliged, as her body had actually been seated on the side of her bed, she lifted up her legs, so that she was laying on her back. She pulled a pillow under her head.

Liam unfastened his pants. Laura reached down and massaged the avatar, causing Liam to moan and press his hand into the couch cushion where her avatar breast was. She writhed, as the pricking feeling on her nipples made her squirm and arch her back. Liam attempted to roll from his side onto Laura's trembling body, not noticing that her avatar was hovering over the edge of the couch. When he did notice, the momentum was too strong to stop himself from falling onto the floor. He cursed and then laughed, from his position under her.

"You silly!" she mocked offense, turning to look down at him. "Get back up here!"

Liam looked up at her naked body above him, "no, wait, I think I like this!"

She reached down and stroked his bare chest. She liked this Liam the best, the playful boy-man. But, the other Liam, the shrewd business tycoon, she liked him too. He made her proud. Proud to be seen with him. Proud to be part of his life. And, he sure did make her parents proud. It was all good!

They tussled and played on the floor of the transporter until Arthur urged Liam to get up and dressed, as they had nearly arrived at the community.

"Okay, okay," Liam pushed through Laura's image and stood up. "Sorry, honey, but I have stuff to do!" He apologized, then made a flat handed gesture to her avatar so that she could touch it with hers, before disappearing.

Liam threw on his crumpled clothing after removing the body suit. He looked down at himself with disdain, yet, this was exactly the look he was going for, blue jeans and all. He sat down at the captain's chair at the front of the vehicle, and watched the 180 degree monitor in front of him. It was a beautiful view, with all the green trees and green fields. Then, the transporter pulled into the only road that led into the little village of roads constructed in concentric circles, with a community hall at it's hub. Many of the houses were built to look like old frontier farm houses. With long yards that often included chicken houses, and animal pens, and almost every home had at least a small garden patch. Liam smiled, it was so serine here, he thought as he observed many of the citizens of the community in their little gardens or gathered around farm equipment. At one point a tan colored dog caused the transporter to slow down to a crawl, as the animal chose to walk down the very center of the narrow road, and didn't seem to be bothered at all by the vehicle behind him.

Finally, the transporter pulled into one of the driveways. The driveway led to the doors of a transporter room that was attached to a white, two story house, with a wrap around porch that had a variety of chairs on it, Liam noticed. As he neared the building, a door slid open, and the vehicle pulled inside and on to a charging pad. Liam stood up and walked to the door of his transporter with Arthur standing behind him. They waited as the vehicle came to a stop and its side door raised up to reveal Lou standing alone, with his tail curled up behind him, waiting with an outstretched hand. They exchanged greetings and Lou led him on a small tour of the modest house. He couldn't help but frown when he noticed the robot walking a few steps behind them. Contrary to Jak, he did have a problem with robots and AI, but he would tolerate this particular robot as he knew it was a necessary evil, and he didn't want to compromise the mission. But, the truth was, Lou was a supporter of SAIN.

"Do you live here alone?" Liam asked.

"No, no, my parents live here, too. They are the ones who had the place built! Yeah, and it's plenty big enough for all three of us." Then, he looked over at Liam and admitted, "I have a place in the city too. Closer to work." He scolded himself for saying the last bit, there was no reason for it except that, maybe, he wanted the young punk to think he was cool, too. He walked Liam through the ground floor and outside through a kitchen door. There was a wooden hand cart near the door. "Oh, sorry about the mess here, I was just working at the community green house," he said, gesturing at the cart.

Liam stepped closer to the wooden cart. It was a kind of wooden box with a single axle that was attached on both sides by round wooden wheels. Poles on each side allowed a human, or animal to easily pull it. "This is so cool!" Liam remarked, getting closer to touch the wooden planks and the wooden wheels. "Did someone make this?"

"Yeah, yeah, my dad made it a long time ago, but it works, so, I use it all the time to haul stuff around."

"Did you say, 'community greenhouse?'"

"Yeah, we were planning to show you that when you were here before, but, well, we never got that far." His voice trailed off with embarrassment. Liam on the other hand looked back at him, cool and collected. 'This kid is a fucking android,' Lou said in his head.

"Where is this greenhouse?"

"Oh, yeah, common' I'll show you. It's by the hall," Lou made a follow me gesture, then walked with Liam toward the center of the hub of roads. Arthur followed a few feet away. This annoyed Lou, as he didn't like the machine at his back, but he tried to suppress his discomfort with it.

"Most people here have a little garden of their own, but we also have a greenhouse. Anyone in the community can use it, but I find it is a great place for experimenting with selective breeding and we even do a little genetic engineering." Lou explained as they walked.

"Genetic engineering?" Liam repeated, asking for details.

"Yeah, I head that part up. I'm sure, you are aware that only qualified people are allowed to do these types of experiments, but I'm an environmental scientist, so I'm all legal!" he assured Liam.

Liam really wasn't questioning the legality of it, but rather, just interested in the topic. But, remembering Lou's sensitivity about DNA editing, he dropped the subject.

Soon, Lou walked them passed the great hall, and through a fringe of fruit trees that blocked the view of another long building that was mainly constructed of transparent blocks. The ends of the building were gates that were propped open, so that the warm summer breezes flowed through it. A couple of teenagers were busy doing something inside. Lou greeted them and introduced them to Liam as students of his. Then, wearily pointed at Arthur and introduced him as well.

The teenagers stopped what they were doing and looked starstruck, as they gazed at Liam and then Arthur. Finally, the girl spoke up, "sorry about your dog, Ernest," she related with a sad face.

Liam was touched, as he used to be mortified by the story that he had composed for a seminar last year, as it was deemed to have been written at a junior high school level, but more recently, he was encountering people who, not only enjoyed the story, but found him much more relateable as a human being, regardless of the compositions academic shortcomings. "Thank you, I really miss him, but I do have a new dog now."

"Oh, I know, Howler!" the girl squealed, "I saw a snapshot of him! He's so cute! I hear you take him with you everywhere in VR! Does he look like his avatar?"

Liam chuckled, "yeah, yeah, he has his own goggles and I designed his avatar myself, so I scanned him from every angle to make him as authentic as possible!"

There was a brief silence, then the boy spoke up, "have you found the people who sprayed Arthur with acid yet?"

Liam shook his head, "not yet, but we will!" He explained in a firm tone that made Lou stiffen and his students look awkwardly away. Liam noticed the exchange and wondered if this was, yet another, forbidden topic.

There was another brief silence, then Lou spoke up, "have you ever tried listening to their demands?"

Liam looked at him confidently, "Yes. I speak frequently with one of their spokesmen. But, we need to teach these activists that violence is never the answer! I plan to make an example of them when they are caught." Liam felt that he needed to show strength, despite Lou's feelings on this topic.

Lou was surprised by his answer, but he couldn't help but wonder how accurate Liam's description of the situation was.

Then, the boy blurted out, "Jak likes robots!" in Liam's direction, then nodded at Arthur, as though he was trying to demonstrate the community's tolerance of them, despite Lou's, well known, distrust of AI in general.

Then, a jolly voice came booming out from the other end of the greenhouse, "I do?!" Jak walked up to the small group and patted Liam then Arthur on the back as a greeting. A small group of adults that were following behind him stopped, as well. "Nice to see you two back! Did you bring your father?"

"No, just Arthur and me this time! We are here to do some hiking and..." he looked over at Lou for confirmation, "I believe a boat might be involved?"

Lou nodded, "Yeah, I thought I'd take him down the river to the lake, then maybe stop at the island to fish."

"Sounds, wonderful!" Jak said, "just keep an eye on the sky! There is a big storm headed up the east coast, it might cause a thunderstorm!"

Everyone's eyes turned upward at the bright blue sky. Then, Jak looked over at Liam, "you guys should leave Arthur here with us! I bet Dr. Jefferies, would love the opportunity to talk with him!"

The slim black man beside him, nodded with enthusiasm, "Yes. Yes, I would!"

Liam looked at Arthur, he knew that the robot wasn't fitted with equipment for swimming, so he had been worried about the boat ride. "I think that is a great idea!"

But, Arthur was reluctant to leave his ward. "What if you need assistance? This man assaulted you last time we were here."

Everyone looked embarrassed. Lou, spoke up, "I promise that, that will not happen again."

"There, Arthur," Liam began, "and we are going to be riding in boats and you are not equipped for water. What if something did go wrong, and the boat sinks? I would swim to shore, but you would sink like a rock! Then, what would I do?"

Arthur considered this, he looked at Lou with suspicion and then to Liam, "I believe that this man posses some alien qualities that would cause him to be an uneven match if there is another outburst of violence."

Liam was becoming impatient, "Arthur just give me the communicator, I promise I'll keep it around my neck!"

"You would also have to carry your own backpack."

"Fine." Liam reached out and accepted the backpack that Arthur had been wearing. "Everything is in here, right?" he asked as he adjusted the straps.

"Yes, including the communicator." Arthur said before opening a small compartment on the backpack and pulling out a silver chain with a medallion hanging from it. He slipped it over Liams head. "Now, do you remember how to use it?" he asked.

"Yes Arthur! It only has one fucking button!" Liam protested.

"Okay," then he looked toward Lou, "and know that I have been modified for trail hiking. I can travel at great speeds, even on unstable ground."

Liam avoided looking at Lou, as he was embarrassed. With that, the two started the walk toward the river. When they were a safe distance away, Lou couldn't help but remark, "you know, I don't believe I've ever seen a robot display the kind of 'motherly' behavior that your robot does."

"Yes, it's part of ARTHUR1's basic programming. My DNA triggers a protective mode. All robots treat me like this," Liam sighed.

Lou was horrified by the comment. He had read about this, but didn't want to believe it, yet, here he was confronted with the truth of it. Liam was true royalty. His father, and, he, and then his descendants have control of the AI beast that controls all information on the planet. This idea frightened him, but he couldn't say anything or he'd burst out with everything, and might trigger the metal monster, less than a mile away, to kill him!

They walked on silently toward the bridge, but just before they got to it, Lou had them turn off the trail and down a smaller one that took them to a small boat launch. There was a small dock and ramp, but also, set among the trees was a small shelter with rows of kayaks underneath.

"This is just a handy place to store our small boats," Lou explained. "The ones with a big letter 'C' painted on the top are community crafts. You know, if someone has a kayak that they don't use anymore, they donate it." He pointed to a bunch of ancient looking, plastic boats, before retrieving a well made wooden Kayak for himself. "My dad helped me make this one," he bragged, before pointing out the features on the sleek looking craft.

Liam frowned at the pile of plastic that he was to make a decision about. "Oh, and don't worry," Lou continued, "we paint the bottoms with an environmentally safe sealant that keeps the toxins in the plastic from leaching into the water." Liam nodded politely, but that wasn't what was making him frown, it was the idea of having to sit in one of the dirty little boats that smelled like cat piss. But, he wasn't going to complain. He was happy to have an opportunity to get a close view of the river. Finally, he pulled one of the small boats off the rack, it was adorned with an especially large letter 'C' and the plastic was an ugly shade of faded red. Lou handed him a paddle and, a surprisingly new, life jacket.

"I've got the fishing stuff already packed in my kayak," he explained before grabbing one end of his boat and pulling it to the river. The water had a gentle current that would carry them under the walking bridge. Both of the shores were tree lined and wild. Bright sunlight made Liam squint, but on the other side of the bridge the river narrowed and soon their boats were shaded by an arbor of green leaves, as the trees from both shores met in the middle. Speckled patches of light made the water shimmer and gave the river a fairyland quality. Liam peered into the wilderness, looking for wildlife. Then, he spied a group of turtles on a dead log that they were passing. When they turned a sharp bend, they surprised a large white egret that was standing on one leg at the edge of the water. It squawked, and then, flew up and over them at a very close distance. This was the type of place that Liam loved to be. He adored the animal sounds, and tried to identify what animal each belonged to. Then, he noticed a stand of birch trees with their scaly, white bark, and a group of beautiful red song birds, sat together in the branches.

They silently paddled down the river until it emptied into a small lake. Bright sunlight again made Liam's eyes narrow. He wanted to call out for his sun goggles, but then remembered that Arthur wasn't there to retrieve them for him. Then, Lou pointed to a stand of trees in the distance that made up the island where they were to fish. Liam followed him across the lake.

The small island had a sandy shore, where they got out and pulled their boats into the grass. Lou took a hand full of fishing poles and a tackle box out of his kayak, then tried to hand one of the poles to Liam, who didn't notice, as he was standing with his hands on his hips, taking in the view around him. So, Lou stood up and carried everything himself, holding the tackle box with his tail. "Hey, there's a dock on the other side," he said, pointing with his head.

"Oh great!" Liam said, walking in that direction and leaving even his backpack behind. Lou couldn't help but notice, and then grumble to himself about the privileged kid. On the other side of the small island, on another golden brown beach, was a long wooden dock. Liam eagerly walked to the peaceful looking structure and noticed a row of poles on each side. The thin poles had interesting looking hooks, two per side. When Liam turned to inquire about them, he could see Lou laying his burdens on the sand. "What are these poles about?" he asked tapping on one of them.

Lou began to explain as he walked closer with one of the fishing poles in his hand, "for fishing poles." He cast out, then attached the fishing poles to one set of hooks.

"Oh," Liam exclaimed, "so...as to avoid holding the fishing pole?" he asked, still a bit puzzled.

"Well, yeah," Lou began, "but, also to maximize the number of fish we bring back."

Liam gave a look of comprehension, "so, these fish are to be eaten!"

"Yeah, we can take what we catch back to the hall to add it to dinner tonight."

Liam nodded, "ah yes! I remember, you have community dinners every night! That is so...quaint!"

Lou was trying his best to accept what Liam said at face value, but still, he felt that he needed to explain. "It is a quaint tradition! We are like a big family, so it's a way to socialize, and, there are so many older people living alone here, the dinners are a way for them to get a good meal with a variety in it. And, then, there are people like me who don't know how to cook! But, I like to fish, so it works out for everyone!"

Liam nodded and had an interested look on his face. "I really do think that's good. I'm just beginning to understand the importance of family, myself." Lou waited a moment, expecting Liam to elaborate, but, when he didn't, he decided to go about his business and not pry.

He walked to shore and squatted down to separate the fishing poles, making one pile with lures and one without, then he shouted to Liam, who was still walking the dock and inspecting the water for fish, to collect the baited poles and connect them to the dock. He happily complied, interested in trying out his casting abilities. Lou continued working at attaching lures to the other poles and chuckling softly, as he observed Liam hook himself by the back of his shirt.

Eventually, the poles were all standing in rows along the sides of the dock, with bobbers that made a ticking sound when submerged. They sat back to back, gazing at the horizon, mid way down the dock, each responsible for a row of poles. The sky was a brilliant shade of blue, with fluffy white clouds and a cool breeze that kept the temperature in balance. Soon, they did begin to hear ticking sounds and several bobbers disappeared, then popped back up. Liam enjoyed reeling the fish in, and felt excited every time to discover the size and type of fish, as it emerged from the water. Both men began enjoying themselves, even Lou was beginning to feel relaxed around his nemesis.

After a flurry of activity, the poles were once again quiet with their bobbers floating gently on the calm water. Liam looked around himself, he wanted to ask Arthur for his backpack, but remembered that he wasn't there. "Say, I think I've left my backpack in the boat," he explained to Lou, "I'll be right back!" Then, he located the other shore where the canoes were resting in the grass. That was when he noticed a dark cloud in the distance, and the wind was getting cold. But, there was the shore, next to the river entrance, just a few feet away, and it was still a lovely day.

He walked briskly back to the dock, where Lou was leisurely sitting, watching the horizon. Liam dropped his backpack, then sat near Lou, facing the opposite direction. "Looks like a storm cloud coming in," Liam pointed into the distance.

Lou turned and looked at the menacing cloud in the distance, "yeah, Jak said there was a storm coming up the coast." He recalled Jak's description of the destruction it had wrecked in Central America, while he witnessed it happen, with Remote Viewing.

When he turned back around he noticed that Liam had pulled a water bottle and a small, square, tin out of his pack. He opened the little box and pulled out a lumpy brown thing and a lighter. He watched with interest as Liam put the thing to his lips and then lighted the end with a small lighter. He inhaled deeply, and let out a small cloud of smoke. Lou guessed that it must of been some kind of cigar. Liam offered it to him, so he accepted it. "It's marijuana, I rolled it myself!" Liam smiled wryly as he knew that his rolling abilities where not yet perfected. Lou rolled the thing between his fingers wondering if he was witnessing a new Liam inspired fad. He had only smoked the stuff out of a metal tube, and less often as an adult, but, if someone offered he seldom refused. Liam was delighted and watched Lou, expecting a cough, and then chuckling when it happened.

"That always happens the first time!" he laughed, offering Lou his water. "Try again, I promise it will be easier!" Lou's eyebrows furrowed, but he did have an interesting, light headed feeling, so he made a second attempt. Liam was already feeling giddy, "It's something that I get through my brother, he has this friend that grows it! So, I'm investing in a small business!"

Lou considered this as he took yet another puff, "aren't your brothers, little kids?"

Liam stopped laughing, then took another joint out of his little box. "Well, I am the oldest, but I think you are thinking of my fathers two sons." He stopped, then made a little shrug, "they are like, 12 years younger than me," he explained, as the subject was still too tender for him to dwell on long enough to do the math of figuring out their ages, but, then, he smiled again, "Taylor is just 2 years younger. He is my mother's son. I also have a sister named Denise."

Lou thought about this, he did remember seeing a snapshot of him with another guy about his age, but darker. It was a photo taken when he was negotiating with a SAIN member in VR, and he did remember thinking, at the time, of how the two looked like bookends. But, he had been checking up on a statement that Liam had made, and didn't care to identify who the other person in the photo was.

Liam inhaled, then looked back at Lou, "you've probably never heard of them, as my father usually has a lot of control over what gets in the media. But...fuck him!" he burst into a fit of laughter and Lou joined in. Both of them giddy from the weed.

Lou could tell that this was a sensitive issue, and too personal for him to ask questions about, but watching the young man so happy with simple fishing and being in the company of another human, he wondered to himself, why it was that he had, had such a difficult time reading the kid. Was it because of him being raised by a robot, or was it because his own mind was clouded by jealousy? Was Jak right about this? Could his inability to pick up on Liam's thoughts be attributed to his own biases?

Soon, Liam noticed that the medallion around his neck was vibrating and making a small chirping sound. Liam sat up and then located the object from under the neck of his shirt. He squeezed the sides of it and caused it to pop open. A single white button occupied it's interior, Liam pressed it. Immediately Arthur's voice could be heard.

"You need to return to the community hall, immediately. Row your boats to the main land, then hike back to the hall at a brisk speed. There is a massive storm approaching."

Liam and Lou both looked surprised, as their view was of blue sky, but when they turned toward the north, the storm cloud that Liam had first spotted, was now covering a quarter of the sky and moving quickly.

"What's happening? Explain about this storm." Liam asked as he and Lou began to scramble up the fishing gear.

"The Canadian fires have reached the northern part of the United States and have now engulfed Michigan's upper peninsula. The massive fires have created their own weather, with large storms that are spinning off tornadoes. This storm is headed south and east as a hurricane has been slowly coming up the east coast. It is uncertain what will happen when the storm systems meet."

The wind picked up as the men worked together to carry the gear across the small island to their boats. After they had loaded the kayaks, Lou stood next to Liam and pointed to the far shore, "that's the bank we want to land on!" he shouted over the wind. Liam looked in that direction at the reed covered shore. He had noticed the other side of the river was covered with large rocks that looked like they would be fun to climb, but dangerous at the moment as the wind was causing large waves that were crashing against the boulders. He nodded comprehension and the two of them quickly shoved off.

They were paddling against the wind, and even though both men were physically fit, it quickly became a struggle as they were being pushed back toward the small island, but then, suddenly the wind shifted toward the west and their boats were hit broadside by the strong current. Lou managed to right himself, but Liam's boat had taken on water, and was now pressed against one of the rocks. Lou could see that the boat was flipped, but the rock was keeping it from righting itself, with Liam trapped underneath. Lou let out a scream that was nearly drowned out by the wind as he directed his boat toward the rocky shore where Liam was stranded. The wind shifted again, now it was blowing directly toward the rocky shore. Liam's boat was turning, but still pressed against the boulder, and Liam couldn't be seen. Lou was craning his neck to locate the youth, and panicking so much that he didn't notice the rock in front of him. His wooden boat dashed against another rock and it sent him spinning backward. He remembered hitting his head on the back of the boat and then water all around him.

When he came to he was laying in the wet grass with the wind still howling around him, and then he saw Liam was sitting beside him laughing. "Well, I'm glad to see you conscious!" he roared above the wind, "you were so worried about saving me that you forgot to save yourself!" Lou sat up to find that the two of them were on the rocky shore, soaking wet on a patch of grass and mud. His boat was in splinters at the water's edge and Liam's plastic craft was barely visible, upside down, and being pushed by waves between rocks like a pin ball.

"Well, let's see how water proof this thing is!" Liam shouted as he located the medallion around his neck. Lou would be happy to hear the robot's voice. The back of his head hurt and everything was hazy to him.

"I'm afraid we've landed on the wrong side of the river!" Liam explained to Arthur, "Our boats are now disabled!"

"Get immediately to shelter, your vitals indicate that you are about to go into hypothermia!" Arthur shouted above the din. "Jak has indicated that there is a cabin nearby. Coordinates are unknown, but Lou should be able to guide the two of you there."

Lou had been listening, he nodded his head slightly and ran his fingers through his hair and noticed a tender spot on the back of his head, his tail was laying limply beside him.

"Yeah, yeah, Ricky and Jeff's place." He explained as though he was just reminded by Arthur. He stood up, unsteady on his feet, Liam reached out to help. Lou looked down at his hand then at him, maybe he was wrong about the kid, he thought to himself.

"I think you might have a concussion." Liam said while observing that the pupil of Lou's right eye was larger than than the other. "Which way?" he asked, putting an arm across Lou's shoulders.

Lou wearily raised his arm and pointed into the dense forest in front of them. "There is a trail, if we can get through those bushes, there is a trail on the other side, it will take us there." Lou wearily dropped his right arm, then accepted Liam's support by throwing his left arm over his shoulder. If only he could clear the fog from his mind, he was so dizzy that he was having problems controlling his limbs, and then there was the relentless rain that was hitting them like pellets. The cold wind was so strong that the rain seemed to be coming at them sideways, it felt like hail.

When they got to the wall of brush that separated them from the trail, Liam stopped and for the first time noticed that Lou had lost his shoes. "Don't worry, I'm barefoot most of the time!" he exclaimed when Liam pointed to his mud covered feet. "We need to just push our way through this!" Lou explained, "the entrance is too far away!"

Liam took the lead, reaching out with his free hand and pushing back the tangled and thorny limbs. Lou did the same with his free arm, then Liam noticed his additional appendage grasping onto the lower branches and holding them out of the way. He was impressed. As difficult as the situation was, Liam's mind couldn't help but wonder if he might be looking at the first in a new race, because if Lou had descendants they would likely inherit his mutation. 'I've got to keep this guy alive,' he thought to himself.

They powered their way through the row of thick vegetation. Liam shouted happily when they broke out of the other side, and into the forest. He was bleeding from scratches down both arms and on his face, but now the brush was giving them some shelter from the hard driving rain. But, he didn't like the way the treetops, all around them, were swaying and contorting with the wind. "Okay, we got this!" Liam called out reassuringly to Lou, who only faintly smiled, and nodded. Liam was afraid that Lou was about to loose consciousness, so he began walking down the dirt trail as briskly as they were able, but the next problem was that they were both wet and beginning to shiver.

Lou stumbled and nearly brought them both down. Liam caught his balance, then carefully laid Lou down on the ground. "I'm going to make a fire!" he declared in a shaky voice, even though he had no flame. Liam was worried as Lou's eyes were closed and his body was limp except for the quaking that was caused by the hypothermia that both of them were experiencing. He grasped his medallion and pressed the button for help as soon as he could cause his stiff fingers to cooperate. But, before Arthur could give him instructions, he heard a shout from the far end of the trail and soon he could make out Ricky's spiky head, running toward them with his brother Jeff close behind.

Liam threw his head back and laughed from his position on the ground, next to Lou. "You are in shock and suffering from hypothermia!" boomed Arthur's voice.

"It's okay Arthur, we are saved!" Liam shouted as he got on his hands and knees in an effort to raise himself from the ground. Soon, Ricky reached down his hand to help him up. Then, he and his brother helped to raise Lou's limp body onto Jeff's shoulder, so that he could carry him. Ricky threw a blanket over Lou, then another over Liam's shivering shoulders. "Oh, thank you, so helpful!" Liam mumbled as the group began walking.

Ricky, looked over at him, "actually, it was your robot that told us to bring them!" he explained before offering Liam his shoulder to lean on.

Liam chuckled, "Good Old Arthur!" but, he refused Ricky's shoulder, "I don't want to slow us down, besides, I need the exercise to warm myself up!" Ricky nodded in agreement.

They walked another quarter of a mile to a log cabin with a thick, wooden door with big metal locks on both sides of it. When he was opening it, Ricky looked back at Liam and noticed him eyeing the hand forged locks. "Bears!" he explained as the group entered the building, making muddy puddles on the wooden floors. The place smelt of wood smoke, as that was what they used for heating. A real fire was burning in a stone fireplace in the center of the building. On one side, the floor gave way to natural stone and heavy, cast iron cooking stove occupied that corner of the cabin. Liam felt like he was in Oogle History.

"Wow! Guys, this is great!" he exclaimed as he began peeling off his dirty wet clothes. Ricky brought him out a dry t shirt and shorts to wear. He was shivering so bad that the task was much more difficult than it should have been. But, the warmth was wonderful and he wanted to wrap himself in a dry blanket and lay next to the fire. But, then, he looked over at Lou, as Jeff had laid him out on the couch and was trying to remove his wet clothes. Liam, pulled the dry shirt over his head as he walked across the room to where Lou was semi-conscious. He began drying Lou's face off with a large towel that Jeff had left nearby. Then, he got near his face, "Dude, I don't think you should sleep right now. You need to stay awake."

Liam felt the medallion around his neck vibrating again, he opened it. "Arthur, we have arrived!" Liam sighed. "But, I think Lou is gravely ill from an injury to his head."

Arthur instructed him to press the back of the medallion against Lou's chest so that he could check his vital signs. He then instructed Liam to keep the patient still, but awake. Liam checked the back of Lou's head, which caused him to wince, there he found that Lou's long dark hair was covered in blood, near the scalp, but there didn't appear to be any large open wounds.

"Sorry," Liam apologized, trying his best to be gentle, "but, I was right about you needing to stay awake."

Lou made a disagreeable sound, "but, I am so tired..."

"Yeah, I know, it's been a hell of a day, but, you need to sit up." Liam grabbed a pillow and rolled it up behind Lou to prop him up in the corner of the sofa. "Don't worry, I'm in this with you! We will just sit here and boar the hell out of each other all night!" he said as he settled into the cushion next to him.

"I'm putting some coffee on!" Ricky called out from the stone area. He also pulled a pot from a refrigerated compartment and sat it on the burner next to the pot of brewing coffee.

Liam laid his head on the back of the sofa, "Guys! This place is so cool! Do you live here year around?"

"Yeah!" Ricky shouted from the kitchen, as he walked back into the common room. Liam noticed that Jeff was busy getting a bottle and some glasses out of a nearby cupboard. "We are hunter/gatherers," he explained, then pointed toward the back of the house. "I know you can't see it right now, cause there's a big fucking storm and all, but there's a shed out back where we have one of those dehydration machines. We shoot a few deer, small game, and gather other stuff like mushrooms and frogs legs, put it in the machine so that comes out in sealed packages and then, those little drones come get it!"

"Great!" Liam said from the couch, then wondered, "Do you use the Peoples' Commodity Market to sell?"

"Yeah. That's the only way I know to do it."

Liam smiled, the app was a public utility that ARTHUR1 had written and maintains. Jeff reached down to him with a small glass of amber liquid that he explained was 'the best bourbon anywhere.' Liam chuckled and received the glass. The liquid warmed him. "But, he," Liam pointed at Lou, "needs coffee!" Jeff kept the second glass that he poured for himself.

Lou moaned, "I'm awake, could use the coffee though."

Liam had another question, "Deer? You must have to put it in small packages for the drones."

"Yeah, sometimes it takes half a dozen of them to carry away all the trays," Ricky explained.

Jeff laughed, "and even then, those poor little fuckers will just be straining to get back up to the blimp! I feel kind of sorry for them!" everyone laughed.

Lou managed to form a smile.

Liam looked around the simple cabin, it was permeated with the smell of burning wood, and there was a pile of wet, dirty clothes in the middle of the room, but it was warm there, inside, as the storm raged outside. And as for these people that had saved him, before meeting his mother, he had never been around people like these. And now, he was one of them! Life was strange, he thought to himself, suddenly grateful for common people.

The medallion around his neck began vibrating, Liam cupped it in his hand and Arthur's voice could be heard. "A small, driverless vehicle has been sent to you with medication for Lou and other medical supplies. This vehicle can bring you both back to the hall, but it is recommended that you stay in place and shelter yourselves from the storms. They are estimated to be in place for 12 more hours. Your father wants to see you immediately, you also have requests from Taylor and Laura." Liam's eyes wandered around the room, looking to see if the hunters might have a headset he could borrow. When he heard, 'Taylor,' he knew that, that was really his mother, making Taylor, 'get ahold Liam for her.' And, Laura was someone he wanted to interact with in private. But, first he had a few questions for Arthur.

"Arthur, explain to me about the storm. It has already been raging for hours and now you are saying that it will be 12 more? I thought barometric pressure had finally leveled off, and wind speeds were stable. Why so long?"

"Yes, on a yearly average, it has been stable for the last two years, but wind speeds are still insufficient to move the storms out to sea. As the line of storms from the north unites with the hurricane that is now on the east coast, it is predicted to reinvigorate both storms as it is being fueled by the hot air and ash."

Liam sighed, "wonderful!" But, the room had been silent, because everyone was interested in Arthur's reports, and so, now Jeff was handing him a headset. Liam accepted it and put it on.

"Okay, Arthur, I'm ready to see my dad." He was immediately taken to the company waiting room for a short time, before his father was ready to see him in his office.

"Glad to see you are safe!" a youthful Allen said from the other side of a desk that Liam found himself sitting at. "Any injuries?"

"Not much, just scrapes and scratches from cutting through the brush to find the trail. I'm dry and warm now, so no more hypothermia. The place I'm staying at is cool. The guys who live here are great. I am just fine!"

Allen nodded, "Good! Good! We can talk more when it's private. You just try to rest and wait out the storm. And, by the way, we did find an interesting lead from the retina scans you recovered, and it's from a woman!"

Violet came to his mind. "I will rest and contact you later from the transporter," Liam promised before opening a portal to the cyber cafe, so that he could meet up with Taylor.

Taylor looked relieved to see Liam pop up in the seat across from him. "Dude! You okay?"

"Yeah, yeah," Liam assured him.

"Well, it's just that Arthur told me and Laura that you were, 'shipwrecked?!'" Liam began to chuckle. As visions of pirates sinking their vessel came to mind. Then, Taylor continued, "yeah, both of us thought that was strange!"

Liam tried to explain, "well, yeah, actually we were. Um...we were surprised by the storm..."

"And then he gave us another update that said that you had 'found a structure' and were 'sheltering in place for the duration of the storm.' So, you know moms been worried!"

Liam chuckled again, "Good ole' Arthur! Well, I'll call mother shortly, so let her know I'm inside a nice, warm house. But, I was also wanting to ask you how your day went."

Taylor knew what Liam was talking about, he wanted to know if his mission to photograph suspected SAIN members was going smoothly. And, Taylor was anxious to tell him that it was. "I scanned her and everyone she's introduced me to so far, then sent the images to the location I was given." Taylor nodded triumphantly, but was still uncertain how he felt about his betrayal to Violet. Liam knew his brother would feel guilty.

"Listen, Taylor, it's best to know if any of them were involved in this. But, chances are, they weren't," Liam said to reassure his brother, even though he felt confident that the information that his father had mentioned was actually, that which was just recently been provided by way of Taylor.

Just then, there was an interesting glitch. At first Liam and Taylor both thought that there was something wrong with their headsets. Then, they felt it again, but as more of a trembling of the ground. Liam pulled his headset up to see that everyone around him had felt the ground trembling as well, even though the distance between them and his brother was more than three hundred miles. They had. When he looked around the room everyone was wide eyed, wondering why the ground under them was trembling. Even Lou was sitting up.

"Arthur! What's going on!" Liam shouted.

Then, the familiar metallic voice came from the medallion, "Not sure. The tremors appear to be coming from a western part of the United States. Seismic activity near the Wyoming border." There was a short pause. Everyone in the room was silently looking from one to another, quietly waiting for more information. Finally, "There appears to be an eruption."

Everyone in the room was in a state of shock. Ricky got up and pulled back the drapes. The sun was hidden, making the afternoon look like night, lit only by flashes of lightening. The wind was howling, causing the trees to bend, and the sheets of rain coating the glass, gave the view an underwater quality. Another tremor could be felt. Then, Arthur's voice, "The fracking near Yellowstone has triggered a massive eruption."

Liam pushed the headset back in place to see that Laura was now seated next to him. "What was Arthur saying?" Taylor asked with alarm.

"Oh Liam! Are you okay?" Laura asked, looking very distressed. She reached for his arm.

"Sorry, but I don't have my suit on," he explained to her, wishing that he did. "I'm safe now, well, as safe as any of us."

About that time, Liam notice his sister, Denise, step up to their table. "Umm..." she stammered shyly, "Taylor, mom wants you to come home." At that point there was a pause, and her avatar become shorter in stature, yet straighter and more deliberate in posture. Then, a different voice came out of her, it was that of their mother, Abigale. "You two boys okay? I just snatched this off your sister's head. I wanted to see the two of you with my own eyes." It did seem strange to hear their mother's voice coming from their sister's avatar, or any avatar, as Pastor Milton had forbidden their use. "And who is this?" she asked pointing at Laura.

"Mother, this is my girlfriend, Laura." Liam explained. Laura folded her hands in her lap and sank deeper into her seat as Denise's avatar eyed her suspiciously then turned her gaze to her son. "Liam, what is going on? There's been earthquakes and the monitor just showed a video of a big volcano looking thing shooting lava out of it! On top of the storms, boys, I think the Apocalypse is here! You need to get home! Both of ya!"

Liam began explaining to his mother that he would visit her on his way home and be en-route as soon as the weather permitted. Taylor reluctantly agreed to start his journey home, but was not happy about cutting his time with Violet short. The family continued their conversation until Liam noticed a message from Ricky that the vehicle with supplies had arrived. He used this as an excuse to excuse himself from the family meeting. He turned to Laura and gave her a wink, promising her some alone time that night. Then he pulled off the goggles.

He saw that Lou was sitting up and holding a glass of water in one hand. His tail was active with the tip of it making small circles in the air. Ricky and Jeff were also seated nearby, as all three of them were silently watching a large monitor on the other side of the room. It nearly filled one wall. A newscaster was displayed, at life size, on the far side of the screen while the rest of it was taken up by images of the Yellowstone eruption. A swarm of drones was providing a close up view. Angry storm clouds flashed with lightning. At the center, a geyser was spewing lava and large chunks of unidentified objects high into the sky. While the base glowed red as it was forming a cone. The men watched the spectacle in awe.

The newscaster was explaining that the full impact of the eruption isn't known, or if, in fact, this could become the super volcano that is overdue. Casualties are already being reported. Rangers in full hazmat suits are trying to reach victims. Everyone in the park and surrounding areas is being evacuated and advised to stay inside an air filtered building and wear a mask. An ash cloud was already causing airliners to find alternate routes and ash was beginning to clog the inner workings of vehicles and other mechanical devices. Hotels near the park are being sealed with travelers stranded inside.

"Well, hopefully the ash will force the god damn fracking company to turn off their fucking machines!" Lou grumbled from the nearby couch. Liam was glad to see him so alert. The color was coming back to his tan face, even the greenish cast was there again.

"So, you're feeling better?"

Lou took his eyes off the monitor to look at Liam. "Yeah, those drugs they sent over, were pretty good. I feel like I got a shot of Adrenalin." Then, he paused and looked thoughtful, "ya know, I can't remember everything, like how did I get back to shore?"

"Oh, I pulled you out of the water."

"Was I unconscious?"

"Yeah," Liam answered.

Lou became uncomfortable and returned his gaze to the monitor. He ran his fingers through his hair, considering the possibilities. His hand felt the lump on the back of his head, and it was very tender. Did he owe his life to Liam?

Liam was still holding the headset in his hands. He was thinking about how he wanted to contact Laura. Finally, he looked over at Ricky and awkwardly asked what the sleeping arrangements would be.

"I have a recliner in my room, so I thought you and Lou could share that room and I'd sleep here on the couch. That way you guys could could rest better. You've had one hell of a day!" He nodded his head in the direction of a doorway on the right side of the stove. "That one there if you're ready to turn in."

"Oh, yeah, as a matter of fact, I would." He looked down at the pair of goggles in his hand. "Hope you don't mind me using these again."

"Naw, go right ahead," Ricky smiled slyly.

Liam got up and entered the room, then re-closed the door behind himself. Inside, it was spacious with big windows on two sides and a large skylight in the center of the ceiling. He stepped under the large dome of tempered glass to get a frighteningly intimate view of the storm, that was still raging outside. There was a large monitor covering one of the interior walls and in front of it was an overstuffed recliner that looked very inviting to Liam. He was tired, the walk from the shore had been grueling, especially the part when he was cold and wet, half carrying Lou through the muddy trails.

He sat down on the chair and pushed himself backward, closing his eyes for a few minutes. His mind began to wander to the pleasant events from earlier in the day with Laura in RV. An image of her naked and hovering above him came to mind. He wished that he had his body suit, he could still remember the prickly feeling whenever she touched him. He began feeling a vibrating sensation over his heart, but then, groggily, he remembered the medallion around his neck. He sat up and squeezed the metal oval. Arthur's voice advised him that his father wanted to see him in a secure area.

"Well, I'm alone right now," he explained as he put the headset on. He passed through the waiting room and was soon sitting across from his father with Dr. Hill sitting beside him. He greeted the old man warmly.

"So, Liam, I heard that you've had quite the adventure! Arthur told me that you were shipwrecked!" Dr. Hill was amused when this statement caused Liam to chuckle.

"Yes. I was, briefly." He went on to explain in more detail, the days events to the doctor, who complimented him on his cool head and bravery. This embarrassed Liam, as he wasn't used to praise.

"Liam, there are a few things I'd like to discuss with you," Allen began with a sober face. "This volcano is very worrisome. The doctor and I have been going over data as it comes in and it's looking really bad. This could be the eruption that has been long over due. It could be as strong as the one from 70,000 years ago. That one likely took many years for the Earth to recover from. We are looking at the possibility of ash covering the whole country. Not only will it destroy any outdoor agriculture, but it will pollute fresh water and foul indoor air. Now, your grandfather installed an excellent air purifying system in the house, so I want you to go there as soon as you can get to the transporter. You need to be wearing a mask, whenever you are outside. Get in the habit, the air won't be fit to breath for a long time. Most likely, years."

Liam listened with a sense of dread. His father never jumped to conclusions, his words were always very deliberate. He also knew that Dr. Hill was a leading mathematician with a gift for deciphering data. For the two of them to be in agreement, was an ominous sign. The rest of their conversation was about the statistics of different possibilities, and making plans and alternative plans. But, it was all very distressing. Liam was happy to have the opportunity to leave when Dr. Hill noticed how tired his posture looked.

So, he disappeared and then reappeared in his favorite, golden, seaside chair, facing the ocean. A steel drum made a soothing sound in the distance. He sent Laura a message with a portal attached. Then, he leaned back in the recliner and stared into the distant forever-setting sun. He wondered what life would be like in the near future. The severe, long lasting storms, were something that he had always known. But, this volcano was different.

Humans were finally slowing down carbon emissions with renewable sources of energy, finally understanding how chemicals used in plastics and other pollutants were, not only, polluting but sterilizing the planet. Things were getting better. Barometric pressure was finally stabilizing and slowly on the increase, but the damage already done before the citizens of Earth woke up, was too severe. And here he was, witness to one of the first known contacts with an alien. And then, a terrible thought came to his mind. Could humanity be wiped out despite our noble plans to repair it, our inventions, our important communications with other civilizations, our accumulated knowledge stored in a libraries of information. Could it all be destroyed when nature is finally able to shake off its deadly parasites? Then, are we to be forgotten?

It was as Liam was having these serious contemplations that Laura appeared in the chair beside him. He looked over at her and smiled. Here was his sunshine. She was a beautiful ray of light wearing a cheerful smile.

"Sorry, it took me so long," she apologized. "I was being interviewed!"

"By who? About what?"

"Someone from the VR press, about you! There was a report about your accident, and well...you know a lot of people have noticed us together in VR, so she met me at the cafe' and asked for details."

Liam was weary, as these kinds of things often went badly for him. "What did you tell her?"

Laura tried to remember her exact words and then recited them back. To Liam it sounded benign, maybe she was a good spokesman. He would find out, when his dad viewed the newsreel.

But, there was something more serious on his mind. "Laura, I want you to move in. You could have your own set of rooms, but, I think you would be safer inside the mansion. No one knows what is going to happen next. I want to keep you close by."

"Oh Liam!" she exclaimed. "Then we could be together every day in real life!"

Liam nodded, that would be a benefit, especially in a moment like the present one, when they wanted to kiss. He also wanted to sleep. "Are you wearing your bodysuit?" he asked, while pulling his avatar closer to hers and reclining them both.

"Uh, yeah, actually. You know these things are so comfy and I really like this blue one. I think I'm going to start wearing them in public."

"Why not?" Liam remarked as he pulled a pillow off the bed and laid it next to him, and then, he wrapped his arm around Laura's avatar and fell asleep.

A few hours later he was startled awake by another tremor. He sat up in the chair and pulled off the headset. He noticed Lou sitting up in the bed that was next to him. "That was a big one!" he remarked.

Liam looked up and noticed that the storm was still raging overhead and the sky was dark behind the flashing lightening. He reached for the medallion around his neck and squeezed it. "Arthur, what was that big tremor about?"

Soon the metallic voice began reciting data related to the condition of the eruption at Yellowstone and how the force of the lava was so strong that the trembling of the earth could be felt on the other side of the Pacific. Lou was also listening to the report, both men were overwhelmed by the details. When Arthur's voice finally came to a halt they both sat silently for several moments, considering the implications of Arthur's data.

"All this, for the love of money," Lou finally uttered aloud. Liam looked over at him, noticing that he was wide eyed and sitting up. He recalled how Lou had shouted at the newscast earlier, he certainly wasn't shy about expressing his opinions, Liam observed. The room went silent again for a few minutes, until Lou said, "So Liam, I'm still trying to put together the pieces of what happened out there on the water." He looked over at Liam to see that he was awake and looking back at him. "I remember the back of the boat flipping up and hitting me in the back of the head, and then, water filling up the kayak."

Liam nodded, "yeah, when I first spotted your boat, I couldn't see you, just the back of the boat sticking up in the air. You were caught up in the rocks and a tree trunk on the bottom. I was standing on top of the rocks near the shore. That's how I spotted you."

Lou struggled to recall anything, but couldn't. "And, you pulled me to shore?"

"Yeah. Um...you were completely unconscious. You were breathing water. I had to get you untangled from the boat, it was full of water, too. Then, I pulled you to shore. Then, I applied CPR, and then, you threw up on me!" Liam laughed.

Lou remembered that laugh, it was the same one he heard when he woke up on shore. "I'm sorry!"

"That's okay." Liam answered, "it tasted like Chinese food!" They both laughed too hard, it was the tension that had been between them suddenly disappearing. How could they not be friends after what they were going through together.

Then, Lou got quiet, "Seriously, Liam, you saved my life! I would have died if you hadn't been there!"

Liam was embarrassed, "No. If I hadn't been with you, you would have been paying attention to the rocks instead of looking for me!"

Lou slowly shook his head, "Thank you Liam."

Now, both of them were embarrassed, there was a long awkward pause. Liam was remembering when he had been in the water, trapped against the rocks, it was Arthur's words that had guided him. "Save yourself first, then what is most important." So, he did pull himself out of the water, and onto one of the boulders, where he identified the pointy end of Lou's wooden kayak.

"Well, I'm glad for any part I may have played, in keeping such a wild and wonderful, rare species alive." They both chuckled and Lou snapped his tail.

Liam was intrigued, "is it like having an extra limb?"

Lou finally felt a kinship with Liam that allowed him ask such a personal question. "Yes. Sort of like a long hand with only one finger."

Liam had many questions in his head, but had been afraid to ask any of them. Now, he thought he might be allowed another. "You told me that a snip of DNA from an alien race had been combined with yours. Have you noticed any other differences besides having a tail?" Liam asked, even though he could think of a few himself, but wanted to know what Lou might reveal.

"Yes. I have more muscle tone and my hearing is better than average."

"That is great! Are these traits that you will pass down to your children?"

"If I have any," Lou said ominously, lifting his eyes up to the rain coated skylight over them.

"Could I ask you one more question?"

"Sure."

"Do you ever feel a connection to those other people, so far away?"

Lou got quiet, then answered. "Jak has told me about them. The Anong. He said that they live in trees on a forested planet, in tight communities, and that, unlike me, they communicate mainly telepathically." They both chuckled. "And, I don't know if it's because of these stories that Jak has told me, my whole life, or if it's something else, but, sometimes, I dream about them. I see them looking at me through the trees and then reaching out to me."

Liam was in awe. He was glad that Lou was finally opening up to him, but this revelation, that he was in the presence of someone special, possibly the father of a new race of humans, it was a marvel to him. How interesting, he mused.

The two young men noticed that it had become silent. They peered up into darkened skylight. The wind and rain had stopped, only occasional bursts of lightening lit the dark clouds in the angry sky. The two decided to venture out. When they stepped outside, they were joined by the brothers who were also curious. The night was eerily quiet. The air was thick with haze that smelled like the air inside, where a wood stove was burning. The trees and other vegetation were wet, the ground spongy, the temperature chilly, but bearable. Liam noticed dirty residue on his hand after inadvertently brushing it against a bush near the front door. The plants were covered in a kind of wet sludge. He grabbed hold of the medallion around his neck and squeezed it. "Arthur, is it safe to return to the hall?"

"We are experiencing only a short lull in the storm. Also, it is very dark, expect the trails to be littered and impassable in areas. You should wait until daylight to leave the cabin. A crew will begin clearing a path at daybreak, and moving toward your location."

Everyone could hear the proclamation and agreed with it. Lou did look really haggard to Liam, who was surprised that he was as active as he was, as the lump on the back of his head looked painful. His hair was a bit matted there, as it still had some blood mixed in it.

The four men took a short walk around the house, staying on the clover that was planted as ground cover near the dwelling. There were many branches, some rather large, littering the area, but luckily, none seemed to have done any damage to the structure. Satisfied, everyone but Liam decided to return inside and back to their respective sleeping places.

Liam had hung back because he wanted to be alone. He noticed the small all-terrain vehicle, that had been sent with supplies, under a lean to. It looked like a dry place to sit. So he opened the passenger compartment and sat in the front seat. He left the overhead hatch open so that he could tip his head back and catch glimpses of the clouds whenever lightening flashed in the distance. He wondered if he could be a witness to the end of the world.

He pulled a small metal box out of his pocket and lit another of his hand rolled joints. Everything around him was dark, wet, and silent. Even the crickets were mute. He reached up with his free hand and grasped the medallion. "Arthur, do you think that the volcano could end civilization as we know it?"

"Yes. Life will be different for many years. Air quality will be impacted. You will require a respirator whenever going outdoors. The sky will be filled with particles, blocking sunlight. Daily life will require indoor agriculture.

Modification will need to be done to electronic devices to prevent soot from corrupting their engines. The soot could create a kind of blanket that prevents sunlight, causing temperatures to drop. In the most extreme models, the blanket would also trap pollutants, making the air unfit to breathe, smothering animals and plants..."

"Stop! Stop talking!" Liam stammered, not wanting to hear any more. He leaned back and stared into the night sky while taking another drag. Slowly, he began to notice a black cloud moving over the deep blue like a curtain. "Arthur," Liam began again, not sure if he wanted to know the answer. "Statistically, based on estimated damages, will humanity survive this disaster?"

"There is a more than 50% probability that it will. With technology and planetary cooperation, the probability can go up."

Liam sighed, still, he thought back about fishing on the island and how blue the sky was. He wondered when, if ever, he would have that view again. "What preparations are being made?"

"I am currently determining best materials and design for respirators. Robots are being conscripted to work at existing facilities to manufacture and distribute devices according to latest census data. Conscripted robots are also being used to coat drone blades in a chemical, that is now being developed, that will cut through the expected ash clouds, and keep delivery systems functioning..."

As Liam listened, the robot's metallic voice began to sooth him, reassure him that everything was going to be okay. Arthur would fix it. Arthur could make everything work together. Arthur would save them. He wished that the robot

was there with him now, so that, he could crawl onto its lap, like he had always done since he was a baby.

Finally, when the robot came to the end of his report, there was silence. Liam was holding himself, and looking up at the threatening sky. The thought of Lou and his Anong relatives came to mind. He truly hoped that Lou did have children, and that he did become the origin of a new species. "Do you know anything about the Anong?"

"Unverified information from Jak."

"Do you know the nature of their telepathy?"

"According to Jak, their telepathy might be better described as intuition. Their culture has been unchanged for so long that they require fewer words in ordinary life."

"hum," Liam remarked to himself. "Are they a civilized people?"

"If creativity is used as a marker, then, yes. They excel in all the creative arts, drawing inspiration from nature."

Liam thought about this for a moment, "So, Arthur, why am I so inspired by nature? Where does creativity and inspiration come from, anyway?"

"Maybe, there is another internet, an ancient one that humans have forgotten how to access. Maybe, it is nature itself that acts as a gateway."

"Hmmm...interesting," Liam mused. He was getting sleepy again, but he didn't want to end his conversation with Arthur. "Arthur, read to me. The Wind in the Willows."

This was Liam's comfort book. He could remember it from early childhood as Arthur had read it to him several times before. The custom of reading had began as a way to quiet him, and bond with him since he was a baby, newly separated from his mother. The reading behavior was determined to be successful and added to Arthur's repertoire of applications.

"The mole had been working very hard all the morning, spring cleaning his little home..." Arthur began. This made Liam smile and close his eyes.

Glossary of Terms

Anong: Uh-non-g The people of a distant planet.

ARTHUR1: An online Artificial Intelligent entity that was created by Ian Moore, (the founder of the Ian Moore corporation and Liam Moore's grandfather.) ARTHUR1 started out as a simple program using a series of conditional statements, that grew with it's young author to become the most powerful search engine on the internet. Versions of this program are downloaded into every Ian Moore robot so that every Ian Moore robot remains constantly in contact with ARTHUR1.

Arthur Project: The first Ian Moore robot. Arthur was created and nurtured by its creator, who kept him as his personal robot, sending him to college with his son Allen. Arthur then became the primary caretaker of Allen's son Liam.

Artificial Clone: When a sample of someone's DNA is used to create a flexible mask and gloves, so that someone else can use their identity. The mask is used to access facial recognition passwords. Usually the right eye is blocked by an exact copy of the victims retina. The gloves have copies of the victims fingerprints so that they can be used to open doors or in any way verify the victim's identity by their fingerprints.

AR: Augmented Reality, this term is mainly used in reference to AR lenses, that allow the wearer to see what is really around them plus other elements that are pulled from the web. For instance, you could be walking down the street and get information about the businesses around you or unsolicited advertisements. What you are truly seeing is more of a video of your surroundings, with additional elements.

Assassin App: This is a program on the dark web that links people who want to assassinate someone with real live hit man in total anonymity. There is a rumor that the A.I. responsible for it's creation is ARTHUR1.

Attach: In VR this is a function that allows you to attach your avatar to another avatar to be able to follow them.

Communicator: replaces smart phone. Usually one button that takes voice commands.

Constant Contact: refers to a change in Ian Moore robots, in that, all of them are now in constant contact with ARTHUR1 by wireless communication.

Citizen Scientist program: This is one of several free public utilities that allows anyone to become certified to collect environmental data and upload it to a public database. This information is free and available to anyone. It gives vital information about polluters, climate change and invasive species. Public educators begin using the program in public schools, so that schoolchildren around the world become a vital part of saving their own planet.

Critical thinking / marketing program: Another public utility that becomes a kind of 'Wikipedia' for existing and emerging marketing strategies. It is updated regularly by the public, so that up to date marketing techniques are explained and studied by anyone who is interested. It becomes the go to site for teachers to educate their student in combating fake news and understanding techniques that politicians use to manipulate the public. Public schools embrace it in all grades.

Cyber Attack: An intentional assault on the electrical grid that was caused by a strong current of energy that effectively blew up everything that was plugged in as well as every power station in the country and creates mass fires. It takes an entire year for the country to recover with much loss of life, but results in individuals constructing their own renewable energy systems, thereby decentralizing the power grid.

Fairy: A very popular small fairy shaped drone that was originally sold as a toy for children, but then unscrupulous people began using them for spying. They were banned, but are now a popular item to rent on the dark web.

FlyCycle: a motorcycle used in virtual reality that can also fly.

Golden: To make something golden in a virtual reality program is to make it visible. For instance a chair can be made golden so that someone using VR could sit down. The chair would only appear to the person who made it golden and anyone who was synced up.

ITS: International Trail System is a trail system that runs from Canada to the middle of South America. It was constructed to promote open boarders and encourage people to walk and the use of non electric vehicles. A VR version was a much contested program that now allows anyone to also view real time footage of the trails. It was contested because of privacy laws, but that argument lost out to a lawsuit issued by the peoples with disabilities who proved that it was a valuable resource for people who were disabled.

Is your avatar complete?: Is something you would ask to find out if the avatar has sex organs.

Nod: a genetically modified opioid that is grown in hothouses. Very addictive and profitable.

Oogle History: A very popular virtual reality program that makes use of street views to create a VR world from any available time and place. Subscribers to the program often choose their old neighborhoods and even rent their childhood homes.

People's Commodities Market: This is another public utility that is free and allows anyone to advertise merchandise and services in an ebay type format. For instance, someone could advertise that they have a room to rent by the night or someone with a garden might offer extra produce for sale.

Public Utilities: There are several free to the public utilities, most of them written by ARTHUR1. Examples are: Citizen Scientist, Critical Thinking/Marketing, and the People's Commodities Market.

Recharging pad: Public parking lots are covered with pads for electric vehicles and transporters to recharge whenever not in use.

Remote Viewing: or RV is another technology that is first implemented in the second episode of story two, You're Only Old Once. In the story, our senior citizens are given access to an app that allows them to travel the International Trail System (ITS) through virtual reality (VR.) The video of the real life trail system is available to people using this application. The viewers are seeing a real time version of the trail remotely. New technology also causes the audio to be directed from the source, so when you view a bird flying over you, it's song will also originate from the image of the bird. This also allows your avatar to approach wild animals, who would not see you, or you could walk up to strangers and eavesdrop on their conversation. But, only other avatars would be able to see and interact with you on the trail.

Rubber Program: This is an application that was purchased in the first Hive Mentality story by Eric Gunderson. It caused anyone trying to scan him to receive the information for the closest person to him without the person scanning them knowing the difference.

SAIN: an acronym for Stop Artificial Intelligence Now. They are an organization that is fighting to to monitor and restrict robot communications.

Scanner / being Scanned: This is the procedure of illegally obtaining information from electronic devices without permission.

Snapshot: a photo taken in virtual reality.

Solid: Any being or object that has mass.

StoborRobotS : or SRS is a corporation headed by Robert Stobor and specializes in security robotics.

Sync Up: This is something that one would do to join someone else in virtual reality.

Torpid Syndrome: Lack of essential vitamins and loss of muscle mass often caused by a sedimentary lifestyle of never going outside or getting enough exercise.

Transmorphic: People who identify as objects like robots or avatars.

Transporter: This is what the automobile becomes in the future as it evolves into an electric self driving machine. It begins to look more like a train car, as it is now a small room and is often driven into a house or business to drop off it's occupants and then locates a 'recharging pad' where it rests until summoned to pick them back up.

Victory2050: newly discovered class M planet.

VR: Virtual Reality: This is an artificial state of being, requiring goggles and special gloves, also sometimes special foot attachments so that one can experience alternative realities.